LEO E. NDELLE

# *BAITING THE BEAST*

# ACKNOWLEDGEMENT

Family… Friends… What will I do without you all? From the setbacks and struggles, to the continuing success, you all have always been there. I could never thank you enough.

I just thought I'd let you all know, even though I tell you in one form or another all the time.

# DEDICATION

For you, my siblings!
There are none better than you folks!

# PART ONE

# SOMEWHERE IN THE GRAND CANYON

**BEELZEBUB SNEERED AT** the vermin prostrated in front of him, chanting his praise repeatedly. He would have wiped them out immediately had he not been distracted by his current claustrophobic, corporeal abode.

The stench of this body. Damnation!

He inspected his hands and arms and raised his legs one at a time and nodded his awareness of the gradual but painful transmutation his new physical form was going through, from the etheric to the subatomic and cellular levels. Painful for the human? Yes. Him? Absolutely not. Beelzebub almost smiled as the essence of the body's former owner howled, shrieked, screamed, writhed, begged and rioted in his head against the takeover.

Sweet melody!

He increased the vibrational frequency of his human host using the power of thought to accelerate the transmutation to completion. He ignored the human's essence rioting against the takeover, putting up the fight of its life, because its life did depend on the fight.

*"Why fight it, puny human?"* Beelzebub asked the human's dying essence through telepathy. *"Resistance is futile. Your human essence stands no chance against that of an archangel."*

Beelzebub shrugged his shoulders.

"And my essence is unlike that of any archangel," he added softly, as if he was speaking to himself. "Mine is that of a fallen archangel afflicted with a curse on my essence, a curse cast upon me by a fellow brother."

He closed his eyes and stilled his mind. The rioting and screaming from the human's essence, whose body he had possessed, had reduced to whimpers.

"At first, I hated this curse on my essence," Beelzebub said audibly as he clenched and unclenched his fists. "But now, I rejoice in it. The curse made me special. It made me unique; the first of my kind."

Beelzebub then flexed his neck, shoulders, arms and legs. The body of the human he had possessed remained unchanged but the essence of the human was not just silent. It was gone. The transmutation of the human's body to one that could accommodate his essence as an archangel was complete; from subcellular to etheric levels. Gone was the claustrophobia. Gone was everything that was and looked like the human, including the human's face. He could not have tolerated another moment in the insult that was human flesh. He stretched and flexed his shoulders again as his shoulder blades heaved once, then twice and on the third time, a pair of yellow-red, smoldering wings ripped through the skin on his shoulder blades and spread out like those of a phoenix. He flapped them twice before letting them hang freely.

Suddenly, three other humans appeared about forty feet away from the other humans prostrated in front of him. Unlike those prostrated in front of him, their eyes glowed in a bright whiteness and they were ready for battle.

"You will return whence you came, demon," Shi'mon spoke with authority as the green crystal on the ring he wore pulsated wildly.

"And you pathetic, bottom-feeding creatures think you can even speak in my presence?" Beelzebub scoffed. "Fools! I existed long before your kind was even a concept."

The prostrated priest whipped his head around, opened his right palm towards Shi'mon and uttered a spell. When nothing happened, the priest pulled back his hand and stared at it in surprise, as if it was not his.

"Sleep," Beelzebub heard the defiant human say.

The priest and the billionaire immediately succumbed to Shi'mon's command.

"Time to put you back in the cage, demon." Yochanan said.

The creature that just spoke charged towards him. Beelzebub turned his gaze towards the sky as this creature took a first step. The sound waves of a clap of thunder pressed against air particles at a painfully slow speed, while a bolt of lightning streaked towards the ground in slow, erratic patterns. He returned his attention towards the charging human, who was still in his second step. It was really not worth the effort, but he wanted to teach these creatures a lesson before ending their piteous existences. He strolled towards the creature as it began its third stride. He grabbed the human by the throat on the human's third stride and twisted the creature's neck sharply in a half-circle to the right.

A bolt of lightning struck the ground before the sound of the snapping of the human's neck reached the other humans' ears and the sound of thunder boomed. Beelzebub met the gazes of the other humans and savored in the horror he saw in their eyes. He held the limp body of their dead compatriot in front of him before letting it slump to the ground. Another bolt of lightning began streaking down. Beelzebub relished in the message he had just sent to these foolish humans.

I am Beelzebub, King of Demons and the annihilation of the humans of Earth Realm.

However, he mistook the look of horror on the faces of his attackers to be based on fear and, to his surprise, the humans whizzed towards him instead.

Your doom! Beelzebub snickered and trotted towards his attackers.

Yehuda saw a blur move and stop in front of Shi'mon. The blur delivered a punch into Shi'mon's gut before Shi'mon could take a second step. He knew a punch powerful enough to send a grown man flying a hundred feet away was going to force out all the air from that person's lungs as well as turn that person's gut to mush. Yehuda returned his attention towards Beelzebub as he, Yehuda, took a second step. He stared into the yellow-red brilliance of the demon's eye sockets and braced himself for the demon's attack.

I may be no match for this creature, but may I be damned for all eternity if I fall without a fight, Yehuda said to himself.

Beelzebub turned his attention towards the last of his attackers and his lips peeled away from his semi-fangs in a grin. He took two steps and threw a confident, unconcealed uppercut towards Yehuda's chin. Decapitation was the intention. And then, Beelzebub's bright, yellowish-red sockets bulged in shock at the spectacle that unfolded before his eyes. In the darkness of this part of the Grand Canyon, a beam of light flashed from Yehuda's body and temporarily illuminated the eerie darkness. Everything moved slowly as Yehuda caught a glimpse into the Dimensions of Time and Energy. A serpent of green light coiled three-and-a-half times around Yehuda's body as he inclined his body away from the path of the punch. Once again, he was a vessel of Kundalini, the Serpent of Consciousness.

He watched as Beelzebub's blazing fist grazed through the air in front of his face, igniting the air particles along the path of his punch with supercharged chi. He turned to face the king of demons and the look of utter shock on the demon's face was priceless. Before the demon could retreat his fist, Yehuda twisted his torso and hips and drove his right fist into the demon's hip. Beelzebub crashed into the ground with so much force that he left a six-inch deep hole in the ground. Another bolt of lightning illuminated the roiling sky, slowly making its way towards the ground. He smiled and returned his gaze towards Beelzebub. He uncoiled his hip and released a brutal left kick into Beelzebub's chin. Bones cracked, vertebrae were severed, but Beelzebub healed instantly.

Yehuda sank the fingers of his right hand into Beelzebub's right trapezius muscle, and before Beelzebub could process the pain, Yehuda flung him a short distance away. As the demon's body smashed into the ground, the bolt of lightning found its mark on the demon's chest. Over 70 million volts of electricity, infused with a tinge of Kundalini's chi that Yehuda sparked using an iota of Kundalini's will, coursed through Beelzebub's body, charring it to a smoldering reddish-blackness. Beelzebub gritted his semi-fangs as he seized and convulsed under the power of this alien lightning strike. Yehuda glided towards the King of Demons and loomed over him.

"What are you?" Beelzebub asked using telepathy as he healed his body through the power of thought.

"What I am is no concern of yours, demon," Yehuda replied in Beelzebub's telepathic frequency, which shocked and stupefied Beelzebub.

"You can speak in the frequency of Lemuria?" Beelzebub gawked.

"I do not care what or where that is," Yeshua replied with sour contempt. "But you will not leave this canyon… Not alive, at least."

"We will meet again, creature," Beelzebub grimaced as he stood up from the ground. "That I promise you."

In a burst of blinding, golden light, Beelzebub disappeared.

Yochanan roused from the ground, massaging his neck and Shi'mon zipped over just in time to catch Yehuda as Yehuda returned to his human form and passed out. He was even weaker than he was the first time he had manifested such power, when they fought against and exterminated the Bright Eyes in the lair of The Twins of Terror. Shi'mon swung Yehuda's arm over his shoulder as the lightning stopped flashing and the skies cleared. The crystal in Shi'mon's ring ceased pulsating as well.

"We will talk about this when we get home," Shi'mon said to Yochanan.

He then turned towards the sleeping priest and billionaire.

"Wake up," he commanded using telepathy.

As the priest and the billionaire roused from their slumber, Shi'mon, Yehuda and Yochanan teleported back to their home in Rome. The priest and the billionaire had no memory of where they were, let alone, why they were where they were. Meanwhile, on Earth Realm, Beelzebub, the fallen archangel and King of Demons, also known as The Beast, had been set free. And he would stop at nothing to finally eradicate what he considered was the most despicable creatures in Creation: humans!

# CHAPTER ONE

# THE WATER-BEARER

**THE YEAR WAS** 31 C. E. Another uneventful, slow day for business was over. Yaakov was already too familiar with these trends in business. Not everyone was crazy about purchasing linens during Passover. Good thing these trends were only temporary. He rode his donkey on his way home. A few waves and casual hellos to a few known faces punctuated the ride. But he was looking forward to saying hello to the only jewel in his neighborhood he cared about; and as luck would have it, Abra was sitting in front of her parents' house, picking grain with her sisters and friends, and chatting the evening away.

Yaakov kept a constant pace and tried to act casual, though he could hardly contain himself. Out of the corner of his eye, he hoped Abra would look his way. He would pretend he was turning his head in her direction at the same time. And by Yahweh, not only did Abra look in his direction, but she smiled so brightly that her smile might as well have been the only source of illumination for the evening. Yaakov almost lost his balance on his donkey. He waved at her, and she waved back.

*Wait. Did she hold up her hand a little longer than usual?*

Yaakov slapped himself mentally and returned to the present. One of these days, he would be courageous enough to ask for her hand in marriage.

Yaakov arrived home, washed up and donned clean garments. Dinner was at a local restaurant, followed by meditation on his mentor's teaching before he hit the sack. The life of a bachelor and an apprentice to Yeshua. He eased himself into his bed later that night, and the last thing on his mind before he plunged into a deep, dreamful sleep was him at a wedding with Abra as his bride. He was happy, she was happy, and so were their families.

Yaakov was walking towards a well to fetch some water. It was odd because men did not fetch water; women did. However, this was a dream, and in a dream, anything was possible. He sighed.

*The life of a bachelor.*

Yaakov tossed the pail made of animal hide into the well and waited for it to fill up. Despite the pressures he faced from family and friends, he would rather marry out of love than out of obligation. Thank Yahweh that habituation tended to spawn immunity. He pulled the rope that was attached to the pail in the well. But when he turned to pour the water into his clay pot, the pail that had been full of water was suddenly bone-dry. He cast the pail into the well again. When he pulled the pail out of the well, the pail was still bone-dry. Multiple repetitions yielded the same result.

"What in the name of Yahweh," he cursed.

Then, someone chuckling on the corner caught his attention.

"Not funny, Master," Yaakov said.

"Oh, it is funny, brother," Yeshua replied amid chuckles.

"I'm just trying to fetch some water," Yaakov almost whined. "Couldn't we train later, please, Master?" Yaakov pleaded.

"Who said this wasn't your training?" Yeshua asked.

"I thought this was just a dream," Yaakov said.

"And who said it couldn't be both?" Yeshua replied, still chuckling.

Yeshua bit into a fruit that Yaakov had never seen before. Yaakov decided to try one more time. He cast the pail in the well and waited until it was full. As he retrieved the pail from the well, a moment of realization struck him. He turned towards his mentor and grinned.

"This is my dream," Yaakov said. "So here, I'm in charge. No more tricks."

Yaakov cautiously poured the water from the pail into his clay pot. When he finished, he let the pail fall freely into the well and wiped his hands on his cloak. Mission successful.

"You've always been in charge," Yeshua said, standing up. "You were the one making the water disappear. Not me."

"I was trying to shift my responsibilities to you, Master," Yaakov conceded.

"The important thing is that you took charge and that was impressive," the Master commended him. "Now, turn around and look behind you."

Yaakov did as he was told to find a dried-up and fissured barrenness as far as the eye could see. The well, neighborhood, everything except for Yeshua, himself and the clay pot full of water were gone.

"What happened here, Master?" Yaakov asked. "What's my lesson?"

"Look," the Master waved his left hand in the air.

The scene changed. Both Yaakov and Yeshua levitated to an aerial vantage point that enabled them to better appreciate the arid panorama that stretched out before them. Suddenly, water gushed from the ground until the wilderness became a sea of water beneath them and two fishes swam freely in it. To the right of the panoramic scene was a man holding a pitcher and filling it with water flowing nonstop through a water gate. Nothing looked amiss.

Then, a creature that looked human appeared between the man with the pitcher and the fish still swimming in the water. But the creature was anything but human. Bright, yellowish-red flames spewed from its mouth and eyes, and it had a spear in its right hand. The creature lifted its spear to strike at the fish, but another creature, with a serpent of light wrapped around his body, appeared from nowhere and punched the creature with the flaming eyes in the face. A fierce battle ensued between the creature with the spear and the one with the serpent. Alas, the creature with the spear thrust its spear into the chest of the creature with the serpent. As the blood gushed from the chest of the creature with the serpent of light, the water was poisoned, exposing the fishes to a slow and painful death. As if to add insult to injury, the poisoned water dried up as quickly as it had appeared, exposing a parched, barren earth once again.

The water from the water gate stopped flowing as well, but the man with the pitcher still had some water in his pitcher. He rushed towards the fishes, with the obvious intent of scooping their flapping, dying bodies from the parched earth. But just as he was about to save the fishes, the creature with the spear struck him down with a powerful punch to his face. The man fell to his knees and let go of his pitcher, which broke, releasing its contents into the parched earth.

The man with the broken pitcher screamed in frustration, and the creature with the flaming eyes roared with joy. The man with the broken pitcher felt utterly useless, powerless and helpless as he watched the fishes flapping wildly towards a slow and horrible death by asphyxiation on the parched earth. Regardless, he crawled towards the fishes, knowing there was nothing he could do. The creature with the spear let the man with the broken pitcher witness the horror that was unfolding in front of him just to entertain its sadistic side. The man with the pitcher finally got to the fishes. He picked up a fish in each hand, stared at them for a few seconds and wept bitterly.

Then, the creature with the spear raised its spear in the air with both hands, pointing its tip upwards. He brought it down to the ground once, and the ground rumbled when the spear struck it. The man with the broken pitcher was oblivious to what was happening. He just cradled the dead fishes in his hands as the tears flowed freely down his cheeks. The creature raised its spear in the air again and crashed it into the ground. The tip of the spear split into two identical tips, and the rumble that followed was even more intense than the first time. The man with the broken pitcher noticed and turned around to face the creature with the spear. Again, the creature raised its spear in the air and crashed it into the ground. A third tip sprang between the other tips, and the spear became a trident. The man with the broken pitcher felt the earth ripple as if he was sailing across the ocean as the rumble in the earth turned into a violent, persistent earthquake. Then, the earth fissured into a deep fault from the point where the trident had struck.

As the earth quaked violently, the last of the waters from the broken pitcher began to drain into the fault. The man with the broken pitcher looked around frantically like a caged, frightened and confused animal seeking escape. But before he rose to his feet, the creature with the trident drove its trident into his chest and pinned him to the ground. Water, instead of blood, flowed from his stabbed chest. As the water flowed into the earth and his life ebbed away, the earth dried up even more. The man with the broken pitcher used the last of his strength and brought the dead fishes close to his chest as he died and turned to dust. The dead fishes also turned to dust.. The creature with the trident then lifted its trident into the air with his right hand and roared in victory before it faded into nothingness.

"Why did you show me this, Master?" Yaakov asked, unable to even begin to fathom the significance of the vision.

"The water and fishes represent the Age of Pisces," Yeshua replied. "On the dawn of every age, a wave of new consciousness bathes the Dimension of Solaris and all the realms therein, including Earth Realm. A living luminary is also born. This is birth by self-realization. Last year, my journey through the Shadow of the Soul occurred during the dawn of the Age of Pisces and it resulted in me becoming both a self-realized being and multi-dimensional being. Therefore I am the living luminary of this age. This is the first time in the history of Creation that a living luminary also became a multi-dimensional being."

Yaakov scratched the back of his head in thought.

"So, what is your purpose then, Master?"

"A living luminary's main purpose is to prepare the creatures of a realm for their next evolutionary leap," Yeshua replied. "But now that I am also a multi-dimensional being, my purpose goes far beyond that now. Do not concern yourself with my purpose, Yaakov. It is beyond your purview."

'Yes, Master," Yaakov nodded and bowed his head slightly in respect.

His mentor's tone of voice was not particularly indicative of a reprimand. Like his mentor said, this was beyond his purview.

A moment of silence went by.

"And what about the man with the pitcher?" Yaakov asked.

"He represents the Age of Aquarius," Yeshua replied. "Normally, the Age of

Aquarius precedes the Age of Pisces. However, because of the Precession of the Equinoxes, we observe the Zodiac across the cosmos in a backward fashion. The Zodiac is the path of the Realm of Solara, the central realm of the Dimension of Solaris, across the cosmos. I'll tell you more about the Zodiac later."

"And I was just about to ask about that," Yaakov smiled. "But that can wait. So, please, continue with your explanation of the vision."

"How polite of you," the Master teased, and both men laughed. "Alright now. Basically, Creation operates by laws and design. It is truly beautiful and perfect in every sense of the word. We are now at the beginning of the Age of Pisces, and the next will be the Age of Aquarius. But there may be discord and complications in this perfect design."

"As representative of the two creatures in the vision?" Yaakov asked.

"Yes," Yeshua agreed. "But I will start with the one holding the serpent. He represents a dimension that is of the same vibrational level as Solaris. But it is neither a part of Solaris nor the twelve ages of the Zodiac. Some consider it to be a thirteenth age in the Zodiac. This is not the case. It is merely a dimension that spans along the equinox of the Zodiac and holds a strong significance of its own. It represents a balance in the Zodiac and is a binary dimension to Solaris. Serpents symbolize consciousness. Hence, the serpent holder in the equinox of the Zodiac simply means that consciousness governs the Zodiac and is not polarized.

"That is why the creature with the spear had to kill it first. The creature with the spear represents a phenomenon, an actual creature, that will move to disrupt this balance in the Zodiac. The serpent-holder did what was natural to it. It tried to maintain order when this creature showed up. But when the creature killed the serpent-holder, it caused a major rift in the balance of the Zodiac."

"And the 'blood' of the serpent-holder became the poison of the Age of Pisces," Yaakov interjected.

"Correct," the master agreed.

"The water was poisoned, meaning the new vibration of consciousness you're going to help release will become tainted if the situation is not addressed," Yaakov continued.

"Correct."

"With misrepresentations and misinterpretations," Yaakov added, scratching his chin through his beard.

"Correct again."

"And when is all this supposed to start happening, Master?" Yaakov asked.

"It's happening already to culminate during the next transition between the ages," the Master replied as he gently rubbed his left earlobe between his left index finger and thumb.

"And that is why the creature attacked at the cusp of both ages." Yaakov exclaimed. "He's trying to strike two ages at the same time."

"You are a lot wiser than you are aware of, brother," the Master said.

"We cannot let this happen, Master."

"And you wonder why I chose you for this lesson," Yeshua nodded slowly.

"The fishes died, as well as the man with the pitcher," Yaakov continued as if Yeshua did not just pay him a compliment. "Is all lost then?"

"A vision represents a possibility and with that possibility is a preclusion of choice," the Master continued. "And every choice leads to an outcome or a set of outcomes."

"What must I do then, Master?" Yaakov asked with a spark of enthusiasm in his demeanor.

"To locate and eliminate the creature with the spear," the Master replied.

"Who is this creature, Master?" Yaakov continued. "Is he The Anomaly?"

"No, he's not," Yeshua replied. "He's one who was cursed and banished. He is one full of hatred for humans. And he is here already, confined and waiting to be released."

"Where?" Yaakov asked.

"You will know soon enough," the Master replied.

Yaakov wondered why Yeshua did not just tell him where this creature was confined. And if this creature was already confined here on Earth Realm, why did the Master not strike this creature down at once?

*Not within your purview,* Yaakov reminded himself.

Yeshua opened his right hand. In it was a ring with a green crystal on it.

"What is this, Master?" Yaakov asked.

"This is what you, or whoever your leader will be, will use to find the creature whenever he is released," Yeshua replied. "It will pulsate with green light and when that time comes, do not hesitate to eliminate this creature. Act immediately. Do whatever it takes. Do you understand me?" Yeshua spoke with a sternness of voice that Yaakov had never heard before.

"You don't have to tell me twice, Master," Yaakov replied and took the ring from his master's palm.

Yaakov slid the ring on his right ring finger. The ring pulsated three times with green light.

"I trust you will do what needs to be done," Yeshua said firmly.

"I will not fail, Master," Yaakov affirmed.

"I know you won't, brother."

Yeshua placed his left hand on Yaakov's right shoulder. He observed Yaakov for a few moments and then nodded.

"I must say, given the gravity of the situation, your reaction is certainly at variance with that of the average person's," Yeshua said.

"How do you mean, Master?" Yaakov asked.

"I cannot tell if you are overly confident that you will succeed in this task or if you are just overly excited about the whole situation," Yeshua replied. "Your demeanor indicates neither worry nor concerned on your part. You react as if I just told you the Sabbath is tomorrow, which is tomorrow, in fact."

"Master, if you feel like I do not fully appreciate the gravity of the situation," Yaakov rebutted. "Then you are correct. I do not. Am I afraid? Absolutely. Do I know what to expect? No. However, I use my fear and uncertainty as motivators, not inhibitors. So, am I confident I will succeed? Yes, I am. Or I will at least die trying, for Earth Realm and beyond."

"Of all my apprentices, you've always shown a higher level of wisdom and courage that gives me great joy," Yeshua smiled with pride at Yaakov.

"You honor me greatly, Master," Yaakov said.

"I only speak the truth, brother," Yeshua affirmed. "It is your wisdom and faith in yourself that will carry you on and see you through this mission. Let these be your guide, and the rest will follow."

"Yes, Master," Yaakov replied.

"The creature of destruction in the vision has a hatred for humans like no other creature in existence," Yeshua's eyebrows furrowed in a mix of frustration and concern. "He has been in incarceration in this realm for tens of thousands of years in non-corporeal form. He will be released, albeit a most foolish mistake. But perhaps in the foolishness of that mistake, the termination of a most soulless beast this realm has ever known will come."

"Beast?" Yaakov asked, a little confused.

"In the metaphorical sense, yes." Yeshua replied. "In fact, in later generations, this creature will be called *The Beast*. Alas, as with many other things in later generations, the identity of this beast will sadly be misplaced; but not to you and your brothers."

"Master, you say he has been here the whole time?" Yaakov asked, unable to contain his shock.

"That is correct," Yeshua replied. "As a non-corporeal prisoner."

"Then why do we not just locate and take him out immediately?" Yaakov asked with the excitement for the hope of a master plan in the making.

*I must know,* Yaakov thought. *Purview or not.*

"A few reasons," Yeshua replied calmly. "Firstly, he has been cloaked. So, though he's here, it would require a special set of spells to locate him. Secondly," Yeshua sighed heavily, "Now that I'm a multi-dimensional being, I'm not allowed to interfere directly with certain affairs, and this is one of them.

This is your fight, as humanity and the most I can do is provide you with tools and counsel."

Yeshua paced back and forth briefly. He traced a symbol on the ground with his left sandal that Yaakov had never seen before.

"Thirdly," Yeshua spoke with a slight edge to his voice, "the timing must be perfect. The best time to defeat The Beast will be on the cusp of the ages. At this time, he will be most powerful and most vulnerable at the same time. So, while using the tools I am providing you may work, in the same breath, wisdom just may end up being the most powerful tool you may have."

The master was right; he still did not fully appreciate the gravity of the situation. But he had wisdom and faith; faith in himself and in the master. And with that faith came fear. He was not afraid of The Beast, but for himself. He was afraid he may go beyond a certain edge that he, himself, may not even know yet. And going beyond that edge might result in him failing.

*No need to worry about that for now,* Yaakov sighed as he thought to himself. *Just focus on training as if your life depends on it, which might be the case, actually.*

Life was beautiful, death was not as beautiful, and he was absolutely in love with the life of humanity.

"Master, you said that the Age of Pisces began last year, right?"

"Indeed, brother," Yeshua replied.

"So, the next age, the Age of…." Yaakov furrowed his eyebrows as he tried to remember the name of the next age.

"Aquarius," Yeshua helped.

"Yes, Aquarius," Yaakov reiterated. "About two thousand years from now."

"Indeed," Yeshua replied.

"Heavens. So, I am going to have to live that long?" Yaakov exclaimed and stared blankly at the ground.

Yeshua smiled and felt more confident in his choice of Yaakov for the special mission. His apprentice did not even ask how he was going to stay alive that long. Yet, his apprentice was unbothered by the idea. This was faith unlike Yeshua had witnessed among his apprentices, including his wife. He patted his apprentice on the back three times with his left hand before giving his apprentices right shoulder a firm squeeze of pride.

"I assume you already have something in mind regarding my long sojourn amongst my fellow man, Master?" Yaakov asked rhetorically, as if to affirm his master's chain of thoughts.

"You sure can read me like the Torah, brother." Yeshua replied.

"I do not know about the Torah, Master," Yaakov said. "But, if you say so…"

Yaakov was pensive for a few seconds.

"If I may guess, will I be losing my soul or something like that?" Yaakov asked.

"I could make you soulless, yes," Yeshua replied. "But given the situation, I think soullessness would not be ideal for you."

"You know best, Master," Yaakov said. "Do what you must. So long as I'm prepared and have your blessing, I'll be fine."

Yeshua smiled and said nothing. He raised his right index finger and touched Yaakov's forehead.

Yaakov's eyes snapped open and the morning rays of Solara were seeping through the wooden pieces of the closed windows of his bedroom. He pulled the sheet from his body and sat at the edge of his bed. He felt as if he had just blinked the previous night and dawn was here already. Yaakov yawned and stretched his muscles at the same time. It felt like paradise. When he brought his right hand to cover his yawn, after the fact, he noticed that he had a new piece of jewelry on his right hand. He fingered the ring with a green crystal. He balled his right hand into a fist and kissed the ring. As he stood up from his bed, ready to seize the day, he smiled and shook his head in amusement. When it came to Master, a very fine line existed between dream and reality.

# CHAPTER TWO

## REUNION

**SASHA PACED BACK** and forth and chewed on her fingernails. Ever since Shi'mon, Yochanan, and her lover teleported away to face Beelzebub, her worry roiled inside of her like a storm-tossed ocean. If this was how she felt, she could only imagine how the other three must be feeling in the presence of this creature, whose name seized their newly-given souls with morbid dread. Sasha had never heard of the demon before, but from the looks on the faces of the bravest men she had ever known, she concluded this Beelzebub creature was no easy foe. She shuddered involuntarily and paced faster as the thought of those three meeting their end morphed into a painful possibility.

She had finally awoken from the nightmare that was the Bright Eyes only to be thrust into a possibility of being permanently separated from the man who had gone further than above-and-beyond for her. Yehuda had died and returned from true death. Yehuda had yanked her away from the cold embrace of death and in Yehuda's eyes, Sasha had seen love like she had never seen before. Silent tears of worry rolled down Sasha's cheeks as her spine stiffened with the icicles of fear that spiked from it.

*They should have let me join them,* she kept saying to herself.

She was as good as Andrew, Shi'mon, Yehuda and Yochanan were, or so she thought. Though she, too, had received an esoteric upgrade like those four had, a dimension of differences separated an esoteric upgrade of one's essence and an upgrade in fighting skills. Sasha was also unsure of what Yehuda had become ever since his return from the Shadow of the Soul. Her gratitude for him being on their side was immense, despite the grimness of her expression.

Yes, their side. Sasha was now an unspoken inductee into their group. She was no longer just an informant for Yehuda, another tool in the shed or a sidekick. She was now one of them. They had welcomed her unconditionally. Sasha could not have been more honored. For the first time since losing her family on the night she was turned into a luper, Sasha had a family again.

What a feeling that was. Sasha shivered involuntarily, and her mind returned to its state of anxiety. She was both grateful and angry that Andrew had stayed behind. She could have followed Yehuda-and-Co's teleportation trail to join them in battle. But Andrew was not only there as a babysitter. He was there as the good friend who had helped her maintain her sanity during her many centuries of being undercover with the Bright Eyes. And now, he was doing the same thing, helping to bring some calmness to the storm that raged in her.

"They'll be alright, you know?" Andrew smiled confidently while he watched her pace back and forth.

"I know, I know," Sasha replied impatiently.

"Your behavior says otherwise," Andrew countered.

"Is it that obvious?" Sasha spat with a heavy dose of sarcasm.

"I've known my brothers longer than you have," Andrew ignored her sarcasm. "We share a bond you don't understand. Whatever they're experiencing right now, I'm also experiencing it through our shared clairsentience. So, if anything was a cause for concern, I assure you that I'd have told you. Better yet, I'd have teleported with you to their location."

Sasha ruminated on Andrew's words.

"You're right, Andrew," she conceded, pulling up a chair and slumping into it. "I'm sorry. I should not have been so rude to you."

"It's alright," Andrew said. "We both care very deeply for them."

"Thank you," Sasha said, gratefully.

Andrew smiled slightly when Sasha averted her gaze to the floor. She was less fidgety and less rigid with worry. His words was a temporary panacea to her psyche. Or maybe it was his façade of calmness that had rubbed off on her like an infectious skin disease. Or maybe it was a combination of both. Regardless, he had to put up this show because one of them had to, given the gravity of the situation with Beelzebub, and Sasha lacked the mental and psychological fortitude to do that.

Andrew envied the fact that Sasha was ignorant of the dire nature of the situation though. Her ignorance provided some sort of protection to her current state of mind. Unfortunately, he was not privy to the luxuries of such ignorance. Prior to their departure to face Beelzebub, the brothers-in-apprenticeship had left their psychic connections open to him. As such, he could perceive and experience everything Shi'mon, Yochanan and Yehuda perceived and experienced. However, despite Andrew's awareness of Kundalini's presence within Yehuda, Yehuda's experience of the manifestation and power of

witnessed from Shi'mon. Marissa wiped the silent tears that flowed from her eyes and slid back into his arms. Shi'mon kissed the crown of her head. The silence said it all and Patrick had to admit that the scene was very moving.

"You've grown so big, my child," Shi'mon said quietly.

"It's only been nearly 2,000 years, uncle," Marissa replied and laughed weakly. "And don't you pretend you haven't seen me in that long," Marissa play-punched him in the lower ribs.

"I couldn't stay away no matter how hard you tried to keep your distance." Shi'mon's arms hung free after he let go of her shoulders..

"With an aura like yours, it's hard not to feel your presence whenever you were around," Marissa retorted. "I lay emphasis on 'WERE'."

"And even after 2,000 years, you still think you could detect my presence without me letting you?" Shi'mon asked and smiled. "The only reason you knew I was around was because I wanted you to."

"We'll continue this conversation later, uncle." Marissa said and narrowed her eyes playfully at her 'uncle'.

She moved from apprentice to apprentice and gave each of them a hug.

"You look just like your father," Yochanan said.

"Absolutely not," Tau-ma rebutted. "Those eyes, nose, and jawline are from her mother. Her father labored in vain."

"Seriously, Tau-ma?" Bar-Talmai shook his head.

"What?" Tau-ma asked innocently.

"You've never been good at jokes, anyway," Bar-Talmai said. "Just stick to regular conversation next time."

Through the chuckles, Marissa moved to Sasha, who extended her hand, unsure of how Marissa would react if she moved in for a hug.

"Hello, I'm Sasha," she began. "You've never heard of me but I've-"

"I know who you are, Sasha," Marissa replied and hugged Sasha.

Sasha shuddered with pleasant surprise and was a little slow to return Marissa's hug. She hoped Marissa did not notice.

*How does she know about me?* Sasha asked herself.

*By tapping into your esoteric signature just now,* Marissa wanted to say to Sasha via telepathy, but changed her mind.

"I'm looking forward to some girl time together if that's alright with you," Marissa added. "We are the only women in this testosterone-infested room."

Marissa made a face. The others shook their heads and some of them rolled their eyes. Tau-ma was about to offer a rebuttal, but Bar-Talmai punched him hard in the stomach.

"What was that for?" Tau-ma dusted the area on his stomach where Tau-ma's punch had landed.

"I know what you were about to say," Bar-Talmai replied.

"What was I about to say?" Tau-ma asked.

*"That she really is master's daughter,"* Bar-Talmai replied telepathically.

*"And what's wrong with-"* Tau-ma began saying and then his eyes bulged slightly with the realization of the unintended implications of his statement.

*"I think it's best I shut up,"* Tau-ma conceded telepathically.

"You would've made a very unfunny joke, and that's all you need to know," Bar-Talmai added quickly to everyone's hearing. "Besides, I don't really need a reason to punch you, do I?" Bar-Talmai added and grinned mischievously.

"I sure could use some distraction from this male-infested conundrum," Sasha sighed and shook her head. "Care to join me?"

"Would love to," Marissa shrugged in exaggerated exasperation before winking at Marissa and heading towards Yehuda. "Boys."

Yehuda was the last person in her path of hugs. She paused in front of him and stared into his eyes. Yehuda stared back and made no move to hug her.

"Shi'mon is right; you have grown so big," Yehuda smiled weakly.

"It is good to see you, Yehuda," Marissa said and hugged him tightly.

Yehuda held her lovingly in his arms and kissed the crown of her head.

"Something very bad is happening to you," Marissa said as she gently stepped away from his embrace and took his face in her hands to study him. "I don't know what it is. But it's very serious."

"It's not as serious as it looks," Yehuda lied.

"But it is much more serious than it looks," Marissa almost yelled.

Yehuda appreciated the concern and care in her haggard expression, which were the reason behind her sudden emotional outburst. But that was Marissa, sweet one moment, fiery the next and had no trouble wearing her emotions on her sleeves when she was around those she considered family. Unknown to her, Yehuda had also been keeping tabs on her and Yehuda was willing to bet that his other brothers in apprenticeship had been doing the same as well. It was a responsibility that came naturally for him and it went without saying that the other apprentices shared similar feelings.

"And we will get to the very bottom of this, my love," Shi'mon interjected.

*"No need to cause more worry, okay?"* Shi'mon spoke to her telepathically.

*"Okay, uncle,"* she complied. *"But what IS going on with him? Do you know?"*

*"No, I don't know yet, my love,"* Shi'mon admitted. *"But we'll find out soon enough and see what we can do about it."*

*"Okay, uncle,"* Marissa said.

Shi'mon was the only apprentice Marissa referred to as 'uncle' and not because he was their leader. Her stare went blank as she recalled how Shi'mon had been a father figure to her when her real father was not there in the flesh.

Come to think of it, her only encounters with her father had been esoteric in nature and even those meetings were too few to not remember every single one of them.

*You have father issues, young lady,* Marissa smiled sadly to herself and raised her blank gaze from the floor towards the wall.

She was oblivious to everything else around her as she reminisced.

*Father,* she thought. *I know you were always there, though not in the flesh. Even before mother reassured me a countless number of times that you were never far away, I could feel your presence via our special bond. That much I understand. That much, I can appreciate.*

Marissa turned her gaze towards Shi'mon, who was having a conversation with Yochanan and Bar-Talmai. Marissa let out a sigh of appreciation for everything Shi'mon had done for her. He spent as much time as he could with her during his visits. Despite his busy schedule, despite the sadness, guilt and hollowness that dominated his persona, despite the mantle of leadership that was heavy on his shoulders, Shi'mon had always been there for her, as a father would for his child. One time, he had even stayed a whole week with her when she had just turned thirteen. Two thousand years later, Marissa's heart warmed with gratitude, as always, at the sweet memories of that period.

Marissa scanned the room with passive abandon. She was not trying to fault the others for not being there for her, their master's daughter, their master's only child. She was grateful that they even came to check on her a few times over the past two millennia, when she was still a toddler. They had tasks to complete and purposes to fulfill, according to the dictums of their mentor. The fate of the realm and humanity lay in their hands and that was far more important than whatever father issues she had. She could not be that selfish.

Marissa scoffed slightly as her thoughts took a detour towards the topic of humanity. She marveled at how the human race had proliferated in numbers. She remembered living in areas that had no more than three hundred people at one time. But today, they were talking about the realm having more than seven billion people. Amazing, indeed. So yes, the others would spend more time with her if they could; but they had over seven billion people to look out for. She appreciated them all, but she appreciated Uncle Shi'mon the most.

Marissa mentally smacked herself. Two millennia should be more than enough time for her to outgrow her petty, only-child syndrome and start acting like the grown, two-thousand-year-old woman she was.

*Look at me,* she chuckled in her head. *I'm a two-thousand year-old drama, attention-seeking queen. I have seen worse, though. Us women can be so vain sometimes. Well, maybe all the time. My 'friends' and acquaintances always had the same complaints and concerns: men, menstruation, and menopause, not forgetting weight, looks, age and everything else that came with the van of vanity. If only they knew how old I am and if only they knew that none of these were ever a problem for me. I'm sure they would've sold their souls to have what I have, literally. If only they knew….*

"Your mother is coming, right?" Yochanan asked Marissa.

"She should have been here by now," Marissa replied, returning to reality.

"It has been a while since I saw her or heard anything about her," Bar-Talmai said. "I know she's doing well and that, just like the rest of us, she's busy with her own affairs. Speaking of affairs, it still amuses me that if I lived a 'normal'-" he gestured with his index and middle fingers on both hands in the air at the mention of 'normal' "-life today, I probably would have been a tax expert, and I'd be charging all of you a special fee to prepare your taxes."

"And by 'special,' you mean extra." Yehuda interjected.

"Hey, what's family for, if not to patronize one's business?" Bar-Talmai said, and everyone laughed.

"You boys having a party without me?" said someone from the door.

The laughter died instantly. They all knew who that voice belonged to.

"The party never starts until you walk in, sister," Shi'mon said.

Shi'mon half-walked, half-ran.

*Now this is another first for you, boss,* Patrick thought and hoped that his boss did not hear his thoughts.

Shi'mon and Miryam collided in a tight embrace. Yochanan was next and, almost immediately, Miryam was at the center of a big, group hug.

*So cute,* Patrick smiled and walked towards where Marissa was standing.

He chose to neither read her facial expression nor to read the colors of her aura. However, if he were a guessing man, he would guess that Marissa was glad to see her mother and that was a little jealous the apprentices gave her mother a much warmer welcome than they did for her.

"I've never seen Father Supreme so happy in all my life," Patrick whispered at Marissa.

She nodded absentmindedly, her gaze still resting on her mother. "Uncle was always very happy when he was with us."

Patrick felt a hand slide over his right palm and interlock fingers with his. He sneaked a quick peek at his hand to make sure Marissa was actually taking his hand in hers. He returned his gaze towards the hugging group of bi-millennial humans and managed a half-mile, away from Marissa's line of sight. He returned her gentle squeeze and, out of the corner of his eye, he detected a smile of appreciation on Marissa's lips. But the smile disappeared as soon as it appeared.

Sasha walked to where they were and stood next to Marissa. Either she did not notice them holding hands or she did not care.

"This looks like a nice family reunion."

"You don't say, girl." Marissa replied.

Patrick raised an eyebrow at Marissa's response and turned to face her. She pretended to ignore his reaction, but she could not resist grinning.

"Oh boy, I don't ever wanna find myself on the wrong side of you two." Patrick shook his head. "You've barely known each other, and you're already doing the *'girl'* thing?"

Patrick laid emphasis on 'girl' and rolled his eyes.

"For your sake, I'd recommend you don't," Marissa joked.

"Aye, aye, ma'am." Patrick played along and turned to say something to Sasha, but his words died in his throat.

Patrick did not need to read her aura to see that Sasha was an epitome of insecurity and jealousy. She was finally in closed quarters with the woman her lover, Yehuda, had had an adulterous affair with. This was Sasha's lover's first love, and God, she was freaking beautiful. Yep. Miryam was an amazingly stunning woman and her simple, light green, fitted, ankle-length gown did nothing to diminish her beauty. Patrick felt a little bad for Sasha at first, but he immediately shrugged off the feeling. He wanted to ask if Sasha was okay and all that, but what happened in the past and whatever might transpire within the next few minutes were not his problem. Sasha was a big girl and she could handle herself just fine, without him checking after her. Perhaps his act of kindness might make her feel even more self-conscious.

Patrick navigated his gaze across the room. Yehuda was not a part of the hugging, chattering bunch. He had been standing in his own corner all this time, and no one seemed to notice. Everyone was focused on the newest center of attraction that was Miryam. Finally, Yehuda took slow, careful steps towards the group of apprentices. Perhaps this was another reason for Sasha's feelings of jealousy. Why had her lover seemed so transfixed by this woman's presence? Maybe after all these centuries, Yehuda still had a very severe weakness for his first love, Miryam?

*And why the hell am I bothering myself with this? Let them hash it out.*

If the group realized the awkwardness of the situation, they revealed nothing. They were still chattering along as Yehuda gave Miryam a slow, slightly lingering hug. She hugged him tightly and kissed him on the cheek, just as she had done to the rest of the group. She then peeled herself from him but held his face in her hands; just like her daughter had done.

*Damn genetics.* Patrick smiled.

"It's really good to see you again, Yeh," Miryam said.

Miryam did not call him 'brother' like she did for the rest of the group.

"It's good to see you too, Miri," Yehuda replied.

*Ooohhh snap. And they got nicknames for each other,* Patrick thought

He could have sworn he heard the gritting of Sasha's teeth and the cracking of her knuckles as she clenched her fists. He fought to suppress a smile. Her behavior reminded him of one of those cheesy Mexican soap operas.

"I'd ask how you've been, but I see you don't fare well at all," Miryam added, turning his head from side to side before taking a step back to examine him.

Her smile slipped, then faded away to be replaced by a concerned frown.

"I'm getting better, honestly," Yehuda tried to argue.

"Uh huh," Miryam replied and turned to look at Shi'mon.

Shi'mon gave an almost imperceptible nod and Miryam understood the silent message loud and clear.. He was aware of the situation and would look into it as soon as possible. But the others must not be apprised of the situation just yet. Miryam acknowledged silently as well. She then shifted her gaze past Yehuda and beamed at what she saw. Yehuda stepped aside as Miryam opened her arms. Marissa ran like a little girl into the arms of her mother. Mother and child locked in a tight embrace, the love was heart-warming to witness. Miryam held her daughter's face in her hands for a second, kissed both her daughter's cheeks and then held her daughter again in her arms.

"I've missed you so much, my child," Miryam whispered in Marissa's ear.

"I've missed you too, mother," Marissa replied. "Nice of you to come out of hibernation."

"Nice to see you're still the same child I breastfed," Miryam replied.

*Good, mommy is here and baby can stop crying now,* Patrick rolled his eyes.

"So, who's your friend?" Miryam asked Marissa nodding at Sasha.

"Her name is Sasha, mother," Marissa replied, and Miryam moved to shake Sasha's hand.

"Hello Ms. Sasha, I'm Miryam, Marissa's mother," Miryam smiled and shook Sasha's hand.

"Pleased to meet you, Ms. Miryam. I'm Yehuda's girlfriend." Sasha spoke with ice in her voice.

"I'm pleased to meet you too, Ms. Sasha," Miryam replied very cordially as if Sasha just told her that the sun was shining on a cloudless noonday.

Her smile was even more radiant and her green eyes beamed slightly, almost as if she was excited for Sasha sharing this piece of information with her.

"And please, feel free to call me Miryam," she continued and rested a hand on Sasha's shoulder. "If you're here with us, then you must be part of the family. So, if you've not yet been officially welcomed, please take this as my own way of saying welcome to the family."

It took everything for Patrick to not erupt in laughter. Sasha had been ready for war, but Miryam had defused Sasha's aggression like a pro. Patrick admired the art unfolding before his eyes. Sasha's aggression and jealousy morphed into confusion and embarrassment. Miryam was a woman who was neither living in the past nor had any time for petty sentiments. He now understood why the others adored her, why their master, whom he'd never met, had chosen her and he could see why Marissa was always going to act like a little girl in her presence. One could not help but love and admire this woman, Miryam, in the purest sense of those words.

"Uh... Thank you," Sasha managed after a few seconds' delay.

Miryam nodded.

"So, aren't you going to introduce me to your male companion?" Miryam asked Marissa.

"Don't get any ideas, mother," Marissa said, shaking her head and smiling. "His name is Patrick. He was the one who brought me here from Paris."

"It is such an honor to finally meet you, ma'am," Patrick said with a smile as he took off his fedora and held it against his chest.

"I like him already," Miryam said to her daughter as she shook Patrick's hand. "It is an honor to meet you too, Patrick. And didn't you hear me tell Sasha to address me by my name? Same applies to you, young man."

Her smile was intoxicating.

"It may take a little while for me to get used to that, ma'am," Patrick said. "In case you didn't know, I happen to be just a few decades old, and where I'm from, we usually don't address our significant seniors by first name only. So, forgive me if I refer to you as 'ma'am' in the meantime."

Miryam cocked an eyebrow at Patrick and spared a radiant smile and a nod before she turned towards her daughter.

"He's a keeper," she said with a wink.

"Mother," Marissa exclaimed, averting her gaze towards the floor..

"My point exactly," Miryam continued, obviously enjoying the fact that her daughter was getting a little embarrassed. "You could barely let go of his hand when you were dragging to hug your mother," Miryam added.

"*Mother,*" Marissa was clearly flustered now.

"Oh, come on now, my love," Miryam soothed. "You know I just miss my little girl so much, right? If I don't tease you, who else will?" she asked.

"It would be my honor to make that my life's mission, ma'am," Patrick offered, and everyone, including Sasha, erupted in laughter.

"Come, sister," Shi'mon said, taking Miryam by the shoulder. "There is much to discuss."

"Of course, brother," Miryam replied. "I want to hear everything."

"Tonight, we act like the good old times when we were still regular people," Shi'mon continued, and everyone agreed.

Yehuda and Sasha chose a private corner. Yehuda had some reassuring to do, despite Miryam's clear communication that she was in no way interested in him. Shi'mon and Miryam chose their own corner, and the two began chatting away. The other apprentices formed their own groups. Patrick appreciated the fact that, at least at this moment, they would all act like Earth Realm, and humanity, were not under any kind of threat. In this moment, they would not talk business. They would all be normal, human beings.

*And holy crap. I'm in the presence of the twelve, no* thirteen *apostles of Jesus freaking Christ. How cool is that?.* Patrick fangirled in his head.

"So, what was that all about?" Marissa asked Patrick.

"I'm sorry, I don't understand," Patrick replied, honestly.

"You know, the theatrics you pulled back there." Marissa said. "Taking off your hat, calling my mother 'ma'am' and all that other crap you said…"

"Those weren't theatrics, Marissa," Patrick explained, chuckling as he did. "I admire your mother, and I was being honest about the culture where I'm from. Or at least, that's how I was raised; to show respect for our elders."

"Yeah, yeah, yeah," Marissa rolled her eyes.

"And for someone who likes the word 'theatrics,' you sure are a drama queen," Patrick retorted, grinning as he did.

"Oh, I'll show you drama queen, mister."

Marissa threw a right hook at Patrick. Patrick calmly channeled her punch in a semicircle with his right hand. Using the same momentum, he fed her right hand to his left hand, bringing his right hand downwards to intercept a second punch Marissa was throwing at him. He wrapped both her hands behind her lower back and pulled her close to his body. Her body felt strong against his, face inches away from his, and her bosom pressed against his chest. Her breathing was steady and her breath was warm against his chest. With each breath, her cleavage heaved as if her breasts were threatening to pop out of her low-cut blouse. Marissa smiled at Patrick and he returned her smile as he let go of both her hands.

She let her hands fall to her side but did not peel her body away from his. Instead, she stared into his eyes and the two of them were still smiling at each other. Sasha was smiling, and so was Yehuda; the easing of minds was a success. The apprentices went on with their chats and occasional bursts of laughter, oblivious to everything else happening in the room.

And as Miryam and Shi'mon were engrossed in their conversations, Miryam noticed her daughter's aura glowing brightly. From her corner of the room, Miryam smiled at the thought that, after close to two millennia, her daughter was finally having a good time.

*Thank you, Patrick.* Miryam said to herself.

# CHAPTER THREE

# MEET MADUK

**WELCOME TO THE** Realm of Nimbu, home of Sinisters. Located in the Dimension of Solaris, the Realm of Nimbu was originally uninhabited until the creatures of Hollow Earth Realm turned it into a prison for Maduk. The etheric composition of Nimbu caused a transmutation of Maduk's esoteric signature, resulting in Maduk becoming the first Sinister. Nimbu Realm was originally sealed from the rest of Solaris until a cosmic shift during the transition from the Age of Aries to the Age of Pisces caused a rift in its esoteric confines about 2,000 years ago. However, it would take nearly five centuries before portals started appearing in these rifts and Nimrud would dare to venture out to other realms within Solaris through these portals. How were these portals created? Neither Nimrud nor Maduk understood. During these visits, Nimrud, and the Sinisters he spawned later, pillaged and abducted creatures to turn them into more Sinisters. This was how the Sinisters increased their numbers over the next 1,500 years. And what, or who, prevented them from permanently living outside of Nimbu?

Maduk.

His orders were strict, and no one dared contest them. No Sinister could go toe-to-toe with their lord and master. No one dared to challenge him and those who were foolish enough to try were ended swiftly and with extreme prejudice. So, in the meantime, the sinisters would remain within Nimbu until the time came to return and reclaim his birthright; Earth Realm. Yes, Earth Realm was his birthright. Earth Realm had been given to his parents, and, thanks to his mother, Earth Realm had been taken away from him.

Maduk stared blankly at a wall in his private chambers. He contemplated on the only beautiful thing in the realm; order. He had created the order, an extension of his personality. The order was a bi-product of his might and will, a glimpse of his ego. He recalled the first and only rebellion that broke out a few centuries ago. Before the rebellion, he was never a man of violence. But thanks to the extreme circumstances that brewed under his jurisprudence, he had been forced to give Nimbu Realm a small demonstration of his capabilities.

Maduk had single-handedly ended the lives of over a hundred and fifty rebel Sinisters so swiftly that the remainder of the rebellion had surrendered and sworn their allegiance to him. But Maduk wanted to gift the Sinisters with a message to be remembered for millennia to come. He personally executed the remaining rebels, ripping off the heads of all 449 of them with his bare hands.

Nimbu cowered in the wake of his wordless message, served with extreme prejudice and swift, savvy savagery. Never again would any Sinister conceive of contesting his leadership or coveting his throne. In Nimbu, Maduk was law. In Nimbu, Maduk was order. In Nimbu, Maduk was judgement. And the Sinisters worshipped him because, in Nimbu, Maduk was god.

Nimbu Realm had never forgotten.

Maduk ignored a knock on the door. If the business was of any importance, the Sinister would knock again. A second knock followed. He sighed heavily..

"Come in," Maduk said.

A Sinister came in and bowed her head to the ground.

"Your highness, a thousand pardons for my intrusion," the quaking in her voice matched the trembling of her entire body and her eyes were averted away from Maduk.

"What is it?" Maduk half scolded the sinister.

"The queen is on her way, your highness," the sinister replied timidly.

The right armrest on Maduk's chair snapped to pieces under Maduk's hand. He cursed silently under his breath and breathed deeply.

"I see," Maduk said after a moment. "Tell her I'll be there shortly."

"Would you like for me to have her wait at the main room, your majesty?" the sinister almost stammered as her voice quaked.

"Yes," Maduk replied.

The Sinister bowed her head and left the room, closing the door behind her. Maduk knew why the queen was paying him an unexpected visit and, like always, her presence was already making him lose his calmness of mind. The queen was the one and only creature in Creation who always got under his skin. The mere thought of her made Maduk want to smash something to smithereens. He was about to get an earful for something that was not his fault. She possibly could not blame him for the ever-weakening esoteric boundaries around Nimbu, could she? It was not his fault that they, the Sinisters, could now leave the realm more easily than before.

Maduk had not stepped outside of Nimbu ever since he was imprisoned in it by the creatures of Hollow Earth Realm. He had let his subjects take care of the menial task of abduction and conversion. But with the next great shift drawing nigh and with the esoteric confines of the realm almost gone, Maduk wanted to see Earth Realm after so many millennia. He knew it would drive the queen mad and the thought made him revel with evil pleasure on the inside. He was not so furious anymore about the queen's visit. Pissing her off always spiced his day. And on his first visit on Earth Realm after so long a period, he was welcomed by the vermin known as Yochanan.

Speaking of Yochanan, the man was one of the 'special humans' who were consistently targeting and executing Maduk's subjects over the last 1,500 years. When he received word on these humans, he brushed it off and assumed they would die after a few decades. But that had not been the case. Of all the realms the Sinisters had visited, Earth Realm was the only realm that could sustain Sinister life. These special humans were a promise of stiff rebellion to come. He would deal with them later because 'the time was not yet perfect', according to the queen.

*Damn her.*

But in their frustration, the Sinisters had also received unexpected but very welcome news.

It started as a rumble in the sky across the realm. Nimbu throbbed was confusion; not even Maduk could discern what was going on. For the first time the rifts were not just temporary and in pockets like they used to be. The entire etheric boundary of Nimbu was gone. At first, the sinisters hesitated. No Sinister wanted to risk going out yet. It could have been a trap, for all the Sinisters knew. So Maduk had tasked his top general, Nimrud, with selecting a handful of Sinisters to investigate the situation. Nimrud selected two hundred Sinisters for the assignment.

Maduk would have gone himself, given that he had not been outside of Nimbu in so long. But he was esoterically bound to this prison of a realm, as opposed to every other Sinister, who was only bound to Nimbu Realm by his command. As such, he could never leave Nimbu unless the entire boundary was removed. So, while every Sinister had sensed a rumble in the realm, Maduk's essence resonated with the unraveling of the esoteric boundary of the realm. And this resonance heralded a sentiment he had not felt in more than 4,000 years: freedom.

With this newfound freedom, he had ventured into Earth Realm, after receiving the all-clear from Nimrud's selection of Sinisters.

Maduk felt a force slowly pulling him, beckoning him, towards the horizon of Nimbu Realm. No point in fighting that force. The force seduced his essence. Over two hundred Sinisters had crossed the horizon and stepped into Earth Realm, at the behest of a commander. There was a small problem on the other side that needed rectifying and a few scores of them would not do the job. Talks of a handful of Sinisters gone prior being responsible for the permanent rift in Nimbu's boundaries spread throughout the realm like an orange dust storm. By extension, these handful of Sinisters had set Maduk free. But how had these Sinisters gained the knowhow to dabble in esoterism as such?

Maduk had emerged from the center of a circular pool of black, blood-like liquid. On four corners, four Sinisters chanted incantations, with their eyes closed and hands raised toward the roof of a dark, stone chamber with very rugged walls, reeking with the rancid smell of myrrh gone bad. He emerged slowly from the pool as the Sinisters continued chanting. When his naked form was out of the pool, the Sinisters threw themselves face down and started humming. Their god was here. Maduk regarded the four creatures as they prostrated in front of him. Their horns all pointed towards him, their tails hung limply between their legs and arms were spread outwards until each Sinister's fingertips touched the other's forming a complete, imperfect circle.

Maduk heard a cacophony of incantations as well as screams and shouts of chaos outside and walked towards the sound, until he emerged from the mouth of the cave on Mount K2 in the Himalayas. A Sinister at the entrance to the stone chamber was chanting incantations. Maduk recognized the Sinister. He thought the Sinister had been killed during their last expedition. He now understood that this Sinister had stayed behind to look for a way to set them free. He made a mental note to promote the Sinister to general upon their return.

"All hail Maduk, God of Nimbu Realm," the Sinister hailed with pride.

And then, a human slashed the Sinister's throat.

Maduk leveled a dispassionate gaze at the dying Sinister before meeting the human's fearless gaze with an indifference that burned colder than that at over 28,000 ft above sea level. Maduk had called the human a pest, and he had made a promise to ensure that this creature and his friends would suffer a harsher fate than that of the rest of humanity will when Sinisters took over Earth Realm.

"Hello, Maduk," a familiar voice that Maduk hated with his existence broke into his reminiscing..

"Hello, my queen," Maduk sneered.

"Do we always have to do this?" Lithilia asked without bothering to hide her exasperation. "You've insisted I address you by your 'proper' title in front of your subjects and you get mad at me for respecting your demands?"

*You were supposed to wait for me in the main room,* he wanted to say but settled for a heavy sigh instead.

"Is that what you think, my queen?" Maduk asked coldly. "Do you think I am mad at you?"

Lithilia took in a deep breath to control herself.

"After all these millennia, you still hold so much resentment towards me," Lithilia spoke flatly. "What more do you want? How many times must I apologize for the past?"

"You still did not answer my question, my queen," Maduk replied with the same icy tone.

"Yes, that is what I think, and more," Lithilia gritted her teeth in frustration.

Lithilia glanced over her shoulders to make sure no one was listening and then turned back towards Maduk.

"You spoiled brat," Lithilia added.

"And you forget that you're in this 'spoiled brat's' territory, my queen," Maduk rebutted calmly and flashed an unpleasant smile at Lithilia.

Lithilia shook her head.

"It's almost impressive how much bigger your pair has grown since your incarceration in this dump," Lithilia decided to drop a low blow.

"In this 'dump', I am at peace," Maduk retorted. "You cringe in fear at the mere thought of her. And no matter where you go, Hell, Nimbu, Earth, anywhere, you will never be at peace."

Bright orange, red flames spewed from Lithilia's eyes and in the palm of her hands. She bared her teeth, and her shoulders heaved rhythmically as her anger boiled over.

"I never knew you had a passion for drama, my queen," Maduk teased.

"You'll find out soon enough if you don't control your tongue, creature," Lithilia warned as the flames in the palm of her hands condensed into bright orange, red spheres.

Maduk scoffed and then looked past Lithilia.

"Kalzak," he called out.

Kalzak rushed into his chambers, dropped to a knee, placed his right fist on his chest and bowed to the ground.

"My king," Kalzak responded.

"Lock my door and clear the hallway," Maduk ordered. "No matter what anyone hears or sees, no one is to interfere. Clear?"

"Yes, my king," Kalzak replied, not moving from his kneeling position.

"Dismissed."

Kalzak beat his chest once with his right fist, rose to his feet, nodded towards Maduk and then towards Lithilia before walking out of Maduk's private quarters. His voice boomed as he bark orders down the hallway, the snick of the lock sounding behind him.

Maduk waited for a moments before returning his attention towards Lithilia. "Now, where were we?"

"I was about to do something I should have done a long time ago," Lithilia replied and raised her right hand slowly in the air.

Maduk burst into hysterical laughter and Lithilia clenched her fists, her jaws and squeezed her eyes shut as her anger flared some more. She uttered a few words but Maduk opened his right hand. The flames from Lithilia's eyes and the spheres of fire from her hands migrated towards his open palm. Lithilia's jaw dropped and her eyes bulged in shock, but she quickly regained herself. She summoned more flames on the palms of her hands but as soon as she did, the flames still migrated towards Maduk. Her gaze danced between her hands and Maduk's before she felt an invisible force yank her body forward. She had no time to react as, she started floating slowly towards Maduk until she was eye-level with Maduk and her face was only a few inches from his. His hot, non-smelly breath washed over her face in a steady rhythm.

"Now what did you say you were about to do, my queen?" Maduk asked.

Lithilia struggled to break free from the invisible clutches that held her fast.

"Maybe a very, very long time ago, in another life, you would have been able to raise your filthy hands at me," Maduk said, icy calm overtaking him. "But not today. Not ever, my queen," he added with a sneer.

Maduk let Lithilia go. She landed on the floor with a thud like a sack of dirty clothes. The look of shock, confusion, and consternation on her face was music to his ego. She was not afraid, just like Maduk had expected.

"Because of your legacy of breaking hearts and causing irreparable damages to others, I'd have gladly put an end to the sad excuse of what you call life," he spat. "But your fate is not mine to decide. I shall leave you in her hands, the one you dread the most. She is your ultimate fate."

"Thanks for your support and encouragement," Lithilia scoffed with sarcasm as she picked up herself from the floor.

"You're most welcome," Maduk replied in kind. "Now, back to business."

Maduk turned around and made himself comfortable in a chair.

"What are you here for, my queen?"

Lithilia heaved a sigh of exasperation and sat down on a nearby seat.

"You never should have stepped out of Nimbu," Lithilia shook her head in resignation. "You were good on heeding to my admonition until recently."

"And why should I be concerned, again?" Maduk asked and rolled his eyes.

"She now can find you, you imbecile," Lithilia snapped.

"And how is that my concern, again?" Maduk asked, with the same level of boredom as before. "I know she's still upset with me. But when it comes to you," Maduk shook his head. "She will tear down Creation itself to make sure you pay for what you made me do."

"You still don't get it," Lithilia choked and briefly buried her face in her hands. "I've finally accepted the fact that I can never earn your forgiveness or love. It has been the hardest thing for me to accept and I've realized hope is overrated."

Lithilia bowed her head and wrestled against the well of frustration she felt like she was drowning in. Tears of sadness streamed down her cheeks and she wiped them with the back of her right hand. She sobbed for a few more seconds before she regained herself.

Maduk remained unmoved by her gesture. For all he knew, she could have been putting up a show.

"All this time, the only thing that has kept me going was that you were safe and protected," Lithilia continued and sniveled. "But now that you're in the open, and since you can't see beyond your hatred for me, I'll wrap up my visit and leave you be."

"Finally," Maduk spat.

Lithilia met Maduk's gaze before she continued.

"I'll face her soon. It will be my last stand to protect you. But, just so you know, if you think she's pissed at me, think of how *he* feels about you."

Maduk's head snapped towards Lithilia. He took a closer look at her to make sure she was not bluffing, and, by the stars, the queen was *not*. Maduk leaned forward in his chair and kept his gaze directly at Lithilia. He looked deep into her eyes and for the first time in forever, he saw the hollowness in them that used to be her soul. This was a woman who had gone beyond the very edges of hope and desperation. This was a woman who had nothing more to lose. This was a woman without any purpose or anything or anyone to live for anymore.

"You *are* telling the truth," Maduk leaned forward, eyes dimming in fear.

"He's here," Lithilia shrugged in resignation. "He has been here for thousands of years. But she hid his identity, always cloaking him. He doesn't even know who he truly is right now. He came back, Maduk. He came back."

The tears flowed freely down Lithilia's cheeks. The desperation in her voice was palpable. But not as palpable as the fear that oozed from Maduk's being, an uncomfortably unfamiliar sensation. He stood up and paced the room.

"You say he doesn't know who he actually is?" Maduk asked.

"No, he doesn't."

"Then my best option is a preemptive strike," his voice quavered slightly with dim hope.

"You'll have to find him first, my king," Lithilia reminded him.

Maduk sensed the balance of power shift from him to her. He sighed heavily. He did not appreciate Lithilia's tone of voice.

"So, what are you saying?" Maduk asked.

He was desperately trying to mask his mounting frustration at his ignorance and stupidity. Once again, this... woman... had him by the balls. He was burning on the inside with a consuming rage as he struggled to control his hands which trembled in fear at her revelation. Maduk had known her for far too long to be absolutely certain that she had this piece of information all along. She was saving it for the perfect moment and that perfect moment was now.

*Damn her. Damn her. Damn her.*

"Are you prepared to listen now?" Lithilia sniveled one more time as she ceased crying, adding some salt to Maduk's blistered ego.

"Will you tell me where he is or not?" Maduk's voice was beginning to rise.

"You'll have to ask nicely, young man," Lithilia replied and even managed a sly smile.

"So you are protecting him?" Maduk asked in classic reverse psychology fashion; although he knew it was pointless against Lithilia.

"I'm doing what I've been trying to do this whole time, you stupid fool," Lithilia lashed. "I've been trying to protect you. Don't you see. I asked you never to come out because if you stayed concealed, she wouldn't sense you. If she doesn't sense you, then she won't be reminded of what happened. If she doesn't get reminded of what happened, she won't want payback. But who's to say she wouldn't let her son have his chance at vengeance anyway?"

Lithilia let the words sink in. She enjoyed every second of Maduk writhing from his growing fear and discomfort until he groped for a chair and slumped into it.

"I'm not a coward," Maduk said after a while.

"It's not about being a coward," Lithilia rebutted. "It's about staying alive."

"And who says he is stronger than I am?" Maduk sounded like he was trying to convince himself. "I can take him on any time, any day."

"And you don't even know who or what you're talking about," Lithilia said. "I can guarantee that you do *not* stand a chance against him."

"Thanks for the confidence," Maduk spat.

"You're most welcome, my king," Lithilia mocked. "I only return that which you have so self-righteously awarded me."

"So, you are really going to hide his identity from me?"

"For your sake, yes," Lithilia replied more slowly.

Maduk chuckled in resignation and shook his head.

"I now see why," Maduk exclaimed and laughed even harder.

"Finally," Lithilia chimed.

"Oh, no, no, no, *no*," Maduk countered. "It is not what you think."

He leaned back in his chair and laughed derisively

Lithilia shook her head.

"You never cease to amaze me, Maduk."

"And neither do you," he retorted, dropping forward to glare at her. "You sit here, acting like you are trying to protect me when you are just trying to protect your sorry self. That is a new low, even for you. I now see why the people of Earth Realm call you Lilith, the demon whore. You will sleep with anyone and anything, both metaphorically and physically, as long as the price is right."

And then, Maduk felt the drop in the temperature of the chamber before he heard the crackle of electricity in the air. A power so dark, it made Maduk's skin crawl, smothered the room. Something had gone blank within Lithilia's essence. Her anger reached levels it had never reached before and it carried her to places she had never been before. Her anger tore down every restriction she ever had: regret, guilt, pride, shame, love, hate, everything. It made her hollower, more void, more soulless. It unleashed a force from within her being that she had never experienced before. Maduk expected to see her mad, and was ready for that. But he was never prepared for what actually unfolded before his eyes.

Lithilia morphed into a human form of bright orange-red flames. The flaming form blazed towards him. He lifted his right hand towards what was once Lithilia but could not stop her. The flaming creature seized him by the throat and flung him across the room. He flew through the door with such force that the door shattered into a million splinters. Before he could react, the human form of flames was upon him, seizing him again by the throat and floating with him in the air. The guards watched, frozen and stunned, as a less-than-six-feet tall flaming human made their over seven-feet-tall god look like a helpless cripple.

Maduk felt the pressure around his neck and felt his body slowly burn inside-out. He felt his life burn away slowly as he locked eyes with those of the creature that used to be Lithilia. He wanted to scream, but not a single sound emanated from his throat. He tried to fight this never-before-seen version of Lithilia. But neither a single ounce of muscle in his frame, nor the tiniest tinge of his will obeyed his command.

"Now you know *exactly* why I am a whore of essences," Lithilia spoke through clenched, flaming teeth in a voice so uncanny it could give a school of children a heart attack.

And Maduk got every single syllable of the message. As Maduk's life slowly burned away, his final thoughts were those of regret; for the way he had treated her these past millennia and for not appreciating her attempts to make up for her past errors. He tried to open his mouth for some final words; but he could not. So instead, in a final gesture, he spoke from his heart; and from his heart, he said four words via telepathy.

*"I am truly sorry."*

The humming from the smokeless, odorless flames on Lithilia's body, forged from the ethers and supercharged with a non-human essence, slowly died off, along with the flames on her body as she gradually became human again. She let go of Maduk, who landed on the ground with a loud thud. Her naked body floated towards Maduk as he coughed repeatedly. Her clothes had been burned away by the flames on her body. She headed back to his private chambers, oblivious of her nakedness, and pulled a seat towards her using telekinesis. She eased herself into it, still uncaring about summoning garments over her body and leveled a cold, hard glare at Maduk on the floor.

Maduk had seen that look too many times to know that she was still furious at him. But at least, she would not kill him. He sat up without taking his eyes off her and began healing himself using the force of will. There was no pain or sound as he used his chi to form new flesh over his charred body; only cold-burning fear seizing his soul. She looked down at him, and this time he saw something new in her gaze: indifference. He might as well have been dead to her; but she would keep him alive just because…

Just because…

Maduk refused to admit the reason why. He was still adamant to believe that Lithilia was capable of such sentiment. Lithilia spun her chair away from him using telekinesis. Maduk stood up from the floor, stumbled weakly past her and sat opposite from her.

"Here's how things will be from now on," Lithilia said sternly. "Nimbu will remain open, but I'll cloak you from her."

"What if Nimbu is attacked?" Maduk asked.

"What makes you think I care about your Sinisters?" Lithilia replied.

Maduk reeled backwards slightly, shocked beyond belief at Lithilia's candid reply. She would sacrifice Nimbu and all the Sinisters as a means of achieving her ultimate plan, whatever the plan was.

"What happened to you?" Maduk asked, still adjusting to the new Lithilia sitting across of him.

"I don't know, and I don't care," Lithilia replied flatly. "But you will be safe. When the time comes, you will face him, and I will face her. This is an inevitability we both must answer to. Now, don't you have something to take care of?"

Maduk nodded. He stood up from his chair and summoned the guards who had witnessed Lithilia almost kill him. They rushed into his chambers and took a knee. Within seconds, he killed each guard with his bare hands and summoned flames using the force of will to burn their corpses to nothingness, as if they never existed in the realm. The God of Nimbu Realm could not allow word to spread about the queen beating him. That would be very bad publicity. Maduk turned around to face the queen.

Lithilia opened her arms. Maduk reluctantly walked towards her, and because he was almost a foot-and-a-half taller than she was, he knelt in front of her. She cradled his head on her bosom and lovingly kissed the crown of his head.

"Now, my son, are we going to work together?" Lithilia asked coldly.

"Yes… mother," Cahen, also known as Maduk, replied as timidly as he used to do many millennia ago.

# CHAPTER FOUR

# MY BETTER HALF!

**LITTLE CAHEN BURIED** his face in the crease of his grandfather's neck, while grandfather gently rubbed his back and spoke words of comfort to the traumatized child. He glanced at the entrance of the huge facility just in time to see his mother running away into the garden.

*Why did mother hurt father? His innocent mind wondered. What did father do? Was it because of me? But I did not do anything. I was just in the corner with my little friend, but mother scared my little friend away. Was I not supposed to be here?*

"It is alright, my boy," his grandfather kept whispering in his ear as he caressed his head. "No harm will befall you here."

Cahen's shock and confusion had rendered him silent. He squinted and wiped his nose on his grandfather's shoulder and spared another quick glance at the entrance of the facility before his grandfather rounded a corner. His mother was nowhere in sight. Little Cahen then rested his head on his grandfather's shoulder and stared blankly ahead. His childlike innocence kicked in and shrouded his psyche from further psychological trauma. Even better, grandfather will protect him from anything that scared him, including his mother.

"What is his status?" Cahen's grandfather asked a woman who was tending to Cahen's father.

"Physically, he is fine, sir," the woman replied. "The scans revealed no internal injuries. Not even a concussion. Just broken skin."

She gestured towards the spot on Cahen's father's head that had been sealed with organic foam and bandaged. In two hours, the organic foam will morph into the patient's skin constituency and heal the wound without leaving a scar.

"Good," he adjusted Cahen in his arms. "Is Sunki on the expedition still?"

"Yes, sir," she replied.

"Okay, I will handle the boy's father's psychological assessment," he said and handed Cahen over to his father.

Little Cahen immediately snuggled in his father's arms. His father kissed him on the head.

"I am glad you are physically well, my son," Cahen's grandfather said.

"Thank you, father," Cahen's father said. "And thank you for taking care of Cahen."

"Of course," the man gave a nod of encouragement. "He is my grandson, is he not?"

"Yes, Father. He is," Cahen's father attempted a weak smile.

Cahen immediately fell asleep in his father's arms.

"Where is she, Father?" Cahen's father's voice revealed a hint of worry.

"Somewhere in the garden," Father replied.

"I have never seen her like that," the man added.

"It was a first time for us all, son," Father agreed. "Do not worry. We will take care of the situation and make sure she understands that her behavior caused plenty of hurt. Alright?"

"Alright, Father," Cahen's father replied.

"Rest up and I will see you later," Father said and turned his attention towards Cahen, who was asleep in his father's arms. "Do you want me to put him in bed for you?"

"No, thank you," Cahen's father said, adjusting Cahen's body in his arms. "He can sleep here with me."

"As you wish," Father headed for the door. "See you later."

Father walked out of the chamber, pressed a button and the door slid shut behind him. Cahen's father was alone with Cahen. A moment later, he pressed a button on the side of the bed. The bed spread out sideways and became big enough to comfortably accommodate both father and son. He stared lovingly at his child sleeping next to him. Cahen's peaceful look was intoxicating. He kissed his son's forehead, closed his eyes and fell asleep almost immediately.

He dreamed of a creature with wings of light. She was beautiful. Her skin flawless, her body toned and eyes so green, deep-set and hypnotic that they made his body go limp with fiery desire, even before she glided towards him. She kissed him deeply and passionately, and he returned the favor. She called him by a strange name. He corrected her several times, telling her that his name was Adamou. But the creature of light was adamant. When he awoke from his dream, he was unsure if his dream truly was a dream.

Father walked into his office and sat behind his center desk. He tapped on some buttons on his table, and four holograms hovered in front of him. One hologram was of a male, the other of a female. Each of the remaining holograms contained notes underneath the hologram of the male and female. Father leaned back and stared at the holograms for a moment. Above the male, the name "Adamou" was inscribed in bold print, and above the female, "Lithilia" was also inscribed in bold print. The man leaned forward and tapped a few more buttons on his desk. The holograms of the male and female merged into one, and the notes merged and form a single set of notes. Father studied the single set of notes, and after a while, his frustration started to get the better of him.

Father was hoping to find something after cross-referencing their records that could help explain Lithilia's sudden, violent outburst. Unfortunately, he did not find anything.

*What could have gone wrong in the design process?* He wondered.

Both subjects had demonstrated remarkable progress and promise. He would get to the bottom of it. The logs and scans revealed nothing abnormal with both subjects. Nothing seemed out of the ordinary. He rubbed his temples and cursed under his breath. His frustration was building up as the prospect of another failed experiment loomed in the horizon. Finally, he sighed heavily and pressed a button on his desk. The holograms vanished.

The door to his chamber slid open and Sunki walked in. Sunki was Father's cousin and second-in-command. The cousins greeted each other brusquely.

"How did the expedition go?" Father asked.

"Very well, Ukni," Sunki replied with a slight smile of excitement as he stood in front of Ukni's desk. "Our initial readings were correct. There are astounding amounts of deposits within an eight-sound-leap radius alone and going a hundred sound leaps below. More than enough to heal our home realm."

"That is great news indeed, brother," Ukni replied.

Their realm, Necheru, was edging towards destruction due to an abnormal recurrence of a set of geological chain reactions; hence why Ukni and his team had journeyed into the dimension in search of possible solutions that could help stop and reverse the geological chain reactions that threatened to destroy their realm. They could evacuate the entire realm, of course, but only as a last resort. Sunki's latest update was great news. Ukni tried to share in the exciting news, but his mind was too preoccupied with Lithilia's behavior. If the experiment failed, again, then Ukni and the rest of his realm would have a more serious problem than just losing their realm.

"What is the matter, brother?" Sunki asked.

"The female showed tendencies of violence today," Ukni said. "Left the male with a gash in the head and a very traumatized child in the wake of her outburst."

"Damn it," Sunki exclaimed, knowing what the long-term ramifications of Lithilia's behavior meant for the mission.

"Believe me when I say my choice of words was not as nice as yours was," Ukni said, shaking his head while Sunki pulled a chair and sat next to Ukni.

"And we do not know yet what is going on, do we?" Sunki asked.

"No, we do not," Ukni replied flatly.

"Okay then, we will have to bring in the female and run some separate tests on her. Maybe we will come up with something," Sunki suggested.

"Agreed," Ukni said and pressed a button on the far right-hand corner of his desk.

A hologram appeared and a face was in the center of it.

"Sir," a young male greeted.

"Bring me the female and take her to Room 6," Ukni said.

"Yes, sir," the young male replied, and the image disappeared.

Ukni returned his attention towards Sunki.

"So, on to more exciting news," Ukni said with a little more enthusiasm than he could muster. "When do you think we can begin extraction?"

"Within the next four to five days," Sunki replied. "I will update the others in the nearby realms of Lunis and Mars."

"Good," Ukni raised his hands to eye level.

He turned them inside out several times, shook his head and smiled.

"What is it, brother?" Sunki asked.

"I am aging a lot faster," Ukni replied, "I think it is because this realm is closer to Solara and the days are a lot shorter here compared to home. You are not looking much younger either."

"You do not say," Sunki agreed, and both men laughed at each other.

They continued chatting for half an hour. Suddenly, a hologram of the face of the young man tasked with finding Lithilia appeared in front of them.

"Sir, we have a situation," he said grimly. "We cannot find her."

"What do you mean you cannot find her?" Ukni and Sunki were on their feet. "Where did you run your search?"

"Started with a radius of ten sound leaps," the young male replied. "There was nothing, sir. Extended the radius to twenty and then to a hundred. Still there was nothing. She could not have covered even a sound leap within such a short space of time, sir."

The young man mopped his sweaty forehead with the back of his hand.

"There is absolutely no trace of her, sir," he added. "Not even esoteric."

Sunki did not even blink when Ukni banged his fist hard into his desk with enough force to split the desk in two. Luckily, the desk was made with an alloy of ionized carbon and reinforced iron. Ukni screamed more profanities than Sunki had ever heard him scream. He began pacing up and down in his office.

"We are still searching, sir, and we will find her," the young man continued. "I just wanted to give you a status update."

"Find her," Ukni screamed.

"Will do, sir," the young male replied, and the hologram vanished.

"Where could she have gone?" Sunki asked, more to himself that to Ukni.

"I will go check on Adamou," Ukni said, choosing to ignore Sunki's pointless question as he headed for the door. "He must be apprised of the situation."

"And I will take over the search," Sunki offered, following his cousin.

The door slid open, and both men walked out of Ukni's office.

Ukni met Adamou and Cahen in the hallway and grinned with delight to see Cahen in a much happier mood. He approached them with a light smile, and when they saw him, Cahen ran towards him. He picked Cahen up, threw him up in the air and caught him on his way down. Cahen went wild with joy.

"You are growing too fast, my child," Ukni said, tickling Cahen's nose. "Soon, I will no longer be able to lift you off the ground."

"Says who, grandfather?" Cahen asked. "You will still be very strong, and you will be able to carry me still like you are now, will you not?"

"We will see when that time comes, my boy," he replied and set Cahen on the floor. "How about you run along and play in the hallway, eh?"

Cahen was gone before he finished the statement. Ukni shook his head and laughed lightly.

"How are you feeling, son?" he asked Adamou.

"Very well, Father, thank you," Adamou replied. "How is she doing?"

"That is why I am here, son," Ukni said. "Walk with me."

The two men walked slowly along the hallway.

"She is nowhere to be found, son," Ukni said, and Adamou stopped dead in his tracks. "We are still searching for her and we will find her, rest assured."

Adamou leveled a frightened and confused gaze at Ukni. He opened his mouth to say something but his throat felt dry. He cleared his throat and averted his eyes towards the floor as if he was in a daze.

"But where could she have gone to?" Adamou murmured before raising a pair of fearful eyes in Ukni's direction. "What if something happened to her, Father?"

"We will find her, son," Ukni tried to reassure him with a firm hand and a gentle squeeze on Adamou's shoulder. "For now, you must let your son know what is going on; that his mother is missing, maybe somewhere beyond the hills. But we are all still searching for her. Okay?"

Adamou's stare was blank and almost lifeless. He remained silent and did not move, but a gentle squeeze and push on his shoulder from Ukni was incentive enough for him to resume walking. They caught up with Cahen and Adamou broke the news to Cahen. Cahen took the news with the innocence of a child.

"I hope mother is doing well, father," Cahen flashed a smile of innocence in Adamou's direction. "She will come back home soon."

A day, then a week and then a whole month went by, and Lithilia still did not return. Hope dwindled by the day and many hearts were broken. Everyone entertained the possibility of their worst fear coming to pass. Adamou envied Cahen's innocence, which seemed to shield the child's psyche from the trauma of the child's missing mother. He was a man torn apart with grief, pain and loneliness. The only thing that helped him to maintain his sanity was his son. He had suddenly become a single parent, and it was a new experience for him. Ukni decided he would wait no longer. It was time to provide Adamou with a new companion.

"We will not use the same procedure as last time," Ukni told Sunki.

"Why not?" Sunki asked.

"I'd rather avoid the possibility of history repeating itself," Ukni replied. "Despite everything he has been through already, Adamou has shown more emotional, psychological and mental stability than Lithilia did. I want to use him as a base for his new partner."

"I understand, and I agree," Sunki said. "When do we begin?"

"As soon as I finish explaining to Adamou that he will have a new partner, and Cahen a new mother," Ukni said. "Hopefully, she will be a better half to him than Lithilia was."

A few moments later, Ukni was at Adamou's home. Cahen was playing outside. Adamou was a pitiful combination of loneliness and heartache. His hair, beard and clothes were disheveled and he stank as if he had not had a bath in weeks, though only six days had gone by since Lithilia's disappearance. Ukni's heart was heavy with pity as he empathized with his creation, Adamou, who was experiencing his first heartbreak.

"I came to inform you that I intend to provide you with a new partner, son," Ukni said after the two had exchanged brief pleasantries.

"I do not want a new partner," Adamou protested. "I want my Lithilia."

"Son, I understand that is what you want," Ukni replied. "I want her back as well. She is my daughter, remember? But I also have to accept the fact that she is no more, and we have to do something."

"But I do not want another partner, father," Adamou protested even more.

"I know you do not," Ukni agreed. "But what about Cahen. Do you not think he needs a mother?"

Adamou chewed on this for a moment. Father was right. He may not need a new partner, but his son needed a new mother. His son was still too young to go through life without the nurturing love of a mother. Ukni saw his opportunity and seized it.

"Everything will be alright, my son," Ukni said. "We are not talking about a replacement for Lithilia, your partner, my daughter and most of all Cahen's mother. We are only talking about a new addition to the family. Who knows? You may grow to love her eventually."

Adamou scoffed and Ukni nodded with a smile.

"I am not saying you will love your new partner any more or less than the way you love Lithilia," Ukni continued. "I am just saying you could eventually grow to love her in some way. I think it would be great for us to have a new member in the family. What do you say?"

"How much time before this happens?" Adamou asked.

His features contorted in slight irritation and aggravation before relaxing into resignation. He did not want to agree with Ukni's logic. The thought of loving another woman, in one way or another, was both strange and sickening to him.

"As soon as I know that you are agreement with me, son," Ukni confessed. "I do need your support in this."

Adamou was moved that Father sought his blessing in this venture. It was one of the many reasons why Adamou truly loved Father so much. He sighed and turned his gaze from the ground to meet his father's eyes.

"I am with you, Father," Adamou said.

"Thank you, son," Ukni said with delight. "We will begin when you are ready."

"When I am ready?" Adamou asked.

"Yes, son," Ukni replied. "This time, we will provide a partner for you from a part of you. This will be the first time we will be attempting such a feat. You have proven to be strong mentally, physically and psychologically, even in the face of adversity. So, we think if we provide a partner for you, from you, then we could avoid a repeat of what happened."

Adamou thought about Ukni's words and seemed to understand.

"As much as I want my lover and mother of our child to return to him," he spoke with his head slightly hung in resignation, "I fear her violence could repeat itself. So, if this new procedure would significantly reduce the risk of a repeat of what happened, then I must make the right decision, if not for myself, then for my son."

Ukni remained silent, preferring to let Adamou continue with his process of rationalizing the situation.

"Alright, father," Adamou replied, squaring his shoulders and turning to face Ukni. "I am ready."

"Excellent," Ukni said. "So, to give you an idea of what we will do, we will put you to sleep for a few hours. You see this right here?"

Ukni poked into one of Adamou's left floating ribs.

"Yes…" Adamou replied, unsure of where Ukni was getting at.

"This rib is a little longer than that on the other side," Ukni continued. "So, we will shorten this rib to match the length of the other. It is causing you some discomfort, is it not?"

"Nothing I cannot handle, Father," Adamou shrugged.

"I know you can handle it, son," Ukni agreed, amused. "You are a tough one. So, when we shorten this rib, we will use the portion we are going to cut off as the base material for making your companion. How does that sound?"

Ukni tried to sound as excited as possible for something he had performed so many times he could do it perfectly while stone-faced drunk.

"It does sound interesting, Father," Adamou confessed. "So, my new partner will actually be a part of me…" he said more to himself.

"Exactly, son," Ukni exclaimed, snapping his finger.

"I think I like how that sounds already," Adamou forced a smile. "My new partner just may be my better half after all."

"And we all will be here to usher her into our world," Ukni interjected.

Adamou nodded.

"Shall we begin, son?" Ukni asked.

"Yes, Father," Adamou replied and stood up. "Let us go and take care of that extended rib."

48

# CHAPTER FIVE

# A SHADOW OF MY PAST

## WHO AM I?

I am a direct descendant of the proverbial first man. Yes, I can easily trace my lineage to that man. He lived a lot longer than most people are aware of. His reputation preceded him, and he was a well-loved, respected and honored man. From what I understand, the humans of today remember him as the first man who 'fell into sin', thanks to his wife. How sacrilegious, disrespectful and abominable. Makes me sick to my essence. The humans of today claim to be so advanced, so savvy, so... everything. But their best today would never compare to our average back then. If I could, I would spit on all of them before ending their miserable lives. But they are not even worthy of such a blessing

Who am I?

I am he who hails from the lineage of the one who never tasted death because 'God himself called him up to the heavenly realms whilst he was still alive.' My ancestor was most favored by God and honored and respected by the people. I am he whose ancestor was swept up to the heavens in a chariot of fire as many witnessed. And just like my original ancestor, the humans of today do not appreciate this ancestor of mine. He is only mentioned briefly in their popular literature, like one would talk about what time of the day it was. When the humans of today speak of him, they do so without reverence, respect or honor. Why, humans, why? If I could, I would spit on all of you before ending your miserable lives. But you are not even worthy of such a blessing.

Who am I?

I am of the line of he who was righteous in the wake of a world wrought with evil and wickedness. I am of the line of he who was tasked with saving humanity from the great deluge that was meant to scourge the world of the rapidly spreading epidemic of evil. And was this deluge born of nature or was it by design? Of course, it was by design. 'God' was angry with us because we were no longer kissing his rear end and licking the poultry poop off his heel. That was the claim. That was what we were told. And, of course, the humans accepted this tale unequivocally. Humans and their puny minds. 'God, the merciful', loved us so much that he gave us free will to use and when we use it, what does 'God' do? Yes. You are a very wise one, are you not? You guessed correctly.

Apparently, this 'God' has children everywhere; in every realm and dimension you can think of, even in Inner Earth Realm. He must have been very busy spreading his seed and populating the realms. I must admit, I do envy him. Such resilience. So, what happens when you have children everywhere, many of whom do not even know they share the same father? Sometimes, they start getting a little too fond of one another and not in a family kind of way. You get where I am going with this, do you not?

And so, it came to pass that the sons of God in the higher dimensions and realms desired the daughters of humans in Earth Realm. And do you know what resulted from this 'desire'? Another story for another day. These sons of 'God' from the higher realms must have taken after their father. I have no doubt about that. After all, the fruit never falls far from the tree, does it? What I find very interesting is the fact that the children of higher realms and dimensions only sought the daughters in Earth Realm surface dwellers. They never ventured into Inner Earth Realm. Now why was that?

Because the creatures of Inner Earth Realm were and are, for lack of a better word, special. They are pure, in a sense, responsible, accountable and live on the principles of love. They refuse to subscribe to the whims of a creature, who calls himself or herself 'god.' They are welcoming but will not tolerate any disharmony or discord. They inhabit a realm within a realm but are of the same vibrational frequency as Earth Realm. As such, Earth and Inner Earth belong to the same dimension, Solaris. They are different in every sense of the word; physiologically, psychologically, mentally and above all, spiritually. They are one with everyone and everything. They coexist and respect everything and everyone in their realm. But... I digress. Let me return to my self-introduction.

Who am I?

I am the result of a union between a 'son of the God' in the higher realms and a 'daughter of God' on Earth Realm. Sounds incestuous, does it not? Thank you very much, human language. But no. Incest was not the word of the day in these unions between the creatures from up there and the women down here. The creatures from up there masked their lust and testosterone-infused egos with theatrics that made them irresistible to the maidens of Earth Realm. They preyed on the naiveté of these girls, and they are supposed to be higher and more evolved than we of Earth are? If you ask me, the only thing that set them evolutionarily apart from us was that they could hold their erections longer than we could. There were whispers amongst the maidens of how… 'incredible and insane' these sons of God were in bed. Kudos to the maidens who enjoyed the pleasures, and pains, their indiscretions with these creatures from up there brought forth.

Who am I?

I am he who challenged the dullness and mundaneness of the life of a human. I am he who would not accept anything without questioning. I am he who would change the world and return control to the humans, one sword at a time. I am he who is special and chosen amongst the many sons and grandsons of my ancestor, amongst those that survived the deluge, for a special purpose, by luck or design.

My focus became sharper than my sword as that purpose became clearer with every battle I won and every land I conquered. My purpose became more evident as thousands threw down their weapons and bowed at my feet. They called me conqueror, warrior, leader, and king. They trembled in my presence and executed orders without question. Fear is always a good motivator, and these fools had become too content in their comfort zones.

But if there was one thing I had in common with these people, it was a common hatred for the gods in the heavens; the gods who lived somewhere beyond the clouds. The hatred was not there at first. But there are few things that proper leadership alone cannot achieve. Perhaps the fear of the wrath of the gods prevented the people from revolting against the gods. Perhaps out of fear of me the people followed me and took on my biggest project yet. Perhaps all they needed was the right leadership, the right voice, to rile them up and yank them from their comfort zones.

Whatever the reason was, the timing was perfect. The momentum of the era had built up to a crescendo, and the time had come to capitalize on it. If the gods could live, then the gods could also die. By the extension of that same logic, the gods could either be chased away or killed. If the gods were chased away, they might return with fortification. But if they were killed…

The second option sounded a lot more appealing and pleasurable.

Who am I?

I am he who subdued humanity and set out to eliminate the gods. Whether my birth father was among them or not was of no consequence. The mission was simple: the gods had to die. Every single, last, filthy, conniving, lying one of them must perish. Be it swiftly or slowly, the gods had to die. They all had to fall by the arrows, the spears, and the swords I commanded.

Who am I?

I am he who chose a piece of land in a city called Babel. I am he who would build The Tower of Babel. There I would commence my biggest project yet; to build a tower so high up that it would reach the sky. From there, we would launch our attack. From there, we would strike down the gods and end their reign and influence over us. I am he who was born to bring a sweeping change and rebirth by the sword instead of water. I am he who was born to lead. I am he who held the key to the future for my kind. I am he who held the banner of promise and the prospect of freedom from the gods. Mine was strength, mine was lust, and mine was power.

I am Nimrud.

But the gods played a trick on me. They played a trick on us all; but because no one else matters, I say they played a trick on me. Damn them, those sneaky vermin. How dare they use wit over my strength. How dare they tear asunder what I had built. How dare they smite the people with the affliction of multiple tongues. Communication was impossible and without communication, progress with the project of completing the tower was stifled. In the end, fighting and chaos became the only languages spoken by the people I commanded until they destroyed the very tower they had built. Damn the gods. Damn them all. Damn them a thousand times over.

I could hear the laughter of the gods reverberating in my mind like a torturous symphony of the soul. Their mockery drenched me like a never-ending, tropical downpour. At the apex of my reign came my worst humiliation. In the peak of my pride, came the biggest blow to my ego. After that blasphemy from the gods, I conquered many more lands and sired many offspring; either out of transferred aggression or just because I could. But nothing was ever the same. Nothing could erase the past and heal my crushed ego.

I was not used to failure or defeat. In fact, I had never known failure or defeat. These were portions I visited upon those I slew and conquered. These were what happened to others, not to me. My pride was pulverized and there was nothing I could do about it. Even for a king and conqueror as mighty as myself, there were certain things I was helpless against; like changing the past.

But, I could either marinade in melancholy or do something about it. As such, I decided to resume the project. This time, I would not use a divided people. I had to use a people who were basically unsullied by anything external, including the gods. It was for this cause that I would journey to Inner Earth Realm to solicit the aid of the dwellers therein. Yes, I was aware of their policies and their aversion for discord. But I am Nimrud, and no one would dare defy or try to defeat me. Unless they were part of the godly entourage, that is.

Damn them. Damn them all.

And thus, I followed the map that legend had left behind for anyone who may want to discover Inner Earth Realm. It was still unclear who the creator of the legend was, given that the history of humanity was still in its infancy then; or so we were made to believe. But this only seemed to strengthen the authenticity of the map. I had nothing else to go by and all the wise men in my kingdom had nothing else to offer. Thus, I set out with nothing more than a small army of fifty soldiers and a map I had little faith in, to search for the doorway to Inner Earth Realm. Twenty-one days and twenty-two nights later, we stumbled upon a most impressive sight fashioned out of pure fantasy. We beheld the beauty before our very own eyes that was inconceivably spectacular and extraordinary.

After three weeks of treading through treacherous terrains and occasionally fending off wild beasts and highway thieves, we arrived at the foot of the *Mountain of Giants*. Its summit was shrouded in the clouds and it was completely covered in white, shiny earth, which glistened in the glare of Solara. We must have just crossed the *Veil of Illusions*, which concealed this megalithic, gigantic structure from the eyes of everyone else. I looked back and saw not the forest through which we just journeyed. In its stead, I beheld an entire valley of greenery, flowers, many strange beasts on the land and fowls in the air. This truly was another realm on Earth Realm. I regarded the faces of my servants and guards. Some of them had fallen on their knees in worship of the gods rumored to dine at the top of this mountain.

"Cowards!" I spat at them and returned my gaze towards the Mountain of Giants. "Let us see if truly giants dwell within this structure."

I stripped my gaze from the weaklings who accompanied me and looked towards the base of the mountain. For the first time, I noticed what looked like a cave at the foot of this mountain.

"I swear, by my name, that this cave was not there when first we arrived," I muttered to myself.

The lone cave at the foot of the mountain was about ten feet high, about two-and-a-half feet taller than I.

A stone's throw into the cave, a wheel of bright, pulsating white light, that was about seven sword lengths in diameter, hovered. It spun around slowly, and the center expanded and contracted rhythmically. Strangely, the brightness of the wheel was limited to only the wheel. The rest of the cave was steeped in pitch blackness. Our minds could not comprehend this phenomenon, but our hearts appreciated its splendor. My soul was awash with a calmness unlike the kind I have ever experienced and my body was gifted with rejuvenation and youth. I dismounted my horse and was about to step into the cave.

"Come no further, mortal man." a non-corporeal voice commanded.

"Why not?" I asked defiantly. "I only seek audience to table a proposition."

"We do not want your kind amongst us, mortal man," the voice replied.

"And what do you mean by 'your kind'?" I demanded in anger at the voice's spiteful contempt.

"The kind with no respect for life," the voice replied. "The kind that thrives on fear, disharmony, and chaos. Be gone now, before it is too late, mortal man."

"Show yourself so we can talk like men," I demanded. "Or are you afraid?"

"Final warning to you all," the voice addressed the rest of the soldiers. "If you even as much as take a single step forward, you will be struck down."

The voice reverberated with an alien authority that the soldiers had never heard before; not even from me. I saw the doubts and fear in their eyes and the trembling in their demeanors. Even I admitted that whoever was behind this voice, his authority dwarfed mine. Yet, my pride dwarfed my wisdom. As such, I unsheathed my sword and marched forward toward the cave. I hoped that if my soldiers saw me lead, they would follow suit.

I was wrong.

"You have sealed your fate, mortal man," the voice bellowed. "Because of your foolhardiness, you will never leave this place alive."

And with those words, a beam of light shot from the wheel and blinded me.

Next I knew, I was behind bars and a very tall man stood outside my prison cell, with his hands clasped behind his back. I rose to my feet and reached for the bars. I tugged and pulled, but the bars just stared at me as if in mockery.

"I demand to be released," I screamed, and the man outside my prison cell looked at me as if I had gone mad.

"Do you know who I am?" I yelled and thrust a clenched fist in the direction of the wheel of bright, white light. "Who do you think you are?"

"Who I am is of no importance to you," the giant replied with infuriating calm. "You should concern yourself more with where you are going from here."

"You will pay for this blasphemy," I yelled. "My army will sweep over you all like a swarm of locusts."

"Your army fled in the wake of your disappearance, which was wise of them," the man said. "Soon, they will spread the word that you are dead and gone, thanks to gravity and the floor of a valley. A tragic accident, indeed."

I glared, yelled and screamed at the man, and he just looked at me like one would look at a deranged pet in a cage. Soon, I realized that I was all alone in a foreign territory full of giants. A short while later, I was taken from my cell and dragged in chains because I would not stop kicking and screaming. I got a quick glance of what I could tell was Inner Earth Realm. What I saw held a promise of immeasurable beauty, but unfortunately, I was preoccupied with more important things; like saving myself from these gentle yet unthinkably strong giants.

I was brought to what looked like an empty hall with nothing but a single beam of light beaming towards me. The guards who brought me to this location let me go. I thought my opportunity for escape was finally here. But when I made to run away, I realized that my body had lost all will to move. I opened my mouth to speak, to demand to be released. But even my lips had lost their will to obey my thoughts.

The light. That was it. The light was not just for illumination. Damn these creatures of Inner Earth Realm.

"For trespassing and threatening the harmony and peace of our realm," a non-corporeal voice said. "Your penalty should have been instant execution. But for the sake of the agreement we have with one of your ancestors, you will be banished instead to another realm for the rest of your existence."

I was immediately hurled through another door and into another hall. In the center of this hall, a perfect sphere hovered in midair. My nameless captor placed a hand on the sphere, and a vortex appeared in the ceiling. He stepped aside and left me standing there by myself. I thought, yet again, that this was going to be a perfect opportunity to make a run for it. Alas, I was wrong, yet again. The vortex slowly descended towards me. I wanted to heave a sigh of surrender, but even that was an impossible feat. Surrender.... An alien term. An alien sensation. It did not belong in my world. But here I was....

The vortex sucked me away and dumped me face-first on an orange-red ground in what appeared to be another realm. My ribs hurt with blinding pain. Perhaps a few broke and pierced into my flesh but I was quickly healed by the atmosphere of this unknown place that might as well be my new home or prison. I stood up and surveyed the area.

*Strange.*

"And rest assured, you will not be going back to Inner Earth Realm anytime soon," a corporeal voice spoke from behind me.

Startled, I whipped around and saw a man walking slowly towards me.

"Who are you?" I asked, fists at the ready for a fight.

At least, this man was almost of the same height and build as I.

"Easy, son," the man said. "If it were not for my map, you would not be here in the first place. It was I who drew that map a very long time ago."

"Who are you?" I asked again, lowering my fists.

"Nimrud, your reputation precedes you," the man continued. "First things first, your current attitude will not get you anywhere. And when you address me, you will do so with respect, son."

"And why do you keep calling me 'son'?" I asked, my curiosity getting the better of me.

"Because, Nimrud," he replied with a patronizing calmness, "I am Cahen, your ancestor and first son of Adamou."

***

Nimrud's eyes snapped open. He had replayed this story in his mind a countless number of times and every time felt like it was the very first time. Over the past too-many-centuries-to-remember, he had become a shadow of his own past, and it still sickened him. He rose from the floor and headed for the door. He meandered along a long, winding hallway until he stopped in front of a door and knocked on it.

"You know you never have to knock," a voice called from inside.

"Nothing wrong with being polite, brother," Nimrud replied as he entered his brother-in-friendship's quarters and closed the door behind him.

"How kind of you," Nimrud's brother said jokingly.

Both men laughed and took seats opposite from each other.

"We are so close now," Nimrud continued. "Everything is lining up perfectly. And to think that they said I could never leave this realm..." Nimrud shook his head amusedly.

"I'm more excited than you are." his brother replied. "Can you feel the changes already?"

"It is intoxicating," Nimrud replied. "Finally, after all these millennia, we will finally reclaim our rightful place and eradicate the humans. They were pathetic then and are even more pathetic now. And I cannot imagine doing it with anyone else but you by my side."

"The honor is all mine, brother," Nimrud's brother replied.

"A well-deserved honor indeed," Nimrud commended. "You have shown strength, loyalty, and resilience throughout the centuries like no other I can think of. That is why, despite your relative youth, I not only made you my protégé, but I call you my brother. I wish I had someone like you during my days on Earth Realm. Things would have been a lot different."

"Well, things are about to get even better,." Nimrud's brother replied. "They can only get better. You, me, Maduk and the queen, we share a common vision and goal. How can anything be more unifying and stronger than that?"

Nimrud looked at his brother and nodded slowly, smiling at the same time.

"And you wonder why I call you, 'brother'," Nimrud said standing up.

His brother stood up as well. Nimrud towered over him by a full head and neck. Nimrud placed a right hand on his brother's right shoulder and squeezed.

"You are not my immediate family, but you might as well be. I will never stop telling you that."

Nimrud patted his brother's shoulder twice before heading for the door.

"I just wanted to stop by and say hello before my meeting with Maduk," he said as he opened the door.

"Thank you," Nimrud's brother replied.

Nimrud nodded and closed the door behind him as he walked out. Yaakov let out the long breath he was holding and wondered if he was running out of time. But more so, if he could keep up with the act much longer. He sighed deeply and pressed a button at the edge of his desk. The door opened and a beautiful, by Sinister standards, female walked in. This one had neither a tail nor horns. She closed the door behind her and walked towards Yaakov. She undid the straps of her garments and was naked in an instant.

"How would you like me, sir?" she asked.

When Yaakov did not reply, she understood he was asking her to take the initiative. So, she knelt in front of him and undid his pants. As his pants made their way to the floor, she took him in her mouth and went to work as if her life depended on it. Yaakov closed his eyes and placed a hand on her head. A few minutes later, she stood up and bent over Yaakov's desk. She pressed a button as Yaakov removed the rest of his garments and took a position behind her. The door opened, and two more voluptuous, exquisitely sculptured female Sinisters walked in, one with horns and a tail and the other without any. They were already naked and ready to please their master in whatever way he wanted.

# CHAPTER SIX

## THE SECOND WOMAN.

**ADAMOU TRIED TO** focus in the glare of the lights in the operating room as the anesthesia wore off. The luminous assault was too much for him to handle yet. The pounding in his head made him slam his eyelids shut. He remembered why he went under the knife and reached for his left lower set of ribs by reflex. The incision was almost completely healed already. Gradually, he reopened his eyes and no longer felt like his head was going to implode. Adamou slowly pushed himself upright and let his legs hang freely off the bed. He then felt both sides of his lower ribs for comparison. Both were of similar length. He cautiously let his feet touch the floor as he slid off the bed.

"You are up already," a lady with a kind face and a radiant smile that revealed sparkly, white teeth said and reached for Adamou.

But Adamou raised a hand to reject her offer for assistance.

"I am fine, madam," he replied. "Thank you."

"I see why Ukni loves you so much," she said as she adjusted her thin, pitch-black dreads behind her ears. "You keep surprising us. Here you are, emerging from anesthesia in half the time and already moving around on your own."

She moved closer to him.

"May I at least walk next to you, Adamou?" she asked.

"Of course, madam," Adamou smiled.

"And you do not have to call me 'madam' all the time," she added, walking alongside Adamou and matching him in height, despite the low pair of sandals she wore. "My name is Meena and Ukni, or Father, is my brother."

"I have seen you around, but I never knew your name," Adamou said with a smile to hide the fact that he was wincing from the slight pain in his side. "Does that make you my aunt, then?"

Meena laughed a little.

"Well, if Ukni is your father, then logically you are my nephew," Meena replied and laughed again. "And, I am not laughing at you. I am laughing at the situation, but not in a bad way. The thought of you being my nephew, and you actually saying it out loud, just sounds funny to me. That's all."

Adamou laughed as well and then said, "To be honest, it feels strange referring to you as my aunt, Meena. I am not sure why; but it is like I want you *not* to be my aunt."

*It is odd but interesting that he is experiencing such conflicts*, Meena furrowed her eyebrows in thought.

"And I think you have a lovely name," Adamou added and smiled.

Meena smiled back and averted her eyes towards the floor.

"Thank you," Meena replied, not understanding why she was feeling a little embarrassed. "That is very kind of you to say."

"I speak honestly. I hope I did not offend you," Adamou added.

"Oh no, you certainly did not offend me at all," Meena replied.

"You know what I just realized," Adamou said. "I am just following you along these hallways. But where are we going?"

"Take a guess, Adam," Meena asked. "Do you mind if I call you 'Adam'?"

It was the first time anyone ever called him 'Adam' and he actually liked it.

"No, I do not, as long as you are the only one calling me that," he replied.

To Adamou, he was just joking. But to Meena, it sounded like Adamou was flirting with her, which was very odd but interesting at the same time. Meena wondered if Adamou not wanting her to be her aunt meant he was developing other… desires… towards her. And was it out of instinct or had Adamou, or Adam as she preferred to call him, been nursing these feelings all along?

*As absurd as it may sound, it is not entirely impossible,* Meena rationalized as they continued walking along the hallways. *Well, everyone keeps saying I look like Lithilia. I do not see the resemblance, but that is just me. Anyway, good thing I keep my dreads. Perhaps, now that Lithilia is no longer around, I somehow remind Adam of her?*

Meena grinned and faced forward as another possibility dawned on her.

*Or maybe Adam was just being a little flirtatious. After all, men will be men, regardless of the realm.*

She made a mental note to observe this new behavior. Perhaps, with Lithilia no longer around, he was learning the art of courtship and seduction. Was this new behavior a mere manifestation of something subconscious? Was it inherited from Ukni's genes or picked up from observing the wanton fraternizing on the facility among her kind? Or was Adam manifesting personality traits that their systems could not detect? After all, he had been showing remarkable evolutionary leaps at a much faster-than-expected rate. Perhaps Meena was overthinking the situation. Well, the only thing that seemed 'wrong' right now was the fact that they had underestimated these subjects in the first place. Ukni would be pleased when she shared her latest observations of Adamou with him. And how would she, Meena, feel if Adam was actually developing deep desires for her?

*One step at a time.*

"As you wish, Adam," Meena played along. "But I cannot guarantee I will be the only one calling you that."

Meena winked at him. She did not expect him to do the same. But when Adamou winked back at her, her eyes bulged in surprise.

The two of them stopped outside a glass partition to a chamber.

"This is our destination," Meena said, gesturing towards the chamber.

Adamou peered inside and then inched closer towards the partition until his breath formed condensation on the glass. Men and women covered from head to toe in white clothing, except for their eyes, were heavily focused on their task at hand. Adamou easily identified Ukni; the one who was in charge.

In the center of the chamber hovered a transparent, cylindrical object, with a rounded top and bottom, that was big enough to contain an adult human being. A white mist was trapped inside the object and it partially concealed anything else. Adamou knew what lay within. A hissing sound reached him, even outside the chamber, and the white mist was aspirated away through a vent at the top of the object, revealing its contents. Adamou inched closer towards the glass partition, as if inching closer would bring him closer to what lay within the cylindrical object. His breathing was steady through his nostrils, and his breath fogged the glass for only a second with each exhalation.

Whether it was a conscious or subconscious gesture, Meena could not tell. She observed him regardless. Adamou opened his mouth to say something, but nothing came out. He just stared at what lay in the cylindrical object. Ukni then turned around, and when he saw Adamou, he waved. Adamou peeled a hand from the glass partition and waved back. He returned to staring hypnotically at the revelation in the chamber.

Adamou's mind went back to the first time he had laid eyes on Lithilia. She, too, was inside something similar, just like he was. The feeling back then was a blend of curiosity and confusion. He neither had any knowledge of anything prior to him waking up in that chamber, nor who the other person in there was. Though the scenario unveiling in front of him felt like déjà-vu, the feelings stirring inside of him were different; for a multiple of reasons too. When he awoke back then for the first time, he was filled with insatiable curiosity. Grunts and guttural sounds were the only languages he knew. He had also awoken with someone who became his partner, his first love. Now, however, he was an observer and this new creation Father and his team were working on was not his first love.

Adamou opened his mouth to speak. He failed again. He swallowed and gawked as he stared unblinkingly, entranced and enchanted by both the science of the situation and the resplendence that lay in front of him; the resplendence created from him and for him. Adamou swallowed and tried not to blink for fear of missing a single moment of this… Adamou had no words.

She was beautiful beyond belief; even more beautiful than Lithilia. She hovered in midair, and her eyes were closed. She was physically perfect. Suddenly, Adamou realized that the more impressed he was about this new partner of his, the more he became aware of the sorrow that had been shoved in the sanctum of his subconscious seeping slowly into his psyche, until he finally submitted to his sorrow. He pressed his forehead against the partition and squeezed his eyes shut. A tear coursed down each cheek, and he sobbed quietly.

Meena's heart fissured and her shoulders slumped, but she did not interrupt him. Her empathy for Adamou's situation was real, genuine and… friendly. She wondered if he wept because he missed his first partner or if he wept because he had finally come to terms with the fact that his first partner was gone for good. Perhaps Adam wept for both reasons. Perhaps Adam was just… She could not find the words.

Meena felt awful for him and could hold back no more as she took a careful step towards him. She placed a soft, gentle hand on his back. Adam turned to face her. Two red, tear-filled eyes stared deeply into Meena's and Meena saw nothing but pain in them. Without thinking, Meena took Adamou's face in her hands and kissed him on both cheeks. A close, loving hug was all she could afford at the moment and Adamou buried his face in the nape of her neck. In all the many millennia of her life, Meena had never heard a man cry so hard.

"Oh, Adam," she whispered as she caressed his thick hair.

From the corner of her eye, she saw Ukni looking at her. Meena nodded at him, and he nodded back.

*"I shall take care of him,"* she said via telepathy.

Ukni gave the thumbs up.

Or maybe the correct phrase ought to have been she was going to handle the subject's psychiatric evaluation until the subject was deemed psychologically fit to handle the latest adjustments in his life. A few moments later, Meena tried to peel herself away from him, but Adamou tightened his grip around her body.

Meena felt his strength, his power and his passion all at once. She resigned to the feeling and gently tightened her arms around him some more. As she reached to rub his back, her hand gently slid over his musculature, and she was genuinely impressed. His sobs had subsided, and her garment had absorbed a good amount of his tears. Meena did not mind. Finally, Adamou gently broke away from her. When Meena made eye contact with him, she smiled weakly and wiped the remainder of his tears away from his cheeks.

"It is alright, Adam," Meena said softly. "I understand, and it is alright."

When Adamou said nothing, she reached for his right elbow.

"Come," Meena said. "Let us go for a walk. Cahen is waiting for you."

Adamou's eyes lit up and his face brightened at the mention of Cahen's name. It was a source of renewed emotional strength for him.

"Yes, he must be worried," Adamou agreed.

"If he is worried, he must have a strange way of showing it," Meena smiled with affection. "He has been keeping the others on their toes the whole time."

"That is my son," Adamou beamed with paternal pride and laughed a little.

Meena laughed as well, happy to see that there was at least one thing Adamou could find comfort in during such a time of great sorrow and pain.

"So, when do I meet her?" Adamou asked suddenly.

To Meena's amazement, Adam easily switched from pain and tears to business quite quickly but did her best to maintain a poker face.

"In about six days," Meena replied. "That is how much time we will need for her to be completely formed and animated."

A few moments later, father and son were reunited, and they returned to their home. Meena met with Ukni later and told him of her observations.

"I cannot say I blame him for flirting with you, you know," Ukni joked.

Meena threw a holographic notepad at her brother. The notepad flew through Ukni's face and the siblings laughed a little.

"He is just being human, I think," Ukni continued. "But you are right; his progress is amazing. I believe we are successful despite everything else, sister."

"I agree, brother," Meena replied. "They certainly are much better than our first creations."

Meena winced at the memory of what had happened a very long time ago.

"Some things are best kept in the past, where they belong," Ukni said and rose from his seat. "And right now, my bones belong in my bed."

"I will continue to observe Adam," Meena said and rose from her seat as well.

"Adam?" Ukni reiterated, raising a mischievous eyebrow.

"Yes, Adam, dear brother," Meena replied, kissing her brother on the cheek and walking out of his office. "I think it is a cute nickname."

"You never gave *me* any nickname," Ukni sulked playfully.

"Good thing I was never your mother, *big* brother," Meena countered

The siblings laughed together, and they bid each other good night.

Six days later, Meena went to Adamou's abode to fetch him and his son. The three of them went to a new chamber in which the new woman was sitting idly, in the company of two minders. The new woman was covered in plain, white clothing that went just above her knees. The people were asking her questions to which she replied verbally and with head movements at times. Adamou was surprised she could speak so quickly.

"Because we used a part of you to make her, we only had to make some minor adjustments to compensate for things like gender," Meena explained, without getting too technical. "Certain things we kept and others we did not keep. Language was one of the things we kept."

"That explains a lot," Adamou replied calmly.

Adamou's eyes never left the woman. His intense stare and focus on her was only matched by the conundrum of emotions within his psyche. His curiosity about her grew by the minute, and so did his pain of missing the woman he once loved. Still loved. Both situations seemed to cancel and enforce each other in a most alien way. But for Cahen's sake, Adamou maintained a calm composure. The two minders who were talking to the new woman stood up and headed for the door. Before the left the chamber, they stopped and mumbled some quick words to Meena. She thanked them and returned her gaze to Adamou, Cahen and the new woman as the minders walked away. An awkward moment of silence hung between them like the shiny source of illumination above their heads and Meena did not want to be the one to break the ice. She was with them strictly as a facilitator.

The new woman rose from the bed and walked towards them. She had a kind, lovely face and a loving smile. Meena studied the new woman's demeanor. If the new woman was consumed with curiosity, just like every other creature they spawned in the lab was immediately after their spawning was complete, then this woman did a phenomenal job at concealing hers. She looked at each of her visitors intensely and then, as if finally making up her mind, she took a step towards Cahen and dropped to one knee. She was now at eye level with the boy. He had a small toy in his arms, clutched to his chest, and he just stared at the strange woman. The strange woman's lips then peeled into the most beautiful smile Meena had ever seen as she reached out to Cahen and caressed his head.

"Hello, little one," she said. "What is your name?"

"My name is Cahen," he replied timidly and managed a weak smile.

"I like your name, Cahen," the woman replied. "Would you like to come sit with me?"

Cahen turned towards his father with eyes seeking encouragement. His father smiled and nodded. Cahen then turned and nodded timidly at the new woman.

The woman then stood up and extended her hand. Cahen took it and walked with her towards her bed. She sat on the bed and propped Cahen on her lap. Cahen smiled and leaned into her bosom. Adamou and Meena gaped in surprise.

*"Brother. You must come and see this,"* Meena exclaimed telepathically.

*"What is it?"* Ukni asked telepathically.

*"Just come here. Quick,"* Meena replied.

The sense of urgency in Meena's telepathic voice made Ukni leap from his table and hurry towards her location.

"What do you have in your hand, Cahen?" the woman asked.

"My toy," he replied. "My grandfather made it for me."

"Very nice," the woman said. "Would you like to show me how it works?

"Yes," he replied gleefully..

He pressed a red button in the center of the toy. A ball of light shone from the toy and started spinning around very slowly. Smaller dots of light of various sizes were going around this great ball of light. There were thirteen smaller balls of light in total. Cahen pointed at the third ball of light.

"Grandfather says we are here," Cahen said. "And this-" he pointed at the thirteenth dot "- is where grandfather and his people come from."

"Oh my, that is so beautiful, Cahen," the woman said. "May I try, please?"

Cahen pressed the button again, and the balls of light disappeared. He handed the toy over to the woman and pointed at the red button. The woman pressed it, and the balls of light shot from the toy once again. Both she and Cahen shrieked with pure, innocent joy. Adamou was still too dumbfounded to say or do anything. But Meena elbowed him slightly, forcing Adamou back to his senses. He walked cautiously toward his son and the woman. The woman looked up and smiled infectiously at him. Adamou smiled back.

"I would give you a proper greeting," she said. "But as you can see, I am being held captive by a most amazing child."

She tickled Cahen who exploded with glee. Adamou laughed softly. He reached for the woman and the two touched lips lightly but sensually. They smiled at each other while Cahen was busy making himself comfortable in the woman's arms. Ukni arrived and stood by the door next to his sister.

"My name is Adamou," Adamou said finally.

"May I call you Adam?" the woman asked with a smile.

Adamou's knees buckled. Meena swallowed, and Ukni nudged her slightly. The eyes in the back of her head glared at him, and his grin was priceless.

"Yes, you may," Adamou replied. "What may I call you?"

"Eva," the woman replied. "You may call me Eva."

"Welcome to the family, Eva," Adamou said.

Adamou placed his right hand on her left shoulder. She reached for his right forearm with her free hand and gave it a squeeze of gratitude and appreciation.

"Are you going to be my new mother, Eva?" Cahen asked out of the blue.

It was if time itself stood still. Adamou's eyes widened with surprise, Meena's jaw dropped again, and Ukni's grin vanished. Cahen's eyes bore the innocence of a child asking a question that, to him, was the simplest question in the world. But to the rest of his immediate world, it was the most abrupt and difficult question anyone could ask, or answer, right that moment. A few seconds went by and these seconds felt like an eternity stuck in a black hole. Finally, Eva spoke.

"Cahen," she said, adjusting the child on her lap and turning him so that they both looked at each other in the eye. "I can only be your new mother if you want me to."

"I want you to be my new mother," Cahen said. "Please?"

"Then I will be your new mother… my son," Eva replied.

Eva kissed the grinning child deeply and lovingly on the forehead before cradling him to her bosom again.

Adamou quickly reached for a chair and sank into it. Meena's throat suddenly felt parched. She swallowed and cleared her throat. Ukni's jaw slowly succumbed to gravity. The two siblings looked at each other and tried to say something, but they could not formulate the words. Eva then whispered into Cahen's ear, but loud enough for Adamou to hear.

"Do you want to show me around, son?" Eva asked.

Cahen leaped from her thigh and took her by the hand. He dragged her out of the room with Eva laughing at his cuteness. As they walked past Adamou, Eva opened her free hand towards him. Adamou took it and was dragged away from his chair. He followed in tow behind his son and his new partner. Meena and Ukni watched speechlessly as the family tried to keep pace with Cahen.

"I think we outdid ourselves this time, brother," Meena said, clapping her brother on the back.

"We certainly did." Ukni replied with unhidden pride. "They might be alright after all."

"Well, this is just Day One, anyway," Meena said, taking Ukni by the elbow and leading him away. "But it sure is a very beautiful Day One."

# CHAPTER SEVEN

# A VESTIGIAL WIFE.

**CAHEN WAS UNLIKE** his usual self. He gave Eva the grand tour of the facility with a little too much excitement. The instant bond between Cahen and Eva was, however, a mystery that eluded the technology of their makers and the logic of everyone else. Adamou was a silent, observant participant in the tour. He watched his son behave with this strange woman as if he had known her all his life. He watched his son treat the strange woman like the friend he never had. He watched his son act with the strange woman as if she were the mother he never had but always wanted. And most of all, he watched and accepted the fact that this strange lady, made from his rib, had taken his son as hers.

Did the fact that she was made from him have anything to do with the instant bond between the woman and her son? Was his son's attachment to this woman a mere projection of his bond that already existed between his son and himself, and all his son was doing was reacting to that already-existing bond? Perhaps the fact that his son's mother was not also around played a vital role in this bonding? By the skies, Lithilia's disappearance left a void in him that was yet to be filled. Watching his son and this new woman act like they had known each other since his son's birth made him realize just how much his son must have missed his birth mother. Cahen was still a child and Adamou's parental instincts reminded him that every child needs a mother and father. He sighed as he walked from a short distance from the two of them.

*Much remains to be understood*, he thought.

When Cahen and Eva walked past a chamber, Eva suddenly stopped. She let go of Cahen's hand and walked towards the transparent partition in the window. She stared intensely at the various equipment and devices therein. Eva zoomed in on a transparent cylindrical object that was large enough to contain an adult-sized human. She raised her left hand as if in a trance and placed it on the partition as she brought her face closer. Cahen stared silently at Eva for a brief moment before lightly taking her right forearm. He slid his hand down until he held her hand. She returned his gesture, but her focus remained glued to the chamber.

"This is where you were made, right?" Cahen asked.

"Yes," Eva replied. "This is where I was made."

Eva turned to look down at Cahen. He shivered involuntarily in her stare, not out of fear, though. A burning in her eyes touched his soul and Cahen felt it, even at his young age. But it was not the kind of burning that made him afraid, like his birth mother's. It was one that bore a promise of protection and love like he could not say he had ever seen before. Something else shone in her eyes, but Cahen did not know what to make of it. All he cared about was that the look in this woman's eyes made him feel secure and cared for, and Cahen could not help but smile.

"I am very glad grandfather made you… mother," he hugged Eva's thighs.

Eva's features softened and her lips spread in a heartwarming smile. She knelt down and held the child against her bosom in a loving hug for a moment.

"Is this all there is to show me?" Eva whispered in Cahen's ear.

Cahen pulled away from her, and she winked at him. He grinned and tugged at her arm.

"This way," Cahen said. "I will show you the kitchen. You should try Aunty Sheena's roasted vegetables."

He smacked his lips and partially closed his eyes.

"They are to live for," he added and scurried away.

Eva laughed and chased after him. Adamou remained a speechless observer.

Ukni settled in his office, and Meena pulled up a chair beside him. He tapped on some buttons on his desk and holograms floated in front of them. He tapped on some of the holograms, and they disappeared, leaving only one hologram. Using his index fingers, he pulled at two corners of the remaining hologram until it was larger than his desk. The siblings observed as Cahen gave Eva a grand tour of the facility, with Adamou walking a few paces away. They noticed how she stopped at the chamber of her creation and how she behaved.

"Did you see the signature spikes?" Meena pointed at the bottom right-hand corner of the image.

Every reading was significantly above normal.

"Yes," Ukni replied calmly.

"Is that not a problem, already?" Meena asked.

"It is an anomaly, but not a problem," Ukni replied. "See this?" he pointed at another bar on the far right-hand corner of the screen. "That bar has been the same ever since we animated her. She has the basic levels of aggression, but she has shown more composure and control compared to Adamou."

"You are correct," Meena replied. "Adam has been unique all this while. But Eva seems to be an upgrade from him."

"Of course, we did more than a little tweaking, remember?" Ukni said.

"But we kept all twenty-four pairs of chromosomes," Meena interjected. "Still, she has been beyond extraordinary so far."

"True," Ukni replied and turned around in his chair to face her. "Do you still intend to keep Adam under your 'personal observation'?" he teased with a wink.

Meena play punched him in the shoulder, and they both chuckled.

"Yes, brother, I still intend to," Meena replied. "But only from a distance. I would rather not interfere in his bonding process with Eva."

"Well, if Eva does not fancy Adamou, then I would gladly and wholly offer my assistance," Ukni said.

"Brother," Meena exclaimed and punched him in the shoulder.

"Let us just say I am willing to do anything, and I mean *anything*, for my creation," Ukni added and Meena rolled her eyes.

"You are unbelievable," Meena said

The siblings returned to monitoring Eva, Cahen and Adamou. Cahen proudly introduced Eva to Sheena and insisted that Eva try Sheena's cooking. It was hard for anyone to say no to Cahen. He was too cute, with his big, black, dancing eyes, gleeful grin and dimpled cheeks and how his voice went up an extra octave with his shoulder-slumping, knee-bending, heartwarming politeness. So, while they were in Sheena's domain, Eva went ravenous over her first solid meal and true to Cahen's word, Sheena's cooking was to live for. Eva ate so much that even Cahen went silent with amazement. Those who observed her could not tell if Eva was only famished or had an extreme curiosity to explore solid food.

"I thought she was well nourished during the procedure," Meena said.

"I assure you she was," Ukni replied, feeling surprised himself.

"Well then, Adam better be ready," Meena said.

"And why is that, dear sister?" Ukni asked, raising an eyebrow at his sister.

"Sometimes," Meena replied with a look of exasperation. "We, women, take out our pent-up 'frustration' on food."

"Pent-up frustration at what?" Ukni asked, still not comprehending. "I mean, she has only been out of the tube for a few hours."

"Be that as it may, dear brother of mine," Meena replied, shaking her head.

"You and I agree that Eva is an extraordinary woman. I am just saying that Adam better be prepared."

"Prepared for what-" Ukni said before the proverbial light bulb went off.

"Ah, I see what you mean. Lucky man," he added and chuckled lightly.

When Eva was finally satisfied, she let out a loud burp, slumped in her seat and conversed with Cahen. Later, she asked if Cahen could take her out of the facility and show her around.

Cahen dashed for the door, knowing that by now, Eva would understand that it was his way of saying 'Follow Me.' So, she dashed after him, meandering along the hallways of the immense facility, despite the buffet she had just wolfed down. Finally, they came to a closed door, and Cahen put on his best theatrics yet.

"Behold, the greatest and most marvelous place your eyes will ever see," he said and stood on his toe tips until he reached a button on the side of the door.

He pressed it and the door parted in both directions. As the evening light from Solara slid through the widening crack in the door and light washed over Eva's face, Cahen added with as much pride as he could summon.

"Behold, the Garden of Aiden."

At first, Eva shielded her eyes from the luminous assault of Solara. She then brought down her hand as her eyes adjusted to the brightness of Solara. She opened her mouth to speak, but no words came out. Though a strange sense of familiarity about the beauty that lay in front of her tugged in the back of her mind, she was still awestruck to speechlessness. She took a careful step forward, enjoying the warmth of Solara caressing her exposed flesh. Adamou's presence loomed towards her from behind. He moved to stand next to her when she did something no one expected. She stripped naked and let her garments pile around her ankles. She then spread out her arms, closed her eyes and spun around slowly. The gentle warmth of Solara's heat was magic on her skin.

Adamou froze and gaped slightly, barely realizing that he was holding his breath. He watched Eva spin around slowly with her arms open wide. The glare of Solara bounced off her flawless, glistening skin, accentuating her curvaceous glory. His primordial instincts flared naturally, sparking desires so fiery he could barely contain himself. He let out the breath he was holding and his chest heaved more than usual as a tingling and warm sensation spread from his nether regions to the rest of his body. He adjusted his stance to curb his extending phallus.

Immediately, Adamou's psyche delved into a quagmire of sexual lust for this new woman and that basic instinct came with feelings of guilt, sorrow, confusion and pain because this new woman was not his Lithilia, who was still missing. He was confused because he was still attached to his wife and yet he was having similar feelings for this new woman, with whom his son had immediately bonded. He breathed in deeply, held the breath for a few seconds and let it out slowly before moving close to Eva. She had stopped spinning and now faced the garden.

"May I join you?" Adamou asked.

"Of course," Eva replied and smiled, without looking in his direction. "You are my partner, are you not?"

Adamou hesitated for a second.

"Yes, I am," he agreed.

Eva ignored his fake smile and took his hand. Her gesture made him feel stupid and immature. The couple followed Cahen who introduced Eva to his animal friends. They walked around the garden. They went through the fields and played in the streams, and he was glad that Eva seemed to relish every single moment of it. Finally, dusk was nigh and they headed to their domicile. Cahen showed Eva all his toys. He even let her play briefly with some of them. Then, Adamou took her to another part of the domicile.

"This is our room," Adamou said, gesturing around.

"This is where you will lie with me," Eva stated instead of asking as she walked around and examined the space.

Adamou hesitated. He opened his mouth and tried to say something, but his throat felt dry, and no words spewed forth.

"Do not worry," Eva continued. "I sense much hesitation in you. Take your time, and when you are ready, we will lie together."

Eva then walked towards him, smiled and kissed him on both his cheeks. Her hard nipples gently stabbed his chest and his knees turned weak, like loose fabric. Then, Eva walked past him and headed towards Cahen's room to play with him.

"Eva," Adamou called after her.

Eva turned around to face him with an expressionless face.

"Yes, my partner?"

"I have something for you," Adamou said and averted his eyes.

Adamou headed for the closet and opened it. Six garments neatly hung from six hangers.

"I started working on these when Father finished making you," Adamou spoke barely above a murmur and his eyes were still averted away from Eva. "Father said it would take six days before you are fully animated. So, I made a garment a day for you while I waited."

Eva's eyes danced with surprise and appreciation as Adamou spoke. She glanced back and forth between Adamou and the garments. His words raced through her mind and made their way to her heart, stirring up deep feelings of appreciation and… desire?

"Last night, I was confident I had done a great job," he continued. "But I felt like you would not like them."

Eva walked past Adamou as he spoke. She took each of the outfits and examined them. She sniffed and held each outfit to her chest. Adamou's passion warmed their way to her heart from the garments, melting her heart even more.

"So, I, uh," Adamou stuttered and cleared his throat.

His hands were trembling from uncertainty. All he wanted was to give his new partner a warm welcome and a gift from his heart, even though his heart was an emotional mess at the moment.

"I, uh," Adamou said before steeling himself. "I made this one last night."

Eva leveled tear-filled eyes at Adamou to find him holding out her gift in both hands. It was the most beautiful of his work. Eva stared repeatedly between it and Adamou. She had emerged from the chamber, filled with the excitement of meeting her partner. She had instantly fallen in love with his son and her maternal instincts had immediately kicked in. Little Cahen was her son, despite her not being his birth mother. However, despite her offering herself wholly to her partner, she had sensed him holding back on her, as if he did not want her but had to be with her, out of a sense of obligation, maybe? She had concealed her disappointment well, she hoped. But standing in front of him, with him holding out this beautiful outfit towards her and hearing the words he spoke, Eva's heart soared with appreciation and, as her soul flooded with hope that everything might be alright after all, tears of gladness and relief flowed down her cheeks.

"Oh no. I am so sorry," Adamou quickly hid the gown behind his back and took a step backwards, away from Eva.

He scratched the back of his head and looked away. How could he have been so foolish. Instead of pleasing his new mate, he had hurt her on the very first day. But before he could say another word, Eva rushed towards him and kissed him with a passion that both stunned him motionless and brought sweet relief. His raging mind stilled, his worry fled, and nothing existed beyond the feel of her body against his. The worst part of all was that Eva's first passionate kiss was, by far, the best kiss he had ever received in all his life. And with this thought, Adamou's body stiffened as his heart was, once again, cast into a conundrum of emotions. Eva peeled her lips slowly away from his and gazed into his eyes.

"My love," Eva said. "You have nothing to be sorry for. These tears are born of the joy that fills my heart for what you have done for me. In this, I feel the hope that, despite your hesitation, you and I will eventually be as one."

She took a step back and held out both arms.

"May I have my gift now, please?" she asked with a sad smile.

"Not yet," Adamou replied.

He approached her, wiped the tears from her cheeks and gently kissed both her eyes before stepping back.

"Now you can have it," he held out her gift once again.

Eva took her outfit with two hands, kissed him again on the lips and slid the gown over her body. She spun around and admired her gift, which was a perfect fit for her physique. She then dashed towards Cahen's room and Adamou was pleased to hear Cahen's pleasant surprise at his new mother's new gown.

And so, it came to pass that Eva lived with her family and embraced the new life she had been given. For the most part, she was very happy; happy with Cahen and Cahen was happy with her. But when it came to Adamou, a different story might be told. Many seasons went by and he still would not lie with her. He was a cordial, friendly and great partner, but he was still averse to engaging in any form of intimacy. It was frustrating for Eva, as was expected, and after several conversations with her partner which yielded no results, she decided it was time for her to make some changes. She would not force him to do what he did not want to; but in the same breath, she would not entertain his behavior any further. She could only be patient with her partner for so long.

"I want to learn how to build a house," Eva told a surprised Ukni one day.

"And why do you want that, my child?" Ukni asked.

"Because I would rather live by myself than share a bed with a partner who treats me like I do not exist," Eva replied.

She was trying to keep her calm, but her frustration triumphed over it.

"I see," Ukni replied, pleased that Eva was not showing any traits of violence. "Could you please give me some time to at least talk to him and hopefully address this situation?"

"You can take all the time you need, but my mind is made up," Eva replied. "I have already had words with him. If he would not lie with me, then so be it. I will not force him."

Ukni did not know whether to commend her for her superior sense of maturity or personally address her needs before trying to find another solution to the situation. But at the same time, his concern that Eva might feel pushed to the edge of her wits grew steadily, and he did not know what could happen after that. Risking the situation was not the best route to take.. As such, he decided that he would grant Eva her request and hope that she might change her mind eventually. While it could take nothing for Ukni and his team to propagate the species, it was vital that they let the species propagate itself. The species needed to mate and mating could not take place with Adamou and Eva residing in separate domiciles.

"Very well, my child," Ukni conceded. "I will teach you how to build a house. But not today; we will commence tomorrow. Alright?"

"Alright, father," Eva replied.

Eva stood up from her chair and left Ukni's office.

*"What is your status, Meena?"* Ukni asked telepathically.

*"Still in progress,"* Meena replied in like manner.

*"Alright, keep me apprised,"* Ukni said and severed the telepathic link.

"I have tried without success," Meena heard Adamou say.

Between Adamou talking and Ukni barging into her mind, she had lost track of her conversation with Adamou.

"I believe you, Adam," Meena managed to say.

Meena wiggled her toes in the stream. She wore a very short pair of pink shorts and a tight, light-blue, strapless blouse. It was hot and humid, or, at least, that was her excuse for choosing the outfit. Adamou sat next to her with his knees folded against his chest.

"I am just trying to find out what is holding you back," she added.

"I am unsure, Meena," Adamou said.

A pause before Adamou's reply belay his uncertainty at the situation and Meena saw her opportunity. She upped the pressure a little.

"And what do you mean by 'unsure'?" Meena asked.

She had chosen the stream because it marked an important turning point in Adamou's life. Even though Adamou and Lithilia had mated here on several different occasions, their first mating here resulted in Cahen's conception. As such, if there was any location that Meena could use to get him out of his comfort zone and open up, this was it.

"I…" Adamou stuttered. "I… I am just not sure."

"About what Adam?" Meena asked and pushed herself off the ground.

Meena knelt in front of Adamou. She looked at him in the eyes, but Adamou avoided her eyes.

"Look at me, Adam," Meena almost commanded. "Please?"

Adamou obliged.

"What is holding you back? Is Eva not attractive enough for you?" she asked.

"Oh, I find her very pleasing to my eyes," Adamou replied.

"Does she treat you or Cahen badly?" Meena asked, though she knew the answer already.

"She gives me great honor, Meena, and she is the best thing that has happened to my son recently," Adamou admitted.

Meena empathized with Adamou's sadness of heart. She was getting closer.

"Then what is holding you back, Adam?" Meena asked.

"Lithilia," Adamou whispered, and tears rolled down his eyes. "I still hold her in my heart, even though I know she is gone."

"You do not have to hold her in your heart anymore if she is gone, Adam," Meena said and took his hands in hers. "Please, let Lithilia go and let Eva in. Eva is here with you *and* Cahen. You will not dishonor her if you lie with Eva. See?"

And without thinking, Meena leaned forward and kissed Adamou on the lips. The kiss was gentle and beautiful. But in that moment, the fine line between therapy and desire disappeared and Meena let him have it all. She kissed him again and Adamou responded in kind. Their lips parted and their tongues touched. Fire and passion burned within their souls. Creator and created locked lips, and for a moment, there was no separation at a non-corporeal level.

Adamou reached for Meena's blouse and untucked it from her shorts. He pulled up her blouse, cupped her exposed breasts and squeezed them firmly. Meena moaned and crashed her body into his. She was on top of him, kissing him madly and caressing him all over. Then Adamou flipped her over and was on top of her. Something so manly, so carnal, and so bestial about his sudden movement made Meena's body go limp with desire.

But in her moment of limpness, reality flared in and the fine line between therapy and desire that had disappeared was replaced by an almost impenetrable wall. She placed a hand on his chest and gently pushed him away. Adamou panted heavily from a sudden awakening of his pent-up passion, feeling caught in a conundrum of his carnality and his craving for something beyond carnal. He tried again to kiss Meena; but her arm stiffened and kept him at bay.

Meena stared into Adamou's eyes, and he stared back into hers. She saw a fire that she had never seen before; one of passion, of desire, of loneliness, of longing and most of all, of letting go. Gradually, his panting eased, and his body relaxed. Meena pulled her arm away as Adamou reached for her blouse and slid it over her breasts. Meena smiled kindly at him and he smiled back at her. Adamou stood up and offered Meena his hand. She took it and Adamou helped her to her feet.

"See?" Meena said weakly as she tucked her blouse back into her shorts. "There is nothing wrong with lying with another woman. Lithilia is gone, and now you have another woman in your life."

Meena was unsure why she could not say Eva's name.

"Now I understand, and I have you to thank for, Meena," Adamou replied.

The strength in his voice and the light in his eyes told Meena that Adamou meant every word he said. Unfulfilled desire burned between the two of them, but more important matters triumphed over their unfulfilled desire. Eva, not

Meena, was created from him for him. As such, he had to commit himself wholly and unreservedly to his new partner. Adamou kissed Meena on the cheek and took her hand. It was such a simple but beautiful gesture that made Meena almost cry. She had been too busy with their mission on Earth Realm that she had lost touch with what they, from their realm, had now come to term as 'humanity.'

Meena and Adamou headed for Adamou's domicile hand-in-hand. They saw Eva playing with Cahen. Meena gave Adamou's hand a gentle squeeze.

"Thank you, Adam," Meena said and let go of his hand.

Adamou said nothing. But the look in his eyes spoke volumes. Meena smiled, turned and headed for the facility. Adamou walked towards Eva and Cahen. Cahen waved when he saw his father and Adamou waved back. When he was close enough, he put his hand on his son's shoulder.

"Could you please give your mother and I a moment?" Adamou asked.

Eva eyed him with sweet mischief and the look of pleasant surprise on her face was more than Adamou could ask for. Cahen grinned and dashed for the domicile. But then he changed his mind and dashed after Meena, who was just retreating into the facility.

"Aunty Meena. Wait for me," Cahen called out.

Meena turned around to see Cahen sprinting towards her. She opened her arms and he accelerated into them. She caught him in her arms, tossed him twice in the air and carried him on her back. He let out an ecstatic squeal. Adamou watched his son and Meena disappear behind the closing doors of the facility.

"May I sit next to you, please?" he asked Eva.

Eva nodded. Adamou sat cross-legged on the ground, next to Eva. He looked at her and smiled weakly.

"Eva," he said. "I know I have not been the kind of partner you wanted me to be. I admit I still had feelings for Cahen's mother, even though she is gone. You do not deserve that, and I am truly sorry."

Adamou took a deep breath and cleared his throat.

"I would like you to give me the opportunity to be the partner that you would like me to be and let me be everything that a partner should be to you. I would like you to be Cahen's mother if that is something you still would like-"

"Yes, yes, and yes I will be his mother," Eva exclaimed with joy.

Eva had been waiting all this while for Adamou's permission to call Cahen her son, even though Cahen had already given his blessing.

"This gives me great joy, Eva," Adamou replied. "Thank you very much. So, will you please grant me the opportunity to be a partner worthy of you?" he asked, and he was as sincere as he could be.

"Yes, Adam," Eva said. "It will make me very happy."

*She called me 'Adam'.* He exclaimed to himself before he grinned.

She had not called him Adam since the day she was created. He picked her up and carried her to their domicile. She giggled all the way. He took her to the room and laid her on the bed. There, they bonded for many hours.

The family was made whole again and with each passing day, their bond as a family grew stronger.

Then one day, Cahen went outside to play. He chased a furry friend of his down to the stream and caught up with the creature. As he turned around to head back to the domicile, a sound in the bushes caught his attention. He turned and looked in that direction. But when he saw nothing, he shrugged and turned around to resume his walk.

Cahen heard a noise again from the same direction and stopped. His curiosity got the better of him and he walked towards the bushes, stroking his furry friend in his arm. Then, something slowly materialized out of nothing, rose from the bushes and stood up straight. The complete materialization, however, revealed that it was not a 'something'. It was a 'someone'. Cahen was paralyzed with so much fear that his furry friend could sense it. The creature sprang from his arm and scurried away. Cahen tried to move, but the muscles in his body would not respond.

"Hello, son," Lithilia said, walking towards her child.

Lithilia knelt in front of Cahen, hugged him tightly and kissed him on the cheek. Cahen remained motionless while leveling a blank, confused stare ahead. She peeled herself away from him and cupped his face in her hands. She smiled, and tears of joy streamed down her cheeks. Her face was the same, but her eyes were different. They glowed with a bright orange-red glow and terror gripped Cahen at the sight.

"Do not be afraid, my son," Lithilia said and hugged him close once again. "I will never, ever harm you."

She wiped her eyes and sniveled.

"I have missed you so much, Cahen. But, I am back and I will never let you go again."

# CHAPTER EIGHT

## SIRING A SCORPION

**"WHOEVER'S OUT THERE**, reveal yourself?" Yehuda called out into the nothingness he floated within.

Silence.

The kind of silence imbued with something that escaped his comprehension. The Shadow of the Soul came to mind, but he quickly dismissed the possibility. This, whatever 'this' was, did not feel like the Shadow of the Soul in any way, thankfully. The energy levels in the 'void' felt familiar but far more powerful and intense than those in the Shadow of the Soul. Innately, he knew no tests awaited him in this... 'oblivion'. He had had enough tests to last what remained of his dwindling existence. He sighed. One moment, a very worried Sasha was snuggling against him and the next moment, he was... here. Wherever or whatever 'here' was. No conscious death, state of deep meditation, deep emotional upheaval or psychological trauma took place to lend some logic to his sudden appearance... 'here'.

"Hello?" Yehuda called out again.

Silence.

The last thing Yehuda remembered was blinking and he was... here. So, if nothing he was consciously aware of was the cause of his sudden appearance... here, then he must have been summoned by... something? No, not 'something'. Some-thing. 'Something' implied an unknown and unspecified. But 'some-thing' implied a presence. And that was what Yehuda was perceiving... a presence. It was there, but where? He searched around and even used clairvoyance but quickly realized the futility of his venture. How does one even begin to search through or within the pitch blackness of such an oblivion teeming with energy, power and life beyond his understanding? Presence perceived but not yet seen. Maybe the presence preferred to remain invisible?

*Where in Yahweh's name am I?* He asked himself.

"Do you know why you are here?" a familiar voice reverberated through the nothingness.

The voice was toneless and genderless. The voice was neither strong nor weak, loud nor soft, aggressive nor soothing. The voice was… dispassionate; devoid of anything but sound. Not sound as in what his perception was accustomed to, but sound as in a reverberation within his being. His every etheric constitution resonated to the 'voice' or sound summoned by this being. Yehuda was so awestruck by the presence of this being that, on instinct, he wanted to drop to his knees before prostrating. However, when he recalled that he was floating within a 'sentient emptiness', he did what he believed was a prostration in reverence. It felt logical and right.

"No, I don't… Kundalini," Yehuda replied.

Every atomic and subatomic particle in his constitution resonated with the energy radiating from Kundalini. Every ether that constituted his entire makeup, from the physical, the psychological to the etheric, pulsated with the vibrations created by the sound of Kundalini's words.

*Yes. Yes. And YES.*

Yehuda had no need to use clairsentience. The power invigorated his soul beyond words. The power was alive beyond words. The power was power beyond words. And an infinitesimal aspect of this power was a part of Yehuda's new and upgraded essence.

"I summoned you to prepare you for your death," Kundalini said bluntly.

"Oh," Yehuda scratched his head.

Yehuda had accepted the fact of his impending death because his body was not ready to host Kundalini. But, in the back of his mind, he had held on to the slim hope of finding a way to prevent his impending death. Alas, Kundalini's words were like an anvil cast into a bottomless ocean, with that slim hope attached to it.

"Your form is dying. There is nothing you can do about that," Kundalini continued. "I could leave your form be, but that will only happen when you have fulfilled the purpose I have for you."

"And what is my purpose?" Yehuda asked.

"Patience, mortal," Kundalini replied.

Yehuda thought he detected a reprimand in that dispassionate voice.

"May I ask you something, please?" Yehuda said.

"Speak," Kundalini replied.

"Who are you?" Yehuda asked.

A moment of perfect stillness lingered. How long? Yehuda did not know. Here, everything, and by 'everything' he meant the nothingness he hovered within, defied all logic of space, time, energy and ether. When the perfect stillness became an uncomfortable silence for Yehuda, he thought about calling out to Kundalini again, but decided not to in the end. The esoteric creature had already given him a stern warning, or what felt like a stern warning, about patience.

"I am Kundalini, the Serpent of Consciousness," it replied.

"So… your real name is Kundalini?" Yehuda asked.

Again, silence.

"I am nameless," it replied. "But I answer to the term 'Kundalini'."

Yehuda nodded and waited for Kundalini to say more.

Silence.

"What do you mean by 'Serpent of Consciousness'?" Yehuda asked.

Silence.

Yehuda sighed in frustration.

"If you're going to take over my body and render me dead eventually, you might as well tell me about you, you know," Yehuda blurted between pursed lips, clenched jaws and a heavy sigh.

Silence.

Yehuda let out an expletive and sat on the… floor. It felt like a floor, but it was oblivion.

"What you ask is… difficult to explain," Kundalini said after a while.

"You mean you do not know who you are?" Yehuda asked with a mixture of sarcasm and genuine curiosity.

"I know who I am," Kundalini replied. "Explaining in your primitive tongue is difficult. I can show you, but you are unable to comprehend."

"And why is that?" Yehuda asked, feeling a little insulted.

"I can show you," Kundalini replied. "But that will be the end of your mortal self. No mortal can behold my true form and live as a mortal."

Yehuda swallowed. Kundalini's words reminded him of a verse in the Torah, specifically from the Book of Exodus 33:20. He swallowed nervously again. He equated getting to know Kundalini to suicide. He was going to die, anyway. But suicide was not going to be his exit route.

"Are you saying that you are not a serpent then?" Yehuda asked.

"I am not," Kundalini replied. "The serpent is just a symbol."

"I see," Yehuda scratched his chin. "Why do you choose the serpent then?"

Silence.

"Okay, I'll tell you what," Yehuda said and stood up.

Yehuda looked around, out of his human habit, to see if he could spot the esoteric entity that was killing him slowly. He realized the stupidity of his actions and shook his head in resignation.

"I can ask you many questions and I may or may not get all the answers," Yehuda said. "My language may be primitive, from your perspective, but it's the only language I know for now, and many other languages on Earth Realm. But you speak it, albeit even better than I do. So, please, do your best to explain to me who you are."

Silence.

Yehuda waited. Silence. He waited some more. More silence. He switched from waiting to being patient. And with that shift came a shift of his energies as well. The ethers that constituted his buildup resonated to a higher frequency and Yehuda knew deep within his essence that he had done something right.

"I am Kundalini, the Serpent of Consciousness," the genderless, formless, dispassionate voice said. "A multi-dimensional being that is neither manifested nor un-manifested, meaning I am somewhere between Creation and the Creator. You may say I am as close to the Creator as it gets."

"Holy –." Yehuda wanted to let out an expletive, but he physically cupped his mouth to stop himself.

And without reservation or hesitation, Yehuda prostrated himself on the… floor. What he felt was beyond a compulsion for worship. Prostrating himself felt as reflexive as breathing.

"Are you…?" Yehuda swallowed nervously. "Are you…?"

"No, I am not," Kundalini replied. "Like I said, I am between the manifested and the Un-manifested; between Creation and the Creator; as close to the Creator as it gets. I permeate all of Creation and, through me, the Creator creates. Like I said, your tongue is primitive. I can only show you; but like I told you before, if I show you me, you will not live as a mortal. You will die. I cannot explain in your primitive tongue any further."

"Okay," Yehuda said, not knowing what else to say.

He felt like a kid who had just opened that closet his parents particularly warned him never to venture near.

"None has ever returned from true death," Kundalini continued. "You are the first in the history of Creation. Your master fulfilled his mission with you. He prepared you well. He knew you were destined for something… special. But he could not see what I had in store for you. No one, not even Akasha, could see what I had set aside for you."

A silence followed that Yehuda dared not even think about interrupting.

"I chose you for a reason and gave you a purpose," Kundalini said. "I needed a soulless mortal from a polarized realm, steeped in the dark but inclined to the light and who had fallen to true death due to a selfless sacrifice. You, Yehuda of Keriyyoth, fit that profile to the letter."

"Why that criteria?" Yehuda asked.

"Soullessness facilitates esoteric upgrades," the multi-dimensional creature replied. "Mortality implies the possibility of transcendence. A preclusion of parity is inherent in polarization. A selfless sacrifice is the perfect soil for the salvation of the only sin there is; identifying with what one is not."

"Thought you couldn't communicate properly in our primitive language," Yehuda blurted before he realized just how rude he may have sounded.

Yehuda let out an expletive and cowered in fear, thinking he was going to be struck down by lightning or some esoteric crap from this serpent he could not see. Nothing happened. Yehuda let out a breath he did not realize he was holding and relaxed.

*Wait. How am I even breathing in this plane of existence in the first place?* He asked himself. He tried to take in a breath and realized there was no movement of air. He sighed at this realization. *Human habits,* he thought.

Nothing was going to happen to him. This was Kundalini, one of the very few multi-dimensional beings in Creation; not some alien from another realm within the planes of existence still governed by polarity, and with the ego the size of the Dimension of Solaris, demanding sacrifices of burnt offering, or barbecue, and promising to rain down fire and brimstone on those who did not entertain their ego with worship and adoration. Kundalini had far more important things to concern itself with than the disrespect from an insignificant mortal from an equally insignificant realm, whether he, Yehuda, was the first in Creation to be resurrected from true death or not.

A moment of silence lingered.

"Why do you choose to manifest as a serpent?" Yehuda asked.

Yehuda chose not to address Kundalini by name anymore because now it felt disrespectful. He did not know how to refer to this creature of immense... everything.

"Symbolic," Kundalini replied. "Creation is made from Consciousness that vibrates at various frequencies. The serpent and its curvy nature is a wonderful representation of the waviness of vibrations as they manifest from the Creator. Creation, everything manifested, is a product of Consciousness as it vibrates. That is why I describe myself, to those who require a description, as Kundalini, the Serpent of Consciousness. I am the vibrations of Consciousness that result in Creation. That is why I permeate all of Creation. That is why I am as close to the Creator as it gets."

Yehuda took it all in. He wanted to ask if Kundalini had ever seen the Creator, been with the Creator, what the Creator looked like and so many other questions. But even as he entertained these thoughts, deep down, he knew these were lines he was not meant to cross. As such, Yehuda chose to ask about something related to Kundalini.

"Why did you curl three-and-a-half times around my body when I was in the Shadow of the Soul?" he asked.

Silence.

"Creation has seen seven Cosmic Sparks so far," it replied. "Creation is about to go through its eighth Cosmic Spark. Each Cosmic Spark represents a perfect cycle. As such, and until the next Cosmic Spark, the number seven symbolizes perfection. However, there exist aspects of Creation that are polarized; light and dark, left and right, right and wrong, up and down, et cetera. When I curled around you three-and-a-half times, as I have done with many other mortals, I upgraded your essence to the level of your purpose. If I curled around your body three-and-a-half more times, then your upgrade would be complete and translate to instant ascension into a realm-dimension such as Akasha or Valla. You would become transmuted into a multi-dimensional being, able to access the four major dimensions of Space, Time, Energy and Ether at will."

"I have never heard of Valla," Yehuda said. "You mentioned Akasha. Does that mean you have curled around her seven times?"

"Do not concern yourself with Akasha's affairs," Kundalini replied.

"My apologies," Yehuda said, still unsure how to address this being.

"The cosmic cluster your kind resides within requires balance," it continued as if Yehuda did not just apologize. "The balance of the twelve dimensions of your cosmic cluster is in peril. The Scribe has indeed turned your cluster into a cog in his grand plan to release the vibration of chaos into Creation; from the Bright Eyes, to The Beast, to the Shemsus."

"The Shemsus?" Yehuda reeled back slightly.

The Bright Eyes had been eliminated and The Beast had just turned up. But these Shemsus of whom Kundalini spoke was an alien name to Yehuda.

"My apologies… Great One," Yehuda said, feeling stupid. "I did not mean to interrupt you."

"The Beast is the least of your worries," Kundalini continued. "He can be stopped, as long as she is ready. But the Shemsus go beyond you and your fellow peers. To hold the balance of your cosmic cluster, you must be ready."

Yehuda knew Kundalini was referring to Sarael when referencing 'she'.

"Rise, Yehuda of Keriyyoth," Kundalini commanded.

Yehuda did as he was told. Kundalini was still nowhere in sight.

"I will now upgrade your form and extend your lifespan," Kundalini said. "Your end is still inevitable, unless I depart from your form. But I will not leave your form until you have completed your task."

Silence.

"I will not curl around you three-and-a-half more times," Kundalini said. "You are not ready. But I will give you something. An iota of my essence will flow through you like venom and this venom will be a source of remarkable strength and power, as well as slow poison to your essence. However, you will not assume a serpentine form. You will assume the form of a scorpion, strong at its claws and deadly with its stinger."

A pair of green, glassy serpentine eyes slowly manifested before Yehuda. A long, twenty-four-foot body of a giant, golden cobra slithered into being. Yehuda appreciated the magnificence and power of Kundalini like he had never before.

"See what I see," Kundalini said.

Yehuda looked up and saw twelve cosmic bodies in a cosmic cluster, each guided by symbolic creatures he innately recognized. The twelve bodies in the cosmic cluster were partaking in a banquet of sorts. There was no disruption of anything. The harmony and balance were perfect.

"Feel what I feel," Kundalini said.

Yehuda's body became infused with chi multiplied a millionfold, initiating the transmutation of his body. Every ether of his makeup resonated to the upgrade of his being. He closed his eyes and surrendered to the moment.

"Rise, Scorpion," Kundalini commanded. "And become the thirteenth member of your cosmic cluster."

And with those words, Kundalini, the Serpent of Consciousness, opened its mouth and sprayed its venom of consciousness all over Yehuda. The venom seeped into Yehuda's body. Yehuda's flesh turned pitch black and harder than the hardest known substance even as his entire body stretched and grew into a gigantic form. His hands enlarged into gigantic claws and his legs broke in several places to become arachnid in structure. His torso also enlarged and two extra pairs of legs sprang forth from his enlarged torso. As Yehuda crashed onto the ground on his eight legs, his lumbar vertebrae exploded from the base of his spine into a very long, curvy stinger.

Yehuda felt no pain as his form morphed from humanoid to pitch-black arachnid. Only an energy of transmutation and invigoration throbbed within his essence as his form became the mystical epitome of a scorpion. He flexed his stinger and snapped his claws repeatedly. The power and life force were there; though these were not as strong as they were right after his resurrection from true death. But it was the second most powerful sensation he had ever experienced in his life.

*Oh, Yes. What a feeling,* he thought.

*"It is done,"* Kundalini hissed telepathically as it gradually dematerialized.

Yehuda, the Scorpion, immediately teleported to join the rest of the cosmic cluster. He partook in the banquet as if he had been a part of them since the dawn of the cosmic cluster. He positioned himself across the diameter of the cosmic cluster instead of taking a position at the circumference. As such, he could ensure stability and balance, in the event of any disruption to the order of the cluster.

And while The Scorpion partook in the banquet, its essence tingled in a prelude to unwelcome tidings afoot. He gave the cosmic cluster an esoteric scan until he found the reason behind his sense of foreboding.

*"I see you,"* he snarled via telepathy to the hearing of the others.

Everything seemed to be under control until the vibrational frequency of the cluster suddenly went out of sync with his, initiating the disruption of the stability and balance of the cluster. It was a herald of tidings to come, a herald of multiple repetitions with similar results. But not this time. In previous times, The Scorpion had not been spawned. That was then, this is now. And now, he, The Scorpion, had been spawned. The cosmic cluster quaked with the ferocity of the cosmos itself. The balance of the cosmic cluster was now tipping over and The Scorpion could not let that happen.

# CHAPTER NINE

## ANOTHER REPLAY

**A LIFELESS PITCH** blackness smothered the land from horizon to horizon. The earth was parched, rock-hard and cracked in a myriad of erratic patterns. The land reeked of loneliness and emptiness.. And except for a single soul that sat cross-legged on the ground, eyes closed and in deep meditation, the land was encased in an aura of death.

Marissa blended with this stillness, becoming one with it. She felt the anima of the barrenness, desolation and death of the land using clairsentience. Her anima resonated with the anima of this plane of existence. Marissa savored this resonance and unity. Then she breathed in slowly and deeply, and a zephyr blew across the land. She slowly exhaled and the zephyr continued to blow across the land. Marissa continued breathing slowly until her breathing synced with the zephyr. Her eyes remained closed. But in her mind, she formed an image of an all-engulfing brightness.

"Let there be light," she commanded in a quiet voice.

Immediately, the darkness was chased away by the light, revealing the dire nature of the land. Marissa opened her eyes and appreciated what she saw. She assigned no labels or judgement.

*I'm getting better,* she thought.

However, her logical mind started doing what it did best; run in every direction of the world it had created for itself during her millennia of existence in the realm.

*Not right now.* She thought, and her mind stilled.

Marissa let it all be. She embraced and accepted it all for what it was. She smiled and felt Mother smiling back at her. At least, her clairsentience indicated that this was the case. All was peaceful; all was serene until the ruckus began.

It started with a violent earthquake that shook the realm like a rag doll. But after a countless number of reruns, Marissa was unbothered by it. She had been petrified the first few times, though, and many mistakes had resulted from that initial fear. But just as practice precedes perfection, she had gotten better. And now, she remained as calm as a mountain in the storm that was the earthquake, as the earth rocked and split under the sheer force of geological spasms. Then, seven hills of equal sizes broke out of the ground in succession and equidistant from one another. From an aerial perspective, if the tops of these hills were connected, they would form a heptagon or an outline of a seven-faceted crystal. Marissa waited for what she already knew was about to unfold.

A ball of fire streaked across the sky like a falling star, leaving a trail of white sparkles in its wake. It streaked and burned across the skies like a cosmic torch and headed straight for the seven hills. It burned brighter as it entered the realm's atmosphere and its acceleration was beyond that of the realm's gravitational pull. The falling star provided more illumination for the already lit, barren realm. Its downward path heralded a promise of apocalyptic obliteration for anything it impacted. One of the newly-formed seven hills suddenly became so big and tall that Mt. Everest would look like a mole hill next to it, and its sudden increase in size was perfectly timed with the collision from the falling star.

A mega explosion more brilliant than those from a hundred Solaras combined followed the impact and half of the mountain was destroyed by the fallen cosmic object. However, the cosmic object, a twenty-four-foot-diameter ball of red-hot, magma-burning fury, remained intact and settled at the bottom of a ten-mile wide and one-mile deep caldera that had just been created in what remained of the mountain. Slowly, as if it had a mind of its own, the ball of fire started rolling up the caldera. It paused at the edge. Marissa was facing this cosmic body of mass destruction and this cosmic body seemed to stare down at her. And then, as if guided by an unseen, malicious force, it slowly tipped over the lip. Once its center of gravity crossed over the edge, it accelerated towards her.

Marissa remained still. The gigantic, blazing ball of fire incinerated everything in its path. Six leagues... Marissa remained still. One league... Half a league... Four hundred fathoms... Three hundred... Marissa did not even blink. She was still; in mind, in body and in her being. She was still by her own nature. When the ball of fire was two hundred yards away, it burst open and a nine-foot-tall creature leaped from its bowels, leaving a trail of fire and smoke as it sailed through the air. The creature landed ten feet away from Marissa in a crouched position before slowly rising to its feet.

The creature appeared mostly human, all nine feet of its smoldering, muscular body, with claws for fingers and toes. It sparked the ethers and a twelve-foot long, smoldering trident coalesced in its right hand. A bright yellow-red flame blazed around its body like a smoldering silhouette. The creature focused blazing yellow-red eyes on Marissa, whose real name was Sarael, and when it opened its mouth to speak, yellow-red flames spewed from its mouth. The creature lifted its trident and crashed the hilt of the trident three times on the ground. A violent earthquake followed each crash and each earthquake was more violent than the previous one. On the third crash, the earth ruptured and fissured towards Marissa in erratic patterns. When the fissure was close to her, it forked on either side of her as if it was forced to do so by an unseen force. Marissa remained still.

"You are getting better," the creature complimented her.

"You bore me," Sarael replied.

"Oh, Sarael," The Beast smirked. "You should learn to lighten up."

"I won't fail this time," Sarael reassured herself and The Beast before levitating in the air.

Sarael sparked the ethers. A golden sword formed in her left hand and a golden shield appeared in her right. She uncrossed her legs and let her feet touch the ground as shoes of gold formed over them. Then she pulled the shield in front of her and placed her sword next to the shield in a battle stance as an armor of gold formed across her torso. A golden hair band appeared behind her head and tied her long, black hair in a tight bun. Green flames then erupted from her eyes and mouth at the same time.

"Today you fall," Sarael promised and lunged towards The Beast.

Sarael swung her sword in a downward arc. The Beast calmly tilted his trident to the right and, with a clang, it deflected Sarael's strike. The smirk on his face reflected his overconfidence, which led to him failing to see that her initial attack was merely a distraction for a more brutal, follow-up attack. From the corner of his eye, The Beast caught a shiny glimmer of Sarael's shield as it raced towards his face. He had no time to react. Sarael had put every bit of emotion, energy, and power she had behind that single motion as she pinned The Beast's right foot to the ground with her left foot as she jammed the golden shield into The Beast's throat. Under normal circumstances, the blow would have resulted in instant decapitation. But these were not normal circumstances and The Beast was no ordinary creature.

The blow, however, was powerful enough to catapult the six-hundred-pound creature off the ground. The body of The Beast was already in a state of motion from Sarael's superhuman blow, but his right foot stayed planted to the ground. Loud, rapid snaps underscored his ankle and fibula fracturing to various degrees in several places while ligaments tore and came apart from sheer wanton savagery. The Beast roared in pain, while Sarael maintained pressure on his right foot. His muscular body landed awkwardly on the hard, parched earth, breaking more bones, ripping apart more soft tissue and causing more excruciating pain around his ankle.

For good measure, Sarael crashed her shield into The Beast's broken ankle repeatedly until The Beast felt numb to the pain. In a desperate move, The Beast thrust its trident at Sarael, but she swiped it away with her sword. However, the move was just a distraction and Sarael fell for it by focusing too much on the trident. The Beast smirked and swept her right foot off the ground with his left leg. Sarael fell to the ground, executed a backward roll and immediately returned to battle pose before using the power of thought to activate her chi to heal her burned leg where The Beast's smoldering leg had struck her. The Beast roared with maniacal rage. He levitated from the ground. Smoldering flames gathered around his shattered ankle and healed it instantly. He snarled, grunted and flared red-yellow flames from his nostrils, knowing that would require more than just outer-worldly flames to heal his badly broken ego.

"Impressive," said The Beast coldly. "But not good enough yet."

He spat a phlegm of fire, which burned into the earth.

"But you really should have finished me off when you had the chance," The Beast added and charged.

The trident arrowed straight towards her torso. She turned her body sideways, bringing up her shield in front of her at the same time. Sparks flew as the trident grazed her shield and pierced the air as Sarael took a side-step towards The Beast. The Beast had also taken a step towards her and thrown a balled fist at her head. Sarael sank her weight as she continued her sidestepping motion. She ducked her head just in time for The Beast's closed, smoldering fist to scrape the crown of her head, singing her hair and scalp with its smoldering heat.

The Beast flared, fumed and swung wildly at Sarael, leaving a clear target for her sword. Her blade penetrated his left armpit and shoulder, until it came to a stop in his left cheekbone. Sarael infused her sword with green, esoteric flames. The sound of flesh burning and the vibrations in her sword from the sound of The Beast shrieking in pain were a priceless symphony to her soul. Sarael twisted and yanked her blazing sword outwards leaving The Beasts left arm hanging from his shoulder by a tiny thread of flesh, like a huge chunk of meat hanging in a butcher's slaughter house. Bright yellow light oozed from his severed shoulder and from his cheek, where the sword had made impact. The Beast slumped to a knee and used his trident for support.

Sarael executed a forward roll and assumed combat position again, while she regrew her singed hair by sparking the ethers and healed her burned scalp using her chi. Smoldering flames gathered around The Beast's almost-severed left arm, forming ligaments, flesh, tendons, and muscle as The Beast healed itself again. He rose to his feet, completely healed but heavily scarred. He leveled a pair of flaming sockets, where his eyes were supposed to be, at Sarael, and the opponents glared flames at each other.

"All hail The Beast in all his scarred glory," Sarael mocked. "Behold the untouchable has been touched by my sword."

Sarael turned around and spat on the ground. Big mistake. The Beast seized the opportunity of Sarael's momentary distraction. He dropped his weight low to the ground and spun around in a complete revolution, with his trident extended. It caught Sarael on her right, outer thigh with enough force to send her rolling twenty feet on the ground. Before she could recoup, The Beast zipped and thrust its trident into the back of Sarael's left thigh. She screamed from the burning, simmering pain that possessed her body. The Beast then scooped her off the ground, lifted her over his head, and smashed her body back down. Sarael tried to heal herself, but The Beast repeated the attack; this time, on her right thigh.

Sarael gritted her teeth and yanked her leg away from the trident. She rolled on the ground to create some space between herself and The Beast, while she tried to heal herself at the same time. Her body sailed helplessly and painfully over fifty feet through the air as The Beast unleashed a ferocious kick into her solar plexus with the force of a high-speed truck. Bone and guts turned into mush. Her body slamming into the ground violently was the least of her worries. The Beast then leaped a hundred feet in the air. Despite her pain, Sarael could only watch in horror and helplessness as The Beast descended on her like the fallen star that he was.

Sarael commended herself for making it this far this time. She had done a lot more than just leave a scar. She had made The Beast furious. It signified progress. The last time, she never made it past the first attack after the earth had split open in front of her. Despite her progress, she was aware time was not on her side

And she needed more time.

The Beast continued his blazing, downwards path towards her. His yellow-red, flaming body grew larger with each distance he covered as he accelerated towards her. The movement seemed to be in slow motion. His trident blazed with yellow flames, held in both hands and raised above his head. A smoldering snarl graced his face and blazing eyes were zoomed on her chest.

She was ready.

Sarael sighed, knowing she would have another chance. Maybe she would succeed next time. The Beast raised his flaming trident higher above his head in a prelude to a deathly blow. But then, the unexpected happened.

A dark flash whizzed past her, and something swiped The Beast from midair. The sheer force of this attack flung The Beast more than a hundred feet away from Sarael. Sarael spun around to face her savior. This was a first. No one had ever come to her aide before now.

"It cannot be," she exclaimed in disbelief when she saw her savior.

Slowly, she stood up and fearlessly approached the creature.

*"Who are you, stranger?"* she smiled, speaking via telepathy. *"I don't know why, but I feel... safe with you."*

It did not move. Sarael reached out with her right hand and placed it on her savior's head. Its one eye was twice the size of her hand. It blinked twice and then, her savior walked passed her, towards The Beast. It had a job to do.

Sarael gawked at the immensity of the creature- an obsidian scorpion that stood nearly eight feet tall and measured at least twenty-four feet in length, from its head to the tip of its stinger. It crawled menacingly towards The Beast, and The Beast assumed combat position.

"You are not supposed to be here," The Beast roared.

"Neither are you," The Scorpion hissed like a snake. "This ends right here, right now. You and your loathsome, evil intent will not have her soul."

"And since when do you care?" The Beast asked. "Are you not supposed to be at some cosmic banquet?"

"I was until you caused a disturbance in my shift," The Scorpion replied with equal sarcasm. "Big mistake."

"Let us end this," The Beast spoke with exaggerated exasperation.

"Just waiting for you to finish licking your wounds," The Scorpion retorted and gestured upwards with its right claw. "She did give you a big, fat scar. We could see it all the way from up there."

The Beast charged with blind fury. The Scorpion also charged.

They came together in a clash of fiery and dark brilliance. Sarael watched as the two creatures attacked each other in a deathly dance of both physical and esoteric rhythms. The Beast struck with its trident, and The Scorpion lashed with its stinger. Both creatures engaged in a duel like Sarael had never seen before. She marveled and shuddered. Yet, she watched, and as she watched, she learned. She pondered upon the verbal exchange between The Beast and The Scorpion. Right now, all meaning eluded her. Eventually, she would understand. She was in deep thought when both creatures infused their bodies; The Beast with bright, yellow light, and The Scorpion with an intense, black light. Both creatures blazed towards each other in one final assault, and as they collided, a blinding flash of light engulfed everything around her.

Marissa leaped from her bed, panting hard. Her thin, white night gown was drenched in sweat and clung to her naked form underneath. Patrick sat next to her, his eyes were averted from her body.

"I'm sorry," Patrick said. "I didn't mean to sneak up on you like that. But I heard you scream and thought something was wrong."

"It's okay," Marissa replied, wiping her forehead with the back of her hand.

She wondered why he was averting his eyes. But when she glanced at her body, she understood and smiled.

"Don't worry about this," Marissa said, gesturing at her body. "You've seen plenty of wet tee shirt contests before, haven't you?"

"You weren't in any of them, though. And I happen to have taken a vow of celibacy," Patrick played along and turned to face her.

"How's that working for you?" Marissa asked and pulled the sheets away from her body.

Marissa slid off the bed and rid herself of the soaked nightgown as if she was alone in the room. She had her back to Patrick; not intentionally, though. She put on a clean, black blouse and pair of jean shorts, without any bra or underwear. Patrick thought it was interesting how he was unmoved by her nude form. He might as well have been staring at a dead tree stump in the woods.

*Damn you, Sara.* Patrick thought and smiled.

He was glad Marissa did not see him smile, lest she misinterpreted his smile.

"I get these dreams every now and then," Marissa said as she pulled her hair back in a bun. "It's basically the same dream, with only minor differences. I can tell you more about them later if you'd like."

"Trust me that much already with your life's secrets?" Patrick asked jokingly.

"It's either that, or I take my life's secrets with me to the grave, you know," Marissa replied. "I must see my mother as soon as possible."

Marissa headed for the bathroom and turned on the faucet at the sink.

"Why's that?" Patrick asked.

Marissa said something, but Patrick did not catch it. She waited as he walked towards the bathroom, meaning to stand by the door so he could hear her better. The tap was also running.

"I was saying," a naked Marissa said as she walked towards him. "That I am horny as hell and I must feed my inner beast before I go see my mother."

Marissa pressed her body against his. Patrick reached around her waist and kissed her neck. Then he reached out, turned on the faucet for cold water and started splashing cold water on her back. Marissa yelped at the sudden shock of the cold water on her bare back and beat him on the chest.

"You're mean, Patrick, you know that?" Marissa said with a grin as she headed for the shower.

"You're not the first to tell me that," Patrick replied.

"How did you know I wasn't going to knock your socks off?" Marissa asked, waggling her eyebrows before stepping in the shower.

"Trade secret," Patrick replied.

"Ooohhh I see," Marissa played along as she stepped into the shower. "And let's just say I was being serious. What would you have done?"

"Only one way to find out," Patrick said as he walked away from her room. "I'll see you later, Marissa."

*"See you later, Patrick,"* Marissa replied telepathically. *"And thank you… For being there when I woke up."*

*"The pleasure was all mine,"* Patrick replied telepathically. *"Literally."*

Marissa could have sworn she heard Patrick laugh in his mind as well.

***

Miryam sat on the porch of her bedroom, staring blankly at nothing. The bond between mother and daughter had only intensified over the centuries. Now, she could feel almost everything that Marissa felt and that even included Marissa's latest dream in every detail. This connection was beyond clairsentience. She had a good idea who The Scorpion was. So she was not surprised when he reached out telepathically.

*"Do you still think my intrusion was too early?"*

*"It doesn't matter anymore, does it?"* Miryam replied nonchalantly.

*"We are running out of time,"* The Scorpion said.

*"You think I don't know that?"* Miryam snapped.

*"I think it was for the better."*

*"And I say the unfoldment of the next events better prove you right,"* Miryam warned. *"Or else, I guarantee you that I will stop at nothing to make you pay should anything happen to my daughter because of your decision."*

*"I respect your motherly tendencies,"* he replied smoothly. *"But if Sarael isn't ready now, she may not be ready in time. You know that and it is not my fault or anyone else's."*

Miryam breathed deeply to calm herself down.

*"I apologize,"* Miryam finally said after a few moments.

Marissa's progress was solely Marissa's responsibility. The pattern of her dreams had to be changed to speed up her progress. The Scorpion knew this, and so did Miryam.

*"It's okay,"* The Scorpion said. *"I have faith in Sarael. She will succeed, and we will all be there to help her."*

*"I never had a doubt,"* Miryam replied. *"On both accounts."*

The Scorpion thought about continuing the conversation but changed his mind.

*"Talk later,"* he said.

*"Yeah, later,"* she replied and severed the telepathic link.

The Scorpion stared blankly through his window. A sleepy female roused in her sleep on the bed next to him. The Scorpion knew what was coming next and sighed as he waited for his lover to say the words.

"Come to bed, my love," she said sleepily.

Yehuda peeled himself away from the window and joined Sasha in bed. As Sasha snuggled close to him, he caressed her hair and pondered on the fact that he too was running out of time. The poison, the essence of Kundalini, was spreading quickly and taking over his being. Soon, Yehuda might be completely erased from existence… and Creation.

# CHAPTER TEN

## LET'S TALK

**ZUKAEL STARED AT** the rock walls that marked the physical boundaries of what used to be his prison. He slowly ran the fingers of his left hand along the wall. Suddenly, he made a fist and punched a six-inch deep hole into the rock wall. Smoldering flames spewed from his eyes and clenched teeth before he let out a scream of rage. He was free from his prison, but he was still a prisoner on Earth Realm. He could not return home. Whatever curse Maziel had laid on him was more powerful than he could handle.

"Maziel," he raged. "I promise you a slow and painful end."

Zukael fumed at the thought of what the new home for the fallen from the rebellion was. Hell Realm. That filth of a realm; the realm they, the creatures of Celestia, used to make fun of and regard with unmalleable disdain. Michael was a sadistic, winged buffoon. Zukael knew Michael was going to cast them out after the rebellion, but he least expected Michael to cast them to Hell Realm. Well, given the alternative, which was execution, banishment to that cesspool of a realm did not seem like such a bad idea in the end. Execution marked the ultimate end. Banishment, on the other hand, spelt hope for another rebellion to come.

When?

He was unsure. Hope for the rebellion coming to pass was merely a concept. No plan to free their leader existed because only Michael knew her location of incarceration. Still, Zukael hoped and felt it deep with his being that a rebellion would ensue somehow, some way.. He retrieved his fist from the wall and let it hang freely.

*And if I am aware of this possibility, then Michael and Celestia must also be aware of it.*

Michael did not have the wings to execute what was left of the rebellion after the war was over. He was too full of compassion and a misplaced sense of honor for that. Raphael, on the other hand... Zukael summoned his wings and flapped them twice to stifle an involuntary shudder as he extinguished the smoldering flames from his eyes and mouth. Good thing Michael, not Raphael, was archangel supreme. If it had been up to Raphael, Hell Realm would still have been a waste of a realm because not a single member of the rebellion would have been spared.

Raphael earned the title *The Ruthless* after the carnage he unleashed on Luciel and her followers during the rebellion. Raphael did not do nearly as much damage as Michael did, but he was the next best thing to Michael. Zukael felt compelled to appreciate Raphael's fiery passion and loyalty towards Michael and Celestia. From one kindred leader to another, Zukael could fold his wings in respect for his binary counterpart, Raphael. However, there could be only one top general of utmost repute and, as such, Zukael looked forward to the chance to do one more dance of death with his greatest rival, Raphael, The Ruthless.

As much as he hated Michael with every fiber of his being, Zukael knew he was no match for Michael on any level; charisma, leadership, combat skills and the list continued. It was interesting how easily deep respect and extreme envy could smelt into hatred. But his hatred for Michael was irrelevant at the moment. Michael was Luciel's primordial interest, the unspoken and former second-in-command in Celestia and leader of the failed rebellion.

Zukael closed his eyes, bowed his head and heaved a heavy sigh. How he missed her so. He could only imagine what Michael might have done to her after the rebellion. Even though Luciel was the leader of the rebellion, Michael would not execute her; could not execute her. And that was testament of Michael's weakness, for which Zukael was grateful.

*Luciel will return, and when she does, another war will follow. The rebellion will triumph, Celestia will fall, and Michael, along with the rest of his loyal followers, will be ended.*

Zukael shook himself out of his reverie. He looked around and reminded himself he was still in his once-upon-a-moment prison. He teleported to another part of the Grand Canyon that was inaccessible to humans. He chose a huge, random boulder and perched on it. He raised his eyes towards Solara and stared directly into it. He thought about teleporting to Solara, but he remembered he could not leave Earth Realm. If he could even teleport to any other realm within the Dimension of Solaris, it would have been better.

Zukael sneered, made a fist and bared his semi-fangs when he realized just how much he hated Earth Realm and the humans. He hated the realm and its creatures even more than he hated Hell Realm. The reason for his hatred was obvious and logical and Maziel knew exactly how to turn that hatred into an instrument of torture. How could an archangel of repute like himself be tasked to being a guardian to the gunge of Creation called humans? Again, he swore to give Maziel a very slow and painful exit. All he needed was the opportunity to meet Maziel face-to-face.

Zukael remembered being contacted by a female, once. How she had known about him and his prison eluded him. She said she had a proposition for him regarding dealing with the humans. She may be vermin, but for the moment, they shared a common interest. And who was that creature who defeated him? He was human alright, but he was not just any kind of human. Whatever he was would be a hindrance to his plan for the humans. After all, they were a part of the reason for his incarceration. His hands suddenly burst into bright, golden flames as his memory went back to the moments after the rebellion was over.

***

The fallen were all lined up on their knees with their hands tied behind their backs with chords summoned from Celestia's light. Michael's hoard stared and glared at them, the fallen rebellion. Luciel had already been tried and sentenced to eternal banishment by Michael, and only Michael knew where she was locked up. A smart move. So long as the rebellion knew their leader still lived, another would not rise in her stead. And if Michael had the leader of the rebellion at his mercy, then he had the rest of the rebellion at his mercy. Too many of his brethren had perished during the rebellion. There was no need to add to that tally by beheading the rest of the fallen. Besides, a psychological blow was more efficient and effective than dealing a physical one. Zukael wondered if this had been Michael's idea or Uriel's.

Regardless, it was a damn smart move.

The exodus to Hell Realm was uneventful. With their leader gone, a vacancy had opened up in leadership, sparking an all-out power struggle. But Zukael and Malichiel chose not to participate in such blasphemy and stupidity. They would wait for Luciel, no matter how long it took. Their loyalty to her was unshakable because Luciel was their true leader. She wanted more for them; to change their status quo, to make them live up to their fullest potentials as archangels and angels. The same could not be said for Michael. As such, both archangels chose to sit back and watch the insanity of the power struggle unfold.

The struggle turned into savagery, albeit savagery on a much smaller scale than the rebellion was. Still, savagery is savagery. When the power struggle was over, Hell Realm had a new leader. Zukael and Malichiel watched as Maziel unleashed wit, smartness and brutality in a fiery and subtle mix that even they had to admit was nothing short of sheer brilliance. Alas Zukael, Luciel's right hand, and Malichiel, Luciel's strategist, had no idea that Maziel's 'sheer brilliance' was about to take a most unexpected turn.

After his coronation, which Zukael and Malichiel found ridiculously infantile, Maziel knew exactly what to do next. He had observed the last two major generals in Luciel's rebellion and had seen nothing but spiteful contempt and mockery for his leadership in their eyes. It was wise to not let such sentiments fester and infect Hell Realm. After all, Malichiel and Zukael were the last two representatives of the old order under Luciel. Hell Realm had a new order named Kazuk, formerly known as Maziel, and the old order had to be wiped out once and for all. Thus, Maziel ordered Malichiel to be arrested and placed under constant surveillance till further notice. As for Zukael, Maziel had something else in store for him.

Kazuk did not want to entertain the slightest possibility for an uprising. Zukael and Malichiel were the last truly loyal and high-ranking archangels under Luciel's leadership, after Maziel had executed the rest of the high-ranking archangels who had sided with Luciel during the rebellion in a public display of ruthlessness and power. Saving Malichiel and Zukael for last was a psychological move on Maziel's part. As shocked and as surprised as Zukael and Malichiel were, they both still had to agree that Maziel's strategy was genius.

Zukael was too surprised to react when over thirty of their fellow brothers and sisters at arms surrounded him. They bit their lips and averted their eyes. They each had the look a loyal soldier has when that soldier has been given an order he or she disagrees with but must execute regardless. Zukael gazed at their faces and nodded, and his nod made them grip their weapons more tightly and grit their teeth almost audibly in suppressed anger and frustration. Some of them even looked away as Maziel walked through the wall of fallen angels and faced Zukael, who remained calm.

"You go down too easily, General," Kazuk said in mockery.

Zukael remained silent, much to Maziel's disappointment.

"Is your tongue now as useless as the authority you once wielded?" Kazuk scoffed as he took a step towards Zukael.

Zukael remained silent, which angered Kazuk.

A slight warmth caressed Zukael's face as he sidestepped to evade Kazuk's right hook. His target no longer there, Kazuk punched through empty space, his momentum causing him to stumble forward awkwardly. He was helpless against Zukael's extended right leg, which tripped him. Kazuk crashed face-first into the ground. Some of the soldiers who had come to arrest Zukael snickered, which infuriated Kazuk. He stood up and summoned a spear and infused it with a kind of flame that was alien to everyone present, including Zukael. It burned purple instead of golden yellow. Zukael stepped back and stiffened, wary of what this purple flame could do to him. Kazuk saw what he interpreted as fear in Zukael's eyes before he snarled and thrust the weapon at Zukael.

But before Zukael could evade the spear, a fallen angel thrust himself between the spear and Zukael. Kazuk's spear went through the fallen angel's back, and its tip emerged from his chest. The soldier's smile of defiance died as he realized something was terribly amiss. His eyes rolled to the back of his head and his knees buckled. Zukael caught his former comrade-at-arms as Kazuk dismissed his spear. He met the wounded angel's gaze, who tried to heal himself with angel light. The healing process failed. He was as astounded as everyone else was. The flame Kazuk had infused his spear with was definitely not of the Dimension of Lemuria and therefore, the flame must be from an extradimensional source.

*How did Kazuk come across such power? Did Kazuk have an ally from another dimension? If this is the case, then Kazuk most certainly must not be trifled with.* Zukael thought while he held his injured comrade in his arms.

"What is your name, brother?" Zukael asked.

"B- Beelzebiel, s- sir," the soldier stuttered weakly as he writhed and squirmed.

Zukael held him firmly, unable to understand what the dying angel was going through on the inside. All he could afford to offer was empathy.

"I swear to you, on my existence," Zukael dipped his finger into the exposed wound in his dying brother's chest. "Your end will not be in vain."

Zukael crossed his forehead with the angel light that oozed from the dying soldier's wound. The other soldiers beat their chest three times in unison.

"S-sir, m-may I ask one- one last favor of you, p-please?" the soldier coughed out angel light.

"Anything, brother," Zukael replied.

"I would rather die by your hand than by Maziel's," the soldier said.

The dying angel's eyes beamed with defiance for Kazuk and a plea to Zukael.

Zukael nodded.

"As you wish."

The dying angel closed his eyes. Zukael boiled with rage as he summoned a dagger and slashed swiftly, separating the angel's head from his body.

Kazuk summoned his wings and flapped them several times in anger. He uttered an expletive for wasting a one-time-only opportunity of using the spell he had been given by some entity known as The Scribe. He would just have to face Zukael and prove, definitively, that he was the best fighter in Hell Realm.

But his fury was nothing compared to Zukael's. Zukael slowly stood and turned. He summoned his sword and archangel battle flame and cast a glare at Kazuk, daring him to charge.

Kazuk steadied himself for an attack and summoned his spear. However, instead of attacking, he had a moment of clarity. If, by some stroke of luck, he ended Zukael, an instant coup was bound to happen, with the soldiers present boiling with rage and on the verge of brimming over with anger and frustration. Even he, Kazuk, would not stand any chance at surviving the coup. Hell Realm was still heavily and overtly loyal to Zukael. So, no. He would not end Zukael; at least not here and certainly not right now. He lowered his spear.

"Seize him," Kazuk commanded.

No one moved.

"I said seize him," Kazuk boomed the command.

When no one followed Kazuk's order, Zukael had his own moment of clarity. He had already defeated Kazuk. It was clear who everyone wanted to be their leader, despite Kazuk's coronation. He had trained many of his brothers and sisters to follow orders to the letter, regardless of the situation. If he defied Kazuk now, then he would be setting a bad example for those who still called him 'general'. Plus, Luciel was still their leader, though she was in incarceration. Thus, he was not going to start a coup. He would wait for her because he was that loyal to her.

*Leadership by example,* Zukael thought.

Kazuk's head will be his eventually. That was a given. No need to rush it now. As such, Zukael dismissed his sword and archangel battle flame and placed his hands behind his back.

"Who's your captain?" Zukael asked at no one in particular.

"I, General," an angel replied from Zukael's right and stepped forward.

Zukael turned his back towards the captain and extended his hands. The captain hesitated.

"It is alright, captain," Zukael said. "You are supposed to follow orders… just like we taught you."

"But, General-" the captain began to protest.

"It's alright, captain," Zukael encouraged the angel. "Execute the order."

Kazuk swallowed the bitter pill of humiliation and made a mental note to exact an even bigger dose of humiliation on Zukael. The captain frowned and bowed his head as he bound Zukael's hands. Arresting his former general was the hardest thing he had ever done.

"It is an honor, sir," the captain said. "Fighting by your side against Michael and doing this now."

"The honor is all mine, captain," Zukael replied and nodded at the captain.

The captain clenched his jaws and turned around to face his compatriots.

"Take him away."

The angels escorted Zukael away and placed him in solitary confinement. Though in solitude, he remained in constant communication with Malichiel via telepathy. They strategized on ways to eliminate Kazuk, who epitomized all that good leadership was not. This was not what they had rebelled against Celestia for. They feared that if they allowed Kazuk's leadership to continue, their chances of reclaiming Celestia would dwindle, even with the return of Luciel. As such, they concluded that inciting a coup was their best bet at preserving whatever bond remained of the rebellion. They had most of the angels on their side already, angels who were scared wingless of Kazuk though. Thus, the coup may not be as easy as they might like it to be.

But as Zukael and Malichiel strategized, Kazuk launched a preemptive strike. Zukael was summoned and brought before a one-angel judge-and-jury trial. Hell Realm looked on, and Kazuk made a public spectacle of the trial of the great General Zukael.

"Zukael, General of Luciel's army," Kazuk bellowed. "I charge you with treason and conspiracy to start a coup. How do you plead?"

"Why not spare us the burden of your insanity and skip to the end, Maziel," Zukael said and noticed how Kazuk flinched at the mention of his angelic name. "We all know how this ends."

"How do you plead?" Kazuk asked, ignoring Zukael's humiliating jabs.

"I plead that you skip to the very end," Zukael replied, with more exasperation than he wanted to admit. "Please. You are boring me to winglessness."

"Very well then," Kazuk stood up from his throne. "Zukael, I find you guilty as charged. You are hereby sentenced to banishment to a lower realm for the rest of your existence."

Kazuk grinned when he noticed the look of confusion on Zukael's face.

"That's right, Zukael," Kazuk continued. "*YOU* are going to a lower realm, where you will remain in incarceration for all eternity."

"And how do you plan on achieving such a feat?" Zukael asked.

"Patience, General," Kazuk replied. "Patience. First of all, you must give us your new name. So, what would you like to call yourself now?"

"Zukael sounds perfect, Maziel," Zukael replied.

"As you wish," Kazuk said and raised his right hand in the air.

Kazuk uttered some words in a language that was alien to the rest of the fallen angelic host. As he spoke, a blue ball of light formed in his palm and grew bigger with every moment. Everyone, including Zukael and Malichiel watched in awe and confusion. Some gawked as the murmuring and tension in the crowd grew. They had never seen anything like this before.

"And now Zukael, you will heed my words," Kazuk called out in a dark, commanding voice. "You will be banished to the lower realms, where you will lose your identity as a creature from Celestia. You will neither be archangel nor angel. I curse you. I curse you to become an abomination unto the lower realms.

I curse the very being that you are. I curse the very essence you represent. And with this curse, I cast you into the lower realm, to remain therein for the rest of your miserable, pathetic existence."

Kazuk cast the blue ball of light at Zukael. Before Zukael could react, the ball of light engulfed him, and in a flap of a wing, Zukael was nowhere to be found in Hell Realm. It was as if he was never even there. When next Zukael opened his eyes, his hands and legs were fastened to a hard surface by ethereal cords, cords he could not break. Pitch blackness surrounded him, and the only other thing that created a sense of physicality was the ethereal cords and the hard surface to which he was bound. The darkness smothered him, making him feel claustrophobic. He could tell his body had undergone a transmutation, though he did not recall the experience of the transmutation process.

*Maziel's curse*, he spat.

His form felt denser. Confusion and panic crept in. He kicked and screamed. But all he heard was himself and all he felt were the wall, floor, ethereal cords that bound him, a smothering blackness and the new essence that was now his.

In his solitude and surrender, a new being was spawned. He would later learn that something called 'time' governed this realm. What he had become was termed by the creatures of this realm as a 'demon,' and the creatures on this realm even usurped from his essence, while others prayed and worshipped him. But some fought against him and what his essence represented, while still others were spawned from him. He would learn of the savagery and ignorance that governed these creatures, and he would grow to hate them even more. These creatures were part of the reason for the rebellion in the first place and, by extension, part of the reason for his fall and demise.

And as the moments slipped by, Zukael endured and looked forward to his day of reckoning. Kazuk would pay. He swore on his and Beelzebiel's existences. In that perfect moment, he will strike, and Kazuk will feel the full force of his blow. He will never forget. He had seen too many of his brothers and sisters perish. But for some reason, Beelzebiel's end was one that struck the deepest chord with him. And so, he decided he would adopt a new name because his new identity and essence warranted one. Making a choice was easy and his choice of name gave him just enough solace to maintain his sanity while he looked forward to his moment of freedom to come. His new name would be Beelzebub.

***

"It's beautiful, isn't it?" Lithilia's voice cut through Beelzebub's reverie.

"You said you had a proposition for me?" he asked, without looking in her direction.

"All business," Lithilia stated, walking from behind him and standing in front of him.

Lithilia's body was a dark, curvaceous silhouette against the glare of Solara. Beelzebub continued to ignore her presence. Lithilia sighed and shook her head.

"Okay then," she started. "I understand you want my husband's head on a platter, no?"

"So you were stupid enough to become Kazuk's bride," Beelzebub scoffed through clenched teeth.

Beelzebub rose to his feet and towered over Lithilia. He wrapped his left hand around Lithilia's neck and squeezed until Lithilia started to choke. Even as he raised her off the ground, she did not fight back.

"Tell me why I should not end your miserable existence right now, you filth," Beelzebub demanded.

Lithilia pointed at Beelzebub's left hand around her throat, and he released his grip on her neck just a tiny bit.

"Speak," Beelzebub commanded as smoldering flames spewed from his eyes.

"Because... I gave... the spells to the cult that... set you free," Lithilia managed to say as she choked.

Beelzebub's shock at Lithilia's answer made the flames disappeared from Beelzebub's eyes and mouth. He let her fall to the ground. Lithilia gasped and coughed for air as she rubbed her neck.

"I'm confused," Beelzebub said finally. "Why would you want to set free the one archangel who wants to end your husband?"

"If only you would let me speak, instead of trying to kill me, then you might get some answers," Lithilia's choked reply was heavy with sarcasm.

Beelzebub clenched his jaw. He teleported to a boulder outside about six miles from the cave and sat down. Lithilia followed his teleportation trail and appeared in front of him. His line of sight was level with her ample cleavage glistening with sweat in the brightness of Solara.

"Alright," Beelzebub spoke firmly to mask the fact that he was losing the fight against Lithilia's seduction. "Speak."

"Such manners," Lithilia replied and rolled her eyes.

Lithilia rose to her feet and dusted her extremely short pair of denim shorts. She also adjusted her blouse that could easily pass for a strapless sports bra.

*She had on different garments just now. How come...?* Beelzebub thought.

He heaved his shoulders, reminding himself that this was the bride of his sworn enemy and, by the extension of that logic, this piece of vermin was also his sworn enemy. He would end her later. A sheen of sweat glistened on her exposed flesh and an ample cleavage beckoned to anyone to partake at the tantalizing sight. Beelzebub shifted his form on the boulder.

"I'll make it brief," Lithilia said. "You want my husband's head, you want to exterminate the humans, my son, Cahen, wants to take his rightful place here on this realm, and he also needs protection from someone who wants his head."

"And what do you want?" Beelzebub asked.

"To keep my son alive," Lithilia replied.

"But you married Maziel for a reason," Beelzebub said. "And it was not to protect your son. I want to know what your real intentions are."

"I'm not lying," Lithilia replied earnestly. "I want to protect my son-"

"But what you said was only a half-truth," Beelzebub cut her off with a wave of his left hand. "If you don't tell me everything, then this conversation is over."

"Alright," Lithilia exclaimed. "I'll tell you."

Lithilia heaved a heavy sigh and masked her aura not to reveal the fact that she was about to tell a terrible lie.

"I want to become a Paradin," she said.

Beelzebub stared at Lithilia for a moment before he burst into derisive laughter. He laughed so hard that tears rolled down his eyes, which surprised him because he had never shed or seen tears before.

*It must be a common phenomenon amongst these creatures,* he assumed as he ceased his laughter, swiped at his right eye and rubbed the tears between his fingers out of sheer curiosity.

Lithilia suppressed a smile at the fact that Beelzebub had bought her fairy tale and uncrossed her fingers, which she did not realize till then that she was crossing. For an archangel, Beelzebub was so gullible; all to her advantage, anyway.

"I've heard of many insane things, but this beats them all," Beelzebub said and wiped his eyes. "And pray tell, how do you hope to accomplish this feat?"

"Leave that to me," Lithilia replied curtly. "I'm here with an offer for you."

Lithilia spoke with so much authority and confidence that Beelzebub rose from his stony seat and cocked an eyebrow. She had his attention.

"So, what are you proposing?" Beelzebub asked.

"I take something from you that will guarantee my son's superiority in every field over his enemy," Lithilia said. "And in exchange, I will undo your curse."

Beelzebub bolted from the boulder and zeroed in on Lithilia, his amusement forgotten in an instant, too caught off guard to reply for a few seconds.

"You know what that would mean, right... Zukael?" Lithilia asked.

"I'll be able to go back home..." Beelzebub replied barely above a whisper.

Eons of homesickness suddenly rained down on him and he felt something he thought he had lost in a very long time. Hope.

"That's right, Zukael," Lithilia insisted on calling him by his angelic name.

"And if you doubt me, remember who set you free in the first place."

Lithilia thought about reminding him that if she could free him, she could also put him back in the hole where he belonged. But, in her experience, offering hope was a better motivator than using threats… sometimes. Beelzebub chewed on Lithilia's words before he finally spoke.

"Just to make sure I understand your proposition," Beelzebub said. "You want something from me that would protect your son and give him a superior advantage over his enemy and, in exchange, you will undo my curse?"

"Exactly," Lithilia replied. "And you will also leave this realm be. My son will inherit this realm, and you will do nothing about it. Do we have a deal?"

"I suppose I could let this realm be for a much bigger reward," Beelzebub shrugged. "We have a deal. So, what are you taking from me?"

"A part of your demonic-angelic essence," Lithilia replied. "I'll fuse it with my son's essence, and he will be a unique breed on this realm."

"And how do you plan on obtaining this essence from me?" Beelzebub folded his arms across his chest and stared down at her. "Why did you not just take from Maziel?"

"Because Maziel is, in essence, an angel," Lithilia replied, as her clothes slowly faded from her body.

Lithilia's naked form took a step towards Beelzebub, who just stood there, transfixed from the sudden change in behavior.

"But you, Zukael, are different," Lithilia added softly and seductively.

Lithilia put her hand on his chest and pushed him back onto the boulder. By the time Beelzebub sat down, Lithilia had burned his garments away. His naked buttocks rested on the hot surface, but Beelzebub was unfazed by the heat.

"You are unique, Zukael," Lithilia continued as she straddled Zukael, who was now resting on his elbows.

Lithilia reached for his pelvic region and was pleased with his erection, which was as hard as the boulder on which he sat. She raised her hips slightly and guided his hardness towards the ready opening between her legs. She then placed a hand on his chest and gently pushed him until his back was on the scorching boulder. Seduction… When was the last time he ever experienced it? She smiled at how his body relaxed under the hypnotic power of her seduction.

"You are special…" Lithilia whispered.

She made Beelzebub's phallus disappear inside of her and planted a deep, passionate kiss on his lips. Beelzebub throbbed inside of her from eons of suppressed eagerness. She tasted the cycles of pent up passion as she gyrated her hips. For the duration of the union of body and mind, Beelzebub was free of his past and future. Beelzebub was simply a creature at peace. And as his body tensed in a parody of angelic ecstasy, Lithilia seized her moment. The common trait with every creature she had bonded with was that at their moment of climax, male or female, the creature was weakest and most vulnerable. It was in that moment of complete weakness that Lithilia was strongest and therefore most irresistible.

His essence was as exposed and beckoning as a fountain of water in the middle of the Arabian Desert. And Lithilia was more than a lone wonderer dying of thirst. She tapped into the very fabric of his demonic-angelic essence with a deep, passionate kiss and in that same deep, passionate kiss, she sucked in a copious portion of his demonic-angelic essence.

Beelzebub felt a part of his essence migrate from him into Lithilia as if pulled away from him by some ethereal suction pump. A sensation of being drained ensued. He tried to resist to no avail. When Lithilia had sucked in her fill, she vanished, leaving Beelzebub naked, alone and desperate for more in the dry, afternoon heat of the Grand Canyon. He looked around as if he could spot her somewhere, though he knew the effort was pointless. Then the anger set in as well as the feeling of being used and betrayed. But as his anger built into a cold fury, he heard Lithilia's voice in his head.

*"Don't worry, I always keep my word,"* she said telepathically. *"I'll free you from your curse, once I fuse your essence with that of my son's."*

*"I should never have trusted you, you whore,"* Beelzebub spat telepathically.

*"Be that as it may, I have other business to attend to right now,"* Lithilia replied calmly. *"I'll leave you to the whims of your hurting ego. But I hope, for your sake, you keep your end of our deal because if I can remove your curse…"* she let her words trail off.

Beelzebub received the message telepathically loud and clear, and he cursed out loud. Then, he summoned garments over his body and teleported to his former prison, where he sat and contemplated his next move.

*Kazuk, his wife, and her son will die very slow and painful deaths,* he promised himself

***

Lithilia appeared outside her son's quarters and knocked on the door.

"Come in," Maduk called out.

Lithilia stepped in and locked the door behind her. The moment Maduk saw his mother, he knew something was amiss.

"What's wrong?" Maduk asked.

For the first time in a long time, genuine concern darkened his eyes. It warmed her heart.

"Come here, son," she held out her arms.

Maduk obliged. Lithilia reached upwards and took him by the neck. He knew what was coming next. He picked her up by the waist, and she wrapped her legs around his hips. She saw the reflection of her eyes in her son's as they glowed in a different hue. Mother ran the fingers of her left hand on the son's right cheek. Worrying about everything and anything related to her son was her status quo and the son could sense the worry in his mother's heart. The mother felt encouraged by the son's nod of approval. The mother took the son's face in both her hands and smiled back. Mother and son inclined their heads and mother and son locked lips in a kiss unlike any she had ever given to anyone before.

The demonic-angelic essence flowed from mother to son. Mother gave it all and held nothing back. In that kiss, the mother poured forth all her love, fear, anger, hatred and every possible emotion she had left in her. In that kiss, the mother let it all go. The son received everything the mother gave. A strange essence fused with his, took complete control of it and transmuted his body and psyche at the etheric level in a surge of energy and power.

In a fusion between Sinister and demonic-angelic essences, a new creature was spawned. When the fusion was complete, the son let go of his mother. His mother landed on her buttocks on the floor as he spread his arms out wide and screamed so loud that the walls of his quarters reverberated to the sound that emanated from his throat. Mother slowly rose to her feet and placed a hand on her son's chest.

"My son," Lithilia said. "How do you feel?"

The son turned his face towards his mother and opened his eyes. He smiled.

"I feel… different," Cahen replied, and his eyes flashed green.

# THE END OF PART ONE

# PART TWO

## FACING A FOE

**THE FEELING OF** being used left an obnoxious aftertaste in Beelzebub's mouth. He cursed and teleported back to the confines of his once-upon-a-time permanent prison. Pacing back and forth, he swore he would make the whore pay for her transgression, but only after she had kept her end of the bargain. But could he even trust her? He raged at the fact that a piece of vermin, and worse of all Kazuk's wife, had him by his archangelic testicles. He, Luciel's top general, was at the mercy of a whore. How blasphemous!

"Enjoying your freedom, Zukael?" a familiar voice asked him.

Beelzebub had been too consumed by his anger and humiliation to notice he had a visitor, or better yet, an intruder. He whipped around to face his unwelcome guest, summoning a sword at the same time.

"By Celestia. My dream is finally about to come true," Beelzebub rejoiced as he prepared to attack. "I've waited a long time for this."

"That moment has not come yet, Zukael," Kazuk replied calmly, without even summoning a weapon of his own. "I did not come here to end you. If that were the height of my existence, I would have done so instead of cursing and banishing your sorry self to this stench of a realm."

"Be that as it may, Maziel," Beelzebub replied as he summoned archangelic battle flames, "*yours* has come."

Beelzebub attacked while Kazuk remained calm. He observed as Beelzebub took one careful step after another in his charge. Kazuk stripped his gaze from his once-upon-a-cycle brother at arms. He observed the particles of dust as they all seemed to pause in the air. Beelzebub took another step. With every impact his feet made with the ground, there was absolutely no displacement of the dust particles in front of him. Beelzebub moved faster than a Bright Eye and even faster than a human eye could see.

Kazuk returned his gaze towards the charging Beelzebub and saw him pull back his left arm in preparation for a deadly sword strike. He smiled and turned his body square to face the attack head on. For a split moment, the look on Beelzebub's face went from angry and focused, to confused, before changing back to angry and focused. And when Beelzebub swung his sword, the look on his face went from angry and focused to utterly stunned and bewildered. His sword went right through Kazuk as if Kazuk were made of air.

"Always all brawn, as usual," Kazuk smirked and relished the look of utter surprise on Beelzebub's face. "Did you really think I would come down here without protection?"

"How did you-?" Beelzebub asked.

"Oh, don't worry about that," Kazuk replied, with a dismissive wave of his hand. "Just a little extra tweak in your curse. I'd explain to you how it works, but intelligence has never been your forte."

Kazuk walked closer towards Beelzebub and stood inches away from him.

"Like I said" Kazuk scoffed. "That moment has not yet come. And I could end you right where you stand, and there'll be nothing you can do about it."

Kazuk took a step backward.

"But then again, where is the fun in that? So, whenever you are ready, you can return to Hell Realm. I'll be waiting for you. And when you do return, I will free Luciel and make her watch how I tear you apart limb from limb, wing from wing. I will make what's left of you watch as I do the same to her pretty, little self. The last thing you two will see before your existences expire will be your severed heads rolling away simultaneously from your bodies."

An intensity lit in Kazuk's eyes that Beelzebub had never seen before. Kazuk had morphed into something that was an uncanny mixture of insanity, obsession, and darkness. Beelzebub knew he had to revise his plans because the Maziel he knew many cycles ago was not the same that stood in front of him right that moment. The Maziel who cursed and banished him was not the same Maziel who just insinuated that, not only did he know where Luciel was imprisoned, but also that he would free her. As much as he wanted to think that Maziel had lost his mind, he was convinced that Kazuk meant every single word he said. Yes, Maziel the Archangel was living up to the new reputation of Kazuk, the King of Hell Realm.

"Just thought I'd stop by to say 'hello' and let you know that whenever you're ready..." Kazuk smiled. "I'll be waiting for you in Hell."

With those words, Kazuk vanished, leaving Beelzebub wishing Lithilia was around to at least leave a very bitter aftertaste of shame and humiliation in his mouth, because her very bitter aftertaste was far sweeter than Kazuk's.

# CHAPTER ELEVEN

## 475 CE

**"LOOK, IT IS** the pale man of the mountain," Ndode whispered.

"Where?" Senge asked out loud.

"Quiet, Senge," Mekumbe hushed her down and pulled her to a crouching position next to him.

"My hand," the seven-year-old Senge whined.

"Sorry, just stay quiet," Mekumbe, her elder brother, said and rubbed her wrist. "We do not want to draw his attention, okay?"

Senge stifled a snivel and nodded.

"They say he is the god of the lakes," Nkumbe scoffed.

"He is not," Ndode said. "He does not fly in the air, does he? He walks just like we do. All he has is pale skin, like a *moukalah*."

"How do you know he does not fly?" Nkumbe smirked.

Ndode ignored him.

"I hear his eyes are black and *moukalahs* do not have black eyes," Mekumbe chimed in.

"And *moukalahs* do not have long, straight, black hair either," Senge added before Nkumbe could offer another sarcastic remark.

The man with the pale skin pulled his sleeves past his elbows, lifted his long, brown gown slightly, and stooped at the edge of the smaller of the twin Muanenguba Lakes at the foot of the Mt. Kupe-Muanenguba. He pulled his hair back in a tight bun and sparked the ethers into a small cord, which he used to tie his hair with. The villagers designated the smaller lake as the male and the larger lake was the female. He had enhanced his hearing so that he could hear an ant walking on the ground a mile away if he wanted to. He listened to the children's conversation while he pretended to wash his hands and face in the lake.

*Such beautiful beings,* he thought.

He smiled at the cuteness of the children hiding behind the bushes.

*"They say he healed Pa Edie using some magical powers."*

*"Nonsense. Were you there?"*

*"I heard Pa Edie telling the story to the elders. He said he slipped and broke his left leg. His bone was sticking out and he was in serious pain. And then, the* moukalah-"

*"Pale man."*

*"Okay, pale man, appeared from nowhere, touched his leg and the bone was healed."*

*"I think Pa Edie was lying. He just wanted free palm wine from Pa Ekane."*

*"The moukalah is a wizard."*

*"Pale man. And I do not think he is a wizard."*

"Children," the pale man called out to them.

He stood up, turned around and faced the bushes where the children were hiding. He used clairsentience and sensed their fear and confusion.

"It is alright, children," he smiled and waved in their direction. "You can come out now. I will not hurt you."

A few seconds later, Ndode was the first to poke his head out of the bushes.

"No," Mekumbe tucked at Ndode's arm. "What are you doing?"

Ndode yanked his arm away and stepped out of the bushes.

"You are going to be in so much trouble," Mekumbe whispered. "Did the elders not tell us not to-"

Mekumbe heard the leaves rustle next to him and realized to late that his sister was already heading towards the pale man.

"Father is going to skin me alive," Mekumbe gritted his teeth and went after his sister.

"Where are you from, Elder Pale Man?" Ndode asked with respect.

"How come you speak our language?" Senge asked, eyes beaming with curiosity and excitement.

"I asked him a question first," Ndode glared at Senge.

"Children, children," the man chuckled. "I will answer all your questions. Here, let us all sit down."

Ndode and Senge sat on the thick, short grass that was dry, despite the fact that it had just poured heavily a few hours prior.

"You too, Mekumbe," the man gestured at Mekumbe. "And hopefully, your friend back there will be as courageous as you all and join us."

"He will not," Senge said. "He is a weakling and has no courage."

"I am not," Nkumbe leapt from behind the bushes and puffed his scrawny chest. "I was just waiting to see what happens to you first before I decide on what to do."

Senge rolled her eyes.

"I see," the man smiled softly. "So, I will tell you children a little about me and then you can ask your questions later. How does that sound?"

The four children chorused their agreement.

"My name is Yaakov," he said. "And I come from a land that is very, very, very far from here."

"From the other side of the mountain?" asked Senge with eyes that danced with childlike innocence and excitement.

"An impatient one you are," Yaakov chuckled. "But to answer your question, where I come from is much farther than the other side of this mountain. I can speak your language because I learned it."

"How?" Ndode asked.

*By accessing a local's esoteric makeup and tapping into their memory. From there, I imprinted your language unto my conscious memory and that's how I learned your language.*

But Yaakov chose a much simpler reply and hoped that the children did not prompt him for more answers.

"I just learned it."

"Did you really heal Pa Epie's broken leg?" Nkumbe asked.

*So much for asking questions later,* Yaakov thought.

"I did," Yaakov replied.

Nkumbe winced visibly from the fact that he was wrong to think Pa Edie was lying while the other children gasped in victory.

"I told you it's true," Ndode cried and wagged a finger at Nkumbe.

"Are you the god of the lakes?" Nkumbe asked.

"No, I'm not," Yaakov replied patiently. "I am neither a god of the mountain nor am I an albino, or a *moukalah* as you call it. I am like you, only of a different skin color."

"But your clothes are different and your beard is so long," Senge rubbed her chin and furrowed her eyebrows.

"I do not tie a loin cloth and walk around bare-chested like the men here do," Yaakov explained. "I prefer to cover up my entire body for now."

"What is that shiny thing on your finger?" Mekumbe asked, not wanting to be left out.

"It is just a ring," Yaakov fingered the green crystal on his ring. "Do you want to touch it?"

Mekumbe hesitated but Ndode was already on his hands and knees, heading towards Yaakov. He placed his left index finger with extreme caution on the

111

ring as if expecting something bizarre to happen. When nothing happened, he giggled and retreated to his spot on the ground.

"Do you have magical powers?" Senge asked.

"There are certain things I can do," Yaakov replied. "But that does not mean I have magical powers."

"What else can you do, besides healing people?" Mekumbe asked.

Suddenly, multiple screams only Yaakov could hear, thanks to his enhanced hearing ability, ripped across the quiet afternoon. He stood up and enhanced his vision so that he could spot a fly five miles away.

*Too many trees,* he thought.

He enhanced the radius of his clairsentience to five miles, while the children stared at him with confused looks on their faces. He detected a major change in the energy levels of the area, the kind of change that can only be born out of an esoteric disturbance from a non-Earth Realm source.

"Come, children," he commanded.

"What is happening Elder Yaakov?" Senge's voice quivered with fright.

Yaakov ignored her question and gathered the children in his arms. They squirmed, trembled and smelled of fear, literally.

"Close your eyes," he commanded.

He teleported them to the village and released them from his hold. Mekumbe stumbled and fell backwards, Senge retched, Ndode collapsed to the ground and Nkumbe was on his hands and knees coughing and sneezing hysterically.

"Stay here and do not come out, no matter what you hear or see," Yaakov said and whizzed towards the sounds of the many screams.

He froze when he arrived. Screaming women ran everywhere with children on their backs and hips, while others held the hands of the grown ones. The men pointed spears and cutlasses towards what looked like a hovering whirlpool of brilliant orange-yellow light. They were waiting, trembling visibly at whatever they expected to come out of that non-Earth Realm portal. A cacophony of words blended with the screams and chaos.

"The *moukalah,*" someone screamed and immediately the men turned around and trained their weapons on Yaakov, while some of the courageous women picked up rocks and sticks and joined the men.

"Somebody keep an eye on that shiny thing," a tall, muscular man cried out.

He seemed to be the leader of the small, impromptu army that had just formed.

"This is all his fault," cried another thrusting his spear in Yaakov's direction. "The gods and our ancestors are angry at us for allowing him to live in our land."

"Elder Pale Man," Pa Epie ran towards Yaakov and threw himself at Yaakov's feet. "Please, help us. You are one of the gods, are you not? If you can use your powers to heal me, surely, you can use your powers to save us."

"Stand back, Epie," ordered the supposed leader. "He is no god. He is a *moukalah* and must be sacrificed to appease the gods."

Suddenly, claps of thunder raged through the air as the center of the whirlpool of orange-yellow brilliance was sucked inwards by a force unseen, creating a dark oblivion in its stead. The villagers cried out in morbid fear and stepped away from the portal before turning around to train their weapons once again towards it. Bodies quavering, beads of sweat trickling down their faces and bodies, weapons shaking visibly in their hands, the villagers waited, aware that the source of the morbid fear was going to appear again at any moment. Yaakov narrowed his eyes, steeled himself and waited with everyone else. His clairvoyance, clairaudience and clairsentience were at the highest levels possible and he was ready for whatever that was going to emerge from that portal.

And then, he saw it.

He knew the villagers left standing only heard screams before they saw the blood and gore. He knew that many of the villages will not be accounted for, solely because these were being abducted. These villagers were powerless and helpless against this creature that came in through the non-Earth Realm portal, moving so fast that, to the villagers, the creature was just an orange blur before it disappeared into the black oblivion of the portal, which closed upon itself. He heard someone scream 'The evil spirit is back'. However, the warning came in a fraction of a second too late. The helplessness, sadness, grief and pain that filled the air like a rejected burned offering to a wicked god broke Yaakov's heart.

*What in the name of Yahweh was that creature?* Yaakov asked himself.

The creature looked human with an orange-tinted body and was a full head taller than he was. It looked like a male, with eyes that burned orange-red with condescension and spite, and claws for fingernails and toenails. Its bare torso revealed a very muscular body and a loin cloth covered his nether region and buttocks. Its hair was blacker than a moonless night. It eviscerated two men, wounded two men, a woman and a toddler, and abducted three young girls and two young men within its brief attack.

*Why the abduction?* Yaakov thought.

"Please, Elder Pale Man, help my child," pleaded the mother of the injured toddler.

Yaakov rushed to the child writhing on the ground in pain. He had deep claw marks across his stomach and chest.

"It is burning, mother," wailed the child. "It is burning."

"Hold his shoulders down," Yaakov said to the mother.

She obliged immediately.

"Please, Elder Pale Man," she sobbed in desperation. "Help him."

Yaakov placed his left hand over the girl's head and his right hand over her chest. He used his chi to activate the girl's chi, which in turn flowed into her wounds. The girl's mother gasped in awe as she witnessed her child's wounds close up slowly until there was nothing left of them, not even a scar. Her child stopped sobbing and she scooped her child in her arms and cried for joy.

"Thank you, Elder Pale Man," the mother bowed several times in gratitude. "Thank you, thank you, thank you."

Yaakov nodded and headed to the next wounded person. He could do nothing for the dead ones, unfortunately.

"I told you," Epie exclaimed his vindication. "I told you he healed me but no one believed me."

"How many times?" Yaakov asked no one in particular as he healed the next injured person.

"Elder?" Epie asked.

"How many times has that… evil spirit… come here?"

"Today is the first time," the supposed leader replied more firmly than needed. "But this was his third appearance today."

"Third?" Yaakov furrowed his eyebrows in confusion. "But why?"

"We do not know, Elder Pale Man," the leader replied, a little less aggressively this time. "We… we hope you could tell us something about this evil spirit?"

"I do not know anything about this evil spirit," Yaakov replied, moving to the fourth injured person.

He realized many more villagers had been hurt to various degrees than he had assumed.

"But, are you not a god of the mountain?" the supposed leader prompted. "You must know everything."

"I am not a god and I am not from the mountain," Yaakov replied dismissively. "That evil spirit is taking some of your people away. If that was his third visit, then be prepared for more."

Yaakov stood up.

"Line up all the sick and injured here," Yaakov gestured at the open space in front of him.

He tuned on his clairsentience, clairaudience and clairvoyance, and scanned the villagers repeatedly. Perhaps one of them knew more about his creature and the portal than they were willing to admit.

*How can he speak our language?*

*Who is he?*

*He is a wizard, an evil spirit.*
*We should sacrifice him to the gods.*
*He is Ifassa Moto.*

So far, his scan on their thoughts, emotions and energy signatures revealed they were all ignorant of the situation. He spread out his arms over the sick and injured, closed his eyes and sparked the ethers around them to activate their individual healing chi energy. A few seconds later, the sick and wounded rose to their feet, completely healed and rejuvenated. The supposed leader was the first to cast down his weapon cutlass and drop to his knees.

"You are the god of the mountain," he cried and prostrated before Yaakov.

The entire village followed suit. Yaakov shook his head, knowing that trying to confuse them was futile.

"Everyone head for the lakes," Yaakov commanded. "Your ancestors therein will protect you."

Yaakov thought if the portal appeared over the lakes, then the creature might be slowed down in the water before it had time to react. Who knew? The creature may even have a deadly aversion towards water.

Out of the original 328 villagers, only 287 remained. The majority of them had been abducted by the creature. Three hours later, the villagers had migrated with barely a few belongings to camp near the lake. The night was peaceful, though most of the villagers could not sleep. In the morning, the women cooked and the community ate as one. Yaakov was treated like the god he was assumed to be and he could do nothing about it. Nothing could convince these villagers otherwise. The children played near the lakes but no one swam in it for fear the ancestors would pull them into the bottom of it.

Then, at a little past high noon, the portal appeared again. This time, over the lake and this time, Yaakov was ready. The creature leapt out of the portal and ran on top of the lake as if the lake was solid ground. Yaakov whizzed towards the creature and speared his shoulder into the creature's stomach as it was about to grab two young maidens. He landed harshly on the ground and proceeded to rain three punches into the creature's face before grabbing the creature's occiput and chin and twisting sharply. With a loud snap, the creature's neck broke.

Yaakov stood up and stared at the immobile creature on the ground. With a deep breath of satisfaction, he turned around and started walking away from the creature.

"I am Nimrud, Conqueror and King," Yaakov froze when he heard the creature speak. "And I will have what I came for."

The villagers cried and cowered in fright as they pointed in his direction. Yaakov whipped around in time to see the creature stand up and flex its shoulders and neck. Yaakov clenched his fist and met the creature's cold, hard stare with one of his.

"Where are you from and what do you want?" Yaakov demanded.

"Nimbu Realm and I want more humans," Nimrud sneered. "No human has ever bested me in combat. And I have a reputation to keep."

Nimrud whooshed towards Yaakov and tackled Yaakov to the ground. The two men wrestled for a few minutes while Yaakov did his best to run an esoteric scan on Nimrud and learn as much about Nimrud as possible. Esoteric scans demand much concentration, a task which Yaakov was having a most difficult time accomplishing during his fight with Nimrud. At last, when he had learned all there was to learn about Nimrud, he sparked the ethers into a six-inch, razor-sharp dagger, pinned Nimrud to his body in a rear, naked chokehold and pressed the dagger against Nimrud's neck.

"I will make you an offer," Yaakov hissed into the seething Nimrud's ear. "I shall spare your life and you shall let these people be. If I ever see you or your kind here again, I will end you without a second thought. Do we have accord?"

Nimrud glared and raged, until Yaakov pressed the dagger deeper into Nimrud's neck, breaking Nimrud's leathery flesh and drawing orange blood.

"Do we have accord," Yaakov enunciated each word.

"Yes," fumed Nimrud.

Yaakov kicked Nimrud away from his body and stood up. Nimrud turned around to level two orbs burning with hatred and anger towards Yaakov.

"Be gone now," Yaakov ordered to the hearing of the villagers. "Before I change my mind."

"This is not the end," Nimrud swore before whooshing away into the portal, which closed upon itself.

Yaakov dismissed his dagger and met the hundreds of pairs of eyes that regarded him with a mixture of awe, fear, worship and most of all gratitude. While he scanned and learned about Nimrud, he realized what was at stake and came up with a plan, a plan that could not come to pass with him living among the Bakossi people. He had to leave.

*Well, they think I am a god,* he thought. *Let me solidify that notion once and for all.*

*"My fellow subjects,"* Yaakov addressed everyone via telepathy.

The reeling, the fear, the gasping and the looks of confusion and bewilderment on the faces of the Bakossi people were expected. Everyone prostrated to the ground in worship.

*"I have defeated the evil spirit and banished it away from this land,"* he continued. *"It will never come here again. Alas, I must return whence I came, to the land of the gods. Rest assured, that I, Pale Man, will keep watch over you for always."*

The supposedly leader raised his head timidly and bellowed.

"Praise be to Pale Man, god of the mountain."

"Praise be to Pale Man, god of the mountain," the Bakossi people chorused.

*"And now, you may look upon me as I depart to the land of the gods,"* Yaakov said.

Those who were courageous enough did as Yaakov commanded. Others dared not gaze into the face of a god.

*"Be well, children,"* Yaakov addressed Ndode, Senge, Mekumbe and Nkumbe via telepathy. *"Take care of your families."*

And with a mighty will, Yaakov slowly lifted all the waters of the twin lakes using telekinesis and carried the lakes with him towards the mountain, while the Bakossi people gawked, gasped and cried in amazement, awe and fear at the sight. They stood up and pointed in his direction as he glided in the air and sailed towards the mountain with each lake flanking him until he disappeared behind the mountain.

"He can fly," Ndode swallowed and fell to his knees in awe and worship.

Yaakov smiled, knowing that the villagers will be even more shocked at the fact that the former location of their venerated lakes will be completely covered up when they woke up in the morning. They will tell this story in their oral traditions across future generations until the story becomes mythology.

Yaakov carved out two new locations for the twin lakes on Mt. Kupe-Muanenguba using telekinesis and placed the lakes in them. He piled the dug-out ground in a huge heap.

I'll use this to fill up the empty holes tomorrow, he said to himself before he locked on to Shi'mon esoteric signature.

*"Brother,"* he said via telepathy.

*"Yes, brother,"* Shi'mon replied.

*"I need access to you current location,"* he said firmly. *"We need to talk."*

# CHAPTER TWELVE

# A BRAVE BROTHER

**"YOU SAY THIS** creature called itself 'Nimrud'," Shi'mon said.

"Indeed," Yaakov fingered the huge ring with the green crystal on his right, ring finger. "His signatures revealed he was telling the truth."

"Nimrud," Shi'mon furrowed his eyebrows. "*The* Nimrud."

"You can take a look at the Akashic Records if you'd like some confirmation," Yaakov sighed. "It could be some other fellow with that name."

"I do not doubt you, brother," Shi'mon relaxed his features. "If I came across that way, then I apologize."

"No need," Yaakov crossed his legs. "Over four-and-a-half centuries is plenty of time to get to know someone well enough."

"Thank you," Shi'mon said.

A moment of silence crawled through Shi'mon's living room.

"Where did you say you were again?" Shi'mon asked.

"Somewhere south of here, near the equator," Yaakov replied and cleared his throat. "A small African village at the foot of a mountain. The mountain is one of the many dormant volcanoes spawned out of a fissure in the earth. It runs northeast through the land from the Atlantic."

Then, Yaakov leaned forward and waggled his eyebrows.

"Have you ever seen two lakes side-by-side?" he asked.

"No, I have not," Shi'mon replied with zero enthusiasm.

"Then you must visit this village," Yaakov grinned. "Two lakes next to each other. The locals call them The Twin Muanenguba Lakes. The ancestors of the Bakossi tribe settled at the foot of this mountain many centuries ago and they venerate the twin lakes and the mountain, deeming them to be the resting places of their ancestors and their gods."

"Why am I not surprised?" Shi'mon almost sounded sarcastic.

"You should not," Yaakov replied, ignoring Shi'mon's disinterest. "Still, I think it would be good for your-"

Yaakov caught himself before he said the word 'soul'. He and the rest of the apprentices were aware of Shi'mon and Yehuda's soullessness.

"It is alright, brother," Shi'mon offered. "I do not take offense to it."

"I just thought I could cheer you up a little," Yaakov explained. "You always look so grim and unhappy."

*How very perceptive of you,* Shi'mon wanted to say, but he opted for something that was less rude.

"I see," Shi'mon spoke with polite nonchalance. "I know you mean well."

Yaakov smiled slightly and waited.

*Always all business,* he thought in reference to Shi'mon.

"So, if this is Nimrud of old, why did you not just end him while you had the chance?" Shi'mon asked, wanting to return to the subject matter at hand. "Clearly, he is no longer human and lives in another realm."

"Though that would have been the most logical line of action, it would have been most unwise to proceed as such," Yaakov began idly stroking his beard.

The two apprentices of Yeshua were sitting in two of the three armchairs in the living room of Shi'mon's two-bedroom cottage in a village located 39km south of Rome. The room smelled of jasmine and sage, sparked from the ethers by Shi'mon. Jasmine was his dead wife's favorite scent. The scent reminded him of her and, by extension, the scent fueled his hatred and lust for vengeance for the reason behind his wife's, daughters' and grandchildren's death: Yehuda. Despite the freezing, winter cold, the fireplace remained flameless and heatless and the two apprentices were impervious to the cold, or any of the other elements of nature, thanks to some of the things they learned during their apprenticeship with Yeshua centuries ago, like manipulating their chi for various purposes, not excluding rendering their bodies immune to harsh weather.

Shi'mon wore a white tunic and his beard was neatly trimmed while Yaakov had sparked the ethers into a brown tunic. Yaakov preferred to keep his beard wild and unkempt.

"I do not follow," Shi'mon said.

"Nimrud was abducting villagers," Yaakov explained. "Why? I do not know. Also, when I explored his mind, I discovered that there is one above him. One he refers to as 'Maduk'."

"If you explored his mind, how come you could not find the reason why he was abducting the villagers?" Shi'mon prompted.

"Because I was more focused on trying to find out who this Maduk is," Yaakov replied with only a tinge of irritation. "If Maduk is his superior, then Maduk is of a much greater importance than Nimrud is."

"I see," Shi'mon frowned. "So, what do you have in mind?"

"To learn more about that sinister," Yaakov replied.

"Sinister," Shi'mon almost chuckled. "Is that what you want to call him?"

"Yes," Yaakov replied with an expressionless face and leaned forward. "Portals opening, a creature that was once human but has now changed to one with orange skin emerging from it and abducting humans, a thing that is not from Earth Realm. A sinister foreboding beckons. A dark time threatens to take over our realm if we do not act now and fast. I think 'sinister' is a suitable name for what Nimrud has become. Who knows? Perhaps this Maduk is the one who turned him into a sinister. Whatever the case, this Maduk poses a much greater threat than Nimrud does. It is imperative that we learn more about him and then, possibly take him out… and the rest of his creatures."

"I am unsure why these portals have started opening up," Shi'mon scratched his beard. "But I have sensed a shift in the energy levels of the realm. Perhaps there is an esoteric change happening in the realm. Perhaps not. Regardless, what I perceive is as real as the creature you battled. The sinister you defeated."

Shi'mon leaned back and closed his eyes while Yaakov rested his elbows on his thighs and clasped his hands. He had known Shi'mon long enough to surmise that the fearless leader was carefully devising a plan to eradicate the sinister.

"Much still remains to be learned about this Nimrud and what he is," Yaakov spoke with calm determination. "Maduk must be identified and dealt with as well. And that can only be done on the inside."

Shi'mon's eyes snapped open.

"The choice is mine, brother," Yaakov held up a hand. "Respectfully, I did not come here to seek your permission. I only came here to apprise you in person and to inform you that I will be going after the sinisters at the next opportunity."

"I can neither stop nor convince you otherwise," Shi'mon leaned forward slightly. "But, it is my duty as a brother to express my deep concerns about this intention of yours."

"I know and I appreciate your candor," Yaakov straightened his shoulders. "But this must be done. I assure you I will stay in constant touch with you."

"How do you plan on infiltrating them in the first place?" Shi'mon asked. "He saw your face. Unless you want to use shape-shifting to change your face?"

"He saw a man with a beard," Yaakov said and dismissed his beard using the power of thought. "Besides, I can only hold a different face for no more than a week. So, shape-shifting will not be the best course of action."

Shi'mon nodded.

"If I did not know better, you do look like a completely different person without your beard."

"I will also require your aide in this mission," Yaakov continued. "Master gave something uniquely special to each of us, his apprentices. I believe one of yours is your ability to perceive the esoteric energy levels of the realm. I would like you to be on the alert and let me know the instant another such portal appears anywhere in the realm."

"Consider it done," Shi'mon nodded.

Yaakov stood up and walked towards Shi'mon.

"Master gave me this in a dream while he still walked with us in the flesh," Yaakov removed his ring and held it out towards Shi'mon. "I believe its purpose is to indicate the location of a major threat to Earth Realm in the future. I entrust it in your care while I am gone."

Shi'mon took the ring and slid it over his right ring finger but the ring would not get past the second joint of his finger. So, he sparked the ethers around the ring to increase the size of the ring until it fit his finger perfectly. He clenched and unclenched his right fist before nodding his agreement at Yaakov. Yaakov returned to his seat.

"Thank you, brother," Yaakov spoke with focused impassivity.

"You are welcome, brother," Shi'mon replied.

A moment of chilly silence passed between the two men.

"So, what brilliant scheme is going through that mind of yours?" Yaakov asked.

"The Roman Empire just fell," Shi'mon rubbed the bridge of his nose. "Chaos thrives everywhere in these lands. We have threats to our realm from both within and without. I believe the time has come to set up a structure, an organization, geared towards dealing with all these present and future threats."

"Master chose well, indeed," Yaakov smiled with admiration.

Shi'mon tried to remain stoic but failed woefully. He grinned.

"Thank you, brother," he said.

"Of course," Yaakov replied.

"I will use this opportune moment of chaos to start building my organization," Shi'mon continued. "We will see how that will go."

"I trust you will succeed exceedingly," Yaakov chimed in. "Do you still hold a grudge against Yehuda?"

"Of course," Shi'mon frowned. "He must pay."

'I will not argue with you," Yaakov diffused the situation quickly. "I believe that is between you, him and Master."

Yaakov stood up and summoned a wild beard.

"I will wait for your signal," he said firmly.

"I will alert you immediately something comes up," Shi'mon assured Yaakov.

"Thank you, brother," Yaakov said. "Until then…"

Yaakov teleported away before Shi'mon could reply.

Several months went by and Yaakov did not hear from Shi'mon. He remained patient though. Meanwhile, he meditated and performed a lot of hatha yoga all in an effort to heighten his level of perception of the esoteric among other things. He did not want to enter a state of conscious death for fear he might miss an opportunity of a portal opening while he was in that state of conscious death.

*Infiltrating the realm whence the sinisters hail,* he wondered. *Is this my special mission of which Master spoke?*

Yaakov was neither afraid, worried nor doubtful of his decision.

*It does not matter,* he thought. *This feels right and that is all I care about right now.*

Then, one day, during the summer solstice, Shi'mon's telepathic voice yanked Yaakov out of a state of deep meditation.

"Portal at Stonehenge," Shi'mon's spoke with urgency. "Hurry."

Yaakov dismissed his beard and teleported to the chaos at Stonehenge before Shi'mon finished saying 'hurry'. Scores of screaming and stampeding pilgrims and pagans, who had gathered at the Stonehenge for worship and tourism, ran in every direction as about a dozen orange creatures moved at superhuman speeds and abducted several of them into the portal. Yaakov wasted no time. He ran at normal human speed towards one of the sinisters and punched the creature square in the jaw with such force that the sinister crashed into one of the megaton rocks at Stonehenge. The sound of its many broken bones were drowned in the cacophony of cries from the mayhem all around.

Three other sinisters noticed their comrade on the ground, who pointed a finger in Yaakov's direction as the sinister healed himself.

*So they can heal themselves,* Yaakov thought as he watched three sinisters race towards him at supersonic speed. *I have your attention now.*

With a snarl, the first sinister slashed at his head with her clawed, left fingers. Yaakov ducked and punched her left hip towards the ground. He heard a pop before her scream of pain as she dropped to the ground with a thud. Then, he spun away from the burly-looking sinister whooshing towards him and unleashed a ferocious kick into the third sinister's genitals. A scream of pain died in the sinister's throat as it grabbed its groin and writhed on the ground in

122

excruciating pain. He then ran towards the portal, before he stopped, turned around and faced the sinisters.

"Who is next?" he baited as his lips stretched in an evil smile.

Four sinisters disappeared into the portal with abductees while the rest of the sinisters directed curious, angry and fascinated eyes towards the human who stared them down with mocking defiance. Growls and grunts emanated from their throats as they slowly converged towards Yaakov.

"What are you waiting for?" Yaakov bellowed.

The last of the pilgrims and pagans disappeared into the nearby forests.

*Good,* Yaakov thought. *Now it is just you and-*

He felt a sharp pain in the back of his head before everything went black.

*** 

"Take them over there," Yaakov heard someone say as he slowly regained consciousness many moments later. "Hurry, you fools."

He activated his chi to bring his body to full alertness but he feigned dizziness.

"That includes you too," said another to him as two strong pairs of hands grabbed him by the forearm and started dragging him along the hard, orange floor of a hallway of what could be a prison or a temporary holding cell.

He let his head hang low and his body stayed limp as two sinisters dragged him out. Cries and screams of fright, panic and confusion echoed along the hallway like a symphony composed by Pan, the god of the wild. Orange-yellow light illuminated these dark hallways but as his captors dragged him along, the light grew brighter.

*It must be the color of the Solara of his realm,* he thought.

His captors tossed him several feet away and he landed in an open field of bluish grass like a bag of wheat. He pretended to be hurt and painfully dragged himself to a sitting position.

"By Yahweh," he exclaimed.

Scores of screaming and petrified humans, men, women and children, were whipped into four lines. A sinister stood at the front of each line waiting for the next human to be brought up to him or her. It was then that Yaakov noticed there were two kinds of sinisters; those with horns and a tail and those without any horn or tail. The two types still had the same orange tint to their bodies. A lone sinister stood about twenty feet behind the four sinisters at the front of the lines. Suddenly, Yaakov heard the crack of a whip and felt something strike his back. He faked pain and fell to the ground with his face.

"On your feet, peasant," yelled a sinister who had just whipped him.

Yaakov slowly rose to his feet and heard another crack before he felt the whip on his back. He let out a cry of pain and arched his back as he stumbled forward. Despite the breaking of his skin and the blood that soaked his tunic, Yaakov had numbed his body to pain.

"Move your lazy self," commanded the sinister.

Yaakov joined a line and marched slowly forward.

*"Brother, I am in the realm of the sinisters,"* he said using telepathy.

*"Good,"* Shi'mon said in like manner. *"What have you learned so far?"*

*"Well, there are two kinds,"* Yaakov replied as he moved along. *"And it looks like I might be here for a lot longer than I thought. I know why they carried out the abductions."*

*"What do you mean?"* Shi'mon could not hide his concern. *"Follow my trail and teleport here immediately."*

*"Sorry, brother,"* Yaakov almost smiled at Shi'mon's outburst that was heavy with worry, which he thought was cute. *"I have a mission and I will see it through."*

*"Why can you not just teleport away?"* Shi'mon yelled in frustration. *"You do not have to do this."*

*"Merge your clairsentience with mine and you will know why I cannot do as you command,"* Yaakov replied as two sinisters held him fast in front of the sinister at the front of the line. *"My turn has come."*

*"You speak in riddles,"* Shi'mon growled.

*"Just do as I say, brother,"* Yaakov prompted. *"You will have your answer shortly."*

"Wait," a familiar voice commanded.

The sinister at the front line froze in place. Nimrud walked towards Yaakov and examined him with a smug look of unfiltered condescension burning across his face. Yaakov then bowed his head to the ground in fake surrender after a few seconds. He did not want to give Nimrud the slightest chance of recognizing him. Nimrud then spun around on his heels and walked away.

"Carry on," he said coldly.

Yaakov felt Shi'mon's clairsentience merge with his as the two sinisters forced him to his feet. The sinister at the front of the line then angled Yaakov's head to the side, bared its semi-fangs and sank them into Yaakov's neck.

As the venom of the sinister coursed through Yaakov's body, he felt every cell of his body pulsate with a kind of energy he had never felt before. His heart raced at five times the normal speed, his skin crawled and burned as if someone was slowly spinning him over a bonfire. But the burn was beyond the physical. Yaakov saw his aura oscillate between various colors, as if trying to decide on the best color type for what he was slowly turning into.

The two sinisters who held him fast tossed him several feet away and, though he landed and writhed on the hard, orange earth, Yaakov did not care. Nothing existed beyond the transmutation of his essence at the etheric level. Nothing existed beyond the transformation of his body at the physical level. Slowly, the writhing and screaming ceased as the pain, internal and external, ceased with the completion of his metamorphosis. Yaakov slowly rose to his feet and examined his hands and naked body. He had no idea what happened to his clothes.

*"By Yahweh,"* Shi'mon exclaimed via telepathy.

Yaakov quickly ran his right hand on top of his head as well as at the base of his spine.

*No horns, no tail.*

Bad enough already, his skin was now orange. Horns and a tail on top of that would have been a greater punishment to his psyche. He let out a sigh of relief and smothered the sorrow that slowly seeped into his psyche at the realization that his transformation into a sinister may be permanent.

*"Now you know why I said I might be here for a lot longer than I thought I would be,"* Yaakov forced himself to sound strong and courageous.

*"Brother..."* was all Shi'mon could say.

*"Do not burden yourself with my predicament, brother,"* Yaakov steeled his resolve. *"This is Day One of my mission. I will keep you apprised promptly. May Yahweh keep us strong."*

Shi'mon steeled his resolve as well. Right now, what Yaakov needed was not his pity or concern. What Yaakov needed was strength and encouragement.

*"May Yahweh keep us strong,"* Shi'mon replied firmly. *"I await your updates."*

Yaakov severed his telepathic and clairsentience links with Shi'mon.

*And now, my mission begins,* Yaakov said to himself.

# CHAPTER THIRTEEN

# A YEARNING

**"SOMETHING WAS DIFFERENT** this time, mother," Marissa said as she sat next to Miryam on a love seat in Miryam's chamber.

"I know, my child," Miryam sipped her green tea.

"So?" Marissa prompted, raising an eyebrow.

"So what?" Miryam asked in turn.

"What's going on?" Marissa asked. "You still haven't told me anything."

"No," Miryam replied. "I haven't."

Miryam placed her teacup on a stool. Then, she faced her daughter. Like a million other times, she could swear she was staring at her reflection, even though Marissa had her father's eyes, ears, and chin. Mother and daughter could trick an untrained eye into thinking they were twins, given their agelessness. However, unlike some of the other apprentices, Miryam and Marissa were not soulless.

"In due time, I will tell you everything," Miryam continued.

"And pray tell, when is this 'due time', mother?" Marissa asked with magnified exasperation after she rolled her eyes. "Do you know how old I am?"

"No, I don't, Sarael," Miryam replied with the same unwavering calm she had mastered over the millennia, and it was driving her daughter insane.

Marissa gritted her teeth and ran her hand harshly through her hair. Her mother had learned that was one of her many ways to calm herself.

"You keep treating me like a child," Marissa snapped.

"You are my child," Miryam rebutted. "And I will treat you like *my* child; but not as *a* child."

"Don't patronize me," Marissa spat.

"Duly noted," Miryam said. "Part of your training is learning to be patient and to trust in others, especially me."

Miryam let the words seep in for a few seconds before continuing.

"Your everyday activities are a part of your training; not just your dreams, or during 'training' sessions, but in every situation. This you must understand."

A sternness and subtle imploring seeped through Miryam's voice that calmed Marissa a little. Miryam watched Marissa bow her head and bite her lower lip. She knew her daughter, albeit, even better than her daughter knew herself. She knew Sarael agreed with her. And she knew that part of Sarael's frustration was stemming from her desire not to fail her mother. Maybe this frustration was the cause of the recurrence of her dreams. Be that as it may, Sarael's misdirected energies were becoming obstacles to her progress. Miryam reached out and took hold of her daughter's hand and squeezed it gently. Marissa squeezed back.

"Look at me," Miryam said softly.

Marissa obeyed.

"I am very proud of you, my child. I want you to know that. I have absolute faith that not only will you be ready, but that you will be ready in time."

"But what if I am not?" Marissa asked almost to herself.

"If my blood runs in your veins, then there is no way in Creation you won't be ready," Miryam smiled and ran her fingers a few times through Marissa's hair.

Marissa smiled back, weakly.

"I'm afraid," Marissa's voice quavered slightly as she averted her eyes towards the floor. "I don't know what I'm afraid of. Just that I'm afraid."

"A natural reaction," Miryam concurred.

"But you don't seem to be afraid of anything, mother," Marissa said and met her mother's confident stare. "How come I'm not as tough as you are?"

Miryam burst into a fit of laughter that surprised Marissa.

"Who says I'm not afraid, my love?" Miryam asked. "I am afraid, but I'm afraid *for* the one you're training to meet. He doesn't know what's coming."

Marissa huffed a little laugh and kissed her mother on the cheek.

"Thank you," she sighed.

"Of course, my love," Miryam replied. "Now, you may go continue flirting with Patrick."

*"Mother,"* Marissa exclaimed, throwing her hands in the air and shaking her head.

"Oh, come on now, you're a two-thousand-year-old woman, and yet you act like a teenager," Miryam chuckled. "He's a fine specimen though, I must admit. Good eye, my child. Good eye."

"Mother, stop," Marissa cried and buried her face in her hands.

"Alright, alright, I will," Miryam said. "Just go easy on him, okay? You know, he's still so young and fragile-"

"I'm leaving now," Marissa said and ran out of her mother's quarters.

"Now why didn't she just teleport?" Miryam asked herself out loud. "For the same reason I'm drinking this tea, maybe?" she said to the empty room.

Miryam reached for her cold, half-empty cup of herbal tea. But before the cup touched her lips, it was full again with a hot, steamy brew, thanks to her sparking of the ethers. She had no use for the liquid, but something about the activity of drinking tea like 'everyone else' reminded her of her humanity. It kept her grounded and focused, and she needed that. The hour was nigh and what Marissa never knew was that she was as ready as she could ever be. All she needed was one more 'procedure', one final stage in her training. If Marissa made it past this final stage, then may Yahweh help the poor creature she would be going after.

And therein lay Miryam's fear. Even though she was honest with her daughter about her fear, her true fear was not for the creature Marissa was fated to go after. Miryam feared that her daughter might be lost to the dark side once the floodgates became open upon completion of the procedure. She sipped on her herbal tea and wished once again, that her lover was there to guide both her and their daughter through the next phase.

***

*"Hey, are you busy?"* Marissa asked Patrick telepathically.

*"Depends,"* Patrick replied in kind. *"Is everything okay?"*

*"Mother asked me to 'go and flirt' with you,"* Marissa replied flatly. *"So, I'm doing what my mother asked of me, like the loving, obedient daughter that I am."*

*"Ah, I see,"* Patrick replied. *"Just obeying momma, huh?"*

*"You know it,"* Marissa affirmed and then paused for a few seconds. *"Well, actually, I need to talk to you when you get the chance, please?"*

*"Alright,"* Patrick replied. *"I'm in the middle of something; just making a quick stop in Thailand. I'll be done maybe in half an hour or earlier. I'll see you then?"*

*"Sure,"* Marissa replied. *"Take your time, though. No rush."*

Marissa knew Patrick could tell she was lying and she did not care. He did not even need to use his clairsentience. The one thing she had picked up from her brief encounters with Patrick was his strong sense of perception, despite his age. Twenty-two minutes later, a gentle knock on her door sounded, and Marissa invited Patrick in.

"Is the dream still bothering you?" Patrick closed the door behind him, before following Melissa to sit next to her on the couch.

"The dream is just a byproduct of what's actually bothering me, I think," Marissa replied. "I'm dying to come out of the dark, you know. I don't know what my mother is preparing me for and every time I ask her, she tells me 'in due time' I'll know. It's killing me. It's like navigating in the dark and my blind faith is wearing thin."

"I don't know your mother as well as you do, obviously," Patrick said. "But I can stake my life on the fact that she'll never steer you wrong. She must have a game plan for you, and when she says you'll know in due time, she really does mean that she will fill you in at the right time. Who knows, she might also be keeping you in the dark for your protection."

"From what?" Marissa sighed. "Assuming that's the case, what's out there that has a hard-on for me? I mean, I can handle my own, I believe."

"Oh honey, you still don't know just how valuable you are, do you?" Patrick shook his head. "You know, most of the world still believes your father never had a wife, let alone a child. Even better, that you two are still around."

"Yes, I know. thank you very much," Marissa rolled her eyes.

"And you wonder why your mother is protecting you," Patrick said. "You think she's not aware of your potential? Whatever's out there must be beyond what you can handle in your current state. And it must be linked to you, somehow. I understand you want to know exactly what's going on, but at the same time learning to have faith and patience could be part of your training."

"You sound like my mother," Marissa said smiling and shaking her head. "She must have infected you already."

"She's a remarkable woman, Marissa," Patrick concurred. "Not gonna lie. From the first moment I laid eyes on her, I've had nothing but the deepest respect and admiration for her. She's just that kind of person."

"Are you trying to make me jealous?" Marissa asked, playfully.

"I would, but you seem to be immune already, O Feisty One," Patrick bowed theatrically. "But seriously... My recommendation's that you stick to whatever training she's got lined up for you. Plus, if you need a hand with anything and you think I could be of any help, just let me know."

He smiled.

"Anything?" Marissa asked, narrowing her eyes in mock seriousness.

"Yes, your highness," Patrick replied. "Anything…."

"Should've kept your mouth shut, o dark knight in rusty armor," Marissa said standing up. "'Cause right now, I need you to do something for me."

"Heaven help me." Patrick said with exaggerated exasperation. "What does her majesty require of me?"

"I want you to take me on a date like no one has ever done before," Marissa commanded and folded her arms underneath her ample bosom.

"When? Now?" Patrick asked incredulously.

"No, in the next cosmic dance," Marissa replied. "Right now, of course."

"Well, aren't you a spoiled brat," Patrick rolled his eyes and grinned. "Looks like someone needs the belt to their butt."

"I might like it," Marissa replied and winked mischievously at him.

"Oh Lord," Patrick sighed and took Marissa by the elbow. "Walked right into that one, didn't I?"

"Like I said earlier, I'm just being an obedient daughter." Marissa grinned.

Patrick rolled his eyes before taking Marissa by the elbow and teleporting himself and her to a spot near the top of a mountain. The winds were relentless at that altitude and the temperatures were below freezing, though no snow covered the mountain top. Patrick and Marissa were unfazed by these harsh conditions. Marissa looked around and admired the dormant volcano she was standing dangerously close to the edge of the steep crater that was about two hundred feet in diameter. She was fascinated by its blackened walls, mainly because she had never visited this part of the realm. She enhanced her vision as she looked into the pitch-black abyss that was the main vent of the volcano. It was probably half a mile deep.

"Too bad I can't see any magma," she called out to Patrick.

"Maybe that's a very good thing," he replied.

The view from the top of this mountain was breathtaking, relaxing and peaceful. For a moment, she was silent and absorbed the allure of the panorama. Unconsciously, she reached for Patrick's hand and gave it a gentle squeeze. Then, unconsciously again, she snuggled close to him without taking her eyes away from the surreal beauty that stretched out as far as the human eyes could see.

"Behold, her majesty stands on Mt. Cameroon," Patrick grinned with pride. "The only active volcanic mountain in Central and West Africa. Oh, it also happens to be the tallest mountain in West Africa. To the south," Patrick said as he pointed towards the south, "is the City of Limbe, my favorite city in this realm. And that's the Atlantic Ocean. The little islands you see are uninhabited."

"It is so beautiful and peaceful," Marissa said softly. "It's so different from the cities I've been to; much simpler, more peaceful and much more beautiful."

Marissa spoke as if she were talking to herself.

"There's more to see," Patrick gently turned her and pointed the other way. "On the other side of the mountain, you will find small towns like Idenau, Debuncha amongst others. Debuncha is among the top ten rainiest places in the realm. Not far from here, you have a waterfall that falls directly into the ocean. Do you know of any other waterfalls in the entire realm that fall directly into the ocean?" Patrick asked with pride as he schooled Marissa.

"Wow, that is impressive," Marissa said. "I had no idea."

"That ain't all, your royal highness," Patrick added. "The main tribe of the mountain is Bakweri. Legend has it that they worshipped the god of the mountain called Efassa Moto. Efassa Moto is described as half-human, half-goat. Sounds familiar?" Patrick asked.

"Um hm." Marissa replied and smiled.

"So much for legends, right?" Patrick continued. "Now, the Portuguese were the first Europeans in recorded history to set foot on this land. When their ship was near the shore, they saw what looked like fire on the mountain. History says that the Portuguese saw the mountain erupting, but who knows. I find it interesting that after they saw the mountain 'erupting,' not only did they describe what they saw as 'The Chariot of the Gods', but they docked on land, anyway."

"'The Chariot of the Gods'," Marissa whispered. "I like the sound of that."

Marissa sat on the ground and pulled her knees to her chest.

Patrick joined her. For a moment, the pair sat there in silence and basked in the serenity of their environment.

"Does this meet her majesty's expectations?" Patrick asked.

"Absolutely not," Marissa replied with a haughty tip to her chin.

Patrick cocked his head. "Is her majesty disappointed then?"

Marissa cupped Patrick's cheek and brought her face close to his. He did not resist as she planted a long, sensual kiss on his lips. Her body melted to the feel of his soft, luscious lips as their lips parted and their tongues touched. She had to pull herself out of the kiss with effort. As their eyes met in a moment of intense gazing, Marissa's soul was laid bare for Patrick to behold eons of sadness, longing, and lack of peace disappearing in a single moment of complete, unreserved and unadulterated gratitude.

"Her majesty's expectations have been exceeded and her majesty is very, very grateful," Marissa said softly, passion tightening her voice around the words.

Patrick nodded and smiled, and Marissa brought her knees back to her chest. She stared blankly and mindlessly ahead. Patrick had been to this mountain a countless number of times before. The mountain was his Zen, and he could understand what Marissa was experiencing. As such, he joined Marissa in silence and serenity of the scenery. Time stood still, and nothing else existed. The only thing that mattered was that moment, and Patrick and Marissa both relished in the moment together, bonding with each other, the mountain and the very earth from which the natural megastructure sprang from.

*"Patrick. In my office. Now,"* Shi'mon's voice tore through Patrick's moment of Zen like a katana through a piece of cotton fabric.

*"Yes, sir,"* Patrick replied.

Patrick tapped Marissa on the left calf.

"Uncle Shi'mon?" Marissa asked with a dose of exasperation.

"More like Efassa Moto at this point," Patrick replied.

They stood up and dusted the black, volcanic dirt off their clothes. Patrick took Marissa by the elbow, and they teleported to Marissa's quarters.

"I hope her majesty enjoyed the date," Patrick said smiling.

"Thank you very much, Patrick," Marissa said and placed another long and sensual kiss on Patrick's lips. "I absolutely did."

Patrick understood she was just expressing her gratitude and he spoke the words 'you're welcome' in her language.

"Good luck with Uncle Shi'mon," she said.

"Thanks," he chuckled before he teleported away.

"See what happens when you listen to mother?" Miryam said.

Marissa was so startled that she almost literally teleported out of her clothes. Miryam burst into uncontrollable laughter at her daughter's reaction.

"Mother. What are you doing here?" Marissa asked, her heart pounding hard, like drumbeats to an African ceremonial dance. "Couldn't you knock?"

"Sorry, my love. Didn't know I had to knock when I was already inside," Miryam managed to say amid fits of laughter. "You were too busy smooching Mr. Chocolate that you didn't even notice me sitting here. But he knew though… He saw me." she added and winked at her daughter.

"This can't be happening," Marissa shook her head with embarrassment.

"Oh, come on now, my love," Miryam gathered Marissa close and cradled her daughter's head on her bosom. "See. You will always be my baby, whether you're as old as time itself or not."

Miryam held her daughter's face in her hands. This was one of those moments when her eyes burned with the kind of love only a mother could have for her child. She kissed Marissa on the forehead.

"Besides, if I don't mess with you like this, who else will?"

Miryam's tone had changed to something that Marissa was not used to hearing. Something in Marissa completely disappeared, and the two-millennia-old woman was once again the five-year-old girl who would not let her mother out of her sight. Marissa melted in her mother's embrace, and the two women hugged each other for a few minutes in total silence, basking in the deep love they had for each other.

It was a phenomenal day for Marissa. First, Patrick had given her the best date she had ever had in all her life, and now, her mother had reawakened something in her that had been lost a very long time ago. She felt somehow reborn and rekindled, and in her rebirth, Marissa felt a dramatic shift in consciousness like she had never felt before, the kind that resulted in a transformation of both the psyche and etheric. Miryam, sensing this shift using clairsentience, peeled herself from her daughter and took her by the hand.

"Come," Miryam said and Marissa obliged.

"You're about to enter the final stage of your training because you're ready. Why don't you lie down, my child."

Sarael laid her head on her mother's lap and made herself comfortable.

"I'm about to take you to a time when you do not remember, to a time before your current lifetime," Miryam began. "I will unlock your memory, and once that memory is unlocked, something else will be unlocked in you and therein will be your final test. Are you ready, my love?"

"Yes mother," Marissa replied. "I'm ready."

"Alright, then," Miryam said. "Close your eyes, and we will begin."

Marissa closed her eyes. She felt the warmth of her mother's hand as it settled on her forehead. A few seconds later, her consciousness seemed to be ripped from her body, and Marissa found herself sitting in the middle of oblivion with a book opened before her eyes. She stared at the blank, open pages of the book until, slowly, images began to form on the pages. Gradually, the images began to move like characters in an animated movie, and as Marissa watched, the walls to the dam of her subconscious exploded, opening the floodgates of her memory, and releasing the waters of her memory, which came crashing on her psyche in a powerful, ethereal onslaught.

\*\*\*

"Father?" Patrick called from the doorway of Shi'mon's quarters.

"Come in, son," Shi'mon beckoned.

Shi'mon stood near his desk. A green folder and a thumb drive sat on top of the desk. When Patrick walked in, Shi'mon pointed at the folder and thumb drive. Patrick swiped the thumb drive and stowed it away in his pocket. He then picked up the folder using telekinesis and started flipping through the pages.

"I take it Beelzebub let him out, huh," Patrick said a matter-of-factly.

"And he wasted no time in making his presence felt," Shi'mon replied.

"I'll take care of him right away, Father," Patrick said and tucked the folder under his armpit. "Do we have a tracker on him yet?" he asked.

"Yes," Shi'mon replied. "The live coordinates will be sent to your phone."

"I best be on my way then," Patrick said and made to leave.

"Son?" Shi'mon called, stopping Patrick dead in his tracks. "If you need backup, let me know," Shi'mon said and his voice bore a tone that Patrick rarely heard; concern.

"Thank you, but I'm sure I'll be fine," Patrick reassured Shi'mon.

"I know," Shi'mon slid into a chair behind his desk. "But just in case…"

"As you wish," Patrick capitulated, knowing it was pointless to argue. "I see we're using his real name?" he added, trying to change the subject.

"Is it not his name?" Shi'mon tapped his left index finger idly on his desk.

"Prince Natas," Patrick scoffed. "I prefer Satan. Has a better ring to it."

"I'll be expecting updates as soon as possible," Shi'mon said.

Patrick knew when he had been dismissed.

"Of course."

Shi'mon appreciated Patrick's enthusiasm and excitement for his new mission: to search and silence Satan once and for all.. As Patrick closed the door to the office, Shi'mon let out a heavy sigh. He was more than concerned for his protégé. On the surface, he looked calm and confident in Patrick's probable success with the mission. His breathing was steady as he stared blankly at the closed door of his office. However, his mind was a raging chaos of panic and fear. Shi'mon was petrified for his protégé. Patrick had assumed that Beelzebub freed Prince Natas. But Patrick could not be more wrong.

# CHAPTER FOURTEEN

# FROM PRINCE TO PRINCIPALITY

**"EXCUSE ME, MISS,** mind if I sit here?" a stranger asked a lady sitting on a park bench.

The lady spared a glance from the magazine she was reading, long enough for her to conclude that the stranger posed no threat.

"No, it's not," she replied and returned her attention to her magazine. "You may sit if you'd like."

She was walking the fine line between rudeness and unfriendly politeness. She clearly did not want to be disturbed.

"Thank you, miss," the stranger said and sat on the opposite end of the bench.

The stranger held what looked like a novel in his hand. He closed his eyes and breathed in deeply, held his breath for a few seconds and then slowly exhaled. He repeated the gesture two more times and smiled to himself.

"Truly a lovely day," he whispered to himself.

Perhaps the lady sitting next to him heard him. Or not. Either way, he would do what he set out to do today; enjoy a few pages of his must-read book on a gorgeous day at the park. He should have brought the other book he had started reading the other day; the first book of a five-novel series. The series was titled *The Soulless Ones* and book one was titled *The Bright Eyes*. Book two, *An Archangel's Ache,* was out already and he was excited to get his copy. The stranger took in the scenery. The pollen-heavy, spring Saturday afternoon was just warm enough for a walk in the park or to chill outside. He opened his book and started reading. Two pages later, he looked at his watch and then resumed reading. Twenty-three minutes later he had to admit he was paying more attention to the woman than his book.

His bench companion was not so much of an avid reader as her demeanor claimed to portray. First of all, no one spent eight minutes on a single page of a magazine; absolutely no one. Well, unless one fancied the art of self-pleasuring. So, the young missy was surely not reading. She was either daydreaming or had a lot on her mind. The magazine was a front, an escape from whatever unpleasant situation that resided *chez-elle.*

The stranger mentally smacked himself.

*Stop using French.*

And what was she reading? *Christian Talks,* a popular, local magazine. Missy was interested in religion; good to know. And Missy had also stolen a glance in his direction at least fourteen times in the last seventeen minutes. Not that he was counting. But for someone trying to radiate a don't-mess-with-me kind of aura, the contrary was a little too obvious.

Just to toy with her, he enjoyed how she jerked back to her magazine every time he faked a shoulder roll. He complimented himself on his retirement from being a professional sniper… of women. But now was not the time to reminisce on his many tales of all the tail he had had the pleasure and displeasure of experiencing. *Tales of Tail.* He smiled at the phrase. Perhaps he could write a book with that title someday. However, the idea died as soon as it crossed his mind.

"Pardon my intrusion, miss," the stranger said. "I couldn't help but notice that you are reading this month's edition of *Christian Talks.* I was curious what their main topic for the month is, if you don't mind me asking."

Her smile lasted quicker than a blink of an eye, but the stranger saw it. Her shoulders relaxed, and her grip of her magazine loosened a little as if she were finally relieved that he had just shattered the iceberg between them.

"It's okay," she said. "This month's edition features a discussion on biblical proofs that the Devil is real, despite what naysayers may think."

"Now *that* is an interesting topic," the stranger said.

He quickly closed his book and set it on the bench, ready for some intellectual banter.

"And do tell, miss, what do you think? Is the Devil real or not?"

"I think he is real," she replied, folding her magazine.

"So the devil is a 'he' then?" the stranger asked, raising an eyebrow.

"Absolutely," She placed the magazine on the bench beside his book.

*This one may be a sapiosexual,* the stranger thought.

"The Bible says the Devil is responsible for the fall of man and is behind every temptation," she added. "He's responsible for all the world's evils. I could quote many scriptures to support these claims. I apologize, are you Christian or practice any religion at all?"

"I was born and baptized a Christian, miss," the stranger replied.

He insisted on calling her 'miss.' A little charm could go a long way.

"But now, I consider myself spiritual and always open to learn and share. It's all about the message, not the messenger or other people's twisted interpretations of the message, if you catch my drift. I appreciate you asking."

"You're welcome," the young lady replied.

"Do you know what else I am?" the stranger asked.

"What's that?" the lady asked, with a look of confusion on her face.

"Neil," the stranger replied.

Neil grinned at how relaxed and less cautious she became.

"Nadia," she extended her hand.

"Pleased to meet you, Miss Nadia," Neil said, shaking her hand.

"Likewise, Neil," Nadia replied. "And please, call me Nadia. The 'miss' thing makes me feel old," she added and laughed a little.

"I will," Neil said. "So, where's your secret fountain of youth?"

"Mighty generous of you," Nadia replied without even as much as a smile. "Thanks, though."

"You're welcome," Neil said, aware that his compliment did not faze Nadia. "So, back to our discussion; you said you believe the Devil is real. I can respect that. And what is his name?"

"He has a few," Nadia replied. "Satan, Lucifer, The Serpent, The Fallen Star or just The Devil. You don't agree?"

"Um, not exactly," Neil replied. "I don't think the Devil, Satan or Lucifer is the one responsible for all the evils of the world."

He adjusted himself on the bench. Nadia's attention was fully focused on him.

"I think, though," Neil continued. "That we are responsible for everything we think, say and do and this responsibility demands accountability. But regarding Lucifer, Satan and even the Fallen Star, I think these are not one and the same person, and they aren't responsible for the sins of the world."

"And what about the temptations of Adam and Eve in the Garden of Eden, and that of Jesus in the desert?" Nadia asked. "It is clearly outlined in the Bible how Satan tempted these people."

"It's interesting that you cited these two situations," Neil said. "Unless I'm mistaken, these are the only two instances in the Bible in which the process of temptation is described in a lot of detail."

Neil paused to let his statement sink in a little. He could see the wheels turning in Nadia's head, and after a brief moment, she seemed to agree.

"In Eden," Neil continued. "The serpent is used to represent the agent of temptation. The serpent carries strong symbolisms that would require another day and time to talk about. But I'll take you to the temptations of Jesus in the desert. In the final temptation, Jesus was taken to a high mountain and shown all the kingdoms and riches of the world, right?"

"Right," Nadia affirmed.

She was waiting for Neil to make his point.

"Now, if one stands on Mount Everest or even the moon, is it possible to see all the kingdoms of this world at once?"

"I see your point," Nadia conceded. "So, the temptation was more of a vision as opposed to Jesus being taken to an actual location. But couldn't one argue that Satan was just trying to seduce Jesus with a vision of the world's kingdoms and all its riches?"

"A valid argument," Neil said. "But that would defy the logic of the entire temptation process, which ought to be valid in all three temptations. Satan wasn't trying to seduce Jesus with riches by asking him to turn stone to bread or to jump from the temple roof. There was a much bigger intent behind these temptations. Jesus was fully aware of the fact that he could turn stone to bread and if he wanted to, he could float down from the roof of the temple, or any tall building for that matter. So what was Satan trying to do? Satan was trying to create a shift in Jesus' level of consciousness by sowing a seed of doubt. If Jesus had done as the Devil tempted him to, his action would have been a profession of doubt, borne out of a shift in his consciousness and awareness of who he actually was. This means that Jesus would have become identified with what he was not and this would have been his sin. What do I mean by that?

"The word 'sin' is translated from Greek and Hebrew words which mean 'to miss the mark.' I forgot what those words are. But it's something that was said when an archer or spear thrower missed his mark back in the day. So, what is this mark? Identity. If you identify with who you truly are, beyond your physiological and psychological processes, then you have hit the mark. However, if you identify with what you are not, then you have missed the mark. This is the only sin there is; identification with what one is not. Every other 'sin' is just a result of this wrong identification.

"So, my humble take is that Jesus, like all of us, had a light and dark side. While in the desert, and right after his baptism, he was only wrestling with his dark side to ensure that his dark side did not get the better of him. This 'wrestling' was purely psychological, hence why I started with the third temptation to establish this 'vision' or psychological aspect of the temptations, and the psychological process only has societal relevance and is a result of accumulated information. The psychological process has no existential relevance. Jesus was aware of the boundlessness truth that constituted his true identity, but he had to face his psychological process regardless. That was his temptation, and it had nothing to do with the Devil, Satan or Lucifer."

"And what about Eve?" Nadia asked.

"Eve merely had a shift in consciousness and became aware of her light and dark sides, good and evil respectively," Neil replied. "Everyone who functions on this plane of life is subject to duality: up-down, left-right, good-bad, right-wrong, et cetera. That includes us and even was no exemption. He just triumphed over this notion of duality or polarization by becoming a self-realized being. Hence, why the Book of Hebrews 4:15 says Jesus '...was tempted in every way, just like we are, and did not sin.' But let's get back to Eve."

Neil adjusted his frame on the bench while Nadia continued to stare at him with unwavering focus and razor-sharp attention. She was soaking everything in.

*Good,* Neil thought.

"The fall did not occur when Eve ate of the tree of the knowledge of good and evil," Neil continued. "The fall occurred when she *beheld* of the fruit, *saw* that it was good to eat, and she 'wanted to become like God', *knowing* good and evil. In other words, Eve lost her 'innocence'."

"Right there, that shift within her, was the fall. Her 'innocence' was symbolic of her not being identified with her physiological and psychological processes as representative of her being oblivious of her nakedness and all that. You know the rest of the story after that, with them hiding from God because they were naked and all that.

"Anyway, once she had that shift in consciousness and wanted to become like God, possessing knowledge of good and evil, she became identified with her psychological processes and body. Eve did not fall because she ate the fruit. Eve ate the fruit *because* she had already fallen, *because* the shift in consciousness had already occurred within her. She lost her innocence, as represented by the fact that she 'realized she was naked.' The knowledge or awareness of good and evil represents the polarization of consciousness and we all, including Jesus, carries this seed of polarization in our essence.

"This logic is valid for the temptations of both Adam and Eve in the Garden of Eden and Jesus in the desert, Neil surmised. "What do you think?"

Neil observed Nadia pondering on his words. He had to admit that he admired her open-mindedness and willingness to learn.

"You know, I never looked at these stories from your perspective," Nadia admitted. "I must say that your logic is solid. I'll have to do some digging later for myself. Thanks for sharing. This conversation has been most enlightening. I've certainly got a lot to ponder on. Hope I can remember much of it, though."

Nadia glanced at her watch.

"I'm sorry to cut our chat short, but I must go. Perhaps we could continue some other time? I really enjoyed talking to you."

"I'd love that very much, Nadia," Neil replied standing up with her.

Nadia retrieved her cell phone from her cheap handbag, tapped on the screen a few times and handed it to him.

"Please put in your number, if it's okay with you," Nadia said and smiled.

Neil returned Nadia's smile and did as she asked. He returned her phone to her and she tapped on the screen once. Two seconds later, his cell phone vibrated in his left pocket. He smiled and pulled it out. Nadia ended the call and typed something on the phone; he assumed it was his name. Neil saved her contact information and returned his phone in his pocket.

"Hit me up some time," Nadia said as she returned her phone in her bag.

"I sure will," Neil replied. "Enjoy the rest of your day, Nadia."

"You as well," Nadia replied, then hurried away.

Neil returned to his seat and pretended to read from his notebook. Yes, it was a notebook, not a novel. Eight minutes later, he rose from the bench and strolled to his car. Nine minutes later, he walked into his house and headed for the basement. He tossed his notebook on the couch and sat in front of his laptop. The outing was a success beyond his expectation. He just needed to remember to use this fake name with Nadia from now until when she decided to dump him. Yes, he already had her by the clit. It was his personal, unbiased opinion. He was neither bragging nor gloating. It was what it was.

The man who posed as Neil moved the mouse until the cursor landed on a folder named 'Ultimate Folder.' He double-clicked it, and it opened. He selected a subfolder titled 'Manuscripts' and double-clicked on it. He then scrolled down and double-clicked one of the many Microsoft Word documents in it. When the document opened, he continued from where he left off, starting a new page on the manuscript. He took a deep breath and played with various titles for the next chapter in his head, and forty-two seconds later, he settled on a suitable one.

He cracked his knuckles and began typing. *CHAPTER FOURTEEN: FROM PRINCE TO PRINCIPALITY…*

## 1800 B. C. E. I

Natas stormed into the temple, ignoring the priests as they bowed and greeted their crown prince. He stripped himself unceremoniously as he marched towards the inner chamber of the temple. A priest fetched his royal garbs from the floor, folded them neatly and placed them on a table. At the entrance to the inner chamber, the high priest, who was the crown prince's best and only friend in the entire kingdom, was waiting for him in full priestly garbs.

"Let the record reflect that I strongly disapprove of the imminent actions of his highness," the high priest said to no one in particular.

"Duly noted, Damas," Natas replied dismissively.

Prince Natas spread out his arms and legs. Four priests gathered around the crown prince and began donning him with ceremonial robes.

Prince Natas was the first-born son of the king and heir to the throne. He had a strong penchant for the occult and, thanks to his royal status, he had access to every ancient scroll and manuscript in the kingdom. His childhood friend, Damas, became high priest at age fourteen, making him the youngest high priest in the history of the kingdom. Fifteen years later, Damas had already earned the reputation of being the most powerful high priest the kingdom had ever known. And as his friendship with Prince Natas grew, Damas taught Prince Natas, often unwillingly, about the secrets of the occult.

And so it came to pass that the kingdom was under threat of a siege from a coalition of six of its once-upon-a-time allies. The king, Kalamas, was ready to sign a truce and spare his people from massacre. But Prince Natas' ego was bigger than his sense of reason. He would stop at nothing, not even at his father's orders, to prevent his future birthright from being seized by a bunch of traitors.

Alas he could not command an army. His father had stripped him of his rank as Supreme General, because his father could not fully appreciate the extent to which he was willing to go for the sake of the kingdom. He needed a way to defeat an army of close to 20,000 men, if not more. Going against such an army as a lone soldier was beyond stupid. Perhaps, if he went as something other than a lone soldier, he stood a chance.

Damas was convinced that his childhood friend had lost his mind. Friendship or not, however, he was obligated to follow the orders of the crown prince. Thus, when Prince Natas ordered Damas to get to work and find a solution, Damas had no choice but to obey his prince.

And so it came to pass that the brothers in friendship did more research and experiments in a month than they had done in both their years combined. They tore through every sacred text, chanted every possible chant, forbidden or not, created and cast too many spells and invocations to remember, but none yielded any fruit. Time was not on their side.

They had two more weeks before King Kalamas signed the truce that would plunge the kingdom into slavery. 'Desperation' was the word of the day. One day, a recently ordained priest was cleaning the library as the crown prince and high priest were doing some research. As he moved to clean behind one of the shelves, he tripped on his broom and crashed into a shelf. The shelf collapsed and landed on the priest. Everyone who saw or heard the crash immediately rushed to the priest's aide.

"Are you alright?" asked Prince Natas.

"No, Sire," the priest winced in pain. "I have a dislocated shoulder and a very badly sprained ankle, I think."

"Take him to the infirmary and tend to his injuries," Damas ordered.

Two priests carried their comrade away. Prince Natas was about to summon some other priests to restore the shelf to its original position when he noticed a badly wrinkled piece of a scroll attached to the back side. He tore it off very carefully and started to read.

"What is it?" Damas asked, noticing the look of surprise on Natas' face.

"I think it is a prayer to a spirit called *Beelzebub*," Natas replied, handing over the piece of the scroll to Damas.

"I have never heard of this spirit," Damas said. "Maybe it is the name of your future wife, sire? Should you decide to take a fair maiden's hand in marriage one fine day?"

Prince Natas glared at Damas and Damas shrugged.

"You are over seven years overdue for a wife, my prince," Damas continued.

"Continue in that manner and I shall have you nailed to a stake," Natas teased.

Natas' eyes bulged in shock. He passed the note to Damas, who also read it. His reaction was the same as his friend's. They both looked at each other for a moment, and without saying a word, they bounded towards the inner chamber and sealed themselves inside.

*These shelves are always moved around and cleaned regularly,* Damas thought. *And no one noticed a scroll of this size until now? Why? Something is amiss.*

"Are you sure you are ready for this, Natas?" Damas asked.

"Between this and slavery, my choice is easy," Natas replied as he stripped bare and lay on the altar.

Damas nodded and began reciting the words on the scroll. Immediately, a luminous silhouette of a human being with wings began to manifest in midair. Goosebumps spread across his body, though it was hot and humid in the inner chamber, and a cold shiver slowly shimmied down his spine at the frightful sight of this creature of light.

"I suggest we stop," Damas pleaded. "I have a bad feeling about this."

"No. Keep going," Natas commanded.

Reluctantly, Damas kept reading from the scroll. The luminous figure grew brighter and floated towards Natas' body. Natas clenched his fist, not knowing what to expect. He was afraid, but his fear was nothing compared to his desire to save the kingdom, *his* kingdom. When Damas pronounced the final words on the scroll, the figure stopped moving. Dark orbs where its eyes were supposed to be stared down at Natas in an unreadable fashion.

What happened next was unclear to both the crown prince and high priest.

Chains of yellow light appeared and seemed to bind the silhouette of light's arms and legs to something invisible. The creature of light let out what sounded like a maniacal scream of rage and fought. But the creature was powerless against its bonds. Suddenly, the bonds gave and the creature rushed towards Natas and disappeared inside him.

Natas screamed and thrashed as his body and essence burned unlike any burning sensation he had ever felt in his life. It came from the inside, as if every iota of his physical makeup and beyond was on smokeless fire. Natas' form rioted against the forced transmutation of his body as his essence slowly resonated with that of the strange creature of light that had just taken over his body.

And then, all was still.

Damas held his breath, not knowing what to think or do, and hoping for anything less than the worst for his best friend and brother. Then, he saw Natas' chest heave upwards before a lungful of air gently escaped from Natas' mouth and nostrils. All was still again for a few seconds and Damas let out the breath he was holding. He hunched over, supporting himself by placing his hands on his knees. His worst night mare had come to pass. What was he going to tell the king? That his son, the crown prince, had died under his watch after being possessed by some… thing? The king would have his head, regardless of what Damas told the king. His heart was rent in twain and a deep, painful sadness and sense of loss enveloped Damas. He took one careful step after another towards the perfectly still form on the altar that was his best friend.

Suddenly, Natas' body was hurled towards the ceiling by an unseen force before it crashed onto the stone altar. Damas screamed and rushed towards the limp form of his friend. No one could survive such a crash against such a stony surface. But before he got to Natas, Natas' eyes popped open. His eyes had no iris and no pupil; just a pair of night-black orbs and when he spoke, it was an alien voice that both frightened and paralyzed Damas.

"Finally, I am free," Natas, or the new resident of his body, cried.

It examined its hands and felt its body.

"I will keep this body until I will have use for it no more."

Then, the 'thing' turned and looked down at Damas as if Damas was trash on the ground..

"You are his friend, Damas," it said to Damas.

"Y-y-yes sir," Damas stammered.

"Your friend is alive," it said. "I need him to be alive for my own survival. But if you are thinking about killing him to kill me, you are wasting your time."

It hovered away from the altar and got dressed. Damas watched helplessly.

"You cannot kill a fallen archangel," it added and started walking towards the door. "You do not have the means."

Hearing these words, Damas mustered some courage.

"Sir," Damas called out.

The creature stopped walking but did not turn to face Damas.

"Who are you?"

"I am Zukael, high-ranking archangel from the Realm of Celestia," it replied. "But in this new form, you may call me Daemon."

"Thank you, sir," Damas replied timidly. "And if I may ask, what are you going to do now?"

"Fulfill your friend's wishes," Daemon said and left the inner chamber in a flash.

*"I have been dying for some action, anyway,"* he added telepathically.

Damas immediately rushed to the library. He thought he might have an idea on how to free his friend.

Meanwhile, at the infirmary, the three priests who were in the other chamber went in, but only one came out. His shoulder used to be dislocated and his ankle used to be badly sprained. The other two had suddenly plunged into a deep sleep, and when they would later awake, they would have no recollection of why they had gone to the infirmary in the first place.

The injured priest, meanwhile, left the temple and entered the city. He took a turn into a street corner and emerged as a man who looked like he had been around for just a little over half a century. The Scribe blended with the masses, pleased with himself for another successful mission. A new species had been spawned and introduced into humanity to later serve as a catalyst when he, The Scribe, unravels all of Creation.

Daemon, the possessed Natas, stormed into the palace while the king was in session with his advisers.

"I must speak with you immediately," he said to King Kalamas, his father.

"What is it, son?" King Kalamas asked, making a mental note to deal with his son's rudeness later. "What happened to your voice?"

"I intend to face your enemies soon," Daemon replied.

"Raise your gaze towards me so I can see the foolishness in your eyes," King Kalamas commanded.

Daemon kept his head bowed towards the floor.

"Enough of this madness already," King Kalamas sighed. "I have entertained this insolence long enough. Guards, seize him and keep him

consigned to his quarters until this situation with our enemies is resolved."
Two guards beat their chests in affirmation and walked towards Daemon.

But as soon as the guards laid their hands on the crown prince, they screamed in heart-rending pain, gouged at their eyes and fell to the ground, burnt out sockets where their eyes used to be. Many gasps of shock reverberated across the palace and the king sat forward in his throne.

"You want me to gaze upon you?" Daemon asked and slowly lifted his gaze towards the king. "Behold, mortal."

At first, Daemon did not care for King Kalamas cringing and cowering in his throne out of fear. Instant fear also seized everyone who gazed upon him.

"Like I said earlier," Daemon spoke with an evil baritone. "I intend to face your enemies soon. I tell you this as a courtesy, not to seek your permission. Your enemies will all be slaughtered, the first of many slaughters to come. This realm will know one ruler, true and all-powerful: me."

King Kalamas swallowed nervously as he watched what used to be his son spin around and march away from the palace. His heart shattered at the pain of losing his son and ruining the prospect of saving his people by signing a treaty. How could one man fight an army of 20,000 men alone? It was a suicide mission, one that came with the bitterness of losing a child.

"Sire, there still is hope," an adviser dared to speak. "Hope to broker a treaty with our enemies."

King Kalamas understood what the adviser was insinuating.

*Deny that my son acted on my orders,* King Kalamas thought. *Shame my son's memory and blame it on his madness. One life to save thousands. It is my duty to see this come to pass.*

"We will wait until we have word of his mission," King Kalamas replied.

And so it came to pass that same day, Natas returned to the palace. Word had already reached the palace that the enemy had been completely decimated by what was described as a 'soldier of the gods'. Word had reached the palace of someone who looked like the crown prince, but was not the crown prince, tearing through the enemy faster than a sandstorm. Not a single enemy soldier was left standing. Even those who tried to flee met a certain end. Every single one of them fell to what was described as 'the wrath of the gods', and the eyes of every single one of them were burned out of their sockets.

The kingdom was free. No longer would there be any talks of slavery. But with this great news came the terrible fear of dealing with this one person who could singlehandedly lay waste an army of more than 20,000 men in just a few hours. Creature or not, King Kalamas and his soldiers would make a last stand against a new enemy spawned within the very walls of the kingdom. And so, when Daemon returned to the palace, he was not given a hero's welcome.

"What do you want?" King Kalamas asked.

"My birthright," the Daemon replied.

"Your time has not yet come," the king said.

"That just changed," Daemon replied. "I declare my time is now."

Daemon walked towards the throne. Suddenly, Damas emerged from behind a group of soldiers, a scroll in his hand. He began reading, and as he read, Daemon started screaming and convulsing. Daemon then fell and writhed on the floor, uttering words in a tongue that no one could understand. Painfully, he flipped himself on his stomach and started crawling towards Damas, face contorted in a grimace of pain and anger. Damas held his ground and kept reading from the scroll. Daemon pulled himself forward but resumed screaming and writhing once again. As Damas read on, the creature of light that had merged with Natas slowly separated itself from Natas' body as if pulled away by an unseen force. When it was completely removed from Natas, it hovered in the air as Natas' features relaxed and his face slumped to the floor of the palace.

"Damn you, vile human!" the creature of light raged at Damas. "Damn you!"

Damas ignored the creature and kept reading until he uttered the final words of the scroll to complete the exorcism.

*"ZUKAEL, BEELZEBUB, DAEMON. RELEASE YOUR ETHERIC HOLD ON THIS SOUL,"* Damas commanded.

And with one final scream, the luminous creature, separated from Natas at both the physical and etheric levels, vanished from sight.

Everyone who had the courage to stay behind remained frozen in place, gripped with too much fear to say or do anything. Natas lay on the floor, alive but too weak to move. He struggled to get up but fell back on the floor. Damas walked cautiously towards his friend and met Natas' eyes. Human eyes. Natas smiled weakly.

"Good to see you, old friend," Natas croaked and cleared his throat.

A single tear rolled down Damas' cheek, but it was not a tear of joy. He knew what was coming for Natas, and he knew Natas knew too.

"Is he human again?" King Kalamas asked.

"Yes, Sire. He is," Damas replied as he helped Natas sit upright.

Damas took a knee in front of Natas and level happy-sad eyes at his friend.. He held Natas' face in his hands, kissed Natas on the forehead before hugging him tightly.

"What is going on Damas?" Natas asked, his voice gaining strength.

Damas released his friend and stared at his friend in the eyes.

"I am so sorry, brother," Damas replied and stood up.

"Seize him," the king ordered, and soldiers converged around Natas.

King Kalamas stood from the throne.

"Natas, my son and crown prince," King Kalamas bellowed. "You have been found guilty of using dark magic to commit treason. You have been possessed by a dark and dangerous entity and can no longer be trusted to rule this kingdom. For the safety of the kingdom, I hereby sentence you to death."

Natas stood speechless. His father's words made no sense to him. Everything he had done, the sacrifices he had made, almost costing him his life, had been all for the kingdom, for the people. If anything, he had been nothing but a true patriot. And this was how his father was going to reward him? By beheading him like a common criminal? Preposterous. Natas was not going to allow that. Confusion turned to anger. Patriotism gave way to a cold burn of fury.

"I lay down my life to save this kingdom, for you all, and this is how you repay me, father?" Natas hissed through gritted teeth. "A charge of treason, a sentence of death and no word of gratitude?"

A surge of energy fill the room, which Damas easily perceived. The hairs of his body stood on end, his eyes bulged and a shudder of apprehension rippled through his body. He screamed in his head before he could open his mouth, but he had no time to warn the soldiers who had seized Prince Natas. Flames erupted from their eyes, instantly burning their eyes away to black ash. The soldiers screamed briefly and clawed at their eye sockets before tumbling to the floor. Their deaths were as instant as the burning of their eyes. Natas charged his father, but Damas blocked his path.

"And you," Natas said, seizing Damas by the throat and lifting Damas off his feet. "I thought you were my friend, my brother. But you betrayed me."

Natas' voice had changed again to what it was when he had been possessed and his body and psyche had been rejuvenated and revitalized by a new kind of energy and power that had taken over his being. As Damas stared at his friend in shock, Natas' eyes, iris, pupils and cornea, turned to inky, Stygian black, just like when Zukael possessed him.

"Yes, Damas," Natas said. "I am a new creature. I am spawned into a new life, and I am the first of my kind. And before you ask; no, I am not Zukael. Zukael is gone, but I am here. I am what Zukael left behind, transmuted and reborn."

Natas was slowly choking Damas to death. Damas clawed at Natas' hands and arms as his legs flailed wildly. His eyes bulged and slowly became lifeless, all to no avail. Natas' tightened his grip as his smirk turned colder. The palace had been thrown into chaos, and no one dared approach both men.

"What... shall... we... call... you... now?" Damas managed to ask.

"Satan. I will spawn many more in my light. We will be called 'demons' and I will be the Prince of Demons," the human formerly known as Natas declared. "And we will erase humanity from the face of Earth Realm."

"Thank... you," Damas replied.

"For what?" Satan sneered.

"The... name," Damas choked.

Damas grabbed Satan's arm. A beam of light burst forth from the point of contact between Damas' hand on Satan's arm, burning Satan's arm with fire summoned from charged chi. Satan screamed in pain and let go of Damas. Damas landed on the floor and gasped for air. But, Satan immediately lunged towards him. Damas uttered a spell and spoke Satan's name at the end. Satan screamed as unimaginable pain seized his body at the etheric level. He fell on the floor and curled into a fetal position. Damas held Satan down with a spell and used another spell to render Satan temporarily powerless.

"*Now*," Damas ordered.

A few soldiers rushed in with a coffin and sealed Satan within the coffin with highly choreographed expertise.

"Mark my words, traitor," Satan raged from within the coffin. "Wherever you are, whenever you are, I will find you and when I do, I will make you pay. I... will... have... your... soul."

"I am so sorry, brother," Damas said.

Damas struggled to stay on his feet, despite the feeling of being drained and exhausted as he bled esoteric energy.

"But there is a reason why I am high priest and you are not."

Damas sparked the ethers and his wooden staff formed in his right hand. He held it in the air and began some incantations. As he spoke, a tiny vortex of light formed out of thin air and started growing larger. It moved over the coffin containing Satan. Satan could be heard kicking and screaming in the rattling coffin, striking fear in the hearts and trembling of the bodies of everyone present, except for Damas. A slight smell of sulphur and iron seeped into the room. At the end of his incantations, Damas struck his staff on the ground. Immediately, the glowing tattoo of a serpent curled three-and-a-half times around his spine and burned into his skin and garments. A vortex of light exploded from the wooden staff in his hand and struck the coffin containing Satan, the Prince of Demons. The coffin was thrust into the light and once inside, the vortex closed and disappeared as if it had never been there. The silence was intense, the relief was heavy, peace was only for a moment as residual fear lingered to remind everyone that they had won the battle, but maybe, just maybe, the war was yet to be won.

And that was how eons ago Satan, formerly a prince named Natas, was banished to the Realm of Porgatoria.

# CHAPTER FIFTEEN

# MY BROTHER'S KEEPER

**"DO NOT WANDER** too far," Eva called out as Cahen ran towards the stream.

"I am just going for a swim, mother." Cahen called back to his stepmother.

"I know, my love," Eva replied.

Eva knew Cahen could no longer hear her. She knew she was smothering him and, while that was not a bad thing, Eva knew the boy needed some space. Sitting outside their domicile, she sighed and craned her neck towards the living room.

"Do you think I am being overprotective?" she called out to her mate.

"I would not have it any other way," Adamou called back.

He was trying to repair a wooden animal toy that Cahen loved to ride on. One of the legs had come loose and his repairman skills were not the best.

"I still have not gotten over how he has taken to you."

"I am made from you, am I not?" Eva replied and turned to face the horizon.

"True, but that is not the only reason," Adamou said.

He changed his position to ease blood flow through his numbing legs.

"It is you, Eva. You are so special. I do not know what it is, but it is there. I am very happy you are with me, with *us*, and I will never stop telling you that."

Adamou set the toy and his tools on the ground and studied the toy.

"What am I missing?" he mumbled.

He swiped a sheen of sweat from his forehead, furrowed his eyebrows and directed a blank stare towards the ceiling.

Eva smiled from her heart. She stood up and entered their domicile. Her partner was where she expected him to be. He was so lost in concentration that he never noticed her standing at the door to their son's room. She observed him for a few minutes with an unwavering smile. Then, she slowly moved forward and knelt at her lover's back and hugged him from behind. The gesture startled Adamou, but only for a moment. As he returned to fixing the toy, Eva kissed him lightly on the ear. Adamou smiled and gave Eva's arm a gentle squeeze.

But when Adamou returned to working on Cahen's toy, Eva reached out and gently placed her left hand on his. Adamou stopped what he was doing and turned around to face Eva. A moment of gazing into each other's eyes, into each other's soul while on their knees, sparked an ember of desire that was fanned into a flame by their love for each other. She moved closer and fit perfectly into Adamou's arms. Adamou kissed her lightly on the lips and gazed into her eyes, which beamed with longing and joy.

*How could I have ever imagined never loving any other woman besides Lithilia?*

His heart melted with love for Eva. He closed his eyes, angled his head and locked lips with Eva. The kiss was slow at first, until the passion took over.

"Cahen may be on his way back," Adamou said amidst deep, intense kisses.

"We have got all the time we need," Eva replied and started rising to her feet without peeling her lips away from Adamou's.

Adamou stood up as well in time to catch Eva as she wrapped her legs around his pelvis. He led her to their room and she barely allowed him the time to disrobe before she took charge. She was already naked and very ready to accommodate her lover several heartbeats before her lover threw her on the bed. An hour-and-a-half later, the couple lay on the bed, spent and satisfied. This session was better than the one they had earlier that morning when Cahen was still fast asleep.

"I should go fetch our fearless leader soon," Eva said as she nestled against Adamou's chest, her happy place.

"You worry too much," Adamou stroked Eva's hair.

Eva moaned when his fingers grazed her favorite spot. Using whatever little, unspent energy she had left, she kissed Adamou, rose from the bed and stepped over her lover. She made a pit stop at the lavatory and emerged a few minutes later, satisfied that nothing would be flowing out of her anytime. She then got dressed and then headed towards the stream to fetch her stepson.

No, Cahen was not her stepson. Cahen was her son and she was his mother.

"Cahen, my love." Eva called out as she approached the stream. "You better be behaving yourself now, young man." she added playfully.

Eva also readied herself for Cahen to jump out of wherever he was hiding and startle her, knowing that she just lost her advantage of surprise by calling out to him. She decided she would sneak up on him regardless, if she could find him first. So, she crouched to the ground, hid behind the bushes and scanned the area for any sign of Cahen. She could not locate the sneaky toddler.

"Where could you be hiding?" she asked herself quietly.

"Right here," replied a voice that was not Cahen's from the opposite side of the bushes.

***

Cahen made his way to the stream. He had been going to the stream more often ever since he met his mother there. Lithilia had convinced him not to tell anyone she was still alive, let alone that he was coming to see her. Her visits were once a week at first. But recently, the frequency of her visits had tripled. It had taken a few weeks for him to get used to his birth mother once again to the point of not fearing her anymore. Lithilia had been patient and her patience had paid off. After all, she was a mother and like any good mother, she would not give up on her son. And so, slowly, Lithilia had succeeded in rebuilding a mother-son relationship that had been lost due to an unfortunate situation.

"Mother?" Cahen called out. "Are you there?"

A figure formed in the air into Lithilia and she dropped to a knee, opening her arms wide. Cahen quickly walked into his mother's arm and wrapped his arms around her neck. She kissed him several times on the cheek and the forehead.

"Mother," Cahen protested and turned his face away to avoid his mother's barrage of kisses.

Lithilia understood and stopped.

"I am sorry," Lithilia said with a grin. "But I can never get enough of you."

"You saw me just recently," Cahen replied.

Cahen turned around and crouched to the ground, picked up a small pebble, stood up and tossed it into the stream.

"And that feels like an eternity to me," Lithilia replied and stood next to him.

Lithilia crouched, selected a few pebbles from the ground and placed them in one hand. She then stood up and offered some to Cahen. He selected a few and then, they started idly throwing the pebbles in the stream.

"So, how is your father doing?" Lithilia asked.

"He is okay," Cahen replied. "He still snores when he sleeps."

Cahen giggled but Lithilia did not join him.

"And is his companion treating him well?" she asked..

"Yes, she is nice to him," Cahen replied

He reached for Lithilia's hand holding the pebbles. There were five pebbles left. He wanted to take all of them.

"Remember," Lithilia said. "You have to share."

"Why should I?" Cahen protested. "Are there not pebbles everywhere?"

"The point, my stubborn love," Lithilia replied. "Is not about whether there are pebbles everywhere or not. The point is that, in my hand, there are just a few pebbles left and you could share them with me so that you and I could play together. Do you understand?"

"No, I do not," Cahen replied. "But I will do as you say, anyway."

"You are very wise for your age, my very intelligent love," Lithilia said and handed Cahen all the pebbles in her hand.

"Why did you give them all to me then, mother?" Cahen asked, with a puzzled look on his face. "I thought you wanted us to share."

"And I am sharing with you," Lithilia replied. "I am sharing everything I have with you. Does that not make you happy?"

"It makes me happy, mother," Cahen said. "But I still do not understand."

"A mother will sacrifice everything and anything to make her children happy," Lithilia replied. "Because a mother's love knows no limits."

"I understand now," Cahen said.

Cahen resumed casting pebbles into the stream as Lithilia watched. It was unimportant whether Cahen understood what she was telling him or not. She was just happy the two of them were getting to spend time with each other more often, which was more than she could ever have asked for. Her time away from the garden had been both trying and rewarding. But that time away had paid off. She had learned so much. One of the things she learned, to consciously teleport, allowed her to visit her son at will. She had to exercise caution, though: no need to arouse any suspicion. Cahen had accepted her wholly; but there was no telling how everyone else would react to the knowledge of her return. Not having her son with her all the time was the hardest thing she had ever been forced to do. However, it was only going to be a matter of time before she had Cahen all to herself for always.

"Is the new woman still treating you nicely?" talking about Eva was the most difficult part of Lithilia's visits.

"She is," Cahen replied. "I like her a lot. She calls me 'son' and I like it when she calls me that."

Cahen's innocent reply made Lithilia wince in pain from the sting of jealousy and clench her jaws; but he did not notice. He waded into the stream as he spoke. He plunged his hands into the stream that rose up to his knees as if he was searching for something. He remained in this position for some time.

"She is so funny sometimes," Cahen continued. "When grandfather had just finished making her, I had to teach her how to use my toys."

Cahen laughed childishly at the thought of teaching Eva stuff.

"She did not even know how to identify where we are in the skies," he shook his head in disbelief. "Can you believe that, mother? She did not know."

"Yes, my son, I can believe that," Lithilia replied and forced a gentle laugh.

Lithilia did everything in her power to hide her jealousy, which was slowly getting the better of her. No matter what Lithilia did, every time Eva came up in their discussion, it felt like a healing sore had just been reopened. It was not enough that this Eva was supposed to be somehow special because she was made from her lover. It was not enough that this Eva was laying with her one and only love. It was not enough that this Eva was so good to her son that her own son referred to this Eva as 'mother'.

It was the entire situation. They were happy. They were content. They were doing just fine without even the memory of Lithilia to bother them.

They had moved on with the notion that she had passed away and that was it. No care, no concern and, certainly, no regrets. Everything was truly going well for them. No one even missed her. They were a complete family. And this irked her the most; that her lover, her son and this Eva, her son's new mother and her lover's new partner, were a complete and happy family. Where she, Lithilia, had failed woefully, Eva had succeeded with flying colors. Lithilia forced herself to return to the present moment. She had little time to spend with her son and she would not let anything, not even this Eva woman, derail her from that.

And so Lithilia played and conversed with her son as moments flew by, which. always went by so fast whenever she was with her boy. *That must be a good thing*, she thought. She suspected that soon, either Eva or Adamou would come looking for Cahen. Eva came most of the time. She was so protective of him. And though Lithilia struggled with her envy, deep down, she knew her son was safe. Deep down, she knew this new woman loved her son to the point that she would never allow any harm to befall Cahen.

*But does harm include me?*

The thought was both comforting and scary at the same time.

They both heard Eva calling for Cahen. Quickly Lithilia hugged and kissed her boy and asked him to go around to the other side of the bush.

"What about you, mother?" Cahen asked Lithilia in a whisper.

"Do not worry about me, my child," Lithilia reassured Cahen. "I will be fine. Go now and I will see you in three days, alright?"

"Alright, mother," Cahen replied and bowed his head as an anvil of sadness hung from his heart.

Lithilia empathized in her son's sadness and even as it rent her heart in twain, she was happy and overjoyed that her son was finally becoming attached to her again. Quickly, she kissed and hugged her son once more before letting him go. He snuck to one side of the bush as Lithilia slowly dematerialized and become invisible to the naked, human eye by increasing her body's vibrational frequency. To buy Cahen some time, she crouched invisibly next to Eva. Once again, she had to admit that Eva was a stunningly gorgeous woman.

And something about this Eva unsettled Lithilia. However, Lithilia could not tell what it was. Even her clairsentience failed to shed some light on this alien vibe emanating from Eva. Still, Lithilia felt it; as palpable as the envy that burned within her for Eva.

"Where could he be hiding?" she heard Eva whisper

Lithilia decided to play a small trick on Eva to allow Cahen the time to sneak up and startle her. The trick worked every time and Lithilia was very happy to see that her son was happy, even when he was with a different mother. Eva could not see her of course, but Eva heard her when she spoke. Lithilia saw Eva's face contort in confusion right before Cahen jumped from the opposite direction of the sound of the faceless voice. But that look vanished from Eva's face when Cahen appeared and her world went ablaze with joy.

Lithilia watched Eva's colors change and every time it happened around Cahen, it still looked as if it were the first time. It was, admittedly, a beautiful sight to see. She watched them play-wrestle on the ground. Eva let Cahen win and she saw how, as soon as Cahen was with Eva, Cahen forgot about her, Lithilia, his birth mother.

Every visit was one of joy and peace, followed by pain, sadness and envy.

Lithilia had tried to make peace with herself for causing the rift in her family, but she was yet to succeed. *Enough with the moping already.* One day, she would have to make sure her son was never away from her anymore. At least, for now, Lithilia consoled herself, Cahen was in great care.

*** 

Eva assumed the voice was Cahen's. So, she leaped from her hiding position and landed behind the bushes, arms spread out, ready to snag the young lad in the air. But no one was there.

"*Ya*," Cahen screamed from her left and leaped on her mother's back, knocking her to the ground.

Eva shrieked with glee and joy at the same time. Mother and son play-wrestled on the ground until the son won, and mother conceded. They returned to the domicile, holding hands all the way. Then suddenly, Eva doubled-over and started retching. Terrified by her violent sickness, Cahen ran ahead.

"I shall fetch father," he called out.

'No, my son," Eva coughed and spat on the ground. "It is nothing, just nausea. It is just-"

But she did not finish her sentence as she leaned forward and retched again. Then, she took a knee, sucked in huge gulps of air and wiped her mouth with the back of her hand. Adamou came sprinting towards her. Cahen ran as fast as he could but he could not close the gap between him and his father. Eva managed a weak smile. She had never seen Adamou so frightened before. He knelt beside and took her by the shoulders. Cahen arrived and stood in front of Eva, making sure he was a few feet away from where Eva just puked. His eyes were heavy and his features rigid with worry and fear.

*What is wrong with mother?* he thought.

"You do not look good." Adamou remarked. "Let father look you over."

"It is alright, my love," Eva replied weakly, wiping her mouth with the back of her hand. "Really, I am alright. It just happens every now and then."

"Wait. What do you mean by 'every now and then'?" Adamou was even more worried now.

"Well," Eva replied a little timidly and rose to her feet. "It started about two weeks ago. But really," she said. "I am fine. See?"

She gestured towards herself and looked from Adamou to Cahen. Cahen was not convinced but the expression on Adamou's face changed.

"When was the last time you had your flow?" he asked.

"About three moons ago," Eva replied.

Adamou made Eva step away from the mess in front of her. He examined her as if he had not seen her in a very long time. Then, his eyes bulged and he grinned like Eva had never seen him grin before.

"Yes, I know. I gained some weight, I think," Eva said innocently. "I had to make some new clothes because the other ones did not fit me like they used to. I do not know why I keep throwing up, though. But I am sure it is nothing."

"No, it is not nothing." Adamou exclaimed. "It is everything."

And then he picked up Eva in his arms and lifted her up in the air as if Eva were a child. He spun her around a few times. Then, realizing that the movements may make Eva more nauseous, he quickly set her down.

"I am sorry, my love," he apologized. "I am sorry. I got carried away by this wonderful tiding."

Eva laughed at his cuteness and was pleasantly surprised and amused by his sudden show of happiness.

"I am not completely sure, but I think you are with child, my love," Adamou added. "*Our* child."

Then he leaped towards Cahen and scooped the child in his arms while Eva unconsciously placed a hand on her tummy.

"You are going to have a brother or a sister, my son," Adamou told Cahen. "You will have a new playmate."

Cahen seemed excited for a quick moment. But then, he realized he did not understand the full meaning of his father's words and his eyebrows furrowed in confusion. At least, he was no longer afraid that his mother was in trouble.

"I am with child…" Eva whispered to herself.

"Yes, my love," Adamou replied and took her by the hand.

And then, as if it finally dawned on her, a tear of joy rolled down her cheek and she hugged her lover. The maternal instincts were immediate. She stared at her tummy as she gently caressed it, followed by some chuckling and tears of joy as she hummed a tune to her unborn child growing in her stomach. She reached for her son and the three clung to one another in a family hug. Cahen still did not understand what was going on, but family hugs were always a good thing.

The family headed to Father's domicile and after Eva was examined, it was confirmed that she was indeed with child.

"Our calculations indicate that your gestation period is about eleven cycles of Lunis," Father said. "So, we should be having a new member in the family in about eight cycles."

Eight moons full of joyful impatience and excitement later, Eva gave birth to a healthy baby boy via a smooth birthing process. Adamou and everyone else was extremely happy. Cahen was still a little confused about the whole notion of having a younger brother, but he seemed happy as well.

"What shall we call him?" Adamou asked Eva.

"Why not let Cahen do the honors?" Eva offered as she cradled the sleeping newborn in her arms.

"You never cease to amaze me," Adamou said and kissed Eva on the lips.

Ukni and his team smiled and beamed with pride. Their experiments were getting better by the moment.

"So, what do you want to call your brother, Cahen?" Eva asked the young lad, who was standing next to Meena, holding her hand.

He looked a little confused and did not know what to do.

"Come on now, big man," Meena gave him a little nudge of encouragement. "It is a great honor to name a child, and when the child is your baby sibling, it is an even greater honor."

"I… I do not know what to call him, grand-aunty," Cahen replied timidly.

He was feeling the pressure from many pairs of eyes and happy smiles raining down on him.

"Whatever you decide to call him, so will it be," Adamou encouraged him.

Eva nodded her approval.

"Alright," Cahen said and walked towards his younger brother as his younger brother sleeping in his mother's arms.

He stared at the tiny human for a few seconds and then uttered one word.

"Ahben."

"*Ahben* it is," Adamou affirmed.

And so, the newborn child was called Ahben. Unfortunately, his baby brother could not play with him yet. He was still too tiny and could not even speak. His eyes were still closed and all he did was cry, sleep and feed from mother all the time. Perhaps this baby brother may not be much of a playmate after all.

"Patience, my son," Eva would say. "He is still a baby. When he grows up to be as big and strong as you are, you two will become the best playmates ever."

Cahen decided he would wait then, because he trusted his parents. And as time passed, Cahen realized that he was really starting to like his younger brother. He would carry his brother in his arms and sometimes even sing to him. A few times over the next few moons, he missed his meetings with his birth mother because he was too enchanted by his younger brother.

Lithilia was not happy about that. Her jealousy had finally reached its tipping point and she decided to do something about it.

One day, when Cahen went to meet his birth mother, he sensed something was off about his birth mother. His birth mother was besides herself. Something troubled her, putting her in a constant state of irritation and even anger. What? Cahen's childlike innocence could not fathom.

But Lithilia was not angry at her son. She was angry at the situation that was causing her son to miss their meetings.

Cahen also noticed that his mother's tone of voice and behavior had changed drastically; a change that began after his younger brother had been born.

*But why would mother not be happy about my little brother?* Cahen wondered. *Everyone except for mother is happy about him. Why? I do not understand mother these days.*

Poor Cahen was still too young and innocent to understand concepts such as jealousy and hatred, and the connection that formed between both sentiments sometimes. As such, all he could think of was that his mother was acting and talking strangely and differently. Cahen did not appreciate this new behavior from his mother.

But one thing he knew for certain was that he would look after his younger brother and he would protect his younger brother from anything that wanted to hurt him… anything and anyone. Even if his father had not repeatedly tasked him with this, innately, Cahen knew that as the elder brother, he had to be his brother's keeper.

# CHAPTER SIXTEEN

# FROM BEST TO WORST

"**I'M SURE HE** has his reasons," Sara said.

"But I've never seen him like this," Patrick argued. "He's never asked if I needed backup for a mission before. He looked... concerned for me."

"Like I said, based on what you done told me about him, he must have his reasons," Sara insisted.

"I mean, I understand this may be one hell of an opponent. But I think I can handle ma own," Patrick continued ranting as he paced back and forth in Sara's bedroom with one arm across his chest and another on his goatee.

"I don't think it's got anything to do with your skills," Sara said. "There's more to this than meets the eye. Maybe when you meet this prince, then you gon' have a better understanding of what's goin' on."

"Hence why I made a pit stop here," Patrick slid into a loveseat.

"And here I was thinkin' you wanted to get your good luck on before headin' out," Sara teased. "Didn't wanna push it by assumin' you actually missed and wanted to see me, ya know."

"You can read me like a book," Patrick played along and shook his head.

"Oh, I can do more than read you, my chocolate mousse," Sara replied.

Sara straddled and kissed Patrick with all that she had. Patrick kissed her back.

"So, did you hear anything about this prince during any of your many travels?" Patrick asked.

Sara kissed him lightly on the lips.

*Such a hopeless romantic.* Patrick thought.

"Heard that," Sara said, suppressing a smile while she pretended to be mad.

"Really?" Patrick said. "Now you're listening to my thoughts?"

"Sorry, baby," Sara said and lowered her eyes in embarrassment. "Didn't mean to. I just tuned in and...." her voice trailed off.

"It's okay, babe," Patrick said and kissed her lightly on the lips. "Not that we have anything to hide from each other. But it's best we don't invade each other's privacy like that in the future. Deal?"

Sara kissed Patrick on the lips and smiled.

"Deal," she replied. "I'm sorry."

"No worries," Patrick caressed her cheek. "Now, back to this prince. Heard anything about him?"

"Matter of fact, I have," Sara replied. "He was, like many young royals at the time, full of life and plenty of testosterone. But there was never any doubt he was a true patriot; proud and pompous, but a true patriot, nonetheless."

"So, what happened?" Patrick asked.

"Didn't live in that kingdom until after his demise," Sara replied, as she played with Patrick's earlobes with her fingers. "But word on the streets was that he meddled with the occult and paid dearly for it."

"So, was meddling with the occult part of his everyday routine?" Patrick asked. "I'd think that a crown prince like himself would be more concerned with the military and chicks, instead of messing with the occult."

"True, but Natas was no average crown prince," Sara said. "His childhood friend later became a high priest, the youngest ever, they said. Dahmes or Damas was his name. So, they grew up to become a powerful pair; a crown prince and a high priest as best friends? Talk about a recipe for mischief."

"Is this your analysis or what actually happened?" Patrick asked.

Patrick was no longer looking at her face. He was very slowly unbuttoning Sara's blouse.

"My analysis," Sara admitted. "Anyway, back to the story. And so it came to pass that the allies of the kingdom of the crown prince colluded to lay siege upon the kingdom. They gave the people two options: slavery or slaughter. The king had a very short time to decide. Desperate times called for desperate measures. Something happened and Natas became possessed, according to legend, by a creature of light that had wings."

"Zukael," Patrick exclaimed and stopped fondling with Sara's breasts.

"Indeed," Sara agreed, squeezing Patrick's hands.

Patrick resumed fondling her breasts. But his mind was elsewhere.

"This was the first time anyone in the kingdom had ever seen someone possessed by an entity," Sara continued her narration with a dramatic flair. "And behold. A new creature was spawned from this union."

"That's why Zukael, or Beelzebub, is called King of Demons," Patrick said.

"True," Sara agreed. "The prince and his friend, the high priest, must have invoked Zukael somehow, without knowing what the outcome was gonna be, maybe. Musta been outta utter desperation 'cause, from what I heard, Prince Natas claimed it was out of love for his kingdom."

"And apparently it worked, right?" Patrick asked rhetorically.

"Yep," Sara replied and resumed her theatrics. "The enemy was decimated by the 'hand of the gods', and the kingdom was saved. It's so sad that the very 'hand of the gods' became the ultimate threat to the kingdom. Prince Natas, or the separated entity of the new creature he had become, was still very much attached to the kingdom, even after its physical form had been banished to another realm.

"After finally realizing that he was no longer going to inherit his birthright, the kingdom, Natas' entity chose a different rout. If he would not have the kingdom, then the kingdom, and those beyond, would know no peace. As such, this separated entity became the mastermind behind much of the chaos in that kingdom and beyond for many years, spawning the myth of Satan going around leading people to sin."

"Wait a sec," Patrick exclaimed. "You're saying that even though he was imprisoned in another realm, he was still active on Earth Realm? How come?"

"His body was imprisoned, but somehow, he became a soulless creature," Sara explained. "Not in the sense of your mentor and his peers, but as in his soul could leave and return to his body at will. It took a few years, but Damas, Imma stick with that name just because it sounds a lot better than Dahmes, found a way to permanently imprison Natas' soul."

"This Damas guy sounds like the real deal," Patrick admitted.

"Well, he wasn't the youngest high priest ever for nothing," Sara peeled her blouse from her shoulders herself since Patrick was taking too long. "I'm guessing you already know the master instigator behind all this?"

"The Scribe," Patrick replied. "And now, Satan has been released."

"And it is your task to see to it that he does not unleash mischief unto seven billion people," Sara said.

"Wait," Patrick narrowed his eyes. "How do you know about The Scribe?"

"How old am I again?" Sara sighed. "I probably done forgot more than what you know, young man."

Sara started unbuttoning Patrick's shirt. Patrick smiled, relaxed and leaned forward slightly so that she could take his shirt off more easily.

"Thanks for the insight, honey," Patrick said absentmindedly.

"Of course," Sara replied, standing up.

Sara slowly began disrobing in front of Patrick. She let Patrick feast his eyes and relished in the changing colors of his aura. Finally, he was ready.

"One for good luck?" Sara asked.

Sara turned around and headed for her bedroom, without expecting an answer from Patrick. But before she took a third step, Patrick zipped and carried her into the room. Two hours later, Patrick left in search of the resurrected Prince Natas.

Patrick floated at the entrance to a cave, thousands of feet in Marianas Trench in the Pacific Ocean. The conditions at this depth was more than what even the latest technologies in the realm could handle. But he was an upgraded human. And this was no ordinary cave. It was a portal to another realm and visible only to certain clairvoyants. Certain pieces of equipment could detect energy signatures from the cave's location and there would be no rational or scientific explanations for such a phenomenon. But only folks, like Patrick, knew that this cave entrance was one of the few portals on Earth Realm that led to the Realm of Porgatoria.

Patrick had teleported directly from Sara's house to the coordinates where the energy surge was recorded. He encased himself in a force field and enhanced his vision to see clearly at this level of the ocean trench so far down and out of the reach of the light from Solara. The bioluminescence from the many undiscovered creatures herein did little to shed some light in the omnipresent, thick, liquid pitch blackness. He took a moment to appreciate the immense variety of undiscovered marine creatures swimming around him before returning his focus to the cave. It was interesting to watch the marine creatures desperately trying to swim through his force field without success, which they must have thought was an open space in their habitat.

*Enough with the distraction.*

Patrick teleported into the cave. He had expected the cave to be flooded with water. But the cave was like any other cave on the surface, only far more awe-inspiring. Strange precious stones, which he had never seen before, lined the walls of the cave. The cave averaged a height of twelve feet and a length of about forty feet from the entrance to a wall in the back which forked into two passageways. He took down his force field and breathed in the air of the cave. It was the freshest, most odorless breath of air he had ever inhaled.

"Not bad at all for a place rumored to be a laundromat of souls too dirty for heaven but not so dirty for hell," he scoffed. "A demon's paradise., perhaps?"

Patrick laughed at his own joke and his laughter echoed off the walls and continued deeper into the cave.

"So this is what the Realm of Porgatoria looks like," he shook his head. "They lied to us at Sunday school."

Patrick was unsure why, but he suddenly realized that when Shi'mon had offered backup, his boss was not offering that Patrick take another agent on the mission with him. Shi'mon was actually offering to *be* Patrick's backup

No other agent had been as specially trained as Patrick had been and the order certainly did not have any base down here in a trench in the Pacific Ocean that could swallow up Mt. Everest and not even bat an eye, a peak or something. Now Patrick was concerned. If his mentor was offering to be his backup, then Satan must be a very powerful entity indeed. Patrick's alertness and focus spiked as he inched his way further into the cave.

Patrick walked into a chamber of rock that was a lot larger than what he had expected. The walls and floor were lined with the same precious metal at the entrance to the cave.

*What's your light source?* He wondered as he gently ran his fingers of his left hand along the wall to his left. *Smooth to the touch.*

The cave was dimly lit from an omnidirectional source of light. In the center of the chamber, what looked like the remains of a coffin lay on the ground. Its chains had been snapped, and the coffin looked like its lid had been shattered from the inside.

He walked further into the chamber until he was close to the center of the chamber. Still, nothing happened, and Patrick started to entertain the possibility that his target may have chosen to look for a suitable host among the seven billion people on the realm.

"In all my days of banishment, I never thought you would be the one to come and visit me, old friend," a voice called out from behind him.

Patrick whipped around and summoned a yellow flame in his right hand.

"You know why I'm here, don't you, demon?" Patrick spat.

"They still call me that?" Prince Natas asked. "I did not know that name would last this long."

"I'd love to stay here and chit chat," Patrick said. "But I'm on a mission. Any last words?"

"My old friend," Prince Natas chuckled in derisive amusement.

He shook his head and regarded Patrick with soulless indifference. The black orbs that had replaced his eyes shone in the dimness of the chamber.

"Do you know why you were sent here?" Prince Natas asked.

"Of course," Patrick smirked.

"You think you know," Prince Natas said. "But you have no idea why you were chosen. You do not even remember."

"Look here, demon," Patrick said with unconcealed cockiness. "I've got many friends, and a demon ain't one of them."

"You poor fool," the demon chuckled again. "Here. Let me show you."

And Prince Natas extended his hand. Patrick took a step backward and raised his flaming hand in the air. The yellow flame burned brighter, and the demon erupted in evil laughter.

"If I wanted you dead, you would have been the moment you walked in here," Satan said. "Now, give me your hand. First, I want you to remember. Only then will I kill you."

Patrick hesitated. His ego demanded he take out this piece of crap and bury him in this cave. Yet, his gut cautioned him to be wiser. If there was anything he had learned from his mentor, it was that he should always go with his gut no matter what. Besides, something gnawed deep within his psychical makeup, beckoning him like a promise of freedom that came with a certain level of… awareness? The feeling was there, so close and yet just beyond the grasp of his conscious mind, and it grew more intense in the presence of Satan. Patrick sighed and relaxed his features, lowered his hand and extinguished the flame without sacrificing caution. He did not approach the demon.

"I assure you that I will derive no pleasure in ending you while you still wallow in ignorance, old friend," Satan said. "Now, take my hand and remember."

Satan stretched out his right hand some more. Patrick still hesitated, but finally, he stepped forward and reached out with his right hand. A million thoughts raced through his mind before he took his adversary's hand. Perhaps these were going to be his final moments. And if that was going to be the case, he would personally escort Satan to hell before he died.

"Now, you remember," Satan said and closed his hand around Patrick's.

Patrick saw a flash of light, and then everything went black.

## 1800 B.C.E II

Damas collapsed to a knee. A few soldiers rushed to his aid, but he asked them to stay their hands. One soldier was particularly insistent on helping Damas to his feet. As the soldier reached for Damas, Damas perceived a malicious presence in the soldier using clairsentience. He whipped his head towards the soldier to find his eyes glazed over in shiny blackness. The soldier raised his dagger-bearing hand in the air to strike, but Damas banged his staff on the ground. An invisible force threw the soldier about thirty feet away. But the man got back on his feet instantly as if nothing had happened to him. Moving at superhuman speeds, he plowed through the other soldiers like a boulder rolling down a hillside. Then he charged towards Damas.

"You traitor. I will kill you. *I will kill you*," the soldier screamed maniacally in an evil, non-human voice.

Damas pointed his staff at the soldier and the soldier froze. Damas lifted him up in the air by telekinesis.

"Who are you, creature?" Damas demanded.

"Look into my eyes and see your enemy, old friend," the soldier snarled, and Damas' shock was more than everyone else's in the palace combined.

"Natas?" Damas exclaimed. "But how?"

"It was his plan," the soldier replied as he struggled against the invisible bonds that held him fast. "It was always his plan."

"Whose plan?" Damas asked.

But the soldier stayed silent.

"Answer me, Satan, Prince of Demons," Damas commanded.

"The priest," the soldier replied and gagged. "The priest with the injured leg. He was no priest. He was or is something else. Something more powerful than a hundred of you put together."

"Where is he now?" Damas asked.

"I... I... do not know," the possessed soldier screamed in pain, scattering spit all over. "All I know is that he planted both spells; one for the incantation and one for the banishment. The accident was staged to get our attention."

Damas turned to one soldier.

"Get another coffin, now!" he barked.

The soldier took three other soldiers with him and headed out of the palace.

"What is his purpose?" Damas asked. "What does he want?"

"Chaos," the possessed soldier replied and winced. "Chaos." he repeated.

"What are you then?" Damas pressed.

Feeling a drain in his level of chi, Damas started losing his hold on the soldier.

"I am a part of his plan," the soldier replied.

"And why are you not in the Realm of Porgatoria?" Damas asked.

He dropped to a knee due to the depletion of his energy levels. His mental fortitude was growing weaker making it more difficult to recharge his chi. The soldiers still held their ground. Damas appreciated their bravery.

"The spell you used to banish me was not meant to keep me imprisoned in the Realm of Porgatoria," the possessed soldier frothed in his mouth like a rabid dog. "It was meant to set my essence free. My body remains imprisoned in the Realm of Porgatoria, but my essence is free."

Damas could no longer constrain the possessed soldier, and, with a violent twist, the soldier broke free. He landed on the ground and immediately bounded towards Damas. Three soldiers launched to Damas' defense and tried to slow the possessed soldier's progress. But their efforts proved pointless against the Prince of Demons. The possessed soldier slashed through his three former brothers-at-arms like a hot knife through butter and leaped for Damas.

Damas calmed his raging thoughts, stilled his mind enough to recharge his chi, and uttered a few words loud enough for the possessed soldier to hear.

Again, an unseen force slammed into the possessed soldier, sending him sprawling several feet away on the floor. Damas rose to his feet and started walking towards the possessed soldier. Scrambling to his feet, the soldier made to lunge again, but froze in his tracks.

A glow of white light encased Damas' body. His eyes blazed with a white brilliance and his wooden staff transformed into a staff of white light. Everyone, who was still courageous enough to remain in the palace and witness the spectacle between the possessed soldier and Damas, recoiled in a mix of awe and fear. Damas took slow steps towards the possessed soldier, and with each step Damas took, infused chi radiated from his body and filled up the palace like a suffocating esoteric smoke.

Energy, supercharged chi, radiated from Damas' body. The energy throbbed with immense power and everyone present, including the possessed soldier, felt and experienced this powerful energy. The possessed soldier made to charge again at the living, breathing power that was Damas. The move was more out of defiance than anything else. But when a pair of green, serpentine eyes appeared and glowed above the head of the high priest, he knew that attacking this new version of Damas would be tantamount to suicide.

Instead, the possessed soldier turned and tried to flee; but before he could take a step, Damas uttered words in an alien tongue. Infused chi beamed from his staff in the form of white light and struck the possessed soldier in the back. A scream ripped from his throat as he crashed to the floor, a green flame encasing his body. Every iota of what constituted his essence roared as pain became his new identity. A red-hot broth of rage, confusion and fear boiled within him and fueled his will to survive. He immediately sprang to his feet and fled from the palace, leaping from one building to another, screeching, caterwauling and fuming incoherently, as if he was immune to gravity.

Damas watched as the essence of his once-best-friend fled the scene. Chasing down the essence of Natas right then might only bring solace and what he needed was a solution, a permanent one. More research and preparation epitomized the prologue of a possible odyssey that beckoned in the horizon. He will catch up with Satan's essence later, no matter the form it chose to possess next. The spells from the impersonator priest did more than spawn a new creature. It also created a link between Damas' and Natas' essences. Damas could feel Natas and Natas could also feel him. As such, Damas knew instinctively that as long as they both lived, wherever and whenever they were, these two would forever share a bond of enmity that was beyond space and beyond time.

\*\*\*

Patrick yanked his hand away from Satan's and tumbled to the ground.

"No. It can't be," Patrick exclaimed as he cowered.

His training was the best anyone in the O.R. had ever received. However, given what Satan had just shown him, his training would amount to naught."

"Now you remember."

A ball of yellow light formed in Satan's left hand. His body became encased in a glowing, black aura and his pitch-black eyes glowed darker.

"And now you die... Damas."

# CHAPTER SEVENTEEN

## SINS OF A SIBLING

**"WHEN DID YOU** grow so big?" Eva asked Ahben.

"Mother," Ahben grimaced as he tried to wrestle away from his mother's arms. "I am now three years old and can bathe myself."

"I know you believe you can," Eva replied enjoying the feel of her son's strong body wrestling against hers.

Oh, the glow of pride and the sparkle of joy she felt for her son growing up strong and healthy.

"But remember what happened when last you tried to bathe yourself?"

"Because you do not let me do it myself often enough," Ahben argued as Eva pinned him gently in between her thighs and started disrobing him.

"Cahen, come give aide to your mother, please," Eva pleaded.

Cahen rubbed his hands together and grinned mischievously.

"Why does he have to bathe me?" Ahben protested.

"Because you are giving mother a hard time," Cahen replied calmly.

A strong sense of authority simmered in his voice that could only come from an older sibling, though Cahen was not even a teen. Yet, he was already so much in charge.

Adamou watched his family from a distance. The simplest situations, such as giving Ahben a bath, were moments of bonding. The new boss was a handful and Adamou would take this handful all day any day. Ahben was a child full of life, who kept his parents on their toes during his non-sleeping hours. But with Cahen, it was a different dynamic. Two words: respect and obedience. Adamou and Eva were not sure why this was so, but they were content with Cahen's influence on his younger brother.

Cahen finished disrobing Ahben and stepped aside. Ahben grumbled and scrambled obediently into his bath.

"I keep telling you Ahben," Cahen said while Eva soaked the sponge in the bath and started working it over Ahben's body. "Mother is being very nice to you only for now. Soon, you will get a scolding from her, and you will know what it means to give her a hard time like that."

Cahen turned around and started walking away.

"Do not say I did not warn you."

Ahben grumbled some more, and Eva smiled in admiration. Half an hour later, Ahben was clean, wearing fresh clothes and was back to being the sweet, affectionate and clingy child that he was. He played with his mother and made his father run around the house. He was growing up in a physically, mentally and psychologically healthy environment. His parents were pleased and proud, and so were Ukni and Ukni's team.

Cahen headed for the stream to meet his mother, Lithilia.

"See?" Lithilia said. "Did I not tell you that they will start giving more attention to their other child?"

"He is still too young to do things for himself," Cahen argued.

"Are you not still too young yourself?" Lithilia countered weakly.

"Yes, I am still too young, but I am older than he is," Cahen argued. "I can feed, bathe and clothe myself, but Ahben cannot do those yet."

"You are still too young to understand these things, my son," Lithilia said. "Soon, they will not have any time for you. They will only have time for him."

"His name is Ahben, mother," Cahen reminded her.

"A terrible name," Lithilia retorted.

"Which *I* was given the honor to choose for him," Cahen scowled, unable to hide his hurt. "And they loved it. Everyone loved it; everyone but you."

Lithilia's heart broke when Cahen turned his back to her and a hand went to his face as he swiped a tear. She felt bad and stupid that her own child was acting more maturely than she was. She sighed, her shoulders slumped and she extended her arms towards him. But Cahen stepped away from her touch.

"I am sorry, my son," Lithilia apologized. "I did not mean it like that."

"Why do you dislike them so much?" Cahen sniveled. "What did they do to you? I have asked you so many times, but you offer no reply."

The negativity he felt around his mother was sometimes too overwhelming for him to handle, and it was not just because he was a child. He could not tell if his mother was hiding something from him or if she had no answer for him. He was unsure which was a better option.

"I have no answer for you," Lithilia replied weakly.

"Yet, you try to fill my mind with distasteful and false sentiments towards father, mother and Ahben whenever I come to spend time with you," Cahen said and took a step towards his mother. "They treat me well. We are a family. They love me, and I love them."

"No, my son. I hope *you* come to see what I am saying one day," Lithilia glared in defiance of her son's wisdom and maturity. "They only pretend to care for you now, but they love their child more than they love you. The time will come when they will abandon you and focus on *their* child."

She took Cahen firmly by the shoulder and leveled a defiant and determined gaze at him. She was going to fight for her son at all cost. No woman was going to come into her former home, take her former husband and then try to take the only thing that mattered to her most; her son.

"And when that time comes," Lithilia continued firmly. "You will see the truth in my words. That Ahben is taking your place but *you* and *your* happiness are all I ever cared about. Not mine but *yours*."

Lithilia took his face in her hands and kissed him in between his eyes before gazing deeply and lovingly into his eyes.

"I love you with everything that I am and have," Lithilia's voice broke with frustration and desperation. "And I am not sorry for that."

"I know you love me," Cahen said, touching his mother on the cheek. "And I know you mean well. Let us abandon this subject and just have a good time, alright? Please?"

Lithilia agreed, only because her son's immediate desire for happier times with her outweighed her jealousy and resentment towards Eva and Ahben. For his age, Cahen showed so much wisdom and courage. Although Lithilia was proud of her son, she realized her task of psychologically conditioning him to her advantage might not be as easy as she had imagined it would be. But she would not give up. She may have to rethink her strategy a little more.

Lithilia's negative feelings were only directed towards Eva and now, her son, Ahben. No matter how hard she tried, Lithilia could never harbor any bad feelings towards Adamou. Instead, her heart ached with guilt and her soul spasmed with sorrow for putting him through so much pain and suffering. She could only hope to face him one day and ask for his forgiveness, if she could summon the courage though. Adamou was the only man she had ever loved and would ever truly love. About this much, Lithilia was certain.

That night, before the brothers went to sleep, Ahben thought it was the perfect opportunity to hit Cahen with a barrage of questions.

"What do you do out there, when you go to the stream?" Ahben asked with more excitement than usual.

"It depends," Cahen replied flatly.

"On what?" Ahben pressed.

"On what time of the day it is and what the weather looks like," Cahen replied with a dismissive shrug.

"So, what did you do today?" Ahben prompted some more.

"Nothing much," Cahen replied. "Just sat by the stream and later, I started throwing pebbles."

"Can I come with you next time?" Ahben asked with excitement and hope.

"Have you not been to the stream already?" Cahen asked with unconcealed exasperation. "There is nothing new there to see."

"But I have never gone there with just you," Ahben replied.

His eyes drooped, and his tone was laden with sadness and disappointment.

"Ahben, we have had this conversation before," Cahen replied. "You are not old enough for us to wonder around by ourselves, yet. Our parents do not think that I am old enough to watch out for you. When you are old enough, then yes, you and I will explore, just the two of us, and we will have so much fun. For now, I ask you to be patient. Alright?"

"Alright," Ahben mumbled sleepily and gently snuggled next to his brother.

Ahben had his own bed. But sometimes, he preferred to sleep next to his brother. Cahen caressed Ahben's head until he fell asleep, which did not take long at all. His father came in and stood by the door.

"Not sleeping yet, son?" he asked.

"Soon, father," Cahen replied while caressing Ahben's head.

"You should go to sleep now," Adamou smiled as he walked into Cahen's room and reached for Ahben. "I shall take your little brother to his room."

"Can he please sleep here?" Cahen pleaded.

"If that is what you want," Adamou straightened and headed for the door. "Sleep well, my son."

"Sleep well, father," Cahen replied as Adamou switched off the lights.

Two years later, the bond between brothers grew stronger. They played, ate, slept, bathed and did everything else together. During these times, Cahen was the coolest brother in the garden. This sentiment only came up when Cahen was not being a disciplinarian. During such times, Cahen was not cool anymore to the point that Ahben would not speak to him; at least for a few hours until boredom and loneliness crept in. Then Cahen became the coolest brother once again. He never laid a finger on Ahben though, despite Ahben trying to initiate fist fights once in a while, believing each time that his big mouth would make him stronger than his much bigger and tougher brother was. Those attempts never lasted more than a few seconds. Yet, Ahben's determination was as stoic as his appetite for food.

"You certainly get that from mother," Cahen always said, resurrecting fond memories of Eva right after she emerged from the chamber.

Despite their time together, Cahen still did not take Ahben to the stream. The reasons were the same and Ahben had to be patient. So, Cahen still went to the stream alone to visit his mother, and with every visit to the stream, the mental poison from mother to son became deadlier. As mentally strong as Cahen was, and with puberty slowly creeping in, he gradually started accepting his mother's loathsome propaganda as truth; that his family did not love him anymore and that his parents preferred his younger brother to him, despite the evidence suggesting the contrary. The adamant nature of an indoctrinated mind, unfortunately. Alas, the seed of jealousy towards Ahben was sown, and it was only a matter of time before this seed began to manifest its fruits.

And so it came to pass that one day, Cahen decided to go to the stream with his younger brother by themselves for the first time. Their parents were hesitant, initially.

"Do not stay too long." Adamou said after he gave them permission.

"Yes, father," Cahen agreed.

Ahben leaped and squealed for joy for several minutes. However, Adamou followed from a distance and kept watch over his boys, out of paternal instincts as opposed to distrust in Cahen's ability to take care of Ahben. An hour later, the siblings headed back home, and Adamou stayed out of sight as he tailed them on their way back home. Day One was a success.

"How did it go, my love?" Eva asked.

"Very well," Adamou slid into a chair next to his mate. "They mostly just tossed pebbles in the stream and played around. Ahben especially seemed to have a great time."

"Perhaps because it was their first time alone out there just the two of them," Eva chimed in. "I am glad they enjoyed it."

"So am I," Adamou agreed. "But I will continue to keep an eye on them during subsequent outings."

Adamou and Eva took turns observing their children from a distance as the children spent time together at the stream. Everything went well, and the parents were satisfied. They never noticed Lithilia watching them, because she hid under a cloak of invisibility. When it was Eva's turn to watch over the boys, Lithilia could think of more than a thousand ways to inflict pain and suffering on this vile woman who stole her man and son from her.

*But where is the pleasure in killing her?* Lithilia thought.

She just wanted to make her suffer many times over. The thought of making Eva suffer gave Lithilia near-orgasmic pleasure. But when it was Adamou's day to watch over the boys, she felt completely different.

Lithilia desperately wanted to reveal herself to him, to let him know she was still alive and doing well. She wanted to run into his arms so many times, to hug him, hold him, kiss him and make love to him over and over. She wanted him all to herself as much as she wanted him to have her all to himself. She wanted to fall at his feet and beg for his forgiveness, to plead with him to take her back into his heart. She wanted to tell him that she loved him with everything that she was and that nothing would make her happier than to be his mate again; that nothing would make her happier than for the three of them, himself, herself and Cahen to be a family once again. But she dared not and that inability to have her wishes come to fruition was the worst form of torture Lithilia had ever suffered.

One day, Ukni received word that there was a lava flow from a mountain very far away, from which the stream took its origins. He warned Adamou and Eva not to let the children play in the stream. They could play at the banks, but they could not play in the stream itself until he ascertained its safety. Adamou and Eva relayed a stern admonition unto their children and Cahen assured his parents that he would see to it that they heeded to their parents' warning.

"Hey brother, let us see what we can build with these pebbles since we are not to go into the stream today," Ahben proposed excitedly.

"Sure. What are we going to build?" Cahen asked.

"I do not know," Ahben scratched his temple in thought. "Anything goes."

"Tough…" Cahen said, rubbing his chin.

"Great. Let us begin." Ahben exclaimed.

Ahben immediately dropped on his hands and knees. Cahen smiled and did the same. A moment later, Ahben gladly presented his final piece.

"Look at what I made, brother," Ahben exclaimed.

Cahen looked up and saw that Ahben had constructed something that was far better than what he had made.

"What is that, brother?" Cahen asked.

"A pyramid," Ahben replied with excitement. "Look. It has seven layers."

"What is a pyramid?" Cahen asked.

He moved closer to look at his brother's handiwork.

"Oh, it is something that grandfather says The Ancients built in lands that are far away from here," Ahben replied with a grin of pride. "He said they are very big structures that are used to generate energy for the realm."

*"Do you see what I was telling you?"* Lithilia whispered telepathically. *"They favor him over you, even grandfather. He teaches this little brat things that he never taught you."*

*"I also know things that he does not, mother,"* Cahen replied via telepathy. *"I am going to learn something new."*

"I could show you how to build it, if you want me to," Ahben offered and sat on his heels, waiting to hear his brother's reply.

Ahben's innocence was the one thing that always kept Cahen grounded and sane in the face of the psychological war that raged within him. as soon as his eyes met Ahben's, the flames of jealousy in his heart quickly died.

"Yes, brother," Cahen replied. "I would like you to teach me, please."

"Yay," Ahben shouted with delight and quickly tore down his pyramid. "Alright, here is the trick to building a pyramid with pebbles."

After a short while and a few attempts, Cahen was able to build a solid seven-layered pyramid. The brothers were happy and continued playing with pebbles. Cahen was not paying attention to what Ahben was building after a while though. Shortly afterward, Ukni came walking toward the stream and was pleased to see that the boys were not playing in the water.

"Hello, grandfather," the boys called out almost in unison.

"Hello, my children," Ukni answered.

Ukni opened a small box he held in his hand. He retrieved a small device and put it in the water. After a few seconds, he raised it to his face and looked at it. The stream was not contaminated.

"Where are your parents?" Ukni asked as he returned the device into the box and sealed the box.

"They are at the domicile," Ahben replied as he stood up and wiped his hands on his garments. "Do you want to see what we just built, grandfather?"

"Of course, my children," Ukni replied and walked towards them.

Suddenly, Ukni stopped in his tracks and furrowed his eyebrows. He thought he sensed another presence, but he was unsure. His clairvoyance was only at the latent stages of development.

"I built a pyramid." Cahen announced, snatching Ukni back to the present.

"That is incredible, Cahen," Ukni replied kneeling beside Cahen's pyramid. "Did you teach your brother how to build a pyramid, Ahben?"

"I sure did, grandfather," Ahben replied and smiled.

"That is great," Ukni replied and patted Cahen on the shoulder. "Great job, Cahen. Great job."

Ukni turned towards Ahben. He did not notice Cahen breathing more erratically and clenching his jaws. Was grandfather saying that he, Cahen, was too stupid to build a pyramid by himself? Why did he just have to assume that Ahben, his _younger_ brother, taught him?

"And what did you build, Ahben?" Ukni asked.

"See for yourself, grandfather." Ahben announced and stepped away from his handiwork.

It was a miniature domicile with three windows and the main door.

"This is incredible, Ahben," Ukni exclaimed.

He knelt to inspect the structure.

"Thank you, grandfather," Ahben replied and beamed with pride.

"You are a natural, my son," Ukni rose to his feet. "You boys keep having a good time. I will let you know when it is safe to play in the stream, alright?"

"Alright, grandfather," Ahben replied.

Cahen did not say anything.

*"Meena, I want a full scan, physical and etheric, on the northern section of the garden, specifically near the stream."* Ukni commanded telepathically.

*"Of course,"* Meena replied in kind. *"Is everything alright?"*

*"No,"* Ukni replied.

Ukni looked around to make sure no one was watching him before he teleported directly into his office.

*"We may have an unwelcome guest,"* he relayed to Meena.

*"Need I say more, my son?"* Lithilia asked Cahen via telepathy.

The anger was sudden, the fury was fiery and the rage was pure and explosive.

"I have had enough," Cahen seethed through gritted teeth.

Ahben turned around to face his brother. His grin disappeared from his face when he saw a look on his brother's face that he had never seen before. Then, the unexpected happened.

Eva was cooking and having a conversation with Adamou when suddenly, she stopped and abruptly stood up. She stared outside through the window, and her body stiffened. A very palpable sense of a bad omen suddenly overwhelmed her. Without even realizing it, she uttered a single word: Ahben. Adamou was also seized by a strange sense of foreboding that something was amiss. Eva turned to look at Adamou, and when he looked into Eva's eyes, he recoiled in shock at what he saw. For the first time, he saw Eva's eyes flash with a greenish brightness, and her body was covered in a green, auric glow.

But what happened next thrust Adamou beyond the edge of his rational mind. One moment, Eva was right in front of him and the very next, she had simply vanished, leaving behind a trail of green light. He fell from his chair, shocked, confused and afraid.

He sat on the floor, not knowing what to do and unable to comprehend what had happened. Then, the very ground on which he sat shook as if rocked by a violent earthquake and the air was filled with the sound of a cry of a mother in the worst possible pain. Adrenaline took over his seeming paralysis. Adamou leaped to his feet and sprang out of their domicile, running towards the stream… hoping against all hope that his fears were false.

Ukni tapped on his desk a few times, and multiple screens hovered in front of him. He tapped on one of the holograms, enlarging it by 50%. His expression hardened, and his heartbeat increased significantly. He then tapped on a series of buttons on this desk and the enlarged hologram split into seven holograms of equal size. He tapped on six of them and they disappeared, leaving only one behind. On the remaining hologram, two small luminescent forms, representing Cahen and Ahben, appeared. But then, a third form was slightly visible. It was a little larger than the boys were, and human. Its features revealed a female. Ukni tried to enhance the image, but the image resolution only got worse. Suddenly, the third form became as luminescent as the other two and raced towards one of the smaller forms.

"Oh no," Ukni exclaimed as he recognized the signature of the third form.

Suddenly, a fourth form appeared on the screen and every reading on the screen went haywire. Ukni could not identify what this fourth creature was, and terror gripped him with icy claws. He reached for a button on the far left hand corner of his desk and pressed it. A spherical console rose from the center of his desk and began pulsating.

"Attention everyone," Ukni commanded. "Intruder with unknown traits on the northwest corner of the stream. I repeat, intruder with unknown traits on the northwest corner of the stream. Possibly hostile and dangerous. Team B, secure parent specimens at their domicile. Team A, meet me at the stream. Proceed immediately and with extreme caution. Ukni out."

Then, Eva's scream pierced his mind and an earthquake that was more violent than any he had ever witnessed on Earth Realm and his home realm followed Eva's scream.

Ahben turned around and the moment he saw the look on Cahen's face, his grinned vanished. He saw what looked like his brother, but it was no longer his brother. What was it that was taking slow, calculated steps towards him? Fear, panic and confusion paralyzed Ahben where he stood as he stared into the flaming orange orbs that used to be his brother's eyes.

"Br- Brother? Are you alright?" Ahben whimpered.

"I... have... had... enough," Cahen growled and stooped as if to take a knee.

Then, without warning, Cahen rushed towards Ahben.

"*Cahen. Nooooo......*" Lithilia screamed and formed out of thin air.

Lithilia whizzed towards Cahen, but she was a step too late. Cahen bashed a rock he had picked up from the ground into Ahben's left temple with such force that Ahben was dead before he hit the ground.

That was when a green, human form of light appeared from nowhere and let out a scream of unimaginable pain and sorrow. The green, glowing figure channeled its pain and sorrow into its closed right fist, dropped to its knees and drove its fist into the ground near the dead child. The ground shook violently as if by an earthquake.

That was when Lithilia knew she had made the biggest mistake of her life.

That was when the boy that was Cahen knew he had done the irreparable.

Even at his young age, Cahen knew he had lost his boyhood and lost everything he ever had, everything he ever cared for and everyone he ever truly loved. The green human form of light wailed. As her light faded, as if put out by her tears of pain, Eva scooped up the lifeless body of her son and cradled him in her arms. She cried, she screamed, she wailed, and her pain was so palpable that every plant life within a half sound leap radius instantly withered to death. Adamou rushed in and stopped dead in his tracks, unable for a moment to fathom what his eyes were beholding. Death was an alien concept to him, but the pain of loss was not. Instinctively, he knew Ahben was no more and, as the seconds ticked with Eva's wail of unimaginable grief, the reality of the situation slowly dawned on him. He approached Eva and the peaceful-looking but bloodied Ahben and knelt beside them.

Ukni, Meena and Team A appeared close by. They saw the bloodied rock fall from Cahen's hands, as well as all the dead plant life around them. Even Lithilia's presence was not as shocking and dumbfounding as the green, glowing form of Eva returned to normal. Adamou seemed to be the only compass of normalcy in this horrific scene.

"Sir," a voice crackled over Ukni's telecom. "Parent specimens are not-"

"They are here," Ukni's voice was heavy with defeat, sadness and a deep sense of loss. "Converge on my location at once."

"Yes, sir."

The cry of pain and sorrow from a grieving mother was more than anyone could bear. Meena and a few of Ukni's team members sobbed silently for the family. Ukni's heart was shattered. Adamou and his family, as well as Lithilia, were more than just mere creations of his. They were his children and grandchildren and he loved them as such. But he was also the leader of the expedition and thus, he had to show strength of mind and emotion. Thus, Ukni reached deep into his psyche, blocked the pain and, with a heavy sigh, he hardened his demeanor and switched to Commander Mode once again. Despite the nuclear reaction of suffering that threatened to tear through his psyche to the surface, Ukni would not shed a tear in public. And then, the unexpected happened.

Eva held out her left hand towards Cahen and Cahen felt an unseen force yank him towards her. His neck fit into her left hand. She locked a pair of green, glowing eyes with Cahen's, wrapped her fingers around his throat and started squeezing. As she choked the life out of Cahen, Adamou took her firmly by the shoulders.

"My love," he pleaded with her, despite his unbearable pain. "Please, do not do this. Giving Cahen the same fate as Ahben will not bring our son back to-"

An unseen force slammed into his body so hard that Adamou was thrown almost a sound leap away. But he immediately stood up and hurried towards the stream, desperately clinging to the hope that he was not going to be too late to stop Eva from doing something she might regret for the rest of her life. He did not care to wonder why he felt no pain from his broken, right tibia and left forearm, and why these broken bones healed on their own.

*"Secure her. Now!"* Ukni screamed via telepathy to Meena, who was the only other member of his team who could communicate through telepathy.

Ukni and Meena tried to subdue Eva using telekinesis but the last thing they remembered before they lost consciousness and slumped to the ground was an instant, smothering blackness. The rest of his team were rendered immobile.

Cahen was forced to stare into the green, glowing orbs of the woman she once called mother and what he saw burned his soul to a frightening surrender. No one and nothing was going to save or protect him from the incinerating fury of this woman's demand for justice. He wrestled and thrashed against Eva choking him to death and he felt his life slowly ebb away. Not knowing how else to proceed, Cahen implored Eva the only way he could think of.

*"Please, mother,"* Cahen pleaded telepathically.

This was the first time he had ever communicated with her through telepathy. He was unsure if Eva could hear him. But death beckoned and desperate times called for desperate measures.

"Do *not* call me mother," Eva growled in a most alien voice.

*"Please, mother,"* Cahen insisted. *"I beg of you, before you end me, look into me."*

Even in her pain-induced insanity and rage, the last vestige of her maternal instinct kicked in, and she did as Cahen had asked by accessing Cahen's esoteric signature and psyche. How she achieved this feat was no concern of hers at the moment. She had greater concerns to address.

In a spark of instantaneity, Eva saw a child, broken from birth who became even more broken in the wake of his mother's outbursts of violence. In a spark of instantaneity, she saw a toddler feel true healing love for the first time when she, Eva, had been made and she saw a once-broken-but-healing child being manipulated by his birth mother. She saw a child's psyche broken anew by his birth mother, snapping into a moment of insane and uncontrollable rage, resulting in that child committing the unthinkable. From this irreparable action, the child radiated an aura of regret, pain, shame and confusion. And in a spark of instantaneity, she made up her mind on what to do next. Her eyes lost their glow and returned to normal and her fingers slowly slid away from Cahen's neck. Cahen, however, did not move. He stood rooted on the spot and bowed his head in regret, shame and most of all, profound sadness.

Eva sobbed wildly. Adamou walked slowly towards her and took her by the shoulders. He did not care about how he covered an entire sound leap on foot within seconds. He was just extremely relieved that Cahen was still alive. Lithilia stood frozen on the spot. She had acquired a few talents during her period of disappearance. But after seeing what Eva, the woman she despised with every fiber of her being, was capable of, Lithilia decided inaction was her best course of action. Whatever this Eva woman was, Lithilia was going to do everything in her power not to find out.

Adamou caressed the blood-soaked hair of his son's head. He pulled back his hand and looked at the blood on it. At the sight of the blood on Adamou's hand, something beyond rage and the rationalizing of possible ramifications ripped through Adamou's core. Without warning, Adamou's body burst into a bright, golden flame. Golden flames spewed from his eyes and mouth, and golden flames sprang from his shoulder blades like the wings of an eagle. Lithilia gasped as a myriad of memories and emotions avalanched through her psyche.

*He did know who she was,* she exclaimed to herself. *He is the same as she is.*

"Why Cahen?" the creature that used to be Adamou demanded in a voice that made Lithilia and Cahen cringe in fear and awe.

But Eva was unmoved by her partner's sudden transfiguration. Whatever her partner was, it was still her partner and her partner would never do her any harm. But she could not say the same for her stepson and the woman Eva identified as her stepson's mother. As such, she reversed her role with her partner and became the voice of reason instead.

"No, my love," Eva said in between heavy sobs and pointed at Lithilia. "Her. It is her fault."

Ukni and Meena roused from their state of slumber. The stood up and the rest of his team resumed mobility. But when they made to move forward, they collided with an invisible shield.

"Your doing, brother?" Meena asked.

"No," Ukni replied and sighed.

Ukni and his team stood behind the invisible shield summoned by Eva.

*What have I created?* Ukni asked himself.

They watched helplessly as the creature that used to be Adamou blazed towards Lithilia, grabbed her by the neck with his left hand and lifted her off the ground as if she was a pillow. Lithilia's eyes bulged as fear for her impending and certain end seized her soul. In the same instant, a sword of golden flames manifested in his free, right hand as he pulled it back for a deathly blow.

"*No, my love. Please, no,*" Eva screamed using telepathy. "*Not like this.*"

"Why not," the creature yelled in an angry, alien voice. "I should end her right here, right now."

"Because," Eva sobbed heavily. "Every child needs his mother. Even the child that took ours from us."

And Eva let out a scream of renewed pain that killed every plant and animal, from the blades of grass in the fields, to creatures, tiny and immense, that walked in the earth and those that sailed the skies, within a two-sound-leap radius. Eva's words dug deep into the creature that used to be Adamou's psyche. The flames from his eyes, mouth and body extinguished, his flaming sword disappeared, and he let the paralyzed, fear-transfixed body of Lithilia hit the ground.

Adamou stared at Lithilia, his former mate and lover, with eyes that were devoid of any emotion other than pain. Silent tears rolled down his cheeks as he turned around and walked slowly towards his lover and their dead son. He knelt and gathered the two of them in his arms. Adamou kissed his wife on the head and took Ahben from her arms. Eva was still sobbing heavily when she dipped her finger into the ground that was mixed with Ahben's blood. She rubbed the mixture of blood and earth on Cahen's head and chest.

"As a mother, and the mother who raised you, I cannot end you, even if I wanted to," Eva spoke in between uncontrollable sobs. "But I curse you and everything you touch. For the pain you have caused me, you will know no peace, you will know no happiness, and you will know no love. You will live in many places; but you will never have a home. You will know no forgiveness or kindness until the day you face justice. Blood for blood. Life for life. This curse, I place upon you, Cahen."

Eva spat on Cahen's face. Her curse was steeped in pain and sorrow, inscribed by the ethers, sealed in space and transcended the confines of time. And Cahen's essence resonated its affirmation of this curse.

Eva's declaration was too much for any essence to contain, talk less of that of a child. Cahen collapsed to his knees. Even at his age, he knew the curse of the woman he had called mother was far worse than any form of punishment he could have received. He wished Eva had killed him instead. Not even death would rid him of Eva's curse.

"And as for you," Eva growled at Lithilia and her eyes became green orbs, "No place in Creation will shield you from my wrath. The only reason you are still alive is because Cahen needs a mother. But until the time when I look you in the eye as I end your existence, I place a curse on you; the same I placed upon your son. But while your son will vanish into the annals of humanity, you will be vilified and shunned wherever you are and wherever you go. You will be a whore for all of Creation."

Eva made a dagger manifest in her left hand, unsure and uncaring of how she could summon something out of seeming nothingness. An unseen force, against which Lithilia was powerless, pulled Lithilia towards Eva. Eyes bulging and body quaking with morbid fear, Lithilia kicked, clawed and screamed against the unseen force to no avail. Alas, her body was forced to kneel at Eva's feet as Eva sliced her own palm. Eva made a fist and squeezed blood out of the open gash in her palm. Lithilia continued struggling until the unseen force rendered her immobile. Eva then opened her palm as the dagger disappeared from her left hand and rubbed her bloody palm on Lithilia's forehead.

"And now, we are forever bound," Eva proclaimed. "Ours is a bond that goes beyond time and space, until the day you pay for this day by my hand for what you have done to my son. Blood for blood. Life for life. This curse I place upon you, Lithilia."

Eva spat on Lithilia's face as green light encased the knife wound in her hand and healed it. She then turned around, buried her head in Adamou's chest and wailed bitterly. Adamou turned a cold gaze towards Lithilia.

"Take Cahen and leave before I change my mind," Adamou said. "And if I ever see you again, I will end you, whether or not Cahen still needs you."

Lithilia was quick to heed to Adamou's words as she took Cahen and both of them vanished. She knew she had lost her chance of ever being together again with her one and only true love. This was tantamount to death by hopelessness, and she had only herself to blame. There was only one thing left for her to do.

As long as she was alive and as long as her son still drew breath, she had to adapt, she had to survive. From that moment, her sole purpose in life gravitated towards self-preservation and protecting the center of her creation, Cahen. As such, Lithilia swore to protect her son at all cost from Adamou. And most of all, she swore to protect herself, even if it meant tearing down Creation itself, from the wrath of the only person who made her cower and cringe in fear: Eva.

"What did we create, brother?" Meena asked.

"I do not know, sister," Ukni replied. "I do not know."

***

Maduk sat in his private chamber, staring at nothing, thinking about nothing.

*Cahen,* a voice called out via telepathy.

He bolted from his chair. He could not believe what he was hearing. He could have sworn he was dreaming. But he heard it again. Millennia had come and gone and his longing to hear that voice had never wavered. A countless number of times, the memory of that voice was the only source of hope he had and the only thread that held his broken sanity into place. He swallowed, not knowing how to respond.

The bearer of the voice understood and gave him instructions on a meeting location. Maduk was there before the instructions were complete. His massive body trembled from extreme excitement, nervousness, happiness, fright, sadness, joy, and pain at the same time. There she was, sitting on a chair with her back turned to him. Maduk slowly walked around to face her. Where he had the courage from, he had no idea. He still could not believe it was her, after all these millennia. She looked different since the last time he saw her. But her etheric signature was still the same. He dropped on both knees in front of her and shed the silent tears of a quagmire of emotions. When she saw the tears on Cahen's face, she, too began to cry.

Cahen, the giant of a creature, slumped into her opens arms and wept like a child. Despite his age, he was a child; her child. At least that was how he regarded himself in front of the woman. It felt right, and it felt perfect.

He kept saying he was sorry, over and over. The woman caressed his hair.

"I know," she whispered. "I know."

Her persona was changeless, and her love was as unconditional, undying and timeless as the very first time she had laid eyes upon him thousands of Earth Realm years ago. Cahen was at peace, like a baby asleep in his mother's arms. She peeled his face from her chest and looked at him in the eyes. She smiled and Cahen wept even more. But this time, he wept for pure, child-like joy.

"I have dreamed of this moment my whole life." Cahen said. "I have missed you so much."

The woman smiled, kissed him lovingly on the forehead and cradled his huge head against her chest once again.

"And I, too, have missed you so much… my son," replied Miryam, who was the reincarnation of Eva.

# CHAPTER EIGHTEEN

# OF PRIEST AND PROTÉGÉ

**PATRICK HEARD SATAN** pronounce his death sentence. He saw a yellow ball of light encased in a black aura form in Satan's right hand. He had one, maybe two, seconds before Satan finalized his fatality. A dark veil of despair draped over him as he realized he was no match for this old-new adversary of his.

In a flash, everything he ever wanted to do, everything he ever wished he had done and everything he wished he had done differently played across his mind. While Patrick knew death was an inevitable music that every mortal in Creation must dance to, he never envisioned himself dying at the hands of an enemy. He should have buried his pride and accepted Shi'mon's offer for assistance. Alas, it was too late. And so, he closed his eyes, made peace with himself and the world, and embraced his fate in a final gesture of complete surrender. But as soon as he completely let go, his eyes immediately snapped open.

Patrick caught a glimpse into the Dimensions of Time, Space and Energy. Everything seemed to move in near stillness. He saw the air he breathed in, their atomic and subatomic constituencies laid bare in their true form before him.. A surge of energy coursed through his DNA, infusing him with power like he had never felt before. Or maybe he had had plenty of experience with this power, but he could not remember. Then, a second, more intense and more powerful surge of energy pulsed through him. It burned and coiled along his spine, three-and-a-half times. When the burn reached the base of his skull, he whipped his head upwards and screamed as his eyes turned into bright white orbs and a beam of energy exploded from between his eyes in the form of bright, white light.

Patrick remained in his body, but he held no will over it. Somewhere within his physical form, the essence that was Patrick was still fully operational and conscious. But even in this state, Patrick knew that his body had been taken over by the memory of who he was in another lifetime, a more dominant essence; and that essence was there to stay.

And as the essence of Damas, the high priest, was reborn in Patrick, Patrick was more than willing to surrender and let Damas have his way. In a flash, Patrick learned a lesson that Shi'mon had been trying to teach him for decades: the power of surrender. The timing could not have been any more perfect. As protégé to Father Supreme, Patrick had no chance against Satan. But as Damas, the playing fields had just been leveled. Damas turned his gaze towards Satan, who was still in mid-stride, moving relatively much slower than he was before, because Damas was still within the glimpse of the Dimension of Time. Satan was bringing down the yellow ball of light encased in a black aura towards him. Damas stood up, flexed and straightened his shoulders, clenched his right fist and raised it past his shoulders before Satan completed his stride.

Damas smiled and crashed his right fist into the ground at a supernormal speed. Thanks to the glimpse into the Dimension of Energy, a powerful surge of energy boomed outward from the point of impact, which lifted Satan off the ground and slammed him into a stony wall of the cave several feet away..

Satan's expression morphed from one of victory to shock before he impacted the rocky cave wall, causing many cracks to radiate on the wall where he slammed into. He landed on the ground in an unceremonious heap. And then, Satan's look of surprise and shock turned into pure, unhinged rage. His aura crackled and dazzled with electricity-like sparks as he flooded his body with supercharged chi. Even the air in the cave lost its freshness and lack of odor, replaced by a faint smell of iron and sulphur. The corner of Damas' mouth rose in a half-smile, even though he was no longer within the glimpse of the Dimensions of Space, Time and Energy. Still, Damas, the high priest, was fully awake and he now had Satan's complete attention.

*This might end up being a fair fight after all,* Patrick thought.

Satan nodded, and the corner of his mouth also stretched into a half-smile. He glared at Damas and Damas glared back at him. The two best-friends-now-mortal-enemies streaked towards each other. Their speeds made that of the Bright Eyes seem like tortoises racing.

Damas and Satan came together with a mighty clash and an explosion of energy. Fists encased in yellow and white flames blazed through the air in deadly attacks and weapons sparked from the ethers clashed. Both men were relentless and motivated. Satan was motivated by pure vengeance at the one who banished and imprisoned him. Damas, harboring Patrick's body, was stoic on finishing what he started. Only one of these mortal enemies was going to make it out of the cave alive.

But as the fight wore on, Satan started having the upper hand because he was getting faster. Better yet, Damas was getting slower. His muscles and mind were no longer in sync, exhaustion started wearing down on his body, his heart raced as if he was having a heart attack, and his willpower was no longer strong enough to even spark the ethers. Patrick's physique and psyche could no longer handle the essence of Damas and, as such, Damas' essence was gradually phasing out, especially after Damas' essence accidently caught a glimpse into three of the four major dimensions without any prior preparation or esoteric upgrade. All these came together in a pot of frustration that was boiling over the fires of the fear of defeat and, therefore, impending death.

Patrick summoned courage from his brimming panic in a final, desperate kick to survive and maybe safe himself. Alas, there was no escaping the sadistic onslaught of punches and kicks from Satan, with the last blow catapulting him into the cave wall. Patrick landed on the ground in a helpless heap followed by several rock pieces from the cave wall where his body had impacted. Satan loomed towards him while he healed many broken bones. He propped himself against the cave wall and awaited a final fatality from his foe.

*"We may be linked, Damas,"* Satan hissed telepathically. *"But today, you die."*

But Damas was gone, and all that was left was Patrick, severely beaten and balled up on the ground in a pitiful, bloody heap. Patrick kissed his hopes of teleportation goodbye, knowing that Satan would just track him down using their shared link. Without any prospect of escape, Patrick decided that before he died, he would set aside his ego and make at least one person in the realm very happy. Thus, as Satan moved in for the kill, Patrick uttered one word from his telepathic lips and infused it with as much emotion as he could summon.

*"Sara."*

A bright, violet flash of light filled the cave even before Satan's ball of yellow flames burned into the nothingness that once contained the body of his enemy. Satan clenched his fist and raged, phasing in and out of physicality. Not only had he missed an opportunity to end Damas once and for all. But now, he could not even track his enemy's teleportation signature because the link he shared with Damas had somehow been severed. And that creature of violet light was the most likely culprit.

*But how? And who or what is that creature?* Satan thought.

Satan searched around angrily, hoping against hope that the bright, violet flash of light was a figment of his imagination. The cold, hard truth hit him like a sucker punch to the solar plexus, and his scream of anger was so supercharged with esoteric energy that it caused the cave walls to crack in several places and the cave began collapsing upon itself.

***

Patrick winced as Sara placed him on her bed. She was a human form of bright violet non-consuming flames, flames which cast a serene, violet glow in her dark bedroom. Slowly, the violet flames died out as she absorbed them into her naked body. She knelt close to Patrick, tears of a myriad of emotions spilling over her cheeks as she softly caressed his head.

"Thought I lost you," Sara sniveled. "Heard your call, and I ain't never been so scared all my life."

Patrick smiled weakly when she chuckled and swiped at her eyes.

"I'm sorry, I-" Patrick started saying as he continued healing himself.

*It's taking longer than normal,* he thought, referring to his slow healing.

"Hush, my love," Sara said. "You're okay, and that's all that matters. Just lie down. So glad you called. Felt like I was the last thing on your mind right before you thought you was gonna die. I could feel your every emotion. As much as I was scared to death, I was so damn happy."

Patrick smiled weakly at Sara, realizing that his action had been the ultimate declaration of his love for her. In his mind, he shook his head, wondering if he had made the right choice; not for himself, but for her. She was not of this realm, and though she had regained some of her memory, much of her history was still lost to her, buried somewhere in her subconscious. He wanted to say something, but Sara silenced him with a deep and passionate kiss.

"Don't worry about it," Sara added, still grinning from ear-to-ear.

"I beg to differ," a voice said from a corner of the room, startling both Sara and Patrick.

Patrick muttered an expletive and Sara immediately flared into a bright violet flaming human body. But even before the entire room was bathed in bright, violet light, Patrick knew who the voice belonged to. The intruder pulled up a chair using telekinesis and made himself comfortable.

"So," Shi'mon said calmly. "When were you planning on telling me?"

"As soon as I gave you my progress report, boss," Patrick replied, propping himself up on the bed.

Patrick grimaced in pain before sparking the ethers to light up Sara's room.

"Wait," Sara beamed with surprise. "Is this your father? Not biologically; but you know what I mean."

"Yes, Sara," Patrick replied. "Sara, meet Fr. Shi'mon, Father Supreme of the O.R. Father, meet Sara, my... friend."

Sara understood the reason for his hesitation and was not offended by Patrick referring to her as his 'friend'. She walked over to Shi'mon with an extended hand as she extinguished the flames on her body.

"It is such an honor to meet you, sir," Sara said with excitement. "Patrick has told me so much about you; mostly good things."

"Pleasure to meet you, Ms. Sara," Shi'mon replied in a flat tone that Patrick knew could mean anything from courteous to extremely cautious.

Shi'mon stood up, shook Sara's hand. Patrick gawked, stunned at how much a gentleman Shi'mon was, despite Shi'mon's hard stare and the circumstances of the moment. But Patrick knew he was not yet out of the water.

"I am flattered that he has told you so much about me. But I cannot say he has awarded you the same honor," Shi'mon let go of Sara's hand.

"For obvious reasons," Sara replied, still smiling. "That's why I said 'mostly' good things. Regardless, it's truly an honor to meet you, sir."

"Thank you," Shi'mon sat down. "Do you mind covering up, please?"

"Oh, my sincere apologies," Sara replied, feeling a little flustered.

She had completely forgotten she was naked, but that changed in a zip.

"So, Ms. Sara-" Shi'mon began.

"Sara, please," Sara offered.

"Sara," Shi'mon said. "Where are you from and what are you?"

"My memory is only slight right now," Sara shrugged and sat next to Patrick on the bed. "Thanks to Ashram. I remember so little. I know I ain't of this realm or dimension, but I certainly ain't no angel."

Sara realized her last statement could have been interpreted in many ways under normal circumstances. But these were not normal circumstances.

"You're definitely of a higher dimension," Shi'mon chimed in. "Which one exactly, I don't know yet. What I do want to know though…"

Shi'mon turned his attention towards Patrick, who now sat on the bed quietly, like a child about to be scolded by a parent for doing something stupid.

"What made you think you could hide her presence from me?" Shi'mon asked in a slightly hissy tone.

"I was just trying to protect her," Patrick replied.

"Not good enough, young man," Shi'mon hissed even more.

"I don't know, Father," Patrick replied and bowed his head in shame.

"Maybe you shouldn't talk to him like that," Sara spat at Shi'mon.

"And maybe you should learn your place, creature," Shi'mon lashed back. "You may have him by the balls, but his loyalty to you will always be secondary to his loyalty to me and the organization."

"How dare you."

Her eye sockets flamed up with violet flames as she rose from the bed.

"And what exactly are you going to do?" Shi'mon rose as well from his chair as his eyes burned with a pure, white brightness.

"Stand down, Sara," Patrick spoke softly.

Sara bared her teeth and clenched her fists.

"I said stand down… Please," Patrick reiterated.

Sara glanced at Patrick, nodded and extinguished the flames in her eyes.

"She was only standing up for me, Father," Patrick apologized to Shi'mon.

"Do I have to worry about her?" Shi'mon asked Patrick without taking his gaze off Sara.

"No, Father," Patrick replied.

Sara sensed what was going on and immediately realized her mistake. She took a careful step towards Shi'mon. Shi'mon was testing her and it appeared she failed.

"Sir, I truly apologize for my behavior," Sara said. "I know I'm way more powerful than you and your kind are. But, I assure you that I ain't never meant no harm to your kind and I never will. The only times I hurt your kind was in self-defense. And I've got 26,000 years to prove that-"

"Twenty-six what?" Shi'mon exclaimed and his eyes lost their brightness.

Shi'mon could not contain his surprise and Patrick could not contain his snickering.

"26,000 years, sir," Sara repeated calmly. "That's how long I been in y'all's realm. Well, it's more like 25,798 years."

"I see," Shi'mon said, trying to regain his composure. "Please, continue."

"Thank you, sir," Sara said. "All I want is to regain my memory fully, and until that time, I just wanna live among your kind in peace. I'm happy with Patrick. I think he's also happy with me. I understand what his duties and responsibilities are, and I assure you that Imma never, ever come between him and his work."

Sara dropped to one knee, bowed her head to the ground and extended her left hand towards Shi'mon. She neither saw Shi'mon narrow his eyes and recoil a tinge nor Patrick raise his eyebrows.

"What are you doing?" Shi'mon asked.

"It's a custom I learned from a village I lived in a very long time ago. A form of apology," Sara's hand remained in the air as she spoke, her head bowed. "I fell in love with this custom and have kept it ever since, for those I deeply care for."

Shi'mon sighed, took her hand and raised her to her feet.

"I accept your apology."

'Oh thank you, thank you, sir," Sara grinned with excitement and relief.

Shi'mon turned towards Patrick.

"See you in my study in two hours," Shi'mon said. "Hopefully, you will be fully healed by then."

He teleported away before Patrick could reply.

Patrick slumped on the bed with relief, pleased that he no longer had to hide or lie about Sara to his mentor.

"That went well," Sara said, trying to lighten the mood.

"Perhaps," Patrick replied. "And that thing about the custom and village-"

"Totally made it up," Sara interjected.

The couple burst out laughing and Sara dove into Patrick's arms. She did not notice Patrick wince in pain. Or maybe she did but she did not care?

*So glad I didn't lose him,* Sara thought.

*I'm lucky to be alive,* Patrick thought as he caressed her head. *Yep, I'm a lucky son-of-a-gun, all thanks to her. And... I'm happy to have her in my life. Crap, I'm a goner.*

He stayed with Sara for about half an hour before heading to see his mentor.

"I had a feeling you would be here sooner rather than later," Shi'mon said.

"I'm not fully healed yet, but I can manage," Patrick replied.

Then, he bowed his head and played idly with his fingers for a few seconds.

"I'm truly sorry, Father," Patrick apologized. "I got carried away and lost sight of something, of everything. I shouldn't have let my ego get in the way."

"You have been losing focus a lot lately, young man," Shi'mon spoke calmly as he toyed mindlessly with the cell phone he carried on him just for show. "You know how dangerous our job is. One slip could mean one's end."

"Like today..." Patrick chimed in and summoned the courage to meet his mentor's gaze

"Like today," Shi'mon concurred.

Patrick nodded and clasped his hands behind his back. He straightened his shoulders and steeled his composure. Once again, he was a student ready to submit wholly to his mentor's apprenticeship. Shi'mon's nod was imperceptible.

"So, when did you know about Sara, Father?" Patrick asked.

"When you met her the first time," Shi'mon replied flatly.

"What? You knew this whole time?" Patrick scowled and recoiled slightly in shock. "How?"

"There is something special about you two," Shi'mon replied. "Almost like you two are kindred spirits, for lack of a better description."

Patrick cocked his eyebrows and was about to smile.

"I was not giving you my blessing," Shi'mon added coldly.

Patrick's smile disappeared immediately.

"What makes you say that, Father?" Patrick asked.

"Not important now," Shi'mon replied.

Patrick nodded and Shi'mon leaned forward slightly.

"You may be my protégé, but there are certain things about me that elude you," Shi'mon continued and tossed the phone aside. "For now, know that I just know, just like I knew you would be no match for Natas."

"And yet you sent me to face him," Patrick could barely contain his shock and confusion. "I could've been killed."

"All part of your training, young man," Shi'mon replied and waved at a chair directly in front of him.

Patrick pouted for a second before he sat down.

"Even if you hadn't called out to Sara, I would have come to your aid. But I wanted you to be humbled and, hopefully, regain some of your lost memory."

"Damas..." Patrick mumbled as the feeling of being toyed with gave way to comprehension. "He kept calling me Damas. He even showed me a scene from a very distant past. Felt like I was there."

"Because you *were* there, Patrick," Shi'mon chimed in. "You were, and still are Damas, the high priest-"

"The sudden surge of energy and power..." Patrick muttered as his mind drifted to his encounter with Satan in the cave.

"For a moment, you became the high priest; but that moment wore off," Shi'mon explained. "I know because I kept tabs on your etheric signature. When Damas took over, your etheric signature was overridden by his. It is time for you to remember who you were in that lifetime so that you can be prepared for your next stance against Satan. I chose you for a reason, Patrick. I groomed you for a reason. And you are my protégé for a reason, a reason which goes far beyond you remembering who you were in a past life. But time is of the essence, and I need to know if you are ready."

Patrick understood that his mentor was referring to him being ready to lose his inflated ego and become a student again. *A full cup cannot be filled,* someone once told him. Who was it again? He wondered.

"Yes, Father, I am," Patrick replied. "And I'm also ready to remember."

\*\*\*

Satan was oblivious to the walls of the cave coming down around him. He had more important things to worry about like why he could no longer feel the link with his archnemesis.

"Seems as if you could use some company," a non-corporeal voice spoke from nowhere and everywhere.

Satan whipped his head around wildly, trying to locate the voice.

"Show yourself," Satan demanded.

"That is no way to treat your liberator, my prince," the voice said.

"I command you to show yourself," Satan barked. "I will not speak with a faceless coward."

"As you wish," the voice said.

In a flash, Satan was back in his prison, locked away by the spells Damas had placed upon him. He struggled against his binds. He cursed, screamed, yelled, and his anger and frustration grew exponentially.

"Let me know when you're ready to show some gratitude and respect," the voice added. "And maybe I might have pity on your despicable self."

After a moment, Satan realized that, ego or not, a free puppet was certainly better than an incarcerated demon.

"Apologies for my foolish behavior, o faceless one," Satan relaxed his shoulders. "I pledge my fealty to your service."

"Now we're talking business," the voice said, and in a flash, Satan found himself in an alien environment.

Satan looked around him but could not comprehend what he was feeling or where he was. He hovered in nothingness. The luminosity of this place seemed to come from the air itself. But in the center of this strange oblivion, a dark, spherical energy body that was about seventy-two feet in diameter hovered.

"You are standing at the esoteric and physical core of Earth Realm," the voice explained. "What you see is the conduit through which new consciousness flows into and through this realm."

A form began to manifest as the voice spoke.

"Your mission will be to access it," the voice continued. "Every creature in this realm is essentially linked to this core. Once you can access this core, you can induce your essence unto that of the core, and as such, you can induce your essence unto that of every single human in this realm."

"You mean, I could turn every human into what I am by accessing and using this thing? This core?" Satan grinned with the feeling of unbelief and excitement buzzing within him.

"I'll have to show you first, you know," the voice said as the form became denser. "But patience now, creature."

Satan was starting to grow weary of his liberator's theatrics. He sighed to calm himself.

"While I wait, could you please tell me who or what you are?" Satan asked.

"Aha. You have indeed learned your manners, and for that you get a pat on the back," said the voice as the form materialized completely.

Satan had no sense of humor and an even lesser tolerance for his liberator's laissez-faire behavior. The creature in front of him appeared human, even looked familiar. Satan dug deep into his memory for an answer.

"Wait. You are the priest, who had the accident at the library," Satan gasped, goggled and pointed a finger at The Scribe.

"Well," the priest said with a slight chuckle. "I can be many things."

"Oh. So, what are you then?" Satan asked, with unreserved exasperation.

"I am a purveyor of purpose," The Scribe replied. "And I just revealed to you why I created you so long ago."

# CHAPTER NINETEEN

## SIRING A SINISTER

**"TELL ME ABOUT** your life after that day, my son," Miryam kissed Cahen's head, which felt massive in her hands.

Kneeling before Eva, whose essence had reincarnated into Miryam, with his head cradled to her bosom, the over-seven-foot tall Father of Sinisters still felt like the child he was during his days in the Garden of Aiden over 4,500 years ago. But Cahen did not say a single word. How could he? What could he say? This moment, this feeling, this… love was all that mattered. This was the woman who had shown him true, motherly love. And how did he repay her?

With murder.

Despite what he had done- an unforgiveable act- this woman was doing the unthinkable; offering forgiveness, healing and the same undying, unconditional and selfless love she once had, and apparently still have, for him. Heart clenching, body trembling, Cahen buried his face in her bosom and stained her pristine white, fitted gown with more tears of regret and sorrow.

"Cahen?" Miryam called softly and tilted his head slightly upwards so that the giant of a child would be forced to look at her in the eye.

Cahen opened his tear-streaming eyes and looked into Miryam's. She smiled, and Cahen was bathed in the purest, motherly love he had ever experienced. The tears flowed again and Miryam cradled his head on her bosom, again. Cahen could not stop sobbing and Miryam decided to let him take his time.

"I am so sorry, mother," Cahen finally spoke between sobs. "I am so sorry."

"Hush now, my boy. Hush," Miryam soothed the multi-millennial man as his tears left more wet stains on her white gown. "It's alright now. It's alright. That was in another lifetime-"

"Not for me," Cahen sniveled.

"Yes, I know, you silly man," Miryam caressed his cheeks. "Still, all is forgiven. Let this be a new day for both of us."

"Just like that?" Cahen sobbed.

"Just like that," Miryam nodded.

A few minutes later, the sobbing subsided, and Miryam pulled Cahen away from her bosom.

"Here. Sit next to me," Miryam indicated the open space next to her. "Your head is starting to feel heavy on my chest."

Cahen chuckled and wiped his eyes with the back of his hand and sat beside her, dwarfing her with his immense stature.

"Now, I want to know everything you have been up to, my son," Miryam said with hint of excitement.

His repertoire as Maduk preceded him, but she was more interested in what happened after he and Lithilia were cast away from the Garden of Aiden.

"After the-" Cahen began, but he could not finish his sentence. "After…"

"After that day…" Miryam offered.

She took his hand and gave it a gentle squeeze of encouragement. Her tiny hand vanished in his giant palm. Cahen would not look at his mother in the face. He was grateful for her encouragement. He returned her gentle squeeze with one of his own.

"Easy on the squeeze now, tough guy," Miryam joked and Cahen let go of her hand as one would let go of a hot metal rod.

"Oh, sorry mother."

Miryam laughed out loud.

"I'm just playing with you," she laced her fingers with his, which were almost twice the size of hers. "You couldn't hurt me even if you tried, big guy. I will lay you down flat like a rug."

Cahen laughed out loud and the slight trembling of his body ceased.

"And, my oh my, you've grown so big. Look at you," Miryam added, sizing up Cahen with her eyes for the first time, like a proud mother would her child. "What have you been eating? I mean, do you eat like a cow a day or what?"

Cahen smiled from his heart.

"There you go," Miryam added. "Now, where were we?"

"After that day," Cahen forced the words to come out stronger. "Mother took me to her home. She was living with the people of Inner Earth Realm. When she ran away from the garden, the day she struck father, she wandered aimlessly across the lands until she found, by accident, a strange cave at the foot of a hill or mountain. I could not remember which one she said it was. Anyway, for all I know, she could have spun the tale with false tongue."

Cahen eyes narrowed and Miryam felt his anger and resentment for his birth mother using clairsentience; a most unfortunate burdensome sentiment to bear for over 4,500 years. The poor child's sentiments were justified, though. She withdrew her hand from his and caressed his head. Her hand was tiny against his head, but her touch was solace to his soul.

"Go on, son," Miryam encouraged him.

"I am sorry I got carried away, mother," Cahen apologized and turned to look at her.

Miryam smiled and shook her head slightly. Cahen understood she meant there was nothing to be sorry for. He smiled weakly back at her.

"Your eyes, mother," Cahen said out of the blue. "They are white."

"Oh yes," Miryam chuckled slightly. "I change them to match whatever the color of the dress I am wearing. It's just something I do for the fun of it."

"Ah, I see," Cahen smiled. "I like this color, though."

"Thank you, my son," Miryam beamed.

"Apologies, mother," Cahen cleared his throat. "I got distracted."

"I'm happy you were," Miryam patted Cahen on the cheek. "Please continue."

"Right. The people of Inner Earth Realm were welcoming, especially to a child who was a psychological and emotional wreck," Cahen continued. "So, they decided to raise me as one of their own. They took good care of me, and as time went by, mother started becoming over possessive of me and jealous of our hosts because they were proving to be better at parenting than she was. But their best was nothing compared to yours and father's."

Cahen leveled a pair of droopy, sad eyes at Miryam. She was close, right there with him. Yet, he missed both her and father so much. Maybe his guilt was still getting the better of him. Maybe it was something else. Still, he missed the life they had together as a family.

Miryam smiled and nodded, as she continued to gently caress his head.

"I grew up to be someone worthy of the people of Inner Earth Realm's respect," Cahen continued. "I was their adopted son. It is funny. I am over seven feet tall. Yet, I was the shortest person in the realm."

"You turned out just fine, my boy," Miryam said. "You do know you're a giant among us on Earth Realm, right?"

"Thank you, mother," Cahen said. "So, after a while, I was told I was free to either stay with them or return to Earth Realm. Mother was reluctant to let me go. But at that point, it was not up to her. I was a full-grown adult and old enough to choose my own path. Besides, I was still furious at my mother for what she had done to me and for what she made me do. I still am."

He scowled and bowed his head in shame.

"It was like she hated everyone but me," he scowled, clenched and unclenched his fists. "She was angry at everyone but me. And she was extremely jealous of you, especially. You were the mother she could never be. You still are. She knew that then, and she knows that now. Told me enough times over the last thousand years. She was always insisting I stay hidden from you."

"Did she say why?" Miryam asked calmly as she retracted her hand from his head and let it rest beside her.

"She said you would end me if ever you saw me," Cahen bit his lower lip.

He closed his eyes and took a deep breath to gather himself before continuing.

"But deep down, I knew you would never do that to me. I knew you were still angry with me, but never to the point of ending me. You did not do it then and you certainly would not do it after all these years. Mother begged to differ, but I knew she was wrong."

Cahen turned a tear-filled gaze towards his mother and then added.

"There is never a single moment when I do not wish I could change the past. To reverse what I did. Better yet, to take the place of Ahben," Cahen sniveled and swiped the tears from his eyes. "The memory of your and father's love has been the only thing that has kept me going all this time."

Cahen fought back the tears, but the weight of guilt and regret was too heavy to bear. He broke down and wept again like a man-child. Miryam smiled and fought back tears of her own. It took every ounce of her strength not to feel the pain of her suffering son, despite the severity of his deed.

"I will never do anything to harm you, my son," Miryam reassured him. "It has taken many lifetimes for me to forgive you completely. Even then, I could never visit any harm upon you. Unfortunately, I can't extend the same sentiment towards your mother. We will talk about that another time."

Her eyes flashed with anger and the air around them suddenly grew warmer from her anger elevating the energy levels of the air molecules around them.

*Another time,* Cahen grinned for the first time since their meeting. *So I will get to spend more time with her in the near future. I cannot wait.*

"Oh, before you continue, why 'Maduk'?" Miryam asked.

"Just because," he shrugged. "No reason."

"Okay," Miryam raised an eyebrow. "I don't like that name, though."

"'Maduk' is for everyone else," he explained. "I will always be Cahen to you."

"Good," Miryam crossed her legs. "Please continue."

"As you wish," Cahen spoke more firmly. "So, I left Inner Earth Realm, and after teleporting to random locations, I settled with a small group of people in the south. They welcomed me into their midst. A year or so later, I took upon a mate for myself. Her name was Fasma. We had three children and lived a simple life. Neither my family nor anyone else in the land knew of my origins. I chose not to tell them because I was unsure of how they would react. Everything was peaceful until mother showed up."

"I can only imagine the scene she caused," Miryam smirked.

"Oh no, mother, you got it wrong," Cahen smiled and his tone of voice edged towards humor for the first time since their meeting.

"Pray tell, son. What did I get wrong, even though I said nothing yet," Miryam joked and nudged him in his thick, almost-concrete triceps. "Good heavens," Miryam exclaimed. "What are you made of? Granite?"

Miryam poked at Cahen with her index finger repeatedly and everywhere until Cahen started twisting and turning his body around.

"Stop," Cahen cried, desperately trying to stifle a laugh. "You are tickling me."

"Oh, please don't tell me all those muscles are just for show, you man-child." Miryam teased and poked some more.

Cahen chuckled some more as he tried to twist and scurry away from Miryam. Miryam chased him around until finally he reached around and held Miryam in a tight, gentle hug. Miryam tried to wrestle away from her son, but he held her firmly against his torso. Mother and son were laughing hard, just like when they used to play-wrestle in Aiden. Their hearts soared, their souls uplifted in a state of letting go and letting love. Cahen reluctantly let Miryam go a moment later. Miryam returned to her seat and shook her head at the thought of two multi-millennial beings acting like children.

"So, as I was saying," Cahen continued. "Mother did not just walk up to our domicile and knock on the door. She had to make a grand entrance. She chose one night and crashed into our land in the form of a huge ball of yellow-orange fire. Imagine everyone's reaction when they saw this flaming creature in the form of a human descend from the night sky, crash to the ground and then casually walk up to our domicile and call me out."

Cahen shook his head.

"Everyone else was terrified of this strange, flaming creature," Cahen added. "And everyone was more shocked than terrified when I walked up to this creature and started arguing with it. Among the many words we exchanged, everyone only cared about two: 'mother' and 'son'. Finally, mother stormed away. But her theatrics had caused irreparable damage to my new life. They feared me. That fear turned to aggression, and they came after me to stone me to death. After giving my human family one final look of goodbye and telling them telepathically that I loved them dearly, I teleported away."

"She must have planned it all along," Miryam interjected.

"Agreed," Cahen replied. "She does not want me to be with anyone but her.

She is extremely manipulative, hopelessly insane and very, newly powerful, too. Anyway, I met her that night in a valley and she told me she had discovered something important; that it was a new life and it awoke certain powers in her that she never knew existed. She said she wanted to show me, to bring me into this new life that she had just discovered. She wanted me to have what she had because I am the only reason why she lives and all the gibberish she usually says."

"And that was when you became a Sinister," Miryam interjected.

"That was when I became a Sinister," Cahen reiterated, and sadness filled his already empty gaze. "Mother kissed me that night, but it was not the kiss of a mother. It burned my essence away and replaced it with something that even mother did not expect. I cannot explain. All I know is that the kiss made me a subject of everything that I am not and everything that I do not want to be. It was a kiss of death and birth; death to an old life that I would have preferred and loved, and birth to a life that I never asked for and can never love."

"My curse upon you came to pass after all, my son," Miryam said sadly. "I am truly sorry. I have spent many lifetimes wishing I could take back those words I said and reverse the curse. I acted out of pain, anger, and grief."

"No, mother. No," Cahen interrupted and knelt in front of her. "Please, never ever apologize for anything. Whatever I am now is my own fault, and I am paying for it. If anything, you and father have been the only ones who have helped me stay sane. If I could rewind time-"

"You can't, and we both have to live with that," Miryam interjected.

Miryam kissed Cahen on the forehead, hugged him briefly and motioned for him to sit down.

"Please, continue, son," Miryam said.

"So, after my…transformation," Cahen sat next to her. "We were suddenly surrounded by a number of soldiers from Inner Earth Realm and without another word, they teleported us straight to their main court. There, mother was judged and found guilty of trespassing and desecrating the holy temple or something like that. I should have known that she would not just have 'stumbled' into this 'new life' without stepping on a few toes. Mother was banished for eternity from Inner Earth Realm, and because what she had done could not be reversed, her etheric self was manipulated upon to the point that she would not be able to hold any unique essence of her own. So, mother became something like…"

Cahen searched the right words to use to describe his mother's condition.

"A whore of essences," Miryam muttered. "I am sorry for using such a word to describe your mother. But that is all I could think of, unfortunately."

"I am not offended," Cahen shrugged his huge shoulders and scoffed. "And, as bad as it sounds, that aptly describes her condition. Your curse has certainly come to pass, again. To be honest, I do not feel bad that your curse came to pass on her."

"Anyway," Cahen continued. "I was told I could return to Inner Earth Realm only after I had returned to 'normal.' As a Sinister, I was no longer welcome amongst them. They understood that mother was at fault for what I had become and that I was innocent. It was they who offered me the sanctuary in another realm called Nimbu. Later, mother sealed off the realm in an esoteric field using one of her later acquired skills. I am unsure what she did or who she double-crossed to acquire those skills."

"I may have an idea, but we'll talk about that later," Miryam frowned.

"Okay," Cahen affirmed. "So, I was alone in Nimbu for a very long time until I received an unexpected guest one day; Nimrud, a descendant of mine. It was pleasing to have some company, though the circumstances of the encounter was less than favorable. Well, that is a summary of life after you, mother."

"You poor thing," Miryam said and squeezed his hand lightly.

Cahen smiled sadly. They sat in silence for a few seconds.

"I'm so glad to see you," Miryam said finally, her words dropping gently into the quiet.

"I am glad to see you, too," Cahen smiled and nodded. "I am finally starting to feel some peace."

"I know," Miryam agreed, "Your colors are changing."

Miryam adjusted herself in her seat, and her expression turned serious. Cahen immediately picked up on her change of mood..

"Is everything alright?" Cahen asked.

"For me, yes. I'm at peace with what I have to do and with what's coming," Miryam glowered. "I'm sorry, son, but your mother must pay. She's responsible for Ahben's death. There's no escape for her and she knows it. I'm at peace with that, and I just wanted to let you know her time has come. She is your birth mother and if you feel like you must do what you must, then please, by all means, proceed. I won't hurt you, but I cannot guarantee the same for Lithilia."

She turned a grim expression towards Cahen.

"Do you understand what I'm saying?"

"Yes, mother," Cahen replied firmly. "You do what you must. I will not stand in your way, and I am at peace with that as well. I do not hate my mother, and neither do I want any harm to come to her. But she has forged far more foes and fiends than friends to the point that all I can do is watch as her world becomes ever more complicated until it collapses upon her. Do what you must. I will not stand in your way, and neither will I judge you."

"Alright then, we have addressed one part of the situation," Miryam said.

"Now, I'm afraid there's one more thing you must know."

Miryam leveled her gaze at Cahen and just stared at him. In that moment of silence, with no words exchanged verbally or telepathically, Cahen knew exactly what Miryam was going to say.

"*No*," Cahen exclaimed and reeled backward as if his worst nightmare had just come to life.

"Yes, my son," Miryam said. "Ahben lives. He will seek you and he will find you. And when he does, there will be nothing anyone can do to protect you."

# THE END OF PART TWO

# PART THREE

## REMEMBER MY DEATH

**THE YOUNG SOUL** swam in a pool of total confusion and shock as it looked around the vast, endless and seamless whiteness that surrounded it. It whipped what it thought was its head around in frantic twists, trying to look for anything that it could relate to.

"Hello," a sweet, formless, omnidirectional voice called out..

Instinctively, it withdrew itself backward, or what it thought or remembered as itself. The young soul expected to hit a wall as it glided backward. But there was no wall and even no way to curl itself into a frightened ball. Instead, it buried its face in its hands, or at least, that was what the young soul thought it was doing. Its preconceived notion of its physicality was nullified in this strange… 'place.'

"I understand you are frightened and confused," the formless voice continued calmly, hoping to sooth the young soul's frightened consciousness as it had done a countless number of times to an innumerable number of other souls since the dawn of Creation. "It is a normal reaction for most souls like yours when they come here."

"I want father and mother," it choked out.

Then the young soul felt what it thought was a hand on its shoulder and it instinctively pulled back. It looked up and saw something with a male's face and the face feminine features? Telling the difference was too difficult.

"Please, do not be afraid, little one," the form said and summoned a smile. "See?" It spread its arms around and did a 360-degree turn. "I can look just like you. May I please sit next to you?"

Vibrations of tension and fear gradually seeped away from the young soul, replaced by vibrations of calm and peace. The young soul relaxed a little. After a short moment, the young soul nodded. The form perched next to the young soul in a Buddha posture.

"Do you know why you are here, youngling?" the sexless form asked with its sweet and calm voice.

The young soul shook what it believed was its head.

"I thought so," the form continued. "I will tell you everything and guide you all the way. Alright?"

The young soul nodded and relaxed what it thought was its shoulders.

"In your dimension, in your realm, where you lived, your existence has ended," the sexless creature said. "But because of the way your existence ended prematurely, without you fulfilling your purpose, your consciousness came here, to this dimension. Here, your consciousness will be rehabilitated and at the appointed moment, it will be released back into the lower realms."

"What about father and mother?" the young soul almost pleaded.

"You will not see them at this moment, youngling," the creature replied.

The young soul spasmed before it buried what it believed was its face in its hands and wailed. It felt as if, or so the young soul thought, the creature was putting its arms over its shoulders.

"You must come with me now, youngling," the sexless one said soothingly, pulling the weeping soul closer to its manifested form. "Be not afraid. I will take care of you, as I have done to many souls like you since the dawn of Creation. Your brother can do you no harm here."

After a moment's hesitation, Ahben's soul allowed itself to be led by the sexless stranger into the white, seamless, endless oblivion that would be his temporary new abode.

Sarael suddenly bolted awake, fury bleeding through her veins, heart racing wildly and body drenched in sweat. It was as clear from her anger and cry for vengeance that this was not a dream. It was a memory... *her* memory. A barrage of expletives exploded from her lips and she raged so intensely that her body temperature spiked to levels that dried off her sweat-drenched clothes almost instantly. Her own brother had killed her in cold blood. Sarael whipped her head to the side as she felt her mother's familiar presence at her bedroom door.

"My daughter, before you do anything..." Miryam spoke as calmly as she could. "There's something you first must know."

"There is only one thing I want to know, mother," Sarael seethed through clenched teeth as green flames engulfed her human form.

Sarael streaked towards Miryam, lifted her off the floor by her neck and pinned her to the wall.

"Where is my murderer?. *Where is Cahen?*"

# CHAPTER TWENTY

# MUTATION

**"YOU LOOK GOOD**, mother," Maduk said.

His back was to the door of his private chambers and his mother was standing at the door.

"Some special eyes you have," Lithilia snorted. "Wish I had them."

"Sarcasm aside, you forget my special talents come from you," Maduk replied coolly, turning around to face Lithilia. "You have been doing just fine all this time without eyes at the back of your head, have you not?"

"Something's off about you," Lithilia narrowed her eyes and searched his face.

"Happier than usual?" Maduk offered.

"Yes, that's it, actually," she agreed, her expression clearing for a beat before suspicion crept over her features like clouds obscuring the blue of the sky.

After all these millennia, Maduk was finally showing signs of a sentiment that had eluded him since; happiness. Lithilia shuddered at the thought.

"Care to share the reason behind this newfound happiness?" Lithilia sat in an empty seat.

"Some other time, maybe," Maduk replied dismissively and sat as well. "So, to what do I owe this visit?"

"Business as usual? Good," Lithilia made a mental note to revisit this subject later. "Time is upon us. I've been in touch with Zukael, The Beast, and I think we should move up our timetable."

"I thought we were not ready yet," Maduk said.

"So did I, but we can't wait any longer," Lithilia replied. "I have a plan, and I know it will work."

"Unless?" Maduk asked, raising an eyebrow.

"Unless Zukael refuses to cooperate," Lithilia replied with a maniacal smile. "He has no choice, though. I have something he needs; something that he would sell his soul to have, if he had a soul, that is."

"I trust you do," Maduk replied nonchalantly. "Your powers of persuasion are phenomenal."

"Thanks for stating the obvious, son," Lithilia spat sarcastically.

*I really raised an ungrateful brat*, she shielded her thoughts from Maduk.

"But there will be a problem," Maduk spoke and leaned forward in his seat. "If Sinisters are to take over, what happens to the demons? I know for a fact that Zukael does not plan on sharing power. So, how do we get rid of him and the demons at the same time?"

"Cut off the head of the snake," Lithilia replied confidently.

Maduk's eyes widened in utter disbelief.

"Are you really talking about ending Beelzebub?" Maduk asked. "I know you are a woman of remarkable capabilities and that, recently, you received a major upgrade. But taking on an archangel is not merely ambitious. It is plain insanity."

"Who said anything about ending him?" Lithilia asked. "Haven't I taught you repeatedly not just to hear but to listen? It's vital in this game of survival."

"Game…" Maduk scoffed, leaning back in his seat. "It is always just a game to you, is it not?"

"Your survival is all I care about-" Lithilia rebutted.

"Survival?" Maduk snapped. "What should I be so worried about? Better yet, who should I be so fearful of?"

*Right now, you are the only threat to me and my sanity*, he wanted to add, but changed his mind.

"You already know the answer to that," Lithilia replied calmly. "And for heaven's sake-" She cut herself off with a scowl. "Can't believe I used that word." Lithilia shook her head slightly before starting over. "For Creation's sake, stop acting like a spoiled brat."

"Now who is the one with the new attitude?" Maduk smirked and shook his head. "Just because you had an upgrade, you are suddenly a lot more confident and scheming for inevitable failure."

"I'll ignore your lack of faith, child-"

"I am *not* a child, Lilith," Maduk spat.

At the mention of her false name, Lithilia's eyes flared and she bared her teeth in fury. Maduk remained calm and stared at his mother. A few seconds later, Lithilia regained control of herself and her anger subsided just enough for her to continue talking.

"Only because you are my child," Lithilia muttered. "Only because you are my child...."

Lithilia inhaled and exhaled slowly a few times, a ritual she picked up from her prolonged stay with the humans of Earth Realm.

"As I was saying," Lithilia continued and shot a death glare at Maduk. "The plan is to eliminate the head of the snake; Zukael. By elimination, I don't mean ending the archangel. I mean granting him the one thing he wants the most, above everything else."

"To go home..." Maduk chimed in and nodded his comprehension of the magnitude of this unexpected possibility.

He cupped his chin and furrowed his eyes in thought.

"You can make him go back to his realm? Really?" Maduk raised his gaze towards his birth mother..

"Yes, I can," Lithilia replied.

"How?" Maduk asked. "I mean, do not get me wrong, I am aware you have extensive resources. But to undo a curse on an archangel and send him back where he came from is something else entirely."

"That's the part of the plan I won't share with you," Lithilia replied firmly. "You are my son, yes. But I don't think you can handle that part."

Maduk nodded his understanding. Protesting was pointless. Over 4,000 years of being his mother's son had taught him that. His mother was as stubborn as she was incorrigible and unapologetic. He tried to maintain a poker face and hoped that his mother was not looking at the colors of his aura that moment. He did not blame her for her reservations. Lithilia was adept at whatever she set her mind to. Being cautious was a default setting of hers. He would just have to trust her this one time only.

Maduk debated using his recent encounter with Miryam as a bargaining chip to earn Lithilia's trust.

*Some other time,* he decided.

He would wait and play things out. He smiled to himself. He was starting to think like his mother.

*The fruit never falls far from the tree, right?*

Maduk mentally scoffed at this human saying. A glance in Lithilia's direction revealed she had been observing him keenly, probably trying to listen to his thoughts using clairaudience, despite their agreement never to do this to each other. Maduk doubted if she ever held up to her end of the bargain, though. He, too, was guilty of trying to use clairaudience on her thoughts sometimes, though he never succeeded.

*She must be shielding her thoughts,* he surmised.

Maduk cleared his throat and squared his shoulders when their eyes met, and his smile turned into a grin. A suppressed scowl, the tightening of the corners of her lips and the narrowing of her eyes: all signs his mother was getting frustrated by something new about him.

*I am happy and she hates it*, he thought and did not care if she heard his thoughts.

Today, he would be the biggest tease she had ever encountered, he hoped.

"Do you have a backup plan, in case the snake's head fails to come off its body?" Maduk asked with the intent of distracting his mother from studying him the way she was.

It seemed to work as Lithilia blinked several times before replying.

"I do, actually. He should be here any moment now."

"Zukael?" Maduk asked, a little surprised, but he knew the answer already.

Maduk certainly did not expect an archangel in his domicile, let alone Zukael.

"Yes," she replied. "I used my powers of persuasion, as you aptly described, on him. I convinced him that I can only initiate the process of undoing his curse from here. It is not a lie, but it is not the whole truth. And whether Zukael believes me or not is irrelevant. He'll show up. His desperation is his pressure point and I'm manipulating that pressure point."

"So, why is he coming here, then?" Maduk could not contain his curiosity. "Or you will not be telling me about that as well?"

"He'll come here because with his help, we'll change your essence and you will become an upgrade," Lithilia replied. "Some of his angelic essence will blend with your Sinister essence. You will become as powerful, if not more, as an angel or archangel. And you will be my backup plan in case the head does not come off the snake."

Lithilia's eyes twitched. Only slightly, but enough for Maduk to catch it. It was hard to believe, but he saw worry in those cold eyes for the first time in a very long time.

*Mother's ambition may have smothered her sense of reason,* he feared.

He rose from his chair and walked around the desk that was in front of him. His gaze was fixed on his mother's eyes. Lithilia averted her own gaze. Maduk sat on the edge of the desk in his private quarters and leveled his gaze at his mother. She did not, or perhaps could not, look up.

"What are you going to do, mother?" Maduk asked firmly.

Lithilia stayed quiet, staring away. Maduk knelt in front of his mother and took her by the shoulders. She still would not look at her son. Maduk took Lithilia's chin and tilted her face towards his. Lithilia's eyes were filled with tears.

"Tell me," Maduk demanded dropping on his haunches.

"Please…" she swallowed and continued. "Please, don't make me do this. The plan is perfect, and it will work perfectly."

"You will tell me now," Maduk insisted.

Just then, a knock sounded at the door, and Nimrud poked his head inside.

"You have a visitor, my king," Nimrud said.

"Who is it?" Maduk snapped.

"He says his name is Beelzebub," Nimrud replied flatly.

He was numb to seeing son and mother in angry and even compromising dispositions sometimes. Nothing surprised him anymore.

"Send him in," Maduk ordered and rose to his feet.

Maduk glared at his mother one more time before returning to his seat. A few seconds later, enough time for Lithilia to dry her eyes and assume an everything-is-alright demeanor, the door opened wide, and Nimrud stepped in.

"My king. My queen. May I present to you, Beelzebub, King of Demons," he bowed and ushered Beelzebub in.

Nimrud left the room and closed the door. Maduk stood up, but Lithilia remained seated. Beelzebub exchanged quick nods with her before turning and facing Maduk.

"Welcome to my abode, Beelzebub," Maduk said in a monotone. "Or would you prefer I call you Zukael?"

"Any would be fine," Beelzebub replied with a tinge of impatience.

The two men exchanged a quick bow.

"I have come to cherish both names almost evenly," Beelzebub added.

Maduk sighed from Beelzebub's sarcasm. He felt his mother's warning glare on his face. Antagonizing Beelzebub right now would not be in their favor.

"Please sit," Maduk waved at an empty seat directly opposite from Lithilia.

Beelzebub expressed his gratitude and made himself comfortable.

"So, I understand my mother wanted us here together."

"Indeed," Beelzebub replied. "I do not trust her, but she has what I need: a way home."

"I am sure this dimension will miss your absence," Maduk replied with a smug look on his face. "You do realize that no one even sought your opinion regarding my mother's trustworthiness, right? So, the next time you feel like talking about my mother like that, flap your wings and shut your mouth, instead."

*I will suffer this disgrace until I am free of my curse,* Beelzebub reassured his splintered ego. *First, a human bested me in combat, next was the whore and now, the whore's spawn dares to insult me in my face. Does he know who I am? Does he know that I am The Beast, King of Demons?*

Beelzebub uncrossed and crossed his legs again.

*Their end will come, he promised himself. I will reserve something very special for these three when that moment is nigh. But as for the rest of humanity, none will be spared.* Beelzebub forced a smile.

"Why don't we proceed with business. You two can compare sizes later," Lithilia said and rose slowly from her chair.

Maduk met Beelzebub's glare with one of his own before they rose from their seats as well.

Maduk and Beelzebub followed Lithilia into Maduk's bedroom. Lithilia walked in front of them, and as she walked, she changed the movements of her neck, shoulders, arms, torso, hips, legs, and feet with each step. The changes were subtle, but the effect on Beelzebub was exponential. She was more than a pro at what she did best and the only immunity Maduk held over her mannerisms was the sole fact that he was her son.

*I am so glad I am not one of her victims. Beelzebub is already at her mercy. How she does that, I will never know, and I do not even want to know.*

Beelzebub's every desire to ravage the creature in front of him that stirred his loins thus was so palpable that it could light a match stick.

Lithilia was pleased with what she sensed in the fallen archangel. She was pleased at how vulnerable the king of demons was slowly getting wrapped around her fingers. She will never tire of this feeling; the feeling of power over another. They approached the bed, but instead of making herself comfortable on it, she made a turn towards a table to the right.

She let her arms hang at her sides, and her long, purple, silk gown glided slowly and softly towards the floor as if she was being disrobed by unseen hands. As the purple gown slowly slid towards the floor, it accentuated every single curve of her physique. Her shoulders became exposed, followed by her scapulae and down to her lower back. The gown continued its descent and when it got to the crack in her buttocks, Lithilia slowly turned around to face the two men. Beelzebub's stare flicked to her face. Lithilia was neither smiling nor frowning. But even a eunuch would have been hopeless to the lust that filled her eyes and electrified the chamber. Beelzebub was gone, and Maduk was speechless at just how easily his mother could make almost any man worship her, literally.

Beelzebub's gaze traced Lithilia's body, taking in every inch of her exposed flesh, from her neck, her ample, exposed breasts, her tight core and... and... Celestia be praised. He drooled from the feeling of staring at the most pleasurable, split triangle that ever existed. He tried to swallow, but even his throat seemed paralyzed. Lithilia took a step backward and slowly sat at the edge of the table. She parted her legs slightly, only slightly, but not before placing her left hand in between her legs, feigning support and concealing the promise of paradise that lay beyond that left forearm.

Beelzebub snapped angrily at her sudden gesture and whipped his head upwards. He glared at Lithilia, but only for the briefest moment until his eyes bore the desperation of a sorely, sexually deprived creature. Once again, her eyes rendered him completely helpless and useless, and he took an involuntary step towards Lithilia as if he were in a trance. As Beelzebub approached Lithilia, he made his garments disappear to reveal a naked and hardened archangel. The corner of her mouth curled into a half-smile as Beelzebub rutted against her arm in front of her crotch, pleading for safe passage into the promise of paradise covered by her arm. When Beelzebub could take it no more, Lithilia pulled the arm away and granted him access to the paradise he desperately sought.

Beelzebub moaned loudly as Lithilia accommodated him. She let him unleash his pent up sexual savagery in whatever way he wanted. The whole time, she held the archangel's head on her shoulder and stared directly into her son's eyes. Maduk stared back, but all he could see was his mother's eyes. Nothing else existed beyond those two orbs. Absolutely nothing else. Lithilia would not let her son watch her as she stole another creature's essence. His psyche had already been through enough and this will not add to the tally.

Lithilia had already given Maduk a part of Beelzebub's essence. But during the transfer, she noticed that the fallen archangel's essence had lost some of its purity. As such, she wanted the transfer of essences to be direct, thereby avoiding any loss of purity that may occur while she acted as a conduit for Beelzebub's essence. Plus, Lithilia also noticed that Maduk was slowly losing Beelzebub's previously transferred essence and Maduk was not even aware of this loss. Hence, Maduk had to be there in person and the transfer of essences had to be as direct as possible to maintain the purity of Beelzebub's essence.

Then, Maduk heard his mother say one word telepathically.

*Come.*

And Maduk obeyed.

Lithilia felt nothing as Beelzebub continued unleashing the carnage from his nether regions, completely oblivious to the rest of Creation. His pleasure built, reaching a crescendo as he approached his climax. Maduk walked slowly towards the pair, and Lithilia extended a hand towards him. He inched closer, and Lithilia took her son by the back of his neck. Beelzebub was thrusting more rapidly. He rammed away as Lithilia drew her son closer towards her. Mother opened her mouth and closed her eyes. Son opened his mouth and closed his eyes. As mother and son locked lips, Beelzebub exploded.

In his moment of explosion, in his moment of greatest pleasure, Beelzebub was most vulnerable. This time, his angelic essence drained from him with greater intensity as Lithilia syphoned copious amounts of it and passed it immediately to Maduk, who quaffed every ether of the cursed, fallen archangel's essence like a starving suckling at its mother's breast. Though Beelzebub wanted to pull away from Lithilia, he was powerless against her seduction and esoteric vampirism.

Every cell, every atomic and subatomic particle of Maduk's body exploded in a surge of energy as Beelzebub's imbibed essence merged with his, sparking a metamorphosis of his etheric makeup. This time, the surge of energy was more invigorating, exhilarating and intense. Maduk's eyes snapped opened and his body burned in a smokeless, non-consuming yellow-orange flame, which gradually turned into pale, golden-green flame. He grabbed his mother by the back of her neck, the conduit through whom Beelzebub's essence flowed, and pressed her lips against his even more. Lithilia freed her other hand from Zukael's back and grabbed her son by the back of his neck as well. Mother and son shared more than love. More than essence. More than life itself.

Zukael was sandwiched in between Lithilia's thighs, still powerless against the whore of essences.

After the completion of the upgrade to Maduk's essence, mother peeled her lips from her son's and gave a mission-accomplished smile at Maduk before teleporting both herself and Beelzebub away. She returned Beelzebub to his abode in the Grand Canyon as if disposing of trash in a dumpster before she teleported away.

*"Don't worry, Zukael,"* Lithilia's voice called out telepathically before Beelzebub could even begin to recuperate from losing so much of his essence. *"I always deliver on my promises and, at the perfect time, I will send you back home."*

# CHAPTER TWENTY-ONE

## PAST AND PRESENT

**TO SAY THAT** defeating Prince Natas, first demon spawn of Beelzebub, was Patrick's most important task was an understatement of lifetime proportions. This assignment was as personal as personal could get and the only appropriate response Patrick could summon then was fear. Yes, pure, unsullied fear. His present skillset summed to naught when facing the Prince of Demons. But as someone else, a previous reincarnation of his, he stood a far better chance at defeating Satan.

And therein was the problem. Patrick did not know how to 'summon' this past incarnation of his called Damas, the high priest. If he had his way, he would pass this assignment over to his mentor. No shame in doing that. Patrick was sure that Shi'mon would have handled Satan himself.

But it was imperative that Patrick faced Satan by himself. This was the next step in his training process; maybe even the final phase. Patrick remembered his supposedly once-upon-a-time best friend say they were linked forever. And he had seen the red-hot hatred in Satan's eyes and he had felt Satan radiate an aura of vengeance that could only be quenched by Damas' blood.

Patrick screamed an expletive.

Denial was futile. Even if Patrick wanted to discount the memory jog Satan had given him during their encounter in the cave, he still felt the burn on his back, where the power of Kundalini had curled along his spine as the essence of Damas overrode his essence. And what a rush of energy, of power beyond words, that was. Patrick had never felt anything like this before. Not even from Shi'mon teaching him about the Breath of Life or from his first bonding in the bedroom with Sara. Patrick managed a wry smile before he returned to reality.

Patrick was at war with a formidable creature of unrivaled notoriety. Of all the creatures in Creation, the creature known as Satan had to be his mortal enemy. No retreat, no surrender and seemingly no way out of this one. Fact: soon, one of them was going to die. He had stared in the face of death a countless number of times before, and he had spat in the face of death every single one of those times. Never had he ever been afraid. For someone who neither feared death nor clung to life, this new variable of fear of facing such a formidable for lent a whole new sensation to the inevitability that was death.

And yes, his mind was orange-red with overwhelming frustration. He dug his fingers into his scalp, wishing for a split second that he kept hair he could pull. What did he have to do to summon Damas, the nemesis to his nemesis? He felt as if he was hiking in pitch blackness with no sense of direction. He considered seeking Sara's help. But Sara had only lived in that area *after* his showdown with the possessed crown prince. She would not be of any more help than she had already been; saving his rear end.

He thought about reaching out to Marissa but decided against the idea. She already had problems of her own. Patrick closed his eyes and breathed in deeply. He held his breath for three seconds before slowly exhaling. He repeated the ritual five more times and then opened his eyes. He felt a little more relaxed. Still, no solution loomed in the horizon of hope for his dire-looking situation. Bottom line, he had to face Satan by himself and as Patrick, not Damas.

*"Having a rough day, I see,"* a voice called from his right via telepathy.

Patrick was neither startled nor surprised. The voice was familiar and friendly. Patrick was glad to hear the voice without a form.

"Hello to you too, Ashram," Patrick said.

*"Ah, the whims of youth,"* Ashram, the Hound of Creation, replied and the form of a larger-and-furrier-than-average wolf materialized next to Patrick.

It sat like the Sphinx at Giza, and Patrick unconsciously started caressing the impressive hound's thick, pristine white fur on its back. He loved the cackling sound and tingling on his fingers as a tinge of Ashram's energy played between his fingers and Ashram's fur. The Hound and the human stared quietly ahead for several minutes.

"Thank you, my friend," Patrick said, breaking the silence.

*"What for, Patrick?"* Ashram asked, as if he did not know the answer to his question already.

"For coming, even though I didn't call you," Patrick replied.

"No need to thank me. It was meant to happen," Ashram said. "I thought I would save us some time and show up sooner rather than later."

"You know me too well, old friend," Patrick said.

*"Do you realize you just said 'old friend' instead of the usual 'friend'?"* Ashram asked.

Patrick sighed and nodded.

*"That is an excellent sign."* Ashram continued. *"It means you are starting to remember, even if those memories may seem obscure at the moment. Or that you may still be in denial."*

"Yeah," Patrick sighed. "But, I don't know how to remember that far, and Father tells me time is of the essence; that the next cosmic dance is nigh. And what do my memories have anything to do with the next shift anyway?"

*"You will know soon enough,"* Ashram replied. *"Your mentor is correct; time is of the essence. That is why I am here; to help speed up the process."*

"Talk about perfect timing," Patrick said with a hint of exasperation. "No time like the present."

He rubbed his temples vigorously in a weak attempt to slow down his racing thoughts, while his chest threatened to explode from a distasteful concoction of fear, helplessness and hopelessness. He was fine with Ashram reaching out to him through clairsentience, a gesture which helped to ease his frustration a little.

*"Time is only an illusion, young man,"* Ashram said and rose to his feet.

Patrick's aura blended with Ashram's as Ashram walked to stand behind him. This was Ashram's doing because Patrick was unable to accomplish such a feat. He expected to feel hot, hound breath on the back of his neck.

"Oh, you don't breathe like we do," Patrick chuckled slightly when he did not feel any breath on the back of his neck.

*"This is going to hurt a little, but you can handle it,"* Ashram said.

"Between a little pain and the fate of humankind, easy choice," Patrick squared his shoulders, straightened his gait and nodded confidently. "Let's begin."

Ashram lowered himself to the ground and sat on his haunches. He then lowered his snout close to Patrick's occiput. He nudged the back of Patrick's head and Patrick angled his head forward in a slight bow so that the back of his neck was more exposed.

*"Are you ready?"* Ashram asked telepathically and closed his eyes.

*"Yes."*

Using the power of will, Ashram tapped into the Dimensions of Space and Time and sparked the ethers into an esoteric time-space bubble around Patrick and himself. To Creation, they were invisible. Even time and space did not have any bearing on them in that bubble. When Ashram opened his eyes, they shone with a bright, white glow. He then bared his fangs and roared the roar of a fierce lion as two of his upper canines became elongated. Then he sank them into the base of Patrick's skull. Patrick's scream was loud and painful enough to melt even the Devil's heart. Every nerve ending of his physical body was on fire as chi, supercharged more than a thousand times over the level he was used to, coursed through his body. Patrick's fingers dug into the concrete floor as if the floor was made of paper. But even that did not ease the pain. Right when he thought he was getting accustomed to the sensation, Ashram sank in his fangs deeper.

That was when a surge of energy… of power… of being… coursed through him. It flooded every atomic and subatomic particle of his protoplasmic constituency. His esoteric self became more alive than he had ever felt before. The pain was gone, leaving behind only one sensation: the sensation of being.

*So, this was what it felt like to be; not to exist, not just to be alive, but to just be.*

Patrick felt a connection to Ashram, the concrete floor, time, space, energy and the ethers, to everything and nothing. He was everywhere and nowhere. He was in the past, present and future in the same moment. He relished the sensation. He felt like he was home, like this was the only reality there was, is and ever will be. And then, his being echoed with one word: *remember.*

Patrick's eyes snapped open, completely glazed over and shining with a white brightness that dwarfed even the brightness of Solara.

\*\*\*

Patrick was a baby in another era. He lay in his crib in his parents' room. The rainy season was in full gear and the night was hot and humid. His parents slept with the windows open, as they did on most nights. The night air was cool, and the breeze gentle against his skin.

As Patrick slept, a form manifested out of the darkness; first, as a pair of glowing, white orbs and then the rest of the body followed. The light from a Realm of Lunis bathed the room. As Ashram walked towards the sleeping baby, the light caressed his thick fur, causing his fur to glitter like a sprinkling of a million diamond pieces. The baby roused in its sleep as Ashram licked its tiny hands. Then, the baby opened its eyes. It saw the Hound and giggled. Ashram licked its tiny hands again.

*"Hello, little Damas,"* Ashram said telepathically. *"Should you not be sleeping like most babies do?"*

*"I was waiting for you,"* Baby Damas replied telepathically.

*"I know, my little friend,"* Ashram said. *"You are making a lot of progress. I am proud of you. At this rate, you will grow up to become someone of invaluable importance to your kind."*

*"And you will be there to teach me, right?"* Baby Damas asked.

Ashram nodded and gently nudged the baby's hand back on its chest.

*"Sleep now, my future high priest,"* Ashram said. *"I will see you later."*

Baby Damas went back to sleep as quickly as he had awoken earlier.

The memories fast-forwarded to when Damas was six years old. He was returning from the market with his mother when a man, donning the garbs of a pauper, attacked them. But the man was no pauper. His hands and feet looked like those of a hawk without scales. His eyes were as black as night and without pupils. His fingernails and toenails were elongated and curled, and his face was like that of a lizard's.

The creature demanded Damas' mother hand over her coin purse, and as she frantically tried to untie the bag from her belt, the creature thought she was trying to play a trick on him. So, he shoved Damas' mother to the ground and reached for the coin purse himself. Damas, seeing his mother under attack immediately rushed to her aide. But the creature swatted him away like a fly. Damas landed hard on the ground twenty-four feet and immediately rose back to his feet.

A slowing heartbeat, sharpened vision, acute hearing, heating palms and a quieting mind. These were the sensations in Damas' body right before his vision flashed in blinding whiteness and every iota of his physical and non-physical self spasmed as a jolt of energy fired from his spine to the rest of his being. Intuitively, he knew something had just been awakened in him. Triggered by what? Damas did not know and neither did he care.

Damas raised a hand towards their attacker and uttered a few words in an alien tongue. The creature was immediately yanked away from his mother's body and lifted to more than thirty feet up in the air.

With a gasp of shock, Damas' mother turned towards her son and saw him with his hand raised towards the creature. His eyes were glazed over in whiteness and, even in the brightness of the day, Damas' eyes glowed brightly. His gaze was fixed upon the creature convulsing and riling midair in pain.

"Damas," his mother called out to him.

Her voice snapped him back to reality. Damas blinked, and his eyes returned to normal. The creature crashed on the ground and yelped in pain from a broken ankle. The reptilian-avian creature hurriedly limped away as Damas rushed towards his mother and helped her to her feet. That same evening, Damas and his family received an unexpected visit from the high priest. After about an hour of conversation with Damas' parents, Damas left his parents' house and went to live in the temple as a personal steward to the high priest.

Patrick watched, within the memory and yet outside it, as Damas grew into a very powerful high priest. With Ashram's help, Damas became wiser and more powerful with the passage of time. He saw Damas forge a strong friendship and brotherhood with Prince Natas. He saw Damas' friend become consumed by a savage lust for control and dominance. He saw Damas' friend become possessed and turn into the first demon spawn of Beelzebub. Patrick saw the first duel between Damas and Prince Natas at the palace. He saw how Damas followed every lead of any story about demons or possessions across the lands.

Patrick felt Damas grasping at the thinnest straws of hope for saving his friend, even if it was just his friend's soul. And even as Patrick felt the hope that Damas had then, he noticed that the same tinge of hope still lingered in him, buried in his subconscious mind. If he could feel that tinge of hope, if he could sense that longing to save his enemy, then those feelings must be coming from something, or someone else. Patrick nodded at this realization and opened his essence to be more receptive of this other presence that was lingering within him.

*"Perhaps it is time for you to let that go and face the reality that Prince Natas is a lost cause,"* a voice said inside of Patrick's head.

*"But there is still hope, even when there is no hope,"* Patrick replied.

*"And even if there is hope, sometimes, one must learn to let go of that hope,"* the voice rebutted. *"I know why you still hope, Patrick. But you must get past that."*

*"It was my fault, Damas,"* Patrick replied. *"I should have stopped him."*

*"I know how you feel, Patrick,"* Damas concurred, and his form manifested in front of Patrick. *"I remember. I was there."*

*"I should have stopped him,"* Patrick repeated as his eyes brimmed with tears. *"I should have done more to prevent him from undergoing the procedure."*

*"And since when did anything ever stop the crown prince?"* Damas asked. *"Perhaps I could have made more effort; but what would that have changed?"*

*"Nothing,"* Patrick replied. *"Nothing could have stopped Natas. He was even more stubborn than Papa Coshas' mule."*

Damas and Patrick broke into heavy laughter.

*"Oh man. You still remember that mule?"* Damas asked. *"I think that mule was the first demon spawn."*

They both burst into fits of laughter once again.

*"He made his choice,"* Damas said softly, referring to Satan.

*"And I have to clean up his mess… again,"* Patrick sighed.

*"Sounds like you could use some help with that, new self,"* Damas said. *"From what I can see, you have forgotten so much."*

*"Different times now, old self,"* Patrick said. *"But you're right. I could use some help."*

*"You forgot to say 'please',"* Damas teased. *"I think we will make a formidable team, would you not agree, old self?"*

*"The Terrible Trio at its finest,"* Patrick agreed.

*"Trio?"* Damas asked feeling a little confused.

*"Me, myself and I,"* Patrick explained, but Damas still did not get the joke. *"Boy am I glad I am not you anymore. Where is your sense of humor, old self?"*

*"Gone with the skills you lost, I suppose,"* Damas rebutted and smiled.

Patrick laughed a little.

*"Touché,"* Patrick nodded slowly.

A moment of silence crawled by before Patrick looked up at Damas with a very placid and peaceful expression on his face.

"*Thank you, Damas,*" he said. "*It's great to meet you officially. Now, let's go take care of the crown prince, shall we?*"

"*The pleasure is all mine, Patrick,*" Damas replied.

Damas extended his hand. Patrick nodded and took it. At once, the form that was Damas glowed into a blinding brightness and exploded as the consciousness that was Damas blended with the consciousness that was Patrick. In that fusion, the past and the present became as one, and when the fusion was complete, Ashram ejected his fangs from the base of Patrick's skull.

Patrick's eyes still glowed with a bright whiteness as he levitated off the ground. He extended the fingers of his hands and power danced between his fingers like flashes of electricity. Patrick let his feet touch the ground as he brought his hands in front of his face. He smiled at the new wave of energy and power pulsing through him.

Ashram nodded with pleasure at what he saw and moved to stand next to Patrick. He removed the time-space bubble around himself and Patrick while Patrick ran his fingers through the Hound's fur.

"This turned out a lot better than I had expected," Ashram said.

"This certainly is very different from what I remember," Patrick said. "Talk about an upgrade."

Patrick dropped to one knee and gazed into Ashram's eyes.

"Thank you, old friend. Thank you for helping me remember."

"You are very welcome, old friend," Ashram nuzzled against Patrick's hug.

"Now, if you'll excuse me," Patrick said as he peeled himself away from his hound friend, "I have a renegade demon to locate and liquidate."

***

Prince Natas hovered in the oblivion that surrounded the core of Earth Realm. The Scribe had shown him what to do when the time came. But he still could not understand why The Scribe could not do it himself, even after The Scribe made mention of something about not having any direct influence in the affairs of the cosmic bodies in Creation.

*Fine.* Prince Natas could let that go. But why did he have to wait? He was ready, according to The Scribe. Yet he had to wait? *Damn The Scribe.* Prince Natas had tried to go ahead and take care of business. But he could not even come near the core; the name he had given that spherical ball of energy. He had to wait until the perfect moment for the next wave of consciousness to flood all of Creation.

Satan stared thoughtlessly at the core. Something soothing and empowering about this energy center felt both seductive and addictive to him. And while he relished the sensations of this core, a familiar energy signature interrupted his private moment.

"By the stars. I cannot believe this," Satan exclaimed. "It is you. Finally. It is you, old friend."

Satan turned around and grinned with excitement.

"Hello, old friend," Patrick said flatly. "What are you doing here?"

"How did you find me?" Satan asked, ignoring Patrick's question. "He said no one would be able to find me here."

"You forget that when I banished you, we became eternally linked?" Patrick asked rhetorically and rolled his eyes.

"Which was severed during our battle in the cave," Satan interjected.

"Oh yes," Patrick recalled. "Well, I traced yours. How about that?"

"It really is you," Satan sneered with evil delight. "Finally, my vengeance will be perfect, and you will not be there to stop me when I wipe away humanity as you know it."

"Let's wrap this up, Natas," Patrick said coldly. "You know why I'm here."

Patrick blinked, and his eyes became two bright, white orbs.

"I know you will try," Satan replied. "But this time, I will end you."

Satan blinked, and his eyes became two black orbs. Both men clenched and relaxed their fists. As they did, a ball of black light formed in each of their hands and, like a synchronized dance of death, both men charged towards each other.

# CHAPTER TWENTY-TWO

# GAME PLAN

**"PLEASE, MY LOVE!"** Miryam pleaded.

She was calm in the face of Sarael's rage.

"Don't you dare," Sarael fumed, still pinning her mother to the wall by the throat. "I can't even believe you're trying to protect him."

"I believe what you should be asking yourself is why are you suddenly so angry over something that happened thousands of years ago," Miryam said.

"Because I just remembered and that refreshes everything," Sarael replied, tightening her grip on her mother's throat.

"You realize that whatever you think you're doing to me is pointless, right?" Miryam said calmly.

With a shake of her head, Sarael released her grip on her mother's throat and did a backward zombie walk to the nearest chair she could find. Miryam remained hovering in midair. When her daughter sat down, Miryam glided towards Sarael and cautiously sat next to her. She waited for a moment, doing nothing but staring at her daughter. She reached for Sarael's hand, but Sarael yanked it away.

Miryam sighed.

"Please listen to what I have to tell you."

"If it's not his location, then I don't want to hear it," Sarael spat.

"And I will tell you, but please-"

"Location," Sarael ordered.

"As you wish," Miryam resigned and straightened her white gown.

Sarael stared blankly ahead, her breathing heavy. She could feel her mother's gaze beckoning at her to turn around and face her. But she resisted. She knew if she faced her mother now, she would succumb to what she had fondly come to describe as her mother's sorcery.

*No, not this time,* she encouraged herself.

"Will you at least look at me?" Miryam asked

Sarael hesitated for a few heartbeats before she obliged, but she could not hold her mother's gaze. She cursed silently.

"Look into my eyes and see your wish fulfilled," Miryam said. "Look into my eyes and find the location of your murderer."

Sarael immediately met Miryam's gaze and held it. A connection was formed between mother and daughter as a thin beam of green light slowly migrated from Miryam's white eyes to Sarael's. With words unspoken, Miryam gave her Cahen's location. And, with words unspoken, Miryam pleaded with Sarael to trust her and not exact vengeance on Cahen, yet. When the transmission was complete, Miryam blinked and Sarael disappeared with that blink.

Miryam shook her head in resignation and tried to come up with a backup plan in case Sarael's current state of mind was going to offset her training. As Miryam's mind raced in every direction, Yehuda appeared in the doorway, bearing the look of someone about to deliver word of unhappy tidings.

"Is it time already?" Miryam asked calmly.

"Yes," Yehuda replied with a grim expression. "We've just received word from Yaakov. The Sinisters are getting ready for an all-out attack."

"Then let's go make sure they fail," Miryam said.

Miryam and Yehuda teleported away.

***

Maduk summoned his grandson, Nimrud, and Yaakov into his chambers.

"Your highness," Nimrud and Yaakov greeted and bowed their heads.

"Sit, you two," Maduk ordered.

The two generals slid into the two chairs in front of them, facing Maduk.

"If I may be so bold, my king," Nimrud said. "There is something different about you."

"Good or bad?" Maduk asked with indifference.

"Very good, your highness," Nimrud replied. "Very good, indeed."

Nimrud hesitated for a second, as if he wanted to ask Maduk something but changed his mind. Maduk nodded dismissively.

"I called you two in here because our plans have changed and the timetable just moved up," Maduk explained. "We are going to initiate our assault soon. The moment has come for the people of Earth Realm to know their time is up and our time is now."

"I could not agree more, your highness," Nimrud chimed in with an overdose of excitement. "Just say the word, and I will lead the attack."

"You will not lead the attack," Maduk replied.

Nimrud bolted forward and let out and expletive, unable to hide his shock. He glared at Maduk and gripped the handles of his seat. Maduk let a few seconds pass before he delivered his punchline.

"Yaakov will lead the assault. He has earned that honor. I have something else planned for you."

Yaakov's eyes bulged in surprise and confusion, and his jaw dropped slightly. He swallowed nervously but said nothing. In the presence of Maduk, he will only speak when spoken to.

Nimrud, however, glowered at Maduk and increased his grip on the handles of his seat until his orange knuckles turned yellow. The handles of his seat came off and he flung the broken pieces on the floor. Fear of his grandfather and respect for his leader were discarded into a dungeon of burning anger and fury. How could Maduk betray him like this?

*For Nimbu's sake, I am his flesh and blood,* Nimrud agonized internally. *What did I do to make him visit such humiliation upon me?*

Nimrud realized that, in the end, he was in the presence of Maduk and the only reason he was still alive after his theatrics was because Maduk was giving him special treatment.

*Family...*

As such, he dared not challenge his ancestor. Such a foolish move will not end well for him. He will play this one out. But soon, Earth Realm will be his. After all, was that not what he had set out to do before his incarceration in these squalid environs of a realm?

He was a warrior. A leader. A conqueror. He took orders from no one but his ancestor... for the moment. He had been patient these millennia as second to Maduk and he could extend that patience a little longer. His time will come and he will make his move. Maduk will be dethroned and imprisoned for all the realm to see, while he, Nimrud, will rise as the new leader.

Nimrud had often wondered if he would execute Maduk publicly or just keep him as a prisoner. Execution would send an instant message to the rest of the realm, which could be quickly forgotten in the annals of history. But if he kept Maduk as a prisoner, it would serve as a constant reminder to the rest of the realm of how great, wise and powerful he, Nimrud, was. Nimrud had fantasized about this day countless times, the day when he would have to choose between a public execution and imprisonment of Maduk. He had looked forward to that day. And just when the day was nigh, Maduk had delivered a low blow to his ego. Yaakov was no match for him, despite proving his loyalty and leadership over their short time together. Still, Maduk's deed was unforgivable.

Nimrud's first few decades in Nimbu had been tough; emotionally, mentally and psychologically. He had to reconcile the aberration between his plans to conquer the realm and his new reality as a prisoner in Nimbu. Worse, that new reality might last an eternity. Nimrud had dived into a dark and deep depression, which he would not reveal, for fear of looking weak in the eyes of the others. Half a century later, Maduk had alluded to a plan to not only return to Earth Realm but to take it. And in Maduk's allusion, Nimrud had found renewed hope, as well as new opportunities to seize.

He would have to proceed cautiously. Instead of doing all the heavy lifting that he was accustomed to doing, he would remain Maduk's second-in-command. And when Maduk had done all the heavy lifting, he would deal a final and fatal blow to Maduk.

*"Yaakov also has to go,"* Nimrud thought. *"His death will be a waste of great strength and wisdom. Unfortunately, it must be so. He would have made a formidable ally, but in the future Earth Realm that will be ruled by Sinisters under my leadership, I cannot afford to have any form of competition. There can be only one leader, one ruler, one god."*

Nimrud once considered sharing his plans with Yaakov. But the risks were too great. Yaakov's loyalty to Maduk was pure and genuine; meaning Yaakov had no ambition of usurping power for himself eventually. And with Maduk gone, Yaakov's profound loyalty would have to be directed somewhere else. Who was to say that Yaakov would not be seduced by the notion of being the leader of the Sinisters, corrupted by the thought of total dominion? After all, Yaakov was once human, just like Nimrud himself had been, and a common trait existed in every human that not even the Sinister essence could erase; greed. Thus, Yaakov would not only become his competition; Yaakov might also become his nemesis and that was unacceptable.

"Nimrud?" Maduk called, wrenching Nimrud back to the present.

"Yes, your highness," Nimrud had to hold in a sneer.

"Is everything alright?" Maduk asked.

"Yes, your highness," Nimrud replied with more confidence than required. "I await your instructions on your special assignment for me."

Maduk eyed Nimrud for a few seconds before nodding slowly.

"I will get to that later," Maduk said. "As I said, Yaakov will lead the attack. And with that in mind," Maduk turned his attention towards Yaakov. "Be on the constant alert. Have the men and women ready. There will be no room for error. We will begin with that organization. Once we take them out, the rest of the realm will be ours to ravage."

"I will not fail you, your highness," Yaakov spoke firmly, hoping that Nimrud would not detect his lie.

Nimrud's eyes narrowed, and the corners of his mouth twitched for just a split second before he forced himself to maintain his composure.

"I trust you will not, Yaakov," Maduk said and leaned forward. "For your sake, at least."

Maduk's voice carried a sternness to it that would have made icicles grow on the spine of any other Sinister: but not on the spines of these two. These two were as tough as they come, and they were already accustomed to the many facets of their fearless and ruthless leader. Maduk leaned back in his seat.

"Dismissed," Maduk waved at Yaakov.

Yaakov stood up from his seat.

"Your highness," Yaakov bowed, turned around and walked out of the room.

When Yaakov was outside, he took long strides down the hallway. He nodded curtly at some Sinisters who saluted him as he strode along.

*"Brother,"* Yaakov said telepathically. *"Maduk will make his move anytime now."*

*"I'll let the others know,"* Shi'mon replied telepathically. *"Just give us the word, and we will be there."*

Back in Maduk's private chambers, Maduk waited a few moments as he stared at the door. As if deciding that it was then safe to have a conversation with Nimrud, he tore his eyes from the door and zoomed in on Nimrud.

"Speak your mind," Maduk said flatly.

Nimrud recoiled slightly from shock.

*What in the name of Nimbu is happening?* He thought. *Is this a trap? Some sort of test?*

"I am not sure I understand," Nimrud replied.

"I have known you long enough," Maduk said. "So, go ahead. Tell me what is on your mind. And fear not; I will not take any offense to whatever you say."

"Very well," Nimrud said and adjusted himself in his seat. "I think I should be the one leading the charge, not Yaakov. I deserve as much for all the centuries of service I have placed at your feet. Apart from you, there is no other who could be better suited to lead this charge. I cannot help but feel humiliated, betrayed and dishonored by your choice of that youngling, Yaakov, over your own flesh and blood."

Nimrud felt his voice begin to rise and decided to end his rant before things got out of hand. Maduk may have promised to 'not take offense' but he could not trust Maduk entirely.

*Best to be as cautious as a snake,* Nimrud thought.

Maduk nodded. He brought his hands in front of his expressionless face and tapped his fingertips repeatedly against one another for a few seconds.

"Like I said, your mission is special," Maduk spoke slowly. "To start with, we will not be striking at the members of the organization in their lair. We will be striking them here, in the Realm of Nimbu."

He paused as Nimrud's eyes widened in surprise.

"The members of the organization will come here to attack us," Maduk continued. "We outnumber them greatly, and even if, by some insane stroke of luck, they manage to go through our numbers, they will not go through me. Your initial observation was correct. Something about me is different."

"Forgive me," Nimrud interjected and swallowed. "But how can you be so sure that they will come to us when they do not even know where we are?"

"Because if everything is going according to plan, right now, they are gearing up for an all-out assault on us as a pre-emptive strike," Maduk replied.

Nimrud's eyebrows furrowed as he tried to make the connection. Suddenly, his head snapped upwards as the meaning of Maduk's words became clear to him.

"I cannot believe this," Nimrud exclaimed.

"Believe it or not," Maduk said. "Yaakov is their informant and a traitor. He will relay my signal to them and, when his friends attack, we will decimate them."

"I love this plan," Nimrud smiled. "But, how will he inform them?"

"Telepathy," Maduk replied.

"What is that?" Nimrud's eyes popped in confusion and surprise.

"The ability to communicate using thought," Maduk replied patiently.

"Oh," Maduk did not know what else to say.

But his mind exploded with a barrage of questions:

*How did Maduk know about telepathy?*

*Can Maduk communicate using telepathy?*

*What else does Maduk know and what else can he do?*

*If Maduk can communicate using thought, does that make him a god then?*

*YES,* he concluded.

Nimrud burned with an all-consuming fire of excitement. The last time he felt this way was when he was building the Tower of Babel. The gods had dealt him a low blow back then, but right here, right now, Creation had presented him with the perfect platter of retribution: a real, live god sat directly in front of him.

*The tales were true then. I am a product of a union between a god and a human.*

Nimrud shifted in his seat in an attempt to contain his excitement for this most joyous revelation.

*At last, I shall have Earth Realm beneath my feet,* Nimrud rejoiced within. *Then, I shall build another tower to the heavens. And, when I am there, I shall cast Maduk's severed head in front of them and feast of their fear before I strike them down one by one.*

Nimrud cleared his throat when he noticed Maduk staring patiently at him, as if studying him. Or was Maduk listening to his thoughts? He almost panicked at the thought.

*If that was true, then I would have been dead already,* Nimrud assessed.

"What is my mission then, your highness?"

"On my command, you are to eliminate Yaakov," Maduk replied with cold nonchalance. "Do you think you can do that?"

"With absolute pleasure… father," Nimrud replied and smiled maniacally.

# CHAPTER TWENTY-THREE

## SINS OF A SIBLING

**SARAEL PACED BACK** and forth in the valley. She thought by now she would be picking up her killer's etheric signature. Nothing. She ignored the sweet smell of freshness around her. The peace and quiet that enveloped these rich fields somewhere in some countryside in New Zealand; whatever the name of the location was, did not strike her fancy. Nothing was more important than seeing her mission accomplished. But her killer was not here like her mother had said he would be. Sarael punctuated her back-and-forth pacing with many expletives. Her patience was wearing thin.

She picked up some movement about a mile away and enhanced her vision for a clearer image.

*I hope it's you, you freaking murderer,* Sarael thought, referring to Cahen.

She let out an expletive when she saw a rabbit was the cause of the movement.

By the stars. Why did Cahen kill her? She had done nothing wrong.

Sarael gamboled between referring to herself in the present as Sarael, and the memory of her past life as Ahben. Ever since the memory of the situation – No. It was murder, not a situation. – returned, she had been torn between these two essences. Granted, the consciousness in her body was the same, but the identities were different. And these two identities riled within her. She was Sarael and Ahben in one body. The identity of a past life, Ahben, had been reborn in her.

*Enough with the mental banter.* Sarael screamed at herself.

Mother. Perhaps mother was playing a trick on her in the name of training? Mother always seemed to know what was best for her, did she not? Granted that drove Sarael insane sometimes. Despite everything, from her pride, insolence and everything else, mother had never steered her wrong. She had always had the best intentions for her daughter, had never failed her. Had, annoyingly, always been right. And most of all, mother will always be her mother. Their relationship was unconditional and undying. Sarael sighed. She had let her emotions get in the way of something mother was trying to tell her, yet again.

*Where in the name of the stars is Cahen, damn it?*

For heaven's sake. She, Sarael, was a bi-millennial woman; not a child. So why did she still feel like a child when it came to her mother? Why? Why? Why? The answer: because it was mother. Only mother could have that effect on her. It was not a bad thing, per se, but it was… Sarael searched for the right term.

*Whatever.*

Sarael thought about calling out to Patrick. Maybe if she talked to him, she could see things more clearly. For a young mortal, Patrick was a lot wiser and more mature than his peers. She smiled shyly as some mischievous thoughts wormed their way through her mind briefly. She shook herself back to reality.

*But he seems like a nice guy… No. Stop. We're here for business.* Sarael snapped at herself. Or was it Ahben? She said 'we'. *Come on, Cahen. Show that animal self of yours so I can get this over with.*

Sarael decided to reach out to Patrick and seek his counsel. He would be able to bring some Zen into the situation, or so she thought.

Sarael reached out by telepathy. No response. She tried again but failed.

*This is odd.*

She tried to trace his etheric signature. Nothing.

*I hope…* she could not finish her thought.

Sarael bit her lower lip and furrowed her eyebrows. It was one thing to be unable to reach someone via telepathy. But when one's etheric signature was untraceable, it could mean one of two things: either the creature's etheric signature was being blocked, knowingly or unknowingly, or the creature was…

Sarael swallowed and her heart raced. For a moment, she forgot why she was in the valley. Maybe Patrick was somewhere that was shielding him. Sarael bit her lower lip again in worry as she paced back and forth. She had only known Patrick for a short time and yet, the idea of the worst befalling him was one that she could not afford to even fathom. Patrick was the one person, in recent times, she could call a friend. And for something that bad to have happened to him… She shuddered at the thought. Finally, Sarael steeled herself, returned to her main reason for being there and reached out to her mother. She could not afford to be distracted from her mission.

*"Mother?"* Sarael called telepathically. *"I still don't see my murderer."*

Sarael's rudeness was even palpable at the telepathic level.

*"That's because he's not there,"* Miryam replied. *"Not yet, anyway."*

*"More of your games?"* Sarael snorted.

*"I'd entertain your childishness if I could,"* Miryam scolded. *"But I have neither the time nor patience for that right now."*

Sarael knew she had overstepped her bounds. She had not heard her mother use this tone of voice in a very long time.

*"I'll tell you this much,"* Miryam continued. *"I've been shielding your etheric signature all this time for your own protection, until such a time when I deemed that you were ready. But now, I will remove the shield. As soon as I do, you will get your wish."*

Sarael could feel Miryam sigh heavily before her mother continued.

*"Cahen will come to you and, just so you know, he may not be the only visitor you will be getting,"* Miryam said. *"His mother may also show up. You've never seen her, and I can assure you that she is not someone you'd want to have any form of association with."*

Miryam paused to let the ramifications of what she had just said sink in.

*"On that note, young lady,"* Miryam added. *"I'll let you have your wish while I go take care of more pressing issues; issues related to Earth Realm and the rest of humanity."*

*"Mother, please,"* Sarael called out as she sensed her mother was about to break the link. *"Could you at least tell me what it is you're working on right now that's so important? I'd like to know, please."*

*"I'd be glad to tell you everything,"* Miryam replied calmly. *"But given your recent display of poor judgement in getting your priorities right, it's clear that you're definitely not ready for this. Besides, I tried to tell you already, and of course, nothing is more important than your need for instant gratification in the revenge you so desperately seek. Anyway, good luck to you."*

And with those words, Miryam broke the telepathic link.

Sarael dropped to her knees and bowed her head, feeling even more foolish than ever. Again, mother was right. Again, she had taken mother for an opponent to outsmart instead of working with her as the best teammate there ever was.

Where was her father when she needed him the most?

But as soon as she started the train of thought, she remembered how her mother used to tell her to take responsibility and stop blaming everyone else. Her father was not around, but that was no excuse to act like a child. Suddenly, Sarael became fully alert. She sprang to her feet and waited. She felt it, a most familiar presence she had not felt in a very long time. In that moment, every last vestige of reason left her and once again, a savage thirst for vengeance consumed her.

"Hello, Ahben," a very masculine voice calmly greeted her from behind.

Sarael felt a presence loom over her as her visitor manifested behind her.

Sarael turned around slowly and lifted her eyes to meet her visitor's.

"It has been a very long time, brother," Cahen said.

***

"Are you sure you have no reservations about taking care of Yaakov?" Maduk asked, already knowing the answer to his question.

"If you want it done now, just say the word," Nimrud replied.

"Very well," Maduk said. "I wanted to make sure. But remember, you make a move only when I give the signal. Is that understood?"

"Yes, father."

"Nimrud?" Maduk spoke slowly but sternly. "*Only* upon my signal."

Maduk leaned forward and shot Nimrud a hard stare.

"Do you understand?"

"Yes, father," Nimrud replied more slowly. "I will only do as you wish."

"Good," Maduk leaned back in his seat. "Dismissed."

Nimrud stood up and bowed before he turned around and left Maduk's chamber, shutting the door on his way out. Maduk sighed and shook his head.

*The poor fool must think he is very smart,* Maduk said to himself.

Maduk was fully aware that Nimrud coveted his throne. Nimrud was the same arrogant fool he was from the first day he stepped foot into the Realm of Nimbu. Clairaudience always had its benefits and Maduk was clairaudient. Not much had changed about the brat, but he will deal with that later. Nimrud was family, but when survival was paramount, nothing else mattered. Not even family.

Nimrud was past redemption and thus, Nimrud had to die. This was where Yaakov came in. Maduk had been fascinated by Yaakov from the start, wondering where Yaakov obtained his skills from. There was more to the 'From constant training, my king' response than Yaakov was sharing. Anyway, Yaakov will have to be the facilitator to Nimrud's fatality, and if Yaakov failed, then he, Maduk, will have to do the work himself. Nimrud was a bad seed that had to be discarded from the sinister populace. Mother Miryam and her compatriots would just have to suffer a loss, in case Yaakov fell by Nimrud's hands.

Suddenly, Maduk bolted upright in his seat. He could not believe what he had just sensed. It was a most familiar etheric signature; one he had not felt in a very, very long time. He stood and breathed in deeply. Finally, the day he had long waited for had come. Maduk vanished, teleporting towards the etheric signature emanating from one who would be his judge, jury and maybe his executioner.

***

"Yes, Cahen, it has been a while," Sarael took a step towards the much larger frame of the creature in front of her. "You look different physically. But your face and filth are still the same."

"You changed a lot," Maduk replied.

"You don't have the right to call me 'brother' after what you did to me," Sarael hissed through gritted teeth.

"The truth is, regardless of what you say or do right now," Maduk replied softly and calmly. "You and I are brothers. We share the same father and your mother was, and still is, as much of a mother to me as she has been to you."

"There's more to family than genetics," Sarael hissed again and took another step towards Maduk. "You have no idea what that is. Family does not murder family in cold blood."

"I see a lot of mother in you," Maduk spoke softly. "She taught me about family in more ways than one. But that is not why I am here, brother-"

"Don't call me that!" Sarael yelled.

She grabbed Maduk by the throat suddenly and levitated off the ground with him as her eyes flashed green.

"Before you exact your vengeance," Maduk spoke calmly. "I ask that you listen to what I have to say."

Maduk's calm reminded Sarael that her grip on his throat had no effect on him, just like it did not affect her mother. She released him.

"Thank you," Maduk remained in the air. "Ever since the... incident-"

"Murder," Sarael snapped. "It was *murder*, not an incident."

"Ever since..." Maduk hesitated before he continued. "The betrayal, I have never been the same. I have lived a life of unhappiness, regret, pain, and sorrow for many millennia until recently I found peace. Mother summoned me. I had not seen her since that day. Just being with her brought me peace."

Maduk had lowered his eyes, but he raised them up as he continued.

"So, I am a man at peace. I know happiness and unconditional love once again and if I die right here, right now, then I die in peace."

He swiped at tears on his cheeks as he slowly glided towards to ground.

"No matter what you do to me today, I am a man at peace. Not only because mother forgave me for what happened that day, but also because Creation has granted me the opportunity to be in your presence again. And even if this may be the last time I may see you, I rejoice in it wholeheartedly."

Maduk then dropped to both knees. He dug the fingers of his right hand into the ground and scooped up a handful of fine, black, volcanic dirt. He stripped his shirt with his left hand and rubbed the dirt across his chest in two directions so that the dirt traced a faint, black X across his chiseled torso. Then, he looked up at Sarael, who stared down at him with cold indifference.

"I am at peace because I have finally gotten the opportunity, the one chance I would give anything to have, to tell you how sorry I am and to ask for your forgiveness," Maduk continued. "My plea for forgiveness may mean nothing to you, but that is alright. My heart soars with joy and today, I feel reborn."

Sarael remembered a day in the Garden of Aiden when she, as Ahben, had a very bad fall and had sprained her ankle. She was wailing from pain and had called out to Cahen instead of her mother. She recalled the look of concern on his face as he crouched next to her and gently took her ankle in his hands. She winced and wailed some more from the pain.

And then, Cahen had met her gaze. The worried look on his face had gone and his smile was as radiant as it was a panacea to her ailment. Somehow, the pain in her ankle subsided significantly as Cahen reached out and caressed his head.

"It is alright, little brother," Cahen had said. "Here, I will carry you on my back to Grandfather. He will make all this go away in no time. Alright?"

Sarael, as Ahben, merely nodded, lost in the all-consuming love that radiated from her elder brother's eyes. He wiped her tears away before picking her up as gently as he could and setting her on his back. Sarael saw that same look in Maduk's eyes right now.

Did Cahen literally take the pain away from her ankle with his loving touch? Sarael considered the possibility and, for an instant, her heart melted and shed the skin of vengeance that had smothered it. But only for an instant because she remembered why she was here in the first place and her heart blackened with a demand for revenge and retribution that could only be quelled by Maduk's blood and death.

"That was then, this is now," she hissed to herself, eliciting no reaction from Maduk. "Today you die, you animal," Sarael flared with a slight tremor of hesitation in her voice.

"As you wish, brother," Maduk replied as he rose from the ground. "I did not expect you to forgive me. Still, I am sorry. I can never be sorry enough."

Maduk sighed heavily and tilted his head towards the sky and closed his eyes. Slowly, he returned his gaze towards Sarael. A solemn serenity graced his features, testifying to his claim that he truly was at peace with himself and that nothing would take away that gift he had craved for so many millennia.

"You will have your wish. But it will have to wait, unfortunately," Maduk said. "There is something I must do first, and after that, I will willingly give myself over to you. My life will be in your hands."

Maduk wiped away more tears that trickled down his face. His heart was still too heavy with guilt and regret despite being at peace that he had finally gotten to meet his reincarnated brother.

"I do not cry out of sadness or the fear of my impending death," Maduk continued. "I cry because I am overjoyed to see you again."

Maduk sobbed lightly and summoned new garments over his bare torso. Sarael stared at him, torn between giving Maduk a quick death or to make him suffer first.

"I have missed you so much," Maduk said.

"Can't say the same for you," Sarael scoffed.

"Justifiably so," Maduk replied and straightened himself. "Unfortunately, I must leave now. I swear to you, when I have done with I must, I will return and hand my life over to you. But for now, I must go."

"And who said I was gonna to let you go?" Sarael asked as green flames spewed forth from her eyes.

"I will not fight you," Maduk replied. "But I will be forced to defend myself, should you continue to let your vengeance blind you to the immense dangers threatening the rest of humankind."

"I've heard enough," Sarael yelled and charged.

Maduk watched as Sarael cocked her fist. Relative to him, she moved in slow motion. He took a step to the left and inclined his body. The space between his body and the path of Sarael's punch, heavy with supercharged chi energy, became electrified, giving off tiny sparks of energy. Her missed attack left many areas of her body open on which he could inflict significant pain and damage, but he let her go.

Realizing that she had missed entirely, Sarael immediately did a half-revolution and shot a haymaker towards Maduk's left temple with her right foot. Maduk watched her foot leave the ground and rise of slowly towards him electrifying the air particles along its path with supercharged chi. He reached out with his left hand. Sparks of ethereal energy crackled between his fingers and her leg like electricity as he took a gentle hold of her foot and caressed it softly, while keeping pace with her speed. When Sarael's foot was finally close to his temple, he let go of her foot and ducked. Her foot whooshed past the space above Maduk's head.

Sarael bellowed an expletive and raged.

Realizing that Maduk was superiorly faster than she was, Sarael upped her game. Green flames flared all over her body as she drew from Earth Realm's energy. The ground tremored beneath their feet and the grass within a six-meter radius of her was burned away, leaving nothing but parched earth in its stead. Maduk, was unfazed by all this. Yet, he readied himself for her next onslaught of attacks. But, with every green streak of fire behind every punch, kick and assault Sarael unleashed, Maduk had a counter. For nearly a quarter of an hour, Sarael raged on until, finally, Maduk let out a heavy sigh of vexation, which angered her even more.

"I grow weary of this," Maduk smirked in annoyance.

"Then let's finish this," Sarael retorted and sparked the ethers into a three-foot long, double-edged sword.

Maduk's eyes first flashed in a yellow-orange hue before yellow-orange flames spewed forth from them. Then, the flames changed colors to pale green, causing Sarael to raise an eyebrow in surprise. But, with a blink, she steeled her resolve and gripped her sword more tightly. Sarael blazed towards Maduk and raised her sword, intending to slice him across his body from hip to torso.

Maduk had read her move and streaked towards her. His green flaming form occupied the space between the hilt of the sword and her body. In the same instant, he grabbed Sarael's right wrist with his left hand and placed his right hand above her right elbow, while flaring up and blinding her temporarily. Riding the momentum of Sarael's swing, Maduk flung Sarael above his head and slammed her body into the ground, stripping her of her sword at the same time. As Sarael did a harsh faceplant on the ground, Maduk stabbed the sword down into the ground close to her neck and pressed a sharp edge of the sword on her neck. As her eyes widened at the thought of being decapitated, Maduk dismissed the sword, leaving a surprised Sarael staring wide-eyed at him.

Maduk rose from his position. Realizing her opportunity, Sarael immediately tackled him to the ground and straddled him. Maduk did not resist as Sarael pummeled his face repeatedly with fists shielded in flesh-burning, supercharged chi and energy she drew from Earth Realm. Every attacked disfigured his face, but his face healed as quickly as it was marred.

*"I am sorry, brother,"* Maduk spoke via telepathy again and again as Sarael unleashed her fury on him.

Finally, as if realizing the futility of her actions and the fact that Maduk was no longer resisting her attacks, Sarael's assault slowly came to a stop and her fists rested limply on his chest. Her shoulders slumped and her head bowed low while the green flames on her body disappeared.

"Why?" her voice wavered as she held back tears of frustration.

"Why what?" Maduk asked calmly.

"Why did you kill me?" her voice broke and tears of anger flowed down her cheeks. "What the hell did I do to you? Why did you freaking kill me?"

Sarael exploded and punched Maduk several times on his face again.

"Because I was jealous," Maduk replied. "Because I was angry. Because I was a child, psychologically broken by his birth mother. I can give you many reasons but none will rewind time, brother. All I know is that I am sorry for what I did. I am truly, truly sorry."

Sarael regarded Maduk for a few seconds. Then, with a punch of frustration to his chest, Sarael stood up, summoned a pair of blue jean shorts and a black tank top over her body before extending a hand towards Maduk. Maduk nodded, took her hand and stood up before summoning a plain brown tee shirt and a brown pair of pants over his body. Sarael hit him twice in his abs and shoved him slightly. Maduk hardly budged.

"I keep my promises," Maduk said calmly. "When I return my life will be yours. But I really must go now."

Maduk made to teleport away.

"Wait," Sarael called.

Maduk froze in mid-teleport before slowly materializing back to his regular physical form. Sarael sighed and lifted her eyes to meet his.

"What is it you are going to take care of?" Sarael asked. "Mother said the same thing, but she won't tell me what it is."

"I would tell you, but mother asked me not to," Maduk said flatly. "She said you are not ready, despite my trying to convince her otherwise. And after what just happened, I must say I agree with her."

"And why does everyone keep telling me that?" Sarael exclaimed throwing her hands in the air. "Everyone thinks I'm still a child."

"This has nothing to do with age," Maduk said and walked towards Sarael. "It has everything to do with your frame of mind and your ability to grasp the dire nature of the threat Earth Realm, the Dimension of Solaris and even the cosmic cluster to which we belong is facing. And you, my dear brother, are in the center of it all."

He took her by the shoulders and bent over a little to stare into her eyes.

"A long time ago, you taught me how to build a pyramid with pebbles. My foolish pride, coupled with loathsome propaganda from my birth mother, led to your death."

Sarael winced as the memories came flashing back. Maduk grimaced and his jaws clenched as he fought to keep his emotions in check.

"May I be damned for all eternity if I do not stop you from putting your selfish pride before your purpose. That is what mother means when she says you are not ready."

Maduk let go of her shoulders and stood up straight.

"Until you have learned to move from here," Maduk added as he touched her left temple with a huge right index finger, "to here," he placed the same huge index finger on her chest, "then you will not survive this. I cannot have that. And neither can mother. Do you understand?"

Sarael bowed her head in shame. The one she had sworn to kill was the same one swearing to protect her in every way he could. Sarael could hear mother speaking through her brother, and suddenly, all her hatred and anger melted away like a drop of water on the sands of the Sahara Desert.

For a moment, she was back in the Garden of Aiden. It was time for her bath, and she was giving mother a hard time, as usual. Mother asked for Cahen's help and, with the authority of an elder sibling, Cahen had not only gotten her ready for her bath, but Cahen had also warned her that one of those days, she was going to hear mother's scolding. This was the same Cahen, the same elder sibling, stepping in for mother, just like he always used to do many millennia ago… And Sarael could not help but listen to her elder sibling. The tears flowed freely as she raised her eyes towards Maduk.

"Brother…" Sarael whispered, taking Maduk's large face in her smaller hands. "Brother…"

And the brothers hugged each other in the tightest embrace they could afford. They held each other as the burden of millennia past was washed away in a sea of letting-go. Sarael's body trembled uncontrollably against his as she cried tears of shame and joy at the same time. Maduk's big, strong arms around her were a panacea to the pain from the past as well as a promise of the new prospects of a bright future together. Sarael could not ask for a better sibling reunion and she wanted that moment to last an eternity. Maduk tried to peel himself away from her, but she held fast. So, they continued hugging each other for many silent minutes. Maduk stepped back and this time, she let him go.

"I really must go now," Maduk said. "But I will see you again. Alright?"

Sarael's body trembled with hesitation borne out of the uncertainty of not knowing what the future held for both of them as they strove to rebuild their relationship. However, with a smile, she sighed, resigning to a new feeling that was slowing brimming in her heart; excitement.

"Can't wait," Sarael replied amid sobs.

Sarael then managed a weak laugh, and Maduk smiled. He kissed her on the forehead and teleported away. She was by herself in a valley somewhere in New Zealand. Only then did she steal a moment to appreciate the vast, natural beauty that surrounded her. It was time to do as her elder brother had said. It was time for her to grow up and be ready for her purpose.

A nod-of-self-assurance later, Sarael sat on the ground in a Buddha pose, closed her eyes and plunged into a state of conscious death.

# CHAPTER TWENTY-FOUR

# ON YOUR MARKS

**"GOOD, SHE'S HERE,"** said Yoch as Miryam and Yehuda appeared.

"Welcome, sister," Shi'mon waved to an empty seat next to him.

"Thank you, brother," Miryam headed towards the empty seat. "Peace and goodwill unto you, brothers," she greeted everyone else with a nod and a wave.

"Peace and goodwill unto you, sister," they chorused in unison.

"I trust Yehuda has already apprised you of the situation," said Shi'mon.

"Yes," Miryam replied. "Yaakov fares well, right?"

"So far, yes," Shi'mon replied, and everyone else nodded. "He says Maduk has given him the special task of leading the Sinisters on their all-out attack on us. At least, his cover is still intact for now."

"Excellent," Miryam kept an expressionless face. "It means the plan is working out perfectly."

Everyone's expression distorted in confusion.

"My statement confuses you all, yes?" Miryam barely smiled.

"Please enlighten us, sister," Yoch prompted.

"Brothers, you already know who Maduk really is," Miryam began. "But what you don't know is that Maduk is also my son."

The apprentices gasped almost in unison. Miryam raised her right hand, and silence followed.

"In a past life, that is," she explained. "I was Eva, the second mate of Adamou. I helped raise Cahen, now Maduk, as my own and to this day, he still refers to me as 'mother.'"

"To this day…" Shi'mon reiterated and furrowed his eyebrows.

"Yes," Miryam replied and turned to face Shi'mon. "I met with him recently for the first time since he killed my son, Ahben, now Sarael in this life. I must say, it was one of the best things that happened to me in many centuries."

"You *met* with Maduk? Recently?" Tau-ma exclaimed, not believing what he had just heard.

"And Sarael, your daughter, was also your son, Abel?" Yehuda asked.

"Ahben," Miryam smiled softly. "But yes, you're correct. Cahen and Ahben, or Cain and Abel, are my sons. Ahben by birth and Cahen by adoption."

"And you withheld this piece of information from us?" Bar-Talmai asked.

"Respectfully," Miryam continued calmly. "It was not your place, or any of your places for that matter, to know. Until the time was right."

There was a mixture of reactions from everyone present, except Shi'mon who seemed to be the only calm in the storm that was gradually brewing. The reactions from the rest of the apprentices were understandable. Feelings of betrayal and distrust, laced with small doses of envy, seeped into the room like an unpleasant fart smell. Shi'mon imagined the many most likely questions racing through their minds and it was best these questions be addressed first so that everyone could focus on the task at hand. As such, he raised his hand, calling for order and quiet before he spoke.

"Brothers," Shi'mon said. "Let sister finish what she has to say first and then we can ask her all the questions we want."

Shi'mon then turned towards Miryam.

"Please continue."

"Thank you," Miryam nodded gratefully.

"My husband and our master chose me for a reason," Miryam continued.

Everyone, except for Miryam and Shi'mon spared a quick glance towards Yehuda. But Yehuda maintained a stoic expressionless demeanor as he stared intently at Miryam. He appeared to be the only one paying attention to Miryam.

"He wanted to summon Ahben's essence to be reincarnated as our child. I'm unsure why he wanted Ahben in particular, but," Miryam chuckled a little and shrugged. "Well, you all know how cryptic Master could get sometimes."

An aura of sadness and longing enveloped the room as everyone related to what Miryam said about their mentor.

"However, the timing had to be perfect and in sync with a specific instant on the Cosmic Clock, which he alone knew," she continued. "That's why I was only with child three years after I was wed to my husband."

Miryam swiped tears from her eyes and everyone's features softened. She fought back the urge to tell everyone how frustrated she was with Yeshua during the first few years of their marriage. Being married to a great teacher and miracle worker like Yeshua did not spare her from the stigma and hurtful gossips that came with being married and childless during that era. She had faith in her husband. But as a young, naïve apprentice, with hormones on fire and the needs of a youthful woman gasping for sexual gratification, her faith in her husband was eventually overridden by her pent-up frustration and lack of sexual satisfaction from her husband. Miryam could only hold on for so long and, as such, she had finally succumbed to Yehuda's subtle seduction.

The affair had lasted for over a year, a year that had taken Miryam centuries to let go of and forgive herself for, despite her husband's constant reassurance that not once did he ever bear any ill-will against her for her infidelity, even after his death. And even when she finally started bonding with her husband, she carried on her affair with Yehuda for three more months. Those final months of her affair with Yehuda constituted the lowest point in her life. The affair was a narcotic to her psyche. She was hooked to that narcotic beyond her imagination. And when she was bedding both her husband and her husband's apprentice during the same period, she was so intoxicated by the rush that came with her double-dipping that what she thought was her essence underwent an esoteric split and her true essence was revealed.

The esoteric split awoke a feeling in Miryam that had been suppressed by the esoteric psychostimulant of the affair; raw, untamed, unsullied guilt. This guilt was so intense that the only reason Miryam did not become soulless was because of her etheric makeup, which was undoubtedly different from those of the other apprentices; different because something clearly outer-dimensional was a part of her etheric makeup. Ahben, now Sarael, also had that outer-dimensional essence in her esoteric makeup. Clairvoyance revealed this, and her green flames and glow affirmed it as well. In Miryam's lowest point, the etheric shell of past lives, which encased her true essence shattered and her true etheric makeup flooded her form. Suddenly, everything became clear to her.

Her life within the three years of her marriage were analogous to the life cycle of a butterfly. She had met her husband as an egg. Her affair with Yehuda was like the gregarious phase of a caterpillar. Sleeping with her husband and Yehuda during the same period was her cycle in the cocoon until her true essence had emerged like a butterfly. She finally understood what her husband was trying to teach her at the time. Miryam had a newfound respect and awe for her husband. And while this new chapter of her life was as exciting as it held so many promises and possibilities, Miryam still had to face a past that preyed on her psyche like a psychedelic parasite.

There was no doubt that Sarael was Yeshua's daughter. She took some of her father's facial features and a huge part of his etheric signature, which included some of Miryam's outer-dimensional essence and much more. That 'more' eluded her entirely. Miryam had to find a way to let go of her past and train in the purpose her husband had shown her. Centuries later, she finally let go of her painful past and focused more on the only thing that truly mattered to her: Sarael. Maybe she was so patient with Sarael because, in a way, she saw a lot of her personality in Sarael. Like they say, the apple does not fall far from the tree. Oh, how she missed her husband more than words could ever describe. Despite her indiscretions with Yehuda, her love for her husband and master, Yeshua, was true and deep.

Shi'mon took her hand and gave it a gentle squeeze, a gesture which jerked her back to the present moment. Her heart heavy with the feeling of missing her husband and the residual pain and sorrow that came from this dark aspect of her past, Miryam bowed her head and interlocked her fingers with his.

"Master's essence was unique, and it changed over the three years I spent with him," Miryam stifled a snivel. "I was never aware of how different mine was until Master taught me clairvoyance and how to perceive essences."

Miryam chose to use 'Master' instead of 'my husband' because everyone in the room could relate to Yeshua as their master.

"All of us from the Garden of Aiden, or Eden as it is called today, have an essence that is mixed with an essence of a creature from a much higher dimension than Earth Realm's," Miryam continued. "That's why Sarael and I have a greenish glow and flame, and part of the reason why Lilith is so different. Back then, she was called Lithilia and I'm responsible for the uniqueness of her essence. When she instigated Ahben's death by Cahen's hands, I cursed her… And Cahen."

Murmurs ensued throughout the room following Miryam's revelations.

"Silence, brothers," Shi'mon called out.

The murmurs died almost instantly.

"I deeply regret cursing Cahen," Miryam continued. "I was blinded by pain and grief beyond words. But I certainly do not regret my curse on Lithilia. In fact, I still have a score to settle with her. That will be for another time."

"Oh, please do," Shi'mon interjected. "It will be good riddance."

"Amen," Tau-ma chimed in.

The apprentices chorused their approval.

"Question," Yoch leaned forward. "If you were the second wife of Adam, who was the first?"

"Lithilia," Miryam replied flatly.

"And if Lilith is the first wife," Yoch said. "Then that makes Maduk…"

His eyes bulged at the revelation. Several gasps and a few expletives erupted across the room.

"Yes, brothers," Miryam concurred. "Lithilia is Cahen's mother. And it was my curses coming to pass that turned Lithilia into the whore of essences that she is, and Cahen into a Sinister."

A near riot erupted in the room. Hands flailed, voices rose, fingers pointed and angry glares were trained towards her. Miryam watched them react. She was as unapologetic as she was in control of the situation. Despite the questions racing through their minds, they would eventually understand, just like they understood that Yehuda never meant to create the Bright Eyes and he could not be held accountable for everything that happened after that. The power of purpose was beyond anything they, including herself, could fully comprehend. But, as a multi-dimensional being, The Scribe fully understood the power of purpose and only after Master had survived the Shadow of the Soul, for the second time, did he fully understand the power of purpose.

"Now that the history lesson is over, I'd like to continue with my initial train of thought, please," Miryam called out to the apprentices.

She did not want them to start asking her too many questions that she was not going to answer. Not that she did not have the answers. They were not ready to handle the truth just yet; like the truth about Sarael and her role in the grand scheme of things. Time and place for everything.

"Like I said, I met with Cahen, and it was a fruitful meeting," Miryam said. "All it took was a mother's love, something he had not had in over 4,500 years, and he remembered that, in essence, he is human; just like the creatures of Earth Realm. So, as we speak, the head of the Sinisters is on our side. This is us cutting off the head of the snake. This was the first stage of the plan."

"Thank you for the update," Tau-ma said with a tinge of impatience and leaned forward in his seat. "I think I speak for us all when I say we never saw that coming. But what is this plan you speak of?"

"I was still getting to that," Miryam said flatly.

Tau-ma raised both hands in an apology for the interruption.

"Cahen said that the Sinisters must all be wiped out, especially Nimrud," she said. "He said that every Sinister after Nimrud seemed to have lost all ties to their humanity. Perhaps the transformation was too much for their bodies to handle. There was no way of either reversing the process or rehabilitating them; at least not to the best of our knowledge."

"If I may interject," Shi'mon spoke calmly but sternly. "I think there might be a way of making the Sinisters human again, using the Breath of Life. But they will have to accept that option. We can talk about that later."

"If this is possible, then wonderful," Miryam said. "Yaakov will also be very pleased and relieved to hear about this. What a brave man he is."

Nods and murmurs of agreement filled the room.

"Yehuda, Aaron, Sasha and I can summon the Breath of Life," Shi'mon said.

"Rub it in, brother," Yoch chuckled. "Rub it in."

"What can I say," Shi'mon smiled.

"Will you teach me, brother?" Miryam's eyes sparkled with excitement. "I was never taught."

Her voice and demeanor revealed no jealousy.

"Neither were we," Shi'mon explained. "Yehuda and I just realized we could do it after Aaron and Sasha died during our standoff against the Bright Eyes. I believe our ability to summon and use the Breath of Life had something to do with our trip to the Shadow of the Soul. And when we brought Sasha and Aaron back to life, they, too, just knew how to do it. But I will find a way to teach you."

"Ok, brother," Miryam said. "Thanks in advance."

"Of course, sister."

"Show off," Tau-ma made a show of pouting. "Taking trips to the Shadow of the Soul and knowing how to summon and use the Breath of Life."

"You're welcome to journey there as well, you know," Shi'mon offered.

"Not in this lifetime," Tau-ma made a face and shuddered.

"I'll inform Cahen, then," Miryam brought everyone's attention back to the main issue at hand. So, here's the plan. The Sinisters want to take control of Earth Realm, which Cahen has made them believe is their birthright. Thus, Sinisters live for that purpose. We are Earth Realm's first line of defense. As such, any plan that appears to lure us into their realm and place us at their mercy will appeal to them. Cahen says his birth mother, Lithilia, has a timeframe in mind for the Sinisters to launch their attack. But he will move the schedule up."

"Nimrud hasn't changed much; at least not behaviorally," Miryam leaned back in her seat. "His ego is his pressure point. Hence, assigning Yaakov as the main general in this assault will do damage to Nimrud's pride and cause him to lose focus. Also, Yaakov has enough time to alert us on their plans to attack. Yaakov doesn't know Cahen has been turned. And yes, before you ask, it was during the meeting that I informed Cahen on who Yaakov really is."

Miryam moved in her seat. Using clairsentience, she felt the disapproval and frustration building in the room. They had every right to feel that way. She had gone out of her way to forge this plan with an enemy without their consent. Worst of all, she compromised Yaakov's cover. She might as well have handed Yaakov's head to Maduk in a silver platter. Cahen may be her son, but Maduk was their enemy. How dare she. Her actions were not only disrespectful; they felt like downright betrayal. But, if she had initially shared her intentions with the rest of the apprentices, they would have killed the plan before she finished explaining. She was confident her plan would work on many fronts and achieve so much in one execution.

"So, with Nimrud suffering from the proverbial slap in the face," Miryam continued. "Cahen would kiss his proverbial boo-boo by letting Nimrud know

239

that Yaakov is with us. And therein will lie Nimrud's special assignment, one that would be even more important than leading the Sinisters in an all-out assault on us; Nimrud would be tasked with taking out Yaakov, but only when Cahen gives him the order. If there's one creature Nimrud dreads, it's his grandfather, Cahen. So even if Nimrud wanted to launch a preemptive strike on Yaakov, he would have to deal with Cahen. And Nimrud cannot afford that right now, not while Cahen is showing no signs of vulnerability that Nimrud could exploit."

"Nimrud knows that Lithilia, whom they refer to as the queen, is untouchable even by Cahen. He doesn't know about Cahen and Lithilia's relationship, and he definitely doesn't know about me. Cahen may have a weakness for his birth mother, but I am his ultimate weakness literally and figuratively. Cahen believes Yaakov can handle Nimrud on his own. With Nimrud taken out, and with Cahen indicating that the Sinister cause is no longer one to be pursued, the Sinisters would be forced to surrender or die. After all, their top general would be dead, and their leader would have ordered them to stand down. If they decide to keep fighting, then we'll finally get our wish and exterminate them all. If they choose conversion, even better."

Miryam paused to allow what she had just explained to sink in and to allow herself a moment to regroup her thoughts. The apprentices relaxed their features as their anger and frustration eased off considerably. Slow nods of approval revealed their gradual appreciation of her plan. Myriam also relaxed, relieved the atmosphere in the room had changed for the better. The plan could only succeed if the rest of the apprentices were wholly on board. The last thing she needed was any form of discord among them. Too much was at stake.

"And you two came up with this plan?" Tau-ma asked with a slight smile on his face.

"Yes, we did," Miryam replied calmly.

"The plan that would let Cahen inform his two top generals about a change in the timeframe for them taking over Earth Realm, which would trigger Yaakov to inform us of this new timeframe, which would in turn trigger us to launch a preemptive strike against them, which would cause them to ambush and try to exterminate us, Earth Realm's first line of defense, leaving Yaakov, the traitor as a perfect target for Nimrud, but Nimrud would be killed because Yaakov can handle Nimrud, and in the end, the Sinisters would be forced to either surrender or face obliteration because we're simply the best at what we do. Did I miss anything?" Yoch asked.

His assessment could have been regarded as sarcasm, but given their bond forged over 2,000 years ago and still going strong, everyone knew better.

"Good heavens," Bar-Talmai applauded. "That was very eloquently put."

Everyone else except for Miryam and Shi'mon joined in the applause.

"I couldn't have said it any better."

"That was very wise and impressive," Shi'mon said.

He reached out, took hold of Miryam's right hand and gave it a gentle squeeze. She nodded her gratitude. If Shi'mon, their leader, gave his blessing, then the rest of the apprentices would fall in line.

"What about Lithilia?" Shi'mon asked.

"She's mine," Miryam replied in a tone so cold, it could freeze Solara.

"As you wish," Shi'mon conceded. "And we also have the situation of the fallen archangel to deal with," he added.

"We will take care of him too," Yehuda replied with extreme confidence and calm. "He will fall next time."

Miryam turned to face Yehuda. But he stared ahead, choosing deliberately to avoid her eyes. She met Shi'mon's glance which reflected her concern back at her. But the three of them would worry about that later.

"Very well," Shi'mon said. "If no one has anything to ask or add, I suggest we go about our affairs but stay alert for word from Yaakov."

The apprentices agreed and teleported away, all twelve of them except for Shi'mon. The Cosmic Clock was winding down and the Great Reset beckoned. He reminisced his days of training and fought back the feelings of doubt that were slowly slithering their way into his psyche; doubts regarding his ability to successfully lead his team through these perilous times. He leveled a detached stare at his ring. It still glowed but not as brightly as when Beelzebub had just been set free. Beelzebub was not just a beast. He was *the* Beast, and Shi'mon did not know how to bait this beast.

*Trust in Creation,* the Master used to say. *It will never lead you astray.*

Right now, trusting Creation was the hardest thing to do, especially when the fate of humanity was in the hands of his team, again. Shi'mon sighed heavily.

*"Whatever you're up to, dear Creation,"* he said to himself, *"it better be excellent."*

Meanwhile, Yehuda was in his chambers, and Sasha lay down with her head on his lap.

"You know you don't have to come, right?" he said softly as he caressed her head.

"Uh huh," Sasha replied flatly.

"Dangerous territory, in a different realm-" Yehuda explained.

"And I'll be damned if I let you go by yourself," Sasha cut him off.

She sat up and looked into his eyes.

"I know you're trying to protect me from something other than the Sinisters. But I assure you that I can handle myself just fine."

She kissed him on the lips.

"Nothing, no one and certainly no creature is taking me away from you. Besides," she straddled him. "I've been dying for some action."

Yehuda shook his head in resignation. He let her kiss him again and he kissed her back. She was right; he was trying to protect her, but not from something or someone. Yehuda had a feeling Kundalini was going to manifest again during their next battle and his body could no longer handle any more manifestations of this multi-dimensional being. And this was his reason for not wanting Sasha to join them in battle. He did not want her to witness his death.

\*\*\*

"Why are you cooped up in here, all by yourself?" Lithilia asked playfully.

"I swear, creature," Beelzebub replied. "If I didn't require your expertise."

"I believe the correct word is 'need'," Lithilia offered with sly innuendo.

She walked into the cave. The walls, ceiling and floor was made of smooth, glistening, hard rock, petrified by the sparking of ethers by an outer-dimensional creature; a true epitome of discomfort despite its geological aesthetics, and if anyone was locked up somewhere long enough... Anyway, Beelzebub's problem, not hers.

"Look, I'm not here to gloat or deride you," Lithilia added. "I came to remind you that I always keep my promises. I will take you back to Hell Realm."

"I grow weary of your trickeries, creature," Beelzebub scoffed from his floor where he sat. "If you have nothing more than your 'assurance,' I suggest you leave me alone."

"As you wish," Lithilia turned to leave but stopped, her back to him. "Just be ready for my signal and please act promptly. The timing has to be impeccable."

Lithilia then turned around to face the fallen archangel.

"We will have one chance to get his right and if we miss-"

"I'm assuming you have a backup plan?" Beelzebub sneered.

"Yes, I do," Lithilia replied, choosing to ignore his tone of voice. "Both plans will work very effectively, but I'd rather indulge in the first plan. The aftertaste of drinking from the cup of the second plan will not be a very good one for some concerned parties."

"Parties?" Beelzebub asked as he finally turned his gaze towards Lithilia. "You now have my undivided curiosity."

"Do not concern yourself with the details of your return home, archangel," Lithilia said calmly. "Leave that to me. Just be ready when I call."

Lithilia stood at the entrance to the cave. The daylight carved her form like an expert sculptor of light. Beelzebub shifted his position, and Lithilia smiled. But he could not see her smile. He could only see her form against the light. The form approached him step-by-step, and he could not help but become paralyzed by his lust for this human. He did not know how she did it, but she was an expert at making him want her in ways he had never wanted any other creature before. Then he remembered what had happened the last two times and turned his eyes away from her. But Lithilia immediately teleported herself further into the cave.

She summoned enough illumination to cast just the right amount of glare and shadows to accentuate her every curve in the most seductive way possible. Everything was customized solely for Beelzebub, just like she always did with her victims. Beelzebub's gaze fell on her naked body and the last of his defenses crumbled like a house of cards. Lithilia walked swiftly towards him and ripped his clothes away from his body with pure savagery. She straddled and accommodated him in a domineering manner. Beelzebub tried to resist and protest until he felt his metallic extension become enveloped in the warm, frothing, gripping wetness that was the promise of ecstasy and paradise. As Lithilia went to work and as The Beast's eyes rolled back into its sockets in pure pleasure, she leaned forward until her lips brushed his left ear.

"Enjoy this while it lasts, archangel," Lithilia whispered. "It's rare for me to do this without any ulterior motive."

# CHAPTER TWENTY-FIVE

# IN MY DEATH

**"MISS?" A VOICE** seemed to call at her from a distance.

"Miss? Miss?" the voice called again.

The voice was a lot closer this time.

*So much for conscious death*, Sarael thought..

Slowly, she opened her eyes. She was still lying on the grass in the valley. She did not remember when she had fallen asleep.

"Are you alright, miss?" the voice asked.

Sarael sat up and stretched.

*Apparently my journey towards conscious death took a detour towards Sleep Ville instead*, she thought and sighed.

She turned to face her unexpected companion. He was a heavily bearded man, who appeared to be in his mid-sixties. He held a wooden staff and was crouched next to Sarael. He placed his staff on the ground and knelt beside her.

"Please, let me help you up," he offered.

But Sarael shook her head.

"It's okay, sir," Sarael replied as she sat in a Buddha posture.

Sarael scanned the valley again for good measure and was disappointed she was nowhere near any ethereal existence. She cursed under her breath.

"Would you like some water?" the bearded man asked, reaching for a water bottle hanging from his side by a strap.

Sarael rubbed her eyes.

"No, thank you, sir," she stretched again. "That's very kind of you."

She read his aura using clairvoyance and realized his auric color was white gold. Such purity was rare in humans. She could not say the same for his clothes though. His brown shirt, tucked into a pair of faded blue jeans, had seen better days and his feet were covered in worn-out black boots. His face was wrinkled and hardened, probably from a life of prolonged physical labor. But Sarael was thankful that the man must have been spending a good amount of time in the shower because, for someone who looked as semi-dirty as this man looked, he certainly did smell nice.

"I don't think I've seen you before in these parts," the man narrowed his eyes behind thick, grayish-brown eyebrows. "Are you visiting family, if you don't mind me asking?"

"I was meeting family here, actually," Sarael replied with a wry smile.

She was not wary of this stranger. His etheric signature did not indicate any reason to be. Though what a strange signature he had.

"My brother," Sarael added. "He just left a few minutes ago."

"Oh," the man said. "Will he be coming back to get you? Or maybe you already know your way back to your home?"

Sarael hesitated for a brief second.

"I'll find my way back home, sir," Sarael replied politely. "I'll meet my brother shortly. And you, sir, what brings you to these parts?"

The man laughed a little at her politeness and sat beside Sarael on the ground.

"I bring my sheep to graze here all the time," the man replied with a smile. "I am a humble shepherd. It is a very personally rewarding profession. Perhaps you don't know this, but there are more sheep in New Zealand than there are people."

*Yeah, that explains the accent,* Sarael thought. *Forgot I was in New Zealand.*

"Where are your sheep?" Sarael asked. "Aren't you afraid of losing them?"

"They are here, somewhere," the man replied. "They come whenever they hear my voice, no matter where they are."

He picked up a small pebble and tossed it in the distance.

"That's a very remarkable talent you have, sir," Sarael forced a smile.

*Poor man, he must be getting senile or something,* she thought. *Or crazy altogether.*

"I understand your doubts, but I could give you a small demonstration if you'd like," the man offered, as if he had read Sarael's mind.

Sarael averted her eyes in embarrassment and shrank her shoulders a little.

"Sir, I uh…" she stammered.

But the old man shook his head.

"It's alright, miss," he assured Sarael. "It's no bother at all. Now, if you'd like, I could give you a small demonstration."

"I'd like that, please," Sarael smiled and straightened her posture.

*Could he really have read my mind?* Sarael wondered.

The man smiled, whistled a note into the air and waited. Fifteen seconds later, there were no sheep and Sarael concluded that the old man was indeed crazy. Two very long minutes of awkward silence later, there were still no sheep in sight.

"Perhaps you did not whistle loudly enough?" Sarael offered in an attempt to break the awkward silence.

"You're still missing the point," the old man said.

Sarael furrowed her eyebrows and turned to look at the man sitting next to her. Something about him that struck her fancy even more. His etheric signature was starting to change to one that was vaguely familiar.

"Who are you?" Sarael asked slowly. "What is your name?"

"Patience, Sarael," the old man said. "This is about patience."

And as soon as he said those words, a herd of about fifty sheep appeared over a ridge, meandering towards them. Some stopped to graze while the rest marched on. They seemed to have appeared from nowhere. Sarael opened her mouth to say something, but her words died in her throat. The old man played with some of the sheep that walked close to him. He rubbed their wool, patted them on their backs and even talked to them as if he was speaking to friends. Sarael watched the old man with unbridled curiosity. The sheep stayed in the area for a few more minutes before marching away into the horizon.

"Who are you?" Sarael asked again. "And how do you know my name?"

"Patience, Sarael," the old man said again. "Patience."

"So, this is not a dream and I'm dead," Sarael said matter-of-factly.

"Yes, you are dead," the man agreed. "Very dead, indeed. I see your mother taught you well. How is she doing, by the way?"

"You still have not answered my questions," Sarael shifted and squirmed a bit with impatience.

And as soon as she said those words, she realized the lesson the old man was trying to teach her. Her impatience dissipated instantly.

"You chose the path of conscious death to break through that frontier that is holding you back," the old man continued. "I find it interesting that you would choose such a path instead of just listening to advice."

"Unfortunately, my listening skills are pathetic," Sarael admitted. "I chose to die so that I could face my situation head-on, whatever my situation is."

"Patience…" the old man interjected.

"Is that what my situation is? Patience or lack thereof?" Sarael asked.

"Patience…" the old man reiterated.

Sarael opened her mouth to speak, but she changed her mind. She closed her mouth and sat for a moment in silence with the old man. Neither of them said a word for several minutes. Sarael was restless, feeling as if invisible ants were having a military march past over her skin.

*Keep calm, girl,* she mentally encouraged herself.

A million and one ideas on how to stay focused and undistracted surfaced into her conscious mind. The more she thought, the more restless she became. Finally, she decided to let it all go and observe her feelings. The moment she focused her attention on her feeling of restlessness, everything became still and peaceful. She finally understood what the old man was saying, as well as the lesson her mother had been trying to teach her for over two millennia without success.

"Finally. I get it." Sarael snapped her fingers as she cried out with excitement and turned to face the old man.

For the first time in her current lifetime, Sarael froze in utter shock and surprise. Her jaw dropped as if it were not a part of her body.

"Your mother trained you well," the once-old-bearded-now-young man said with a soft smile. "I'm very proud of her and you too, my child," Yeshua added.

"Father?" Sarael did not even know how she could formulate the word.

Sarael stared at Yeshua before crashing into his open arms and tackling him to the ground. She hugged her father so tightly that if Yeshua was a normal human being, his ribs and spine would have been crushed. Yeshua returned his daughter's hug and bathed her with pure, fatherly love by merging his clairsentience with hers and transducing his feelings for her through their connected clairsentience. Sarael's being floated freely in the energy of love her father immersed her in. She squeezed her father in her arms even tighter and sobbed for joy. This moment was the happiest she had ever been for as long as she could remember.

"I've missed you so much," Sarael said amidst sobs of joy.

"I've missed you too," Yeshua replied. "Though I've always been around."

He pulled her gently away from him, wiped her tears away and appraised her.

"You are so beautiful. Even more beautiful than your mother."

"Thank you," Sarael replied and grinned.

"I must say I labored in vain, though," Yeshua added. "You look nothing like me. Well, except for your ears, but who's paying attention anyway."

"Father," Sarael exclaimed and play-punched him in the arm.

Yeshua laughed out loud and took his daughter in his arms again. They hugged each other for a few more minutes.

"You've come to the end of your training now, my child," Yeshua said as he set her away from him. "Your mother and I can only take you so far."

Sarael's body tensed up before she relaxed, but she held on for a second longer before letting go.

"Before the Cosmic Clock completes its countdown, which will be very soon, you'll face a very dangerous adversary," Yeshua continued. "Even if you run from him, he will chase you down because you have something that he needs. There is no escaping, and this is why you have been training all your life. You know this already, my love."

Yeshua tried to sound as calm as he possibly could, but the seriousness in his tone underscored the gravity of the situation at hand.

"Yes, father, I do," Sarael replied. "I'm not afraid. I was angry. With Mother, with Cahen, even with you for not being there in person."

"I know," Yeshua said and kissed the crown of her head. "I was there. I have always been there. I have never left your side, even though you could not detect my presence."

"It's okay now," Sarael assured him. "In one day, I made peace with Cahen, and got to spend time with you. Couldn't have asked for a more perfect day."

Yeshua smiled and hugged his daughter again. No words were spoken for several minutes, and no words were needed. What was said between father and daughter was beyond what words could describe.

"You must go now," Yeshua urged. "Time is of the essence."

"Will I ever see you again?" Sarael asked, eyes pleading and full of hope.

"Yes, you will, my child," Yeshua replied with a smile as he caressed her head. "And once all this is over, you will see me more often, alright?"

Sarael grinned as her heart overflowed with happiness at her father's promise, dwarfing the prospect of possibly impending death at the hands of The Beast.

"Alright."

"What about that guy? Patrick," Yeshua teased.

Sarael buried her face in his chest like an embarrassed child. She understood her father was trying to lighten up the situation; hence, why he brought up Patrick at the end of their conversation. However, her worry over Patrick's sudden... absence... returned and her expression became grim.

*Maybe father is trying to tell me something?* Sarael thought. *That Patrick is alright, after all? I hope so.*

Yeshua kissed the crown of her head.

"Go now, my two-thousand-year-old child," Yeshua said gently stripping his daughter away from him. "And remember, I am always with you. I love you so much, Sarael."

"I love you too so much, father," Sarael replied.

When Sarael blinked, Yeshua was gone. The air suddenly felt cold on her skin, her heart went cold and even the skies seemed to darken as a deep sadness and longing enveloped her, which she quickly brushed away. Returning from a state of conscious death could be unceremonious sometimes.

*No more wasting time. I have a job to do.*

Sarael locked on to her mother's etheric signature and teleported just outside her quarters. She knocked on the door.

"Come in," Miryam said nonchalantly.

When Miryam saw Sarael, she smiled, and her eyes welled up with tears. Mother and daughter ran into each other's arms.

"You saw him, didn't you?" Miryam asked already knowing the answer.

"If I never see tomorrow, then it shall be with joy and peace in my soul, mother," Sarael said. "I met Cahen and father, on the same day."

She pulled away slightly from her mother.

"What are the odds of that happening?"

"Well, given this particular circumstance, I'd say 100%," Miryam took Sarael's face in her hands. "I see him all over you. Your father, I mean. He alone has this distinct etheric aroma."

Miryam examined her child as if it were the first time she had seen Sarael in a very long time. She relished in the hovering 'scent' of her lover's etheric signature. How she missed that feeling... how she missed him.

"And no, you look nothing like him. Well, except for those pointy ears."

"Oh no, he said the same thing," Sarael exclaimed and the two women burst out laughing. "Cahen is a giant. My goodness."

"Oh yes, that is one big man," Miryam agreed.

"I felt like I did not even exist standing next to him," Sarael added.

Then she looked around as if searching for something.

"Where's everybody?" Sarael asked, quickly sweeping her gaze across the room. "I don't feel them close by."

"They've gone ahead," Miryam answered.

Sarael nodded slowly. Her demeanor had evolved from that of a whiny brat to that of a focused adult, who had a profound appreciation and gravitas of what awaited her shortly.

"I was waiting for you. I knew you'd make the right choice and that you'd be ready in time. I've never, ever doubted you and your ability to learn and grow."

Sarael hugged her mother.

"I know, mother. Thank you."

"Of course. You are my child," Miryam replied.

Miryam glanced past Sarael to find Yeshua standing a few feet away. A connection of gazes, a fusion of individual clairsentience with each other's, a merging of souls and a unification of beings transpired between husband and wife. A silent tear of longing, joy and love traced a path down each of her cheeks. She extended a hand towards her lover, and he took it. Sarael could not see him, but she could feel him using her clairsentience. Yeshua held his lover and his daughter. He kissed Sarael on the crown of her head and Miryam on the lips. Then, Yeshua took a step back and nodded at Miryam. She nodded back at him.

*"I love you, Yeshua of Nazareth,"* Miryam said telepathically.

*"I love you too, Miryam of Magdala,"* Yeshua replied and disappeared.

Where and when Yeshua went, Miryam had no idea. She could not trace his teleportation link. But that was okay. He was always around, whenever and wherever they were.

"Let's go take on some sinisters now, shall we?" Miryam offered.

"By all means," Sarael replied with a smile of confidence and spunk.

And with those words, mother and daughter teleported away to the Realm of Nimbu.

# CHAPTER TWENTY-SIX

## IMMOVABLE

**PATRICK AND SATAN** threw their spheres of black light at each other at the same time. Their spheres of black light collided in midair and caused a small, temporary vacuum which collapsed unto itself. Had any of the spheres come in contact with anything solid, that solid object would have been trapped, sucked in and erased from Creation.

Both men continued dashing towards each other. Satan's body angled to the left in a prelude to a side-step, placing the bulk of his weight on his left leg. Patrick was unsure of what Satan was planning until Satan clenched and cocked his left fist. Patrick's upper lip curled to the right in a wry, half smile. He side-stepped to the right, angling his body at a forty-degree angle. The stance generated and stored potential energy. Satan's left uppercut, imbued with supercharged chi, flared past the space where his head used to be, sparking the air particles in its path into dazzling specks of energy which burned a trail on Patrick's black, leather jacket.

*That was my favorite jacket,* Patrick thought as he unleashed a counter.

Patrick's left hand went up and, with a feather-soft touch, he placed it on the back of Satan's clenched, left fist and rode Satan's punch. As soon as Satan's arm became fully extended, Patrick sparked the ethers into 50,000 volts of electricity and stunned Satan with it. Satan quickly absorbed the electric shock but failed to realize that Patrick only meant it as a distraction. He grabbed Satan's left hand and transformed the potential energy stored in his stance into kinetic energy by taking a step backward with his left leg and uncoiling his torso. Satan's arm jerk forward and his hand open, with his palm facing upwards. The howl of pain and the sound of bones breaking were sweet music to Patrick's ego as he drove his right forearm upwards perpendicularly into Satan's elbow, shattering it to many jagged pieces, many of which tore through Satan's flesh.

Satan's arm dangled like a piece of rope thanks to shattered elbow joints. But Patrick was not done yet. He moved his right hand to Satan's left wrist, and as he did a backward cross-step with his right leg, he sank his weight, thereby dropping his center of gravity and giving his torso more strength for his next move. As he uncoiled his body from his cross-step, he yanked on Satan's wrist and threw Satan over his shoulder. The sound of Satan's skull cracking followed Satan's harsh faceplant on the hard ground. He pulled Satan outward. Satan's body flew over Patrick and crashed face-first into an invisible hardness close to his feet. Then, Patrick placed his right leg on Satan's scapula as he laced Satan's left forearm in between both his forearms and pinned it on his core. He spun around in a complete revolution as he pulled his forearms in a scissor fashion. Soft tissue ripped from bone on Satan's useless elbow and scapula accompanied by snapping of many bones on Satan's shoulder. The entire attack was a swift, smooth and synchronized choreography of displeasure and pain.

Satan's screech of agony reached a new crescendo. Patrick encased his cocked fist with black light. The entire attack sequence was a buildup to cause just enough distraction for him to deal a fatal blow at Satan. His intended target for his final strike was the back of Satan's neck, below the base of the skull. The black light would engulf Satan's neck and part of Satan's skull in an etheric vacuum, thereby severing Satan's head from his body. It would be mission accomplished.

But just as he was about to unleash his final blow, Satan teleported away in a final act of desperation and survival. Patrick's fist drove into nothingness. An expletive escaped from his lips. He rose to his feet, and his white orbs stared into the black orbs of his mortal enemy. He watched as Satan cradled his battered left arm, infusing it with healing chi until Satan's arm was completely healed within seconds. Satan flexed and stretched his left arm, stared at his foe and nodded, as an evil smile formed on his lips.

"Either you have developed some new fighting skills," Satan scoffed. "Or I have been away for too long."

"You don't have to do this," Patrick said, ignoring Satan. "You don't have to temper with the Core. Not sure what The Scribe told you, but I wouldn't trust that creature if I were you. He's bad news for everyone but himself."

"Do you really think I care about what happens to everyone?" Satan asked, flexing his left arm again. "That I care about what happens to this realm?"

"Then why are you doing this, Natas?" Patrick asked. "If you don't care for humanity or the realm, why go through all the trouble?"

"I was crown prince," Satan replied and stepped forward. "I was supposed to take over the kingdom when my father died-"

"And I asked you why you're doing this," Patrick barked and stepped closer. "I don't need to hear what I already know."

"You do not need to be rude, you backstabbing mule," Satan's expression turned smug with derision as he clasped his hands behind his back and puffed his chest. "I am doing this for me. I gave everything to save my people and what did I get in return? A life of incarceration in the Realm of Porgatoria and not even a word of gratitude. Humans took everything away from me and left me out there to die. You, whom I called my brother, betrayed me. You and the rest of humanity must pay."

"'Blessed are the meek; for they shall inherit the earth'," Patrick said.

"What did you just say?" Satan asked

Patrick's words seemed to have thrown him off course.

"I'd tell you," Patrick replied. "But you're too caught up in your insanity to understand."

"Let the insanity continue then," Satan sneered.

Two spheres of black light encased Satan's hands. He immediately shot them in rapid succession towards Patrick, but Patrick caught them in his hands. The spheres slowly disappeared into his hands as he absorbed their energy. Patrick caught a zip motion out of the corner of his eye. He turned towards the direction of the zip motion and saw Satan charging towards him, wielding a sword with both hands. Patrick raised his hands in the air as he sparked the ethers to form a similar sword in his hands.

In a clash of blades they came together. However, Patrick relaxed his hand just enough to cause Satan's blade to clang along his blade and away from his body. Many metallic sparks leaped from their clashing blades. In the same motion, he did a forward cross-step, twisting his torso from his hips and almost instantly releasing the potential energy buildup from his torso twist. Satan realized that he would be too slow to counter Patrick's counterattack. The air whizzed as Patrick's blade raced towards Satan's neck for a decapitation. Again, Satan teleported away and Patrick's sword sliced through empty space. The two men squared off across the room.

"We can do this all day," Patrick smirked and shrugged in arrogance.

"You really think I cannot beat you?" Satan scoffed.

"Do I think the sun rises from the east?" Patrick replied with intense sarcasm. "You're no match for me now. I'm Damas and Patrick in one body."

Patrick took a step forward as he made his sword disappear. His eyes then glowed with an intensity that made Satan shiver involuntarily

"You and I are linked. You know that already. Wherever you go, I follow, and I will put you down like the rabid dog you've turned yourself into. If I have to, I will follow your teleportation link wherever you teleport to, even to

Porgatoria. It ends right here, right now. Only one of us is leaving this place alive."

"So full of yourself, Damas," Satan hissed. "Where are your moral and ethical lines now, huh? What about all those rules you used to have? What about 'respect for all life'?"

Satan turned and spat into the oblivion he expected to be the ground.

"You are a hypocrite, and you do not even have the courage to admit it. I embrace who I am. I make no excuses for it. Who are you to judge me?"

"You are the exception to all my rules," Damas hissed in return, taking control of Patrick's body. "I tried to save you."

Natas' eyes narrowed with hesitation and self-doubt as Damas' words wormed their way into his psyche. He averted his gaze away from Damas.

"I journeyed to all the corners of Earth Realm to find a solution, a cure, for you. I never gave up on you. My new purpose in life was to save the one I once called 'brother.' I failed. And you have the nerve to call me a traitor. Tell me, 'brother', who's the traitor between the two of us?"

Satan hesitated for a moment. He opened his mouth to say something, but nothing came out.

"Answer me," Damas demanded.

"You may have tried to save me once, brother," Satan said quietly. "But you failed. Even now I have come to realize you are still trying to save me."

Satan moved closer.

"There is no saving me, brother, because I do not seek salvation. I am already too far gone to even want to turn back."

"But you don't have to give up," Damas said softly but firmly. "There's still hope. We can find a way. You don't have to do this by yourself. Trust me."

Satan lowered his head as if trying to make up his mind. He remembered the first time he had met Damas. They were both barely in their teens, and Damas had made him look stupid over something really childish. He had immediately gotten into a fist fight with the young priest. Damas never fought back. The royal guards had quickly stepped in to separate the two. Natas smiled at the memory. It was Natas who was always up to some mischief, and Damas would be there to cover up for him.

"Have I ever let you down, brother?" Damas asked.

He extended his right hand towards Natas.

"Take my hand, and see for yourself," Damas offered.

Natas' gaze moved back and forth between Damas' face and his hand. Finally, as if dispelling any last hint of hesitation, he reached for Damas' hand. At once, he established a full esoteric link with Damas and had complete access to all of Damas' memories and Natas experienced Damas' complete past in a flash.

Damas abandoned his role as high priest, much to the shock of everyone in the kingdom. He journeyed throughout the entire globe, across land and sea, in times of peace and peril, seeking ways to bring Natas back. He sought the council of sages and followed every rumor and myth to no avail. Eventually, when he was frail of body due to decades of subjecting his body through the harshest of conditions, Damas returned to the kingdom, preferring to expire in his homeland than on foreign soil. And even then, Damas did not relent in his efforts to seek a solution for his friends salvation, poring through every manuscript he could lay his hand on. Alas, the cold hands of death had finally won, and Damas had died with the sorrow and disappointment at himself of having failed in finding a way to save his friend.

Natas' hand slid off Damas' as Damas severed their esoteric link. His stare was as blank as one who seemed to be lost in deep thought.

"You abandoned your position as high priest?" Satan was incredulous.

He averted his eyes and looked away, unable to hide his shame and guilt.

"Why?" he asked.

"You know why," Damas replied calmly. "You saw for yourself."

Satan stepped away and stared blankly at the oblivion beyond his feet. He seemed to be lost in wondering contemplation.

"I ask you again," Damas spoke solemnly. "Have I ever let you down?"

The words tore through Satan's reverie. Patrick resumed control of his body, walked towards him and placed a hand on his shoulder.

"Have I?" Patrick asked.

"I…" Satan hesitated. "I was… wrong about you, brother."

Satan gently cupped his friend's hand and met Patrick's gaze. His eyes turned from black to normal. Both men looked at each other, smiled and hugged. Shock waves of emotion shuddered through Satan as he remembered his past even more. He gave Patrick another tight squeeze before he spoke.

"Thank you so much," Satan whispered. "Thank you."

"Of course, brother," Patrick flinched slightly from pleasant surprise at the thought of rehabilitating Satan and tried to peel himself away, but Satan held fast.

Patrick stayed in his position and relaxed. And as soon as he relaxed, a jolt of energy ripped through his spinal column and radiated across his body, temporarily paralyzing him. He screamed and collapsed into Satan's arms, jerking, spasming and raging at himself for letting his guard down so easily.

"I am sorry, brother," Satan said as he gently let Patrick's paralyzed body hover in oblivion. "But I am beyond redemption."

Satan turned and glided towards the Core and hovered as close to the Core as he could.

"You tried your best, and I will never forget that," Satan stared into the energy form that was the Core, shoulders slumped and heart heavily burdened. "That is, in fact, the only reason why you still draw breath."

"No… Please," Patrick struggled to say, but he kept choking on his own words, his mouth and throat no longer working.

Patrick watched with horror as Satan summoned a giant sphere of black light between himself and the Core. He knew exactly what Satan planned on doing and was helpless to stop him. He struggled to move, to talk, to scream, to teleport, but nothing worked. He fought with all his will and might to no avail. Then, Satan turned around and looked down at him one last time.

"I am so sorry, brother," Satan said softly. "I hope you forgive me one day, if you will still be alive or even remember who you are by the time I am done."

And with those words, Satan raised his hands in the air and commanded the giant sphere of black light to move forward and engulf the Core. Patrick's regret, weakness, disappointment, powerlessness, and, most of all, feeling of failure magnified so much that they almost had a life of their own.

*There's nothing else I can do.*

Patrick stopped struggling and let it all go, accepting his fate, the situation, the past, and his concept of the future, and he totally surrendered them all away. In that moment, peace engulfed him, and in that same moment, everything came to a standstill, as if someone had hit the *'PAUSE'* button to Creation itself.

*"Tell me, mortal,"* a formless, omnidirectional voice said. *"Why are you here?"*

*"Who are you?"* Patrick demanded, brimming with a mix of confusion and awe.

He whipped his head around at the paused scenery around him. He realized he was no longer paralyzed.

*This must be an alternate reality,* he thought.

*"Your penchant for rudeness is most astounding, mortal,"* the voice continued.

Patrick realized that this was no ordinary 'voice.' He could sense a power far greater than anything he had ever experienced. The power behind this voice dwarfed Sara's in every way. As such, he cowered and bowed his head.

*"I apologize…"* Patrick said and hesitated, not knowing how to address this conscious, powerful presence. *"My rudeness was uncalled for."*

*"Why do you fight?"* the voice asked, ignoring Patrick's apology.

*"Because I want to stop Natas from destroying the Core, humanity and Earth Realm,"* Patrick explained, and as he did, he felt a little foolish.

He was unsure why he felt foolish. He just… felt that way.

*"Pray tell, mortal,"* a feminine voice continued. *"What makes you think that I need*

*your protection or any protection, for that matter?"*

*So, it's a she. And does she mean she's the...* Patrick rationalized. He tried to answer the voice's question, but he could not seem to find the words.

*"You see, mortal,"* the voice spoke in a monotone. *"I don't need your help. I am, in your primitive tongue, the consciousness of the realm. So, tell me, how do you harm consciousness? How do you add to or subtract from it? How do you even quantify or measure it? I am an extension of the consciousness of Creation itself. There is nothing you, your friend, or any other creature can do to me. The realm can be destroyed, but that is as far as that will go. Consciousness is boundless, timeless and limitless. It is omniscient, omnipotent and all-loving. Do you understand anything I just told you, mortal?"*

*"I understand you do not need our help..."* Patrick replied, still not knowing how to address the voice. *"And thank you for your lessons. I truly appreciate them..."* he added with a copious dose of sincerity.

*"You are quite welcome, mortal,"* the voice replied in an almost friendly manner. *"Now, I shall let you continue with your... troubles."*

As soon as the voice said those words, everything resumed its normal course of action as if nothing had happened. The big black sphere of light slowly made its way towards the Core. He thought about what the voice just told him; about not needing his help and how even if everything was destroyed, Consciousness would move on; not because it did not care, but because it was boundless, limitless, and timeless, and, therefore, nonpolarized and non-identified. But he, Patrick, was very polarized and identified with humanity and Earth Realm. The consciousness of Earth Realm may not need any protection or saving, but Earth Realm and humanity needed protection and saving; and Patrick would be damned if he just stood by and watched his home, his people, get destroyed.

As such, Patrick made his decision. In a move that was steeped in a bizarre mix of total self-preservation and complete selflessness, Patrick unconsciously broke free from his paralysis. Without thinking, without knowing, without planning, Patrick moved as if drawing from a well of innate knowledge he was not consciously aware of; not even as Damas.

He teleported towards his unsuspecting enemy and grabbed him from behind. As the big sphere of black light glided closer towards the Core, Patrick teleported directly into the sphere of black light with Satan. As the two men became absorbed into the sphere of black light, Patrick let go of Satan, clenched his right fist, imbued with all the supercharged chi he could summon and crashed it into his chest. The rationale behind his course of action eluded him and he did not care for this rationale either. His action was spawned out of something more innate and fundamental beyond his logical mind and that was all that mattered.

*Trust your instincts,* Shi'mon used to tell him. *They will never steer you wrong.*

A tremendous amount of etheric energy exploded from Patrick's eyes, mouth, and chest in the form of a bright beam of white light until the brightness engulfed both men completely. The etheric energy then returned to Patrick's chest in a powerful suction, pulling Satan, the sphere and finally Patrick into what can only be described as an etheric blackhole that collapsed into itself. The Core was saved and the etheric blackhole disappeared, leaving nothing behind; not even the esoteric signature of either Satan or Patrick.

*"Well done, mortal,"* the formless, omnidirectional voice said softly. *"Well done."*

# CHAPTER TWENTY-SEVEN

## IN SINISTER LAND

**"ASSEMBLE EVERYONE!" MADUK** ordered Yaakov.

Yaakov affirmed and relayed the order to the Sinisters reporting to him.

Seconds later, a loud bell went off and within minutes, tens of thousands of Sinisters in the Realm of Nimbu assembled in front of the main balcony of Maduk's palatial abode. His giant yellow-orange body was a stark contrast against the castle built out of white, marble-like rocks held together with dark, grey mortar forged from mixing orange, superheated Nimbu earth with ice-cold water. Every man, woman and child burned with longing, purpose and most of all, a sense of accomplishment. In their minds Earth Realm was already theirs and, in a few days, humanity will be extinct. Not conquered, not enslaved; extinct. It was not like the humans had not already been on a path to self-extermination with their stockpiles of weapons of mass destruction, anyway. The Sinisters would just be helping in speeding up the timeline for humanity's inevitability, albeit without turning Earth into a barren, uninhabitable, radiation-poisoned realm.

A full-scale assault on the military facilities of Earth Realm's most powerful nations would render Earth Realm almost defenseless. From there, it would be surrender or die. Fear was always a good motivator. Their leaders would have fallen by then, and the rest of humanity would succumb to Maduk's rule. When that happened, the Sinisters would then initiate the rapid extinction of the human species, not by death, but by conversion. Seven-plus billion humans turned into seven-plus billion Sinisters. Even better, Sinisters could procreate. One realm, one species, one mind, one heart, one life under one leader, one god… Maduk.

His impressive figure was covered in a fitted black t-shirt and a black pair of jeans. A white trench coat rested perfectly on his body like a well-done plastic surgery. He glowed visibly, and every Sinister could tell his colors were slightly different, an indication that he was no longer just a Sinister. He was something… more. Some Sinisters prostrated themselves before their leader, their king, their god. Others cowered.

Nimrud stood with proud bearing to Maduk's right while Yaakov was at the assembly ground, standing at the forefront as the first general in the upcoming assault on Earth Realm. Nimrud standing by his ancestor's side instead of leading the assault seemed to suggest that Maduk was already endorsing him to be his undisputed next-in-command. He smiled at the notion that should misfortune befall their fearless leader…

*Patience,* he told himself. *Patience…*

Yaakov started banging the hilt of his spear repeatedly into the ground, and the rest of the Sinisters followed suit. Those who preferred to use their fists as weapons banged their fists into the palms of their free hands. Nimbu's army swayed rhythmically like a yellow-orange sea with the rising crescendo of their prewar cry. No armor, no shields. Nimbu nation had no need for these. They hailed their leader as adrenaline rushed through their bodies. Every man, every woman and every child of Nimbu were ready for battle, for conquest, for glory, for domination.

Maduk allowed his gaze to sweep over them, and his heart was burdened with sorrow, an emotion he had not felt for some time. This would be the last march for most of them, but there was nothing he could do. He could not reverse the process and turn them back to their human form. They were here because of him, and now he was leading them to slaughter. May the heavens have mercy on the last vestige of what he called his soul.

He raised his right hand and an immediate blanket of silence smothered the rising chants.

"My fellow Sinisters," Maduk tapped into the vibrational frequency of the realm as he spoke so that every Sinister could hear him as clearly as if he were speaking directly across from them. "It is time."

Another cheer arose from the masses until he raised his hand once again to silence everyone.

"My fellow Sinisters," Maduk continued. "No more hiding. No more waiting. Our day has finally come. The humans have a saying: the meek will inherit the Earth Realm. They think that saying is for them. But today, we will show that just how wrong they are, how wrong they have been. We are a special breed. We are superior to the humans and today we will inherit Earth Realm."

Suddenly, in the space that lay between Maduk's citadel of a home and the crowd, three humans manifested. Angry murmurs erupted from the Sinisters, and a few on the front line made a move to attack the intruders. But Yaakov raised his spear in the air. The sinisters held back, but their snarls, glares, bared teeth and glowering revealed the palpability of their anger as well as their lust for human blood. It had taken a life of its own.

Shi'mon, Yehuda, and Yochanan scanned the sea of Sinisters spread out in front of them. And then, Shi'mon levitated in the air so that he was at the same level with Maduk.

"Hello, Maduk," Shi'mon said casually.

"Human," Maduk acknowledged.

"I'll make this simple for you and everyone here," Shi'mon said. "You and your... kind... should stand down. If you do there will be no massacre and, in turn, we will offer you a cure."

Maduk's stare burned with an icy feel, while Nimrud erupted in derisive laughter.

"So, we are infected, are we?" Nimrud scoffed. "Not only do you come into our realm unwelcome, but you arrive with insults?"

Nimrud shook his head in derision and his eyes glowed orange.

"You have just sealed your fate and those of your comrades, human."

Shi'mon turned to face the crowd of Sinisters. He floated a few feet forward and then addressed them. He tapped into the vibrational frequency of the realm, just like Maduk had done.

"Listen, everyone," Shi'mon said. "I have a cure. I guarantee your safety if you accept our offer. You will no longer be under the snare of Maduk. You will be human again and even better, we will take you back to Earth Realm. I give you my word. You have nothing to fear from us if you accept."

Shi'mon paused and let his words do their job. Using clairsentience, he sensed confusion and indecision slither through the minds of many sinisters. Now he just had to ride that wave and offer proof of his promise.

"And to lay claim to my boast," Shi'mon added, turning towards Yaakov.

Yaakov levitated towards Shi'mon and an outcry of shock spread across the Sinister populace accompanied by thrusting of weapons and clenched, angry fists in Yaakov's direction. Nimrud gripped the edge of the balcony until his knuckles turned red and eyes glowed red in anger. Maduk, on the other hand, maintained an eerily calm demeanor while his stare burned colder than before.

"Traitor."

"Liar."

"Scum."

"His head is mine," cried Sinister nation.

Shi'mon held Yaakov by the throat, without squeezing and opened his mouth. The Breath of Life flowed as a bright white mist from Shi'mon's mouth into the general's mouth. Yaakov's body convulsed as the Breath of Life infused with his essence, gradually burning off the sinister essence that had taken over Yaakov's essence. The general slowly and completely lost the yellow-orange color of his body as the breath flowed and consumed him at the atomic, subatomic and esoteric levels. The burning was unlike that from a flame and it hailed from the breath, rebirthing him into a new and upgraded human. Once the transformation was complete, Yaakov's body had returned to its original complexion and glowed in a bright whiteness. Shi'mon then released him, and Yaakov dropped into the ground. His body lay there in the lifeless pile of limbs.

Many Sinisters gasped and a few at the frontlines rushed forward; some out of sheer curiosity, others not so much. No one dared touch him though.

"Is he dead?"

"I want to skin him."

"Is he human again?"

"Good riddance."

Yaakov rose to his feet. His eyes remained closed as he turned around to face what used to be his army of Sinisters. When he opened his eyes, they glowed with a blinding light. The sinisters recoiled and staggered away from him out of fear at first, before a few summoned the courage to shove their fear to the side.

"Liar."

"Traitor."

"Kill him," they snapped, snarled, barked and cried in an angry cacophony, silencing those who wanted the cure and become human again.

Nimrud turned and faced Maduk, begging with his eyes for Maduk to give the order. Maduk, grim and silent, nodded. With a nod, Nimrud, leapt over the two-hundred-foot-high balcony and stirred up some orange dust with a majestic landing on both feet. He made his way towards the army of Sinisters while Shi'mon descended slowly towards the ground.

The look in his eyes said everything. Nimrud had something very special reserved for Yaakov. For his part, Yaakov held his stare, unflinching. Nimrud turned his attention towards his army of Sinisters.

"My fellow Sinisters," Nimrud's voice boomed. "Your eyes do not deceive you. You have seen for yourselves. These humans come to our realm and treat us like vermin. They say we are infected because we are who we are. And behold the 'cure'."

Nimrud gestured towards Yaakov, a sneer curling his lip.

"He was never really 'infected' like they say we are," Nimrud continued. "He has been one of them all along. We, Sinisters, do not levitate. But he did. He is a traitor and I will deal with him personally."

"Traitor."

"Kill him."

"Death, death, death, death," Sinister nation chorused in fury over and over.

Nimrud raised his hand in the air and silence doused the raging cries from Sinister nation..

Shi'mon closed his eyes to drown his pity for the sinisters. Nimrud had just put forth solid, albeit not entirely true, arguments that had nullified Shi'mon's promise of a cure and consequently saving Sinisters who wanted to be saved.

"It was our mistake to think of this abomination as one of us," Nimrud continued, referring to Yaakov. "It was our mistake to welcome him into our midst. But the best part of this mistake is that it can be rectified. Rest assured, my fellow Sinisters, the fix will be permanent."

Cheers erupted in a roar that echoed off Maduk's castle.

"So, I ask you all, right here, right now," Nimrud paused for effect.

A deathly silence smothered the realm.

Shi'mon and his team bowed their heads in regret, knowing exactly what was going to happen to these Sinisters. Poor souls.

How easy it was to manipulate them. This was far worse than the day they exterminated the Bright Eyes. The Bright Eyes were not even up to a thousand. But the Sinisters were tens of thousands, and they were all under the spell of one of the greatest generals and conquerors of ancient times.

"Who is ready to seize their birthright?" Nimrud's voice thundered its way into the very egos of every single Sinister of the Realm of Nimbu.

The Sinisters chorused their answer with a cry for blood and glory that rocked the very ground on which they stood.

"I ask again; who is ready to seize their birthright?"

Nimrud turned and looked at Maduk.

Maduk's face bore no emotion, but his heart was being torn asunder. There really was no saving his spawn. Guilt tried to drag him down with them, but no. He could order them to get cured, but that would reveal him as a traitor.

*Two factions will arise,* Maduk rationalized. *Mine and Nimrud's. The way I see it, most will side with my grandson. If their hearts remained unchanged after what they just witnessed, then they are beyond redemption. They had their chance and they chose unwisely. Not my doing.*

Maduk nodded his go-ahead.

"Sinisters," Nimrud called out. "ATTACK."

A third of the Sinister army broke off and headed straight towards the portal while the rest of the army charged towards the three apprentices and Yaakov. And as they charged, six more apprentices crashed in random patterns in their midst like meteors. The force of the combined impacts was supercharged with chi. It eliminated a fifth of the army and caused scattering, yelling and screaming amongst the Sinisters. The Sinisters briefly lost their formation.

Shi'mon, Yehuda, and Yochanan blazed towards the Sinisters, but Yaakov stayed right where he was. His entire focus was on Nimrud, as was Nimrud's on him. Yaakov's eyes glowed white and Nimrud's eyes glowed orange. Then, both men whizzed towards each other.

Shi'mon preferred to start his attack with his fists. He swung and swiped as he zipped amidst the Sinisters and with each attack, a Sinister's head was torn off its body. Sinister's heads rolled with each swipe of Yehuda's ten-inch, double-edged, razor sharp daggers. Those who were not immediately decapitated were left with at least a missing limb.

Yochanan's seven-foot staff, with a foot-long, double-edged, razor-sharp blade with a pointed tip at the end gave him an advantage of reach. He struck from a distance. Tau-ma and Aaron held the entrance to the portal and both men preferred Samurai-sharp katanas as their weapons of choice. Headless, limbless and eviscerated Sinisters fell in the wake of the assault from Shi'mon's squad.

The sinisters battled on, lured and blinded by the trophy called Earth Realm that lay beyond the portal. Despite their supreme fighting skills, the apprentices held little advantage over the overwhelming numbers of the Sinisters. After all, it was just eleven of them versus an army of thousands. The Sinisters dropped dead by the hundreds, but it was still not good enough.

The Sinisters were scrambling now, each trying to seize the opportunity provided by the distraction of their fallen comrades to make it to Earth Realm and never return to the Realm of Nimbu. Tau-mu and Andrew gave their all, but they were losing their stronghold with each passing second.

With a blinding glare, Sarael appeared through the portal and slammed into the swarm of orange-bodied creatures gathered at the entrance. She was a human form encased in green flames, with two whips of green flames extending from her hands. Sarael thrashed, turned, leaped, charged, thrashed and thrashed some more in a violent, beautiful display of skill. She did not stop until every Sinister close to the portal was either decapitated or torn in twain as her fiery whips met their mark with surgical precision.

*"Thanks, Marissa,"* Tau-ma and Aaron spoke in unison via telepathy.

*"Anytime,"* Sarael replied flatly in like manner.

Sinisters swarmed towards Yehuda by the hundreds, hoping to overwhelm him with their numbers. The daggers were not serving him so well and Kundalini had not taken over his body; for which he was immensely grateful. Out of the corner of his eye, he caught a flash of movement as a Sinister leapt in the air, a spear aimed at him. He could teleport away; but he was a blink too late already. He saw his imminent death as if it were slow motion and accepted his fate. But then, out of nowhere, something blurred past him and his assailant ended on the ground, headless and dead. The blur stopped close to him as Sasha took a battle stance beside her lover. Yehuda smiled his gratitude.

"You can thank me later, you stubborn mule," Sasha said, though her gaze remained hard and steady on their mass of opponents.

"Oh woman, I shall do more than thank you later," Yehuda replied, and the deadly duo raged on in their assault against the Sinisters.

*"There's too many of them,"* Yochanan spoke with urgency via telepathy as he absorbed a punch and a kick from two Sinisters.

*"It's an act of desperation,"* Shi'mon replied in kind while parrying an attack. *"They're down to just a few thousand now, based on my clairsentient scan."*

*"They're crazy about you, from what I see,"* Yochanan rolled away as warm air from a red-hot mace graced past his face.

*"How observant of you,"* Shi'mon winced and quickly healed his sliced right bicep and three broken ribs. *"I've got over 500 about to blanket the life out of me right now."*

*"I'll come give you a hand but-"*

Suddenly, an explosion of green light filled the air and the green, flaming figure of Miryam appeared. The Sinisters took a step back from this new foe.

"Let this be fair warning," Miryam said to them through the frequency of the realm. "Surrender now or die."

The Sinisters roared in defiance and raged towards their new enemy. She summoned a burning sphere of flames around her form and bulldozed through the Sinisters. Every Sinister caught in her ball of green flame instantly burned into a pile of ashes.

The Sinisters continued to attack regardless, but their concentration had shifted from Shi'mon and Yochanan to Miryam and the other green, flaming form. Shi'mon and Yochanan decapitated the last of the sinisters who still fought against them and turned their attention towards the two green, flaming figures that attracted the Sinisters like insects to a burning flame. Their weapons clanged on the ground and vanished in a puff of grey smoke. Both men regarded each other before returning to the spectacular, deadly display of efficiency and grace. The green flames from Miryam and Sarael were all-consuming fires that burned the sinisters instantly into ashes upon contact. Screams and smoke from burned Sinister bodies rose upwards like an offering to a god of death and destruction, combining with the magnesium-iron smell of sinister blood to give the air in the realm a dire odor of despair and death.

When they were done, Miryam and Sarael resumed their normal human form and joined the others. Everyone sparked the ethers into clean clothes after ridding themselves of Sinister blood.

"May I never find myself on the bad side of either of you two," Tau-mu said to both Sarael and Miryam. "Whatever you two are…"

Tau-mu left the statement hanging.

"You should've come earlier, sister," Yochanan rolled his eyes. "This could've been over sooner."

"Thought you boys could handle them just fine," Miryam replied. "Besides, we have an enemy much worse than all the Sinisters combined. I had to make sure Sarael was ready above anything else."

"Is it time yet?" Yehuda asked.

"Almost," Miryam sounded more resolute than concerned. "I can sense him approaching. I suggest we recharge our levels of chi, regain our strengths and ready ourselves."

Meanwhile, Yaakov and Nimrud battled each other for their lives. Both men appeared to be evenly matched in style and strength, but the difference came from their respective source of motivation. Nimrud raged from the loss of his army but fought for the prospect of seeing his vision come to pass regardless. Yaakov's was simpler: stop Nimrud at all cost. Centuries of training together resulted in each enemy being able to almost predict the other's moves two steps ahead., but the level of passion invested in this final stand was different for both men. Yaakov was relatively calm. However, Nimrud funneled the ravenous, visceral feelings of betrayal into a cauldron of maddening wrath that boiled over into a ferocious savagery of thwacks and deadly assaults..

"You're done, Nimrud," Yaakov said. "There's nothing left for you. You have nowhere else to go."

"Oh, I have one last thing to do," Nimrud spat. "I must have your head."

"I'm giving you a chance to do the right thing," Yaakov pleaded, holding Nimrud in an elbow and shoulder lock. "Be wiser than the rest of the Sinisters, I implore you. Don't end up like them."

Yaakov gestured at the piles of ashes and decapitated, headless and decimated Sinister bodies around them.

Nimrud staggered away from Yaakov as Yaakov released his arm and pushed him away. He stopped several feet away from Yaakov before accelerating towards Yaakov, who teleported and appeared behind him. Nimrud froze.

"He can teleport," Nimrud mumbled with is head bowed to the ground. "He is… one of them? One of the gods? Or a child of the gods? I… I cannot…"

Nimrud straightened and slowly turned around to face Yaakov. He appraised the realm, full of dead, dying or pile-of-ash sinisters. An anvil of disappointment dropped in the pit of his stomach and a yoke of shame settled on his shoulders.

"So, this is where it ends," Nimrud spoke in calm surrender.

Yaakov saw the acceptance in his eyes.

"But you waste your time, Yaakov. I will be damned if I let you turn me back to a form I have come to despise with every fiber of my being," Nimrud added and quickly seized a sword that lay near his right foot.

"And I will be damned if I fall by your hand."

And with those words, Nimrud placed the tip of the sword at his neck and dove on it.

Yaakov thought about teleporting and snatching the sword away from Nimrud; but Nimrud was beyond salvation. A deep sense of sadness smothered his soul as he walked towards Nimrud's headless body, which twitched on the ground as it gushed its life away from the exposed stump of its neck until it heaved one last time and stopped twitching. Yaakov sighed and closed his eyes. Despite being undercover, Yaakov had developed an attachment to the Sinisters and, most of all, to Nimrud. He looked towards Maduk, who still stood unmoving like a statue on his balcony.

*"May I?"* he asked via telepathy.

*"You may."*

Yaakov nodded. Using telekinesis, he brought Nimrud's severed head to his hands and flipped Nimrud's headless body over so that it lay face-up. He held Nimrud's head for a few seconds and heaved a very heavy sigh. Then, he used telekinesis to place Nimrud's head on the exposed stump of his neck.

"Farewell," Yaakov said almost emotionlessly.

Then, he sparked the ethers into a flame and watched it consume Nimrud's body into a pile of ash. Deep down, he wished he could have done better and saved them all. He summoned a gust of wind using telekinesis and blew Nimrud's ashes away. And, as Nimrud's ashes disappeared in the air, so too did Yaakov's attachment to the sinisters and to Nimrud.

# CHAPTER TWENTY-EIGHT

## THE BEAST

**BEELZEBUB LAY ON** the floor, looking more sexually sated than he could ever remember. Lithilia lay next to him. Her thoughts were anywhere but in the previous few hours.

*Men. No matter the dimension or realm, they are all the same.*

Beelzebub rolled to his side to face her. His eyes were closed, but his hand wandered to her nether regions. She resisted the urge to rip his arm off.

*Maybe later,* she said to herself.

"Are you ready?" Lithilia asked coldly.

His wondering hands on her were starting to become unbearable.

"Ready for what?" Beelzebub groaned.

Lithilia shook her head in disgust.

"If you prefer to stay here, let me know," Lithilia replied.

Beelzebub's eyes snapped open and the feral, soulless look she was used to seeing in them returned. His pupils dilated, swallowing the irises until bottomless black orbs gazed back at her. The sex-deprived creature was gone, and the cursed, fallen archangel was back.

"Of course," Beelzebub replied, his tone of voice indicating his surprise and excitement.

He had arrived at the conclusion that Lithilia did not really plan to live up to her word. Hearing her say this now was a pleasant and unexpected surprise.

"Good," Lithilia stood up. "We're going to the Realm of Nimbu."

A loose-fitting purple gown formed over her naked features and she pulled her hair back in a tight bun. Lithilia felt Beelzebub's horny stare digging into her back, trying to disrobe her.

"I'd love to stay in these squalid surroundings of yours and gyrate your genitals forever," Lithilia spoke with enough sarcasm to cause an eclipse of Solara. "But I have a promise to keep."

Beelzebub smiled, stood up and summoned a white gown over his physique.

The pair teleported to the Realm of Nimbu. Lithilia gaped at the carnage and desolation all over the realm consisting of thickening, dark, yellowish blood and gore that were the dead, dismembered, disemboweled and headless bodies of thousands of Sinisters.

Sixteen gazes, including Maduk's, zoomed in on them. Lithilia did a quick assessment and narrowed her attention to the three people she deemed highest priority: Maduk, her son, a young lady whose etheric signature was very different from the others, but similar to that of an older woman whose etheric signature made Lithilia tremble visibly. Beelzebub broke into a slow, maniacal grin.

"I shall enjoy this very much," he hissed.

He scanned the group until he laid eyes on Yehuda and his grin vanished. He narrowed his eyes and clenched his fists.

"Hello Lithilia," Miryam spoke with a serene calmness. "It's been a long time."

"Cahen," Lithilia beckoned to her son, ignoring Miryam's words. "Come."

Lithilia's quavering voice overshadowed her projection of confidence. Myriam stepped forward and tucked some strands of hair behind her left ear.

"Please, Eva," Lithilia begged and fell on her knees. "Don't hurt my son. Do whatever you want with me, but please, spare my boy. I beg of you."

Cahen regarded his kneeling mother, who was trembling with fright like a leaf floating in the wind. For a moment, his features softened with pity for her. He walked towards Miryam and put an arm around her shoulders. Lithilia cupped her mouth, held her breath and stifled a scream.

"Fear not, mother," Cahen said. "As you can see, mother-"

Cahen hesitated, realizing the awkwardness of the situation. He shrugged and then continued.

"Mother-Eva is no longer angry with me. She has forgiven me and thanks to our collaborated effort," he waved at the rest of the apprentices, "the Sinisters have been exterminated."

Cahen walked toward Lithilia with steady, confident steps.

"I did not lift a finger against my followers, though," Maduk continued. "I could not, even if I wanted to. They were offered a way out. But they chose to go like this instead. And you no longer have to be afraid of her, mother. She has helped me find my peace, and I think if you let her, she will help you too. You no longer have to run away from her. You no longer have to-"

"Stop," Lithilia yelled and jumped to her feet. "Just stop it right there. Do you even hear yourself?"

Lithilia closed the distance between them, reached up and grabbed the lapels of his white trench coat.

"Do you know who she is and what she is capable of?"

"Let him go," Miryam ordered, and a green glow surrounded her body.

The rest of the group, except for Sarael, reflexively took a few steps backward. Lithilia eyed them with wide eyes, her throat suddenly parched and freezing talons of fear strengthened their grip around their spine. If those who were with Eva were also wary of her abilities, then what else was there to do? She, Lithilia, stood no chance in Creation against Eva. No mélange of essences borrowed or stolen would give her any form of advantage over Eva. She swallowed convulsively.

"I said let him go right now," Miryam ordered.

"Who do you think you are?" Lithilia yelled at Miryam with false bravado. "You think because you raised him for a few years you're now his mother?"

"It only took me those years then and a few hours now to give Cahen the one thing you could never give him," Miryam replied.

Lithilia's eyes flashed in an orange-yellowish hue as her jealousy-fueled anger flared. The truth in Miryam's words stung like a knife stuck deep into the thigh. Maduk seized his mother by the shoulders and forced her to look at him.

"Mother," Maduk spoke firmly. "You do not have to like her. You do not even have to speak with her after this. Just do not go against her or Ahben."

Lithilia tried to look past her son, but Maduk jerked her shoulders back so that she was facing him again.

"Mother," Maduk yelled. "For once in your life just listen to me and do as I ask. Trust me. Please."

"And thanks for making him kill me, by the way," Sarael interjected.

Lithilia's eyes returned to normal immediately when she heard Sarael's voice, and she turned her attention slowly towards Sarael.

"Ahben...?" Lithilia spoke as if she were in a daze.

"I'd say pleased to meet you, but I'm a poor liar," Sarael replied.

"But... your etheric signature...," Lithilia said as she took dazed steps away from Maduk towards Sarael. "It's so... *different*."

"Same mother, different father," Sarael shrugged. "What can I say? Esoteric genetics can be very interesting."

"Stay right where you are, Lithilia," Miryam ordered. "Don't come any closer to my child, you esoteric vampire."

"Yes," Beelzebub said beside Lithilia.

She had almost forgotten The Beast's presence.

"I see it now. This is perfect indeed."

Beelzebub leaned forward as if to sniff something in the air. The rest of the group instantly assumed fighting stances.

Lithilia retreated towards Beelzebub as she extended her hand towards Maduk, beckoning him to join her. But Maduk backed towards the other group. Her hand dropped to her side as her heart shattered into smithereens as if her son had just pulled the pin to a grenade, glued it to her heart and walked away, uncaring of the carnage he left behind. However, somewhere inside her psyche, Lithilia found the strength and resolve to quickly reassemble her shattered heart and return to the reason why she and Beelzebub came to Nimbu in the first place.

"Mother," Maduk called out to her. "What is Beelzebub saying?"

"Remember how I told you I had a plan to send him back?" Lithilia asked without expecting an answer. "The one who gave Kazuk, the king of Hell Realm, the spell that cast Beelzebub out is a multidimensional being known as The Scribe. Only a being from a dimension that is higher than the Dimension of Lemuria, where angels dwell, can break the curse and set Beelzebub free."

"How did you come to know this?" Maduk demanded.

"Not important right now, Cahen," Lithilia replied. "All you need to know is that I've been to many realms and dimensions and met many creatures."

Lithilia scanned her opponents using clairsentience and clairvoyance. She then turned and pointed a finger at Sarael.

"And whoever her father is, fits that criteria," Lithilia continued. "Plan A was to find a creature that fits the esoteric requirements, obtain their essence and infuse it with Beelzebub's essence. I have a feeling that Plan A is certainly not an option right now."

"What makes you think she has a choice?" Beelzebub interjected.

Beelzebub relished at the shocked look on their faces, including Sarael's. But the one called Miryam remained unmoved. Her focus was more than razor-sharp and directed at Lithilia and himself. He wondered if this creature could actually withstand him in any way.

Aspects of her etheric signature summoned memories of a very distant past. But how was that possible? Did that mean she was not even human? And if she was not human, did she stand a chance against him? He smiled as he answered his own question: he was about to find out.

"Is this true, mother," Sarael asked her mother.

Sarael's voice trembled as she spoke.

"Is this why you have been shielding me all this time?"

Miryam did not reply.

"I see," Sarael nodded.

"You are not seriously considering this. Are you, mother?" Maduk asked.

"I deliver on my promises, Cahen," Lithilia replied. "And everything I do, I do it for you. Remember that."

"From this moment forward," Maduk hissed as pale green flames spewed from his eyes and mouth. "I no longer want to be associated with you. You are no longer my mother."

"Cahen?" Sarael eyes bulged in excitement. "Your eyes... So cool."

"Sister, get Sarael out of here right now," Shi'mon yelled. "We'll slow him down and buy you some time."

The rest of the group nodded and took battle stance as their eyes glowed.

"No, brother," Miryam replied calmly as she turned into a green-flaming human form.

Sarael's transformation was instant as well.

"It ends here and now. Or we will never be at peace, knowing that we are being hunted by this pitiful creature."

Lithilia realized that Miryam did not care to mention her name. So, her hour had finally come; she was going to face her judge, jury, and executioner. She was responsible for Eva losing her son Ahben in the Garden of Aiden. And now, she was about to sacrifice Miryam's daughter, Sarael, over to Beelzebub. Same scene, same cast, different scenario and most likely a similar outcome.

"See why I said you should have-" Yehuda started saying, but Sasha cut him off with a deep passionate kiss.

When Sasha peeled herself away from him and looked into his glowing eyes, a tear traced a path down each cheek from each glowing eye.

"I love you," Sasha said and turned to face their common enemy without waiting for a reply from Yehuda.

"Damn you, woman," Yehuda replied and turned to face Beelzebub.

The twelve apprentices and Sasha charged towards Beelzebub in unison. Beelzebub, with vague dispassion, watched thirteen pairs of legs move towards him as if they were walking. He smiled and shook his head in amusement.

*Apparently, they never learned from the last time.*

Beelzebub strolled towards the vermin that were crawling towards him. He would toy with them for a little bit before he ended them one-by-one. That would entertain his ego long enough before his departure. Yes, his departure. And with the thought of finally returning home, Beelzebub moved into a jog.

Beelzebub attacked with prejudice; not extreme just yet. His attacks were precise, concise and surgical. Beelzebub wanted them beaten and broken so badly that they would require several minutes to heal themselves. He wanted them to watch helplessly as he possessed Sarael and take her essence.

Her essence was the key to his release and nothing was going to stop him from taking it. Not Maduk, the other woman, and definitely not Lithilia. She was wrong to have trusted him in the first place. He was Beelzebub, King of Demons and General of Luceefa's army. Earth Realm was going to pay upon his return from Hell Realm.

*And I cannot wait.*

By the time Beelzebub finished his assault, the thirteen were sprawled on the ground, mired in their blood and writhing from excruciating pain spawned from crushed internal organs and many jagged pieces of broken bones protruding from various parts of their bodies.

"Take a moment to heal yourselves," Beelzebub sneered at them. "I will take what I came for and then, I will destroy you all."

He turned his attention towards Maduk, Sarael, and Miryam. He looked from one to the other as if deciding who to attack first. He smiled mischievously and made up his mind. Might as well get what he came for first, before moving on to the others. As such, Beelzebub zoomed in on Sarael and prepared to charge.

But even before Beelzebub moved, Maduk was already upon him. With a spear dive, Maduk lifted Beelzebub several feet in the air and drove the fallen archangel into the ground with such force that the king of demons' body ended up buried three feet into the ground. Capitalizing on Beelzebub's shock, Maduk landed three successive punches to his face, with each punch driving Beelzebub's head deeper into the ground.

However, on the fourth punch, Beelzebub caught Maduk's fist and twisted sharply and unleashed a knee into Maduk's groin at the same time. Maduk yelled in pain as Beelzebub tossed him to the side. Maduk crashed into Lithilia, and mother and son landed in a heap several feet away.

Beelzebub sprang to his feet. He summoned his archangel's battle flame and charged towards Sarael.

Miryam summoned a sphere of green flames around her and slammed into Beelzebub like a wrecking ball, knocking him several yards away. Her esoteric flames stuck to his body, overriding his archangel battle flame and burning deep into his flesh. Screams of burning pain and rage escaped from Beelzebub's throat. He quickly regained his composure and sparked the ethers to heal his burning body. He gaped at how much slower his body was healing.

Miryam dismissed the sphere and blazed towards Beelzebub again, whose pitch-black eyes widened in surprise at her speed. Miryam threw some punches and kicks in succession, but Beelzebub either diverted or blocked them all. He realized that he had significantly underestimated this creature he was dueling with and upped his attack to the highest level possible. Before Miryam could react, white, hot pain pulsated throughout her body with each of Beelzebub's repeated strike to her diaphragm, temples, solar plexus and spine until she slumped to the ground from physical paralysis. The amount of time needed to completely heal herself was 9 seconds, which would be 8.99 seconds too many since Beelzebub was already moving in for the kill. Myriam watched helplessly as his cocked, red, smoldering right fist accelerated towards her face.

A whip of green flames wrapped around his fist and yanked back with a savageness that wrenched his shoulder from the socket. Before he could process what just happened, Sarael drove her knee into his chin. His head jerked violently upwards and backward. Sarael yanked the whips of fire over her head to her left and brought it down sharply. Beelzebub's body crashed into the ground with reckless abandon. She repeated the same sequence. This time, she whipped his body to her right before leaping in the air and yanking Beelzebub upwards in the process. She then whooshed downwards and slammed his body again into the ground. She did a forward roll and wrapped flaming whips around Beelzebub's neck. She was about to yank his head off when something slammed into her, knocking her away from him.

"No," Maduk cried and zipped towards Lithilia.

Maduk grabbed his birth mother by the neck and threw her to the side as if she was a pillow of feathers.

"I do not want to hurt you," Maduk said. "But if you *ever* lay a finger on Ahben again, I will end you."

The look in Maduk's eyes was the only indication of the irrefutable truth in Maduk's words that Lithilia needed.

*He really has changed in every sense of the word: physically, psychologically and esoterically*, Lithilia thought as she held back tears of pain and anguish.

"Then I guess it's time to initiate Plan B," Lithilia said.

Lithilia looked towards Miryam's direction who was already rising to her feet. She pursed her lips to steel her resolve before teleporting to Beelzebub.

"You're a demon. So, do what you do best," she exclaimed.

Beelzebub looked at Lithilia as if she was insane but then he hesitated when he realized what she meant.

"You can't take her essence even if you tried," Lithilia added.

Beelzebub nodded. Lithilia was right. For now, he could not get to Sarael to take her essence. But he will return and next time, he will not be alone. Sarael's essence was something that he ultimately had to have, even if it meant burning Earth Realm to the ground, which was already part of his plan anyway.

*Because I still need to be free of Kazuk's curse and her essence holds the key, like the woman said earlier*, Beelzebub thought.

Thus, Beelzebub wasted no time. He grabbed Lithilia by the neck and stared into her eyes. Lithilia stared back into his as his body slowly disintegrated into millions of red-yellow embers before transmuting into golden yellow light and flowing into her mouth. Lithilia's body convulsed as the yellow golden light slid into her mouth. Every cell, subatomic particle and etheric aspect that constituted Lithilia surrendered to the new essence that was taking full possession of her. Finally, Lithilia's body jerked violently and levitated in the air. An explosion of blinding golden light signified the completion of the possession. She landed on the ground and lay there for a few seconds as if she were dead. Then, she slowly pushed herself to her knees before standing upright. When she opened her eyes, her eye sockets burned with a soulless pitch blackness, and when she spoke, her voice was as deep and as hollow as evil itself.

"My son, this was always the plan, even though it was Plan B," Lithilia said. "He will use my etheric signature to return to Hell Realm. I have become his new host, and it will stay like this until I find a way to free myself."

Lithilia shifted her gaze towards Sarael and then to Miryam.

"If I had told you about this before, you would have tried to stop me, because you love Cahen too much. You're too good, even after what I did to you. At least, this way, he will return to Hell Realm, and I will be away from you."

Lithilia returned her attention towards Maduk.

"I may have failed you as a mother, but I will never stop loving you," Lithilia said. "This is the start of my atonement for all the evils I have perpetrated during my existence. Goodbye, my son. I love you."

With those words, Lithilia lifted her gaze to the sky and teleported to Hell Realm, without even giving Cahen the chance to say something in return or to try to stop her.

# CHAPTER TWENTY-NINE

# FUTURE PAST

**THE YEAR WAS** 2102 B.C.E. Two guards stood at the entrance to a small community temporarily settled near an oasis about 6km south of Damascus. A guard swiped beads of sweat from his forehead with the back of his hand. The burning heat in the desert during the day was not uncommon. Today, however, the heat was merciless. Soon, his shift will be over, though.

*And then, I will rid myself of this armor and cool off with Aliya in my tent,* he grinned mischievously.

He mopped his face with a kerchief he retrieved from his belt. When he made to return the kerchief to his belt, he recoiled slightly from surprise. A man was barely a stone's throw away from them and nothing but hot sand stretched across his vision for leagues.

*But how did he...?* he wondered. *How could I have missed that?*

He shot a sideways glance at his companion, who seemed to be unmoved by this stranger's sudden appearance.

*I must have missed him then,* he shrugged, though his rational mind screamed for a logical explanation to this stranger's sudden 'appearance'.

The stranger's robe was pristine white, ankle length, most likely silk and very intricately sewn. He appeared to be in his mid-forties, with a thick beard and a turban matching his white robe wrapped around his head. A gold necklace, at the end of which a gold pendant depicting Solara with rays streaming from it, hung from his neck. He held a tray of food and drink. The guard tightened his grip around his spear, suspicion born of the subtle authority and power that this stranger radiated gripping him.

"Hello, sir. I would like to speak with your lord, please," the stranger said to the guard standing in front of a huge tent.

The guard straightened, staring the man down.

"Be gone, peasant. Our lord is not accepting gifts at this time."

"I understand, sir," the stranger said. "Before I leave, could you kindly let your lord know that Melchizedek was here?"

The guard wrinkled his nose in condescension, though something about this stranger did not sit well.

"Of course," the guard replied a little less aggressively, feeling a subtle compulsion to relax. "I will inform my lord of your visit."

"Thank you, sir," Melchizedek replied. "I bid you good day then."

He turned with his tray of food and drink and walked away from the tent.

"What is going on out there?" a deep voice called from within the tent.

The guard rushed inside and beat his chest in salute.

"Nothing my lord. Just a peasant bringing gifts."

"Ordinary peasants do not wear such sweet-smelling perfume," the guard's lord replied.

*And command such respect and awe,* he thought. *Who was this man?*

"Did he say what his name is?"

"Melchizedek, my lord," the guard replied.

The guard was almost knocked to the ground as his lord sprang past him. The guard cowered, fearing that he was in deep trouble later. He stepped out of his lord's tent. When he saw his lord catch up with this stranger called Melchizedek and kneel at Melchizedek's feet, the guard raised his eyebrows and gawked in confusion and surprise.

"Oh no," he gasped, cupped his mouth as his eyes nearly popped out their sockets. "My lord is going to roast me like a lamb later."

"My deepest apologies, Sire," the guard's lord bowed with his face touching the ground. "My guard knows not who you are. Please, forgive his transgression and mine."

"Rise, Abram," Melchizedek chuckled slightly. "Do not burden yourself with such minor transgressions. As you said, your guard knows not who I am."

Abram rose to his feet, head bowed slightly in respect and offered to take the tray from Melchizedek.

"No," Melchizedek said. "I will properly offer this to you once we are inside."

"As you wish, Sire," Abram replied, still bowing slightly. "Please, follow me."

When they were at the entrance to Abram's tent, Abram asked his guards to fetch everyone in the camp. He then parted the drapes at the entrance to his tent.

The tent was fashioned from white linen and 2.5m tall at the apex and 1.8m tall at the entrance. A rug spread across half of the floor. The image of a lamb and a shepherd holding a staff in a green field was stitched into it with superb expertise. The walls of the tent remained bare and an armchair sat idly at the far end of the tent, directly opposite from the door. A small grey rug with two, deep blue equilateral triangles interlocking perfectly with each other draped over the back of the chair. Two red pillows lined either side of the tent from the door. Inside the tent was around 15 degrees cooler than outside and smelled of a sweet blend of jasmine and sage. A sword in its scabbard rested next to the armchair and a small mattress lay on the far right corner of the tent.

"If it pleases his majesty, it will be my honor to welcome him to my humble abode," Abram said.

"The honor is mine, Abram," Melchizedek said and entered Abram's tent.

Abram quickly snatched the rug draped over his armchair and replaced it with his finest cloth made of silk. He then humbly offered his seat to Melchizedek.

"You are too kind," Melchizedek said and sat down.

"I am honored beyond words to have you in my abode, Sire," Abram replied.

"My lord," a guard called from out of the tent, before fearfully sticking his head into Abram's tent. "Everyone is here."

"Good," Abram replied. "If his majesty could kindly follow me."

Melchizedek set his tray of food and drink on the floor and followed Abram. Everyone in the camp had gathered outside, their faces full of curiosity.

"Everyone, behold Melchizedek, King of Salem and High Priest of the Most High God," Abram bellowed. "You will all address him as 'king' and give him all the respect he is due as king and high priest of the Most High."

Abram was the first to kneel in front of Melchizedek before the rest of his camp members did the same.

*So much for subtlety.* Melchizedek thought.

He did appreciate Abram's humility, though. Abram did, indeed, seem to be a good man and the hand of the Most High was truly upon him. Abram's auric colors were almost golden, indicative of his goodness of heart. Melchizedek had seen Abram's future by glimpsing into the Dimension of Time, and he thought it would be a great opportunity to visit this man of promise as the man embarked on his path towards a purpose unknown to him... yet.

"Rise, Abram," Melchizedek commanded.

Abram rose to his feet.

"You may dismiss your people now."

Abram dismissed his campers and retreated into his tent with Melchizedek. He sat on one of the pillows on the ground and folded his legs in as Melchizedek eased himself into Abram's armchair.

"That was an impressive feat you accomplished with your men last week," Melchizedek said, crossing his legs. "Defeating four kings with so few fighters."

"Praise be to the Most High, my king," Abram replied humbly. "It was by His mighty hand that we defeated our adversaries."

"Praise be to the Most High, indeed," Melchizedek reiterated.

He then regarded Abram for a moment and gave Abram an esoteric scan.

"You know me as king and high priest," Melchizedek said. "These are but titles given to a man by other men. Alas, before I am king, before I am high priest, I am but a servant of the Most High, just as you are. What you do not know is that I am chosen to be the living luminary and anointed of this Age of the Ram, the Age of Aries. My purpose is to prepare humanity for the next evolutionary leap, which will not be in my time."

Melchizedek then reached for the tray he brought with him and removed the cloth that covered its contents.

"Take these gifts of bread and wine," Melchizedek said. "They are symbols of the illusion and truth that is Man and a herald of future tidings to come."

Abram dropped to his knees, bowed his head and accepted the gifts from Melchizedek. He did not understand what Melchizedek had just said but he was honored beyond words. Not only was he hosting the one and only king, sage and magus of unprecedented renown of his era, but he was also receiving gifts from this venerable icon. Abram was a righteous man of great reputation, born from him being specially called by the Most High to be the ancestor of a chosen people. But, compared to Melchizedek, the perfect blend of royalty, wisdom, holiness and enigma, Abram felt insignificant.

"Gratitude, my king," Abram said. "If it pleases my king, I would like to break this bread and drink of this cup with him."

A kind smile formed behind Melchizedek's thick beard.

"Thank you, Abram," Melchizedek said. "But I am afraid I must decline."

"Oh," Abram's voice was heavy with disappointment and confusion. "Did I offend his majesty?"

"On the contrary," Melchizedek chuckled. "You honor me greatly. Alas, this gift is for you, from me. It comes with my blessings and the blessings of the Most High."

Abram set the tray on the ground next to him and bowed in gratitude with his head touching the feet of the king. Melchizedek placed his right hand on

Abram's head and a jolt of energy flooded through Abram's being. Abram jerked and scrambled backwards in awe and exhilaration.

"My king…," Abram tried to speak, but he could say no more.

"Rise and sit, A-Brahma," Melchizedek said.

Abram did as he was told. For a moment, he thought he heard Melchizedek say his name incorrectly, until it dawned on him that Melchizedek's words were deliberate.

*But why?* Abram wondered. *Why would he refer to me as 'A-Brahma'?*

His gaze was averted towards the floor as he pondered on the name.

*I do not know what it means,* he concluded. *But if the high priest of the Most High calls me thus, then so be it. I will receive this blessing with all my heart. Praise be to the Most High.*

"If my king would not break bread and drink wine with me, perhaps my king could accept a humble token from me and my people," Abram offered.

Melchizedek did not want to break Abram's heart by refusing Abram's offer. He already had more riches than any other mortal on the realm. He could have more, if he wanted to. He sighed at the thought about how humans spent their entire lives seeking things that withered away and never cared about the things that really mattered in life; like awakening to the ability to have all of Creation in the palm of one's hand.

"It will be my honor," Melchizedek replied.

Abram glowed and grinned with delight. He dashed out of his tent and barked a series of orders to his servants. A few moments later, a man poked his head through the curtains of Abram's tent.

"My lord, everything is ready."

"If his majesty could follow me, please," Abram gestured at his guest.

Melchizedek followed Abram outside the tent and was welcomed by kneeling servants and a huge stack of gold, silver, precious stones and many other very expensive artifacts.

"Your majesty," Abram said with pride. "Please accept our offer of a tenth of the spoils from the war. I hope it pleases his majesty."

"It pleases me greatly," Melchizedek replied. "Thank you, A-Brahma."

*"Your highness, apologies for the intrusion,"* a voice said telepathically to the high priest. *"But there has been a disturbance at the inner temple."*

*"I will be there shortly,"* Melchizedek replied in like manner.

"I must return now," Melchizedek said. "There is something I must attend to with urgency."

"Of course, your majesty," Abram replied. 'I shall have my servants fetch your carriage for you."

"No need for that," Melchizedek replied. "I did not bring a carriage."

Melchizedek did not wait for Abram to say anything. He lifted his index fingers and traced two circles in the air. When he opened his palms forward, two wormholes of light suddenly burst forth and widened.

Some onlookers gasped and clasped their mouths, others stumbled backwards and fell to the ground, a few prostrated themselves in worship, while the rest ran for their lives. Two men in black robes walked through the portals and took a knee in front of Melchizedek.

"*Take these to the treasury,*" Melchizedek said telepathically, waving a hand at the gifts he had been presented.

The two men rose and spread their palms towards the riches. The piles divided into two and the two men lifted each using telekinesis. Each pile floated in front of the men as they directed the spoils through the portals. Then, they walked through the portals which closed behind them.

Melchizedek then turned and smiled at Abram.

"Stay on the right path and the Most High God will always be with you," he said. "Peace and goodwill on to you, A-Brahma."

As Abram gawked in awe, Melchizedek sparked the ethers into another portal and walked through it. When the portal closed behind him, everyone jerked slightly and stared around as if in a daze. Their faces twisted in confusion, unsure of what was happening and why they had no recollection of why they were all on the ground in the first place. Abram surveyed his people as his mind raced in every direction, unable to make sense of what had just happened.

"*Do not burden yourself, A-Brahma,*" Melchizedek said telepathically. "*They will not recall me ever being there and they will never recall what just happened. But you will. It will guide you as you journey through your purpose.*"

Abram had so many questions for which he knew he would not have answers at the moment. This was Melchizedek... *the* Melchizedek.... The greatest sage and high priest of the time and most favored by the Most High.

"*Go now, and be the man you are destined to become,*" Melchizedek said. "*Go with the blessings of the Most High.*"

Melchizedek appeared in the inner temple of his temple in Heliopolis. Every cell in his body tingled to the disturbance of energy in the inner temple. The disturbance was non-threatening. It felt more like a presence that was... familiar? He gave the inner temple multiple esoteric scans. He detected a tinge of an etheric signature, but no form, physical or etheric, was attached to the signature. Finally, he decided to take another rout.

"Show yourself," Melchizedek commanded.

"As you wish," a voice said, and a form manifested in front of the sage.

Melchizedek and the intruder stared at each other for a moment. Neither said a word until the intruder broke the silence.

"Hello," the man said.

"Who are you?" Melchizedek asked.

"I am you," the man replied.

Using clairsentience, Melchizedek detected that this man was telling the truth. But what did the man mean by those words?

"Where are you from?" Melchizedek asked.

"The important question is when am I from," the man offered.

Melchizedek furrowed his eyebrows in confusion.

"I am from the Age of the Fish," the man replied and took a few steps towards Melchizedek.

"My name is Yeshua," he said. "Your next incarnation and your descendant by many generations. Like you, I am the chosen luminary of the realm in the Age of the Fish, or Pisces."

Melchizedek reached out cautiously and touched Yeshua's face, not knowing what to expect. Then he felt Yeshua's shoulders and arms. Yes, Yeshua was as real as the air he was breathing, and his etheric signature was... Melchizedek had no words to describe Yeshua's etheric signature.

"I never dreamed a day like this would come to pass," Melchizedek said. "To behold a future incarnation in the flesh. But... how?"

"Shadow of the Soul," Yeshua replied. "You have been preparing a long time now for that journey. In the next Solara cycle, you will journey there, face your trials and triumph over them. Then, you will receive an esoteric upgrade up to the purpose of your current existence."

Melchizedek narrowed his eyes and pursed his lips.

"Upgrade," Yehuda repeated. "Like an improvement. Sorry, it's a term from the future. Don't worry. Me telling you about this now changes nothing about this event to come."

"Ah, I see," Melchizedek exclaimed and laughed a little. "Thank you."

"You're welcome," Yehuda smiled and folded his arms across his chest. "So, as I was saying, when I went to the Shadow of the Soul. I passed all the tests and received my... uh... improvement. I am now a multi-dimensional being and can access the Dimensions of Time, Space, Energy and Ether at will."

"You can what?" Melchizedek exclaimed.

"You heard me well, my past incarnation," Yeshua grinned like a proud, intelligent scholar. "It took some practice and some getting used to, though."

"And I thought I would never behold anyone..." Melchizedek spoke as if he was in a daze.

"Best you believe, my fellow incarnation," Yeshua said. "It is very possible, and *you* achieved it, through me, of course."

Melchizedek beamed, pride filling him like a fine wine in a beautiful pitcher at the notion that, though he was not going to be able to access those dimensions in his current lifetime, that would change in the next age. A deep sense of peace and letting go came with that.

"These are great tidings, indeed, Yeshua," Melchizedek said.

Melchizedek's expression changed as he realized that Yeshua was not there for a friendly visit.

"Pray tell, why are you here?" Melchizedek asked.

"The fate of Creation lies in our hands," Yeshua replied. "Long story and I won't bore you with the details. Not your place to know now. I apologize."

"I understand," Melchizedek said. "There is no need for apologies."

"I am re-writing the path of Creation to prevent the vibration of Chaos from becoming dominant across it," Yeshua said. "And I need your help."

"Anything," Melchizedek replied with unbridled resolution..

"Beneath the lion's paw lies the key to it all," Yeshua said. "Beneath the lion's paw lies the last piece of The Scribe's plan for turning our realm as a catalyst for his grand plan."

"The Scribe?" Melchizedek asked.

"Another multidimensional entity, like I have become," Yeshua explained. "He is also known as Chaos. He wants to undo Creation and I am his nemesis."

"I see," Melchizedek rubbed his chin, unable to fully grasp the portentous nature of the situation. "The lion's paw..."

"Indeed," Yeshua affirmed. "This is me, us, re-writing that script. Your task will be to find a way to send the message I will be giving you shortly. I trust you, we, will find a way."

"So... go to the lion's paw and send a message..." Melchizedek reiterated. "A message to whom?"

"To me," Yeshua replied. "The 'me' living in a realm and dimension much higher than that of Earth Realm."

"Oh," Melchizedek bit his lower lip. "Very well. I shall. And when I am at the lion's paw, what will I find there?"

"The ultimate catalyst of the vibration of chaos," Yeshua replied. "The herald of the end called... The Darkness."

# CHAPTER THIRTY

# HOME

**LITHILIA, NOW POSSESSED** by Beelzebub, appeared in Hell Realm. Beelzebub thrashed and roiled within her, feasting on and concocting a mélange of essences from a buffet of essences she had imbibed and stored within her. All the essences she had stolen, used, kept and discarded from creatures from various realms and dimensions had left their imprints on her essence; some more than others. Her main essence remained dominant, though. She was not a whore of essences for nothing. And now, a part of her ability to consume other essences became imprinted on Beelzebub's during the possession, enabling Beelzebub to make certain copies of the imprints of essences etched into hers.

Hell Realm was abuzz with more excitement than usual. Lithilia's gut knotted with a strange sense of foreboding. She teleported to the main court outside where the crowd had gathered.

*"By Celestia,"* Beelzebub exclaimed within her.

*"What's going on?"* Lithilia asked.

*"Why spoil the surprise,"* Beelzebub replied.

Lithilia grew impatient. When she tried to reach Kazuk and failed, her fears magnified a thousand-fold. Lithilia grabbed a creature by the arm and forced it to turn and face her.

"Tell me what's going on," she demanded.

"You should go to the courts and see for yourself," the creature replied.

Lithilia let go of the creature's arm and stood frozen in place, not knowing how to proceed. Her gut begged her to flee, but her twisted sense of integrity demanded that she stay and keep her promise to Beelzebub. Her husband was unreachable and the creature did not address her by her title of queen as Hell

Realm was accustomed to doing. The atmosphere of Hell Realm suddenly had an ominous feel to it.

*"Are you going to stand there and bore me with your noisy thoughts or are you going to do as the creature suggested?"* Beelzebub asked with too much excitement in his voice.

*But why? Why is he so excited?*

A few seconds went by as Lithilia assessed her next move.

*"Screw this,"* Lithilia exclaimed.

Lithilia-Beelzebub teleported to the main court and instantly regretted it. She should have listened to her gut and fled. Screw whatever sense of integrity she was fooling herself she had. Too late, alas. No turning back now.

The King of Hell Realm was on his knees, hands bound behind his back with bonds of angel light. Lithilia's eyes met his. His eyes were heavy with sadness at her foolish decision to show up in the courts that moment. His gaze pleaded with her to run if she could.

*He can't reach me because they're jamming his telepathic link,* Lithilia gasped. *But who could possess such power? Oh no!*

Lithilia's gaze migrated from her husband to his captors, and a whirlpool of emotions stirred within her, threatening to suck her under as she answered her own question even before her eyes validated her answer. She glared at her mortal enemy; the one creature she had sworn to kill. The one creature who was the root cause of all her woes. The one who initiated the chain reaction that spiraled her life out of the paradise of the Garden of Aiden.

This creature was the other binary center of her existence- an aberration that harbored nothing akin to selflessness, care or love. The creature was the existence that epitomized the darkness inside her in its purest form. It was the part of her that was birthed in paranoia and could only be quenched by blood and death.

Lithilia had dreamed of this moment. She had longed for this opportunity. She had lived for it. Everything she had done, everything she had been through, subjected herself to and become, had boiled to this singularity. And now that the opportunity was here, it was far from perfect. Here she was, trapped in the center of a countless number of creatures in one of Creation's many cesspools. Worse, that feeling was nothing compared to that of being trapped by the King of Demons, who had found the right blend of essences within her to give his own essence a little tweak to his advantage. And worst still, Lithilia was face-to-face with the one Beelzebub and Metatron reverently referred to as their general.

Luceefa loomed over a glaring, fearless, defiant Kazuk.

When Lithilia appeared in the courts, the excitement in the air was instantly drowned in a deathly quiet. Luceefa turned slowly and met her glare. Lithilia expected Luceefa to reply with a glare of her own. Instead, Luceefa regarded her as if she was looking *into* Lithilia. She did not care about the creature that stood in front of her. Maybe she did not even recognize the vermin that housed someone of invaluable importance to her. She took slow steps towards Lithilia, as if moving any faster was going to ruin the moment. Her seductive eyes bulged and glowed in surprise and her perfectly shaped lips parted in a radiant grin that revealed brilliant, white teeth. She sensed a presence within Lithilia that she thought she was never going to sense or see again.

"Brother?" Luceefa called softly.

Luceefa gently ran her fingers across Lithilia's cheeks and then quickly withdrew her touch. Joyous shock retreated behind an angry scowl. She whipped her head towards Kazuk.

"Release him," Luceefa commanded. "*Now.*"

"First cut me loose," Kazuk replied softly.

In a swift motion, Luceefa summoned her sword and brought it down on Kazuk's bonds. He stood up, rubbed his sore wrists and walked slowly towards his wife.

Lithilia looked into her husband's eyes and knew she was as doomed as he already was. Kazuk gave Lithilia a slight nod of reassurance. He placed his right hand on Lithilia's forehead and spoke in a tongue that was alien to everyone present except for Lithilia. As Kazuk spoke, a tingling spread throughout Lithilia's essence and the energy signature that resonated with her essence was as familiar as the language she was hearing. The Scribe sometimes left traces behind, when he wanted to.

Suddenly, Lithilia shut her eyes, tilted her head upwards and screamed. Every nerve ending of hers lit up in pain, as though fire consumed her. She screamed and opened her arms as her body arched forward. A golden mist oozed gently out of her screaming mouth as Beelzebub's essence was ripped away from hers. The mist coalesced into a humanoid silhouette without form.

*"He is free at last,"* Lithilia sighed as the last of the golden mist left her lips and the pain in her body died away, as if it was never there in the first place.

A foreboding of dark times to come for her seized her soul.

The silhouette resonated with the vibrational frequency of the Dimension of Lemuria and summoned a new form. Beelzebub stood in the flesh, no longer as a cursed and banished demon, but as a renewed and upgraded archangel.

Luceefa could barely wait for Beelzebub to complete his materialization process before crashing into his arms. Beelzebub summoned a dark, grey gown over his naked body. Metatron joined the pair and the three held one another in a tight group hug.

"Oh, brother," Luceefa exclaimed with unimaginable joy. "I have missed you so very much."

"I have missed you too, sister. So very much," Beelzebub replied. "And you too, brother. It feels so good to be back."

"This moment could not be any more perfect," Metatron chimed in. "Here you are. Both of you, before my very own eyes. I do not know what to say…"

"Then say nothing," Beelzebub said and squeezed them closer.

Beelzebub stepped back and took Luceefa's face in his hands.

"I have a gift for you."

Beelzebub then turned towards Lithilia.

"Thank you. For bringing me back home and for letting me possess you because whatever you are, whatever your essence constitutes, it is a lot more powerful than you're aware of. And when I possessed you…"

Beelzebub trailed off, grinning mischievously. And Lithilia's eyes widened with horror.

"No," Lithilia screamed and lunged towards him, but she was quickly stopped by demons and held down.

She knew exactly what Beelzebub was going to do next. And given his new and upgraded form, there was going to be no stopping him now.

"Please. No," Lithilia begged as she wrestled against the demons grips. "I beg of you, don't do it. Please. I'll do anything. *Anything.*"

But Beelzebub ignored her.

"Come, sister," Beelzebub said taking Luceefa by the hand. "Let me take you to your gift."

Beelzebub extended his right hand, and Luceefa took it, beaming with anticipation. He teleported with her to the Realm of Nimbu. The apprentices and Sarael were healed and in a group discussion. The dead bodies of slain sinisters were still scattered around by the thousands. A mixture of gore and ash eerily punctuated the distasteful butchery in the realm. When the group saw Beelzebub and a different woman manifest suddenly, they quickly took battle stance.

"Sister. Behold Cahen and Ahben," Beelzebub said, pointing at Maduk and Sarael respectively. "Behold the sons of Adamou."

"Oh, brother," Luceefa cooed. "This is a perfect gift indeed."

Luceefa appraised Maduk and Sarael as if those two were the only ones present. The rest of the vermin held no importance to her. Their fates were sealed already. But ending those two, Cahen and Ahben, held a much bigger significance than the two were aware of. Shi'mon's team knew they had much bigger trouble now with not just one, but two archangels. And no way Beelzebub was going to return with just any angel. Given his demeanor around this archangel, and with this archangel calling him 'brother', it could only mean one thing: this archangel was no other than the one many religions in Earth Realm referred to as Lucifer. So, Lucifer was out of The Abyss. Therefore, humanity and Earth Realm's destiny just took a dire turn towards a perdition of apocalyptic proportions..

Luceefa and Beelzebub summoned their respective archangel battle flames and flaming swords.

"I shall truly enjoy ending the sons of Michael," Luceefa hissed with diabolical excitement before she and Beelzebub flared and charged.

# THE END OF PART THREE

# AUTHOR NOTES AND CONTACT INFORMATION

Thank you so much for reading **Baiting The Beast**, Book Three of **The Soulless Ones.** I hope you enjoyed reading it.

Follow me on social media: **@elonendelle**

Amazon/Facebook Page: **Leo E. Ndelle**

YouTube Channel: **Eloverse**

Visit my website for more information about me and the series:

**www.eloverse.com**

Rate and review.

Please also take a moment to read a sample of Book Four of the series titled **Celestial Crisis.**

# BOOK FOUR

# CELESTIAL CRISIS

**LUNOK WALKED TOWARDS** Emok's prison cell. The cell was sparked from the ethers and infused with Shemsu technology that released frequencies which dampened the generic Shemsu esoteric signature. However, the dampeners in Emok's prison cell were customized to adapt to Emok's changing essence. The darker, or more powerful, Emok became, the greater the dampening effect of his prison cell. Or was it the more the darkness took over Emok's essence...? Lunok stayed his thoughts.

Lunok marveled at this top-secret piece of technology and wondered how much more The Council was hiding from the public. *Good thing The Council has given me unrestricted access to every database in the realm,* Lunok thought. Hopefully, The Council was truthful about this 'unrestricted access'. There was only one way to find out. He hoped to find nothing that would shake or break his faith in The Council. However, given what he had just learned about them, he was more open to expect anything from any Shemsu; anything as in ANYTHING!

Emok's prison cell was guarded by four Shemsus who had summoned an extra energy field around the cell. Emok seemed calm but that was only on the surface. Lunok met Emok's eyes and smiled his encouragement at Emok.

"How are you doing, old friend?" Lunok asked.

"I honestly do not know, old friend," Emok replied.

"I understand," Lunok said and stepped closer.

"Soon, you will be transported to your realm of confinement while I work on a possible solution for your condition," Lunok said. "I might have an idea on how to rid you of this entity."

There was a glint of excitement in Emok's eyes as Lunok spoke.

"What do you mean?" Emok asked.

"I spoke with The Council," Lunok said. "They showed me some of the files in the hidden databases you were trying to access. You're not the first of us to go through this, brother. I was surprised myself. They preferred not to show you the files because of certain concerns."

"What kind of concerns?" Emok asked.

"The kind with cataclysmic possibilities," Lunok replied.

Emok nodded his understanding.

"The Council wants me to be a part of the solution," Lunok added. They were impressed by the way I handled the situation in Celestia. Yes, that one!"

Lunok smiled kindly and Emok managed a weak smile.

"I think I understand their lack of success with helping our fellow brethren stricken with the same affliction, brother," Lunok continued.

"I won't even ask what happened after those failed attempts," Emok said and shook his head.

Lunok was silent. He realized that, by mentioning The Council and the videos he watched, he may have inadvertently created a situation that could aggravate Emok. However, Emok was too resigned to the hopelessness of his situation to do anything else.

"I wonder how they did it, though," Emok continued. "Given that there are no records of any Shemsu's existence coming to an end."

Again, Lunok was silent. He could only hope that Emok's thought process did not translate to a cause for concern. The four specially trained Shemsus, and him, were there to ensure that. Still...

"Anyway, tell me why our infallible leaders were unsuccessful," Emok said.

"Their approach was wrong," Lunok replied. "Mine is different and better. All I ask is that you don't give up on me, because I am not giving up on you. Can you try that, old friend?"

"I can," Emok replied with little enthusiasm. "No guarantees, though."

"And that is all I am asking," Lunok said.

Lunok then stepped back and nodded at his four comrades. They returned his nod and then turned to face Emok. It was time to go. Lunok summoned a glyph of light of a seven-faceted crystalline structure on his left palm. He then held out his left palm and the four Shemsu guards each projected a beam of golden light from their forehead, in between their eyes, unto the glyph. Lunok then turned his left palm towards his face and projected a beam of golden light from his forehead, in between his eyes, unto the seven-faceted crystalline glyph. The glyph glowed brightly and Lunok closed his fist. This would be the key to Emok's prison cell.

"Let's go!" Lunok said and made to teleport away.

"Wait!" Emok cried.

Lunok gestured to the other four Shemsus to wait.

"May I please see the team before I am taken away?" Emok pleaded. "I just want to say goodbye, given that I may never see them again."

Lunok understood his request. He summoned the team via telepathy and within a blink, the team appeared on sight. They stared at their former leader, not knowing what to say nor do. Emok was like a distorted image of his former self. They stepped closer towards the energy field. Emok looked at each of them in the eye until, finally, he managed a weak smile.

"I'm happy for this opportunity to bid you all farewell," he said weakly.

"You speak as if we will never see you again," Hikok said. "We have not lost our spirits and neither should you, Emok."

"There are still many realms and dimensions out there calling our name," Obok chimed in. "They're not going to populate themselves, you know!"

For the next few moments, they spoke words of encouragement and hope to their former leader. Emok was grateful and expressed his deep appreciation for everything they were trying to do for him. He assured them that he will do everything in his power to not give up. He had found renewed hope.

"We must go now, Emok," Lunok said.

"I understand," Emok said and then turned his attention towards the rest of the team. "Thank you all so much. I will see you all soon. Good bye now!"

Emok then turned around and gave Lunok a nod.

The six Shemsus teleported away to an extremely dense realm in a dimension of extremely low vibrational frequency than theirs. Lunok and the four Shemsu guards reduced their vibrational frequencies to resonate with that of the realm. They were on the dark side of the realm. Emok tried to do the same but failed. He was unsure why and for some reason, he began to panic. The four Shemsu guards immediately took up formation, ready to do more than just contain Emok, if it came to that.

"Be calm, old friend," Lunok said. "This cell contains some very sophisticated technology. It is infused with frequency dampeners that can do so many things, including maintaining your confines at the Shemsu vibrational frequency, while adjusting to any changing esoteric signatures your essence may undergo because of the darkness. You'll be safe within these confines and this realm is uninhabited. Only a Shemsu, or a creature from a realm higher than ours, could perceive this energy field, and, by extension, your esoteric signature. But I alone will have the key. And by 'I', I mean my essence. So, you're safe and will remain undisturbed until I find a cure for you, brother!"

Lunok summoned the seven-faceted, crystalline glyph on his left palm and placed it on the energy protection field. The energy field glowed, pulsated seven times and then lost its glow. The four guards then detached themselves from the energy field but the field stayed in place. Lunok closed his fist.

"Your containment is now your Shemsu home on this realm," Lunok said. "I have the key and because the five of us imparted a part of our essences unto this key, we are now connected to the energy protection field around your cell. We'll be updated of everything happening within this field."

Lunok then stepped closer.

"I will not rest until I find a solution, brother," he said.

Lunok smiled and waited for Emok to say something. Emok closed his eyes and when he opened them, he spoke words Lunok did not expect to hear.

"I'd suggest you never return," something that looked like Emok said. "You should forget about me, because you are already too late."

And Emok glowed in a bright blackness that neither Lunok nor the other Shemsus had ever seen before.

"Emok! Just hang in there, old friend!" Lunok pleaded.

"The one you call 'Emok' is no longer here, creature!" said the entity that had taken over Emok.

Its voice was so deep and infused with Shemsu energy laced with something so dark it made Lunok and the other four Shemsus take an involuntary step back. But Lunok steeled himself. He was not going to back down so easily. He glared and his eyes glowed in a bright violet-gold hue as he stepped forward towards the energy protection field.

"Who are you and what have you done with my friend?!" Lunok demanded.

"Patience, creature! Patience!" said the entity that had taken over Emok. "You will know me soon enough! This is my promise to you!"

Lunok screamed and punched towards the sky. He was too late and he knew it. A bolt of energy surged from the skies, struck the energy protection field, and started burying the prison cell deep into the ground. As the prison cell accelerated into the ground, Lunok and the four Shemsus could hear the darkness screaming and writhing in essence-chilling fury.

*"You have not seen the last of me, Lunok!"* the darkness raged via telepathy.

*"I'm counting on it,"* Lunok replied in kind and with vengeful rage at the darkness that had taken over his friend.

*"I swear by the entity I am and the essence I have taken over,"* the darkness promised. *"I will be free again and when I am, I will destroy you and everything else; from the Core, to your dimension and beyond!"*

*"I'll be waiting!"* Lunok replied.

Lunok and the four Shemsus shot beams of purple light from in between their eyes. The beams merged in their center and formed a palm-sized sphere of purple light. Lunok opened his right palm and the seven-faceted crystal glowed purple. He summoned the purple sphere via telekinesis. The sphere migrated to his open palm and Lunok closed it. Then, Lunok crashed his right fist into the ground as a bolt of purple lightning struck from the sky and sealed the darkness and its promise of chaos in the earth!